Drop Dead Handsome

A Flower Girls Mystery

REBECCA BURNS ALDRIDGE

A friend may well be reckoned the masterpiece of nature.
Ralph Waldo Emerson

For my beloved parents, Zula Mae Green Burns and Lacy Harvey Burns, who gave me life, and for Julian, who made that life worth living.

Table of Contents

Book One: The News
Part I: Tootsie

Part II: Bippy

Part III: Penelope

Part IV: Rosemary

Book Two: The Meeting

Acknowledgments

Special thanks to my children, by nature and by marriage: Rebecca (with special appreciation for her vision of the cover), Mack (for medical advice), Burns (for all things realty-related), Rich, Elizabeth, and Anne for their unswerving support of both me and my writing and for unanimously settling once and for all–at least for me–the spelling of "email." To them also I owe permission to capitalize "Southern." Everyone should have such cheerleaders!

To my grandchildren: Liza, Virginia, Caroline, Campbell, Burns, and Mary Thomas for making life sweeter than I ever dreamed it could be.

To Pat Jurgens and Patty Slorah for invaluable publishing advice and optimistic encouragement.

To Dr. Bessie Chronaki for her expert grammatical decisions.

To Ted Blain, whose writing, critiquing, and friendship I value and whose encouragement pushed me to publish.

To my cousins, Linda and Ann, and long-time friends, Nancy Jo and Janet, who, with me, form a loosely-defined online reading group.

And to my friends: Bibba, Ginny, and June, and many, many others who have encouraged me across the years to do this.

To my sisters-in-law, Lucy and Ginna, for their unfailing love. They are sisters in all the ways that count.

And, most of all, to Julian. Just because.

Prologue

Jake Tillman noticed it with a strange sense of foreboding: the sleek sky-blue and white twenty-six foot Tanzer sailboat with no one aboard, bobbing like a cork in the murky waters of Serene Lake. He stopped a minute, took off his hat, and ran his fingers through his graying red hair. He whistled through his teeth. A Tanzer! It was a dandy boat, all right. Yes indeedy, a real beauty! But something about it, so solitary and deserted, caused the hairs on the back of his neck to stand up. *What the heck!* he thought, shaking his head and trying to dismiss his first reaction. He popped his hat back on his head. *What's the big deal?* It wasn't so unusual, after all, to see an unattended boat. People often left their boats to go for a swim, especially here in this quiet, out-of-the-way cove, his own favorite fishing spot. But at this time of year? October?

Still, he thought, *it isn't that cold in the daytime in Mississippi yet, and there are always a lot of nuts who just cannot seem to let go of the summer season, taking dips right up until November.* He scratched the back of his neck. *Shoot, those crazy people up in Boston—or was it New York or Chicago?—somewhere up North—even swim in the middle of winter. What is it they call themselves? Polar Bears? That's it. Yeah, that could be the explanation. Or, the owner could have gone fishing in a little john boat that he'd pulled behind the Tanzer. Oh, it could be a lot of things. Sure it could.* Then what was it that struck him as odd?

Hunter interrupted his thoughts. "Granddaddy, will you put this fly on the hook for me?"

"Need a popper bug? Sure, Partner," he said, putting his own rod down in the bass boat. "Let me see it. Okay now, where's your weight?

You're missing your weight, son. Gotta have that. Without it, there's nothing to hold your line in place." As soon as he said it, he knew what had bothered him about the sailboat. *Weight!* He straightened up and looked again at the boat drifting to and fro, not far away. Holy mackerel! That's what was wrong. Nothing was holding it in place. It wasn't just temporarily abandoned. It flat out wasn't anchored. Floating aimlessly on its own, it was now a good fifty feet from where he had first spotted it, and there were no swimmers or sunbathers anywhere in sight. Anchored and empty is one thing, but untethered and empty is something else. Why would someone go off and leave a nice boat like that loose? Those Tanzers don't come cheap. He knew that for a fact. He'd wanted to buy one once, but the price was way out of his budget. Yeah, something about that just didn't seem right.

He pulled a new weight from his box and attached it and the fly to the boy's line. "All right now, there you go, pal. Throw that baby in the water as far as you can, and let's catch us some fish. I'll bet those bass are just holed up down there waiting for you."

The small boy cast his line with all his might and sat holding it, smiling up at his grandfather's face. "Some fun, huh, Granddaddy?"

"Sure is, son. It'll be more fun if you catch a big one, though, won't it?"

"Yes sir!" Grinning, he leaned his freckled face onto one fist, propped against the edge of the boat, holding tight to the rod with the other. Soon, he gazed off into the distance.

Jake studied the small red head, a clone of his own, bent away from him and then affectionately mussed the hair. "Missing your folks?"

Hunter shrugged his small shoulders and then nodded. "A little bit. Not as much when I'm fishing with you, though." He managed a smile.

Jake smiled. "Well, they'll be back soon. This was an important business trip for your dad, you know. He had to go, and he needed your mom with him. He gets lonely, I'm sure, when he has to travel by himself. Besides, it gave her a chance for a nice little visit to London. She'll see all the sights while your dad is in his meetings: the Tower of London, Big Ben, Buckingham Palace, Trafalgar Square. Probably buy you something real nice—maybe a toy—from one of those places. Anyway, I'm happy as a June bug to have this time with you. I've been a bit lonely since your grandmother passed away." *More than a bit*, he thought. *A whole lot more!* "How I miss that dear lady!" He took off his hat, turned it in his hands for a minute, and put it right back on, pulling it snugly down on his head.

Hunter patted his grandfather's hand and nodded silently. "Me, too, Granddaddy. Grandmomma was so sweet. And she baked the best cookies!"

Jake looked away, swallowed, and then quickly added, "And since you all moved to Charlotte, I don't see you as much as I'd like. Not near as much."

"Yeah," Hunter sighed.

"One of these days soon, I'm going to come to Charlotte, and we'll go fishing out on that Lake Norman you're always talking about. You can show me all the ins and outs of fishing there. How about that?"

Hunter brightened as if the sun had suddenly popped out from behind a cloud. "Really? You mean it?"

"Sure do."

"Wow! That would be great. When, Granddaddy?"

"Soon. Real soon. Meanwhile, I'm glad your mom felt comfortable leaving us men alone. It's fun batching it—just us two guys, isn't it? We can eat pizza every night if we feel like it, can't we?"

"You bet! And popcorn for breakfast." Suddenly, the gentle drifting of their idle boat caused Hunter's line to go taut. He sat up. Was something pulling on his line? Yes, he definitely felt a resistance as he tugged. "Granddaddy!" he yelled excitedly. "I think I've got something."

Jake grinned. "Attaboy. I knew you'd get a bite directly. Remember what I told you about mending your line? Mend it and then relax it. Mend and relax. Pull it in slowly. No jerking. Slowly, now."

Hunter tugged, relaxed his line, and tugged again. "I can't. It won't come. What do I do now? Help, Granddaddy."

Jake laid down his rod and put his own strong hands around Hunter's. Together, they pulled. After tugging unsuccessfully for several minutes, they saw a piece of yellow material float to the surface. "Oh, heck!" Hunter said. "I've just caught trash."

"Happens to me, too, all the time. Well, we have to free your line anyhow, so we may as well get it free any way we can," Jake said. He pulled harder and then tried little, brisk jerking motions, creating a riffle in the water. Suddenly, their line broke loose, and not twenty feet from their boat, the object of their struggle surfaced.

Jake heard the sharp intake of breath from his grandson even as his own brain refused to acknowledge what he was seeing. "Granddaddy!" Hunter shrieked. "It's a lady!"

"Dear Father in Heaven!" Jake exclaimed, leaning his tall frame over to peer more directly at the body, which was now floating closer and closer to their boat. It appeared to be that of a woman, all right, but the pale face, lapped by the water and framed by wild red hair, was terribly, grotesquely bloated. Green eyes, like two marbles in a fishbowl, were wide open and staring, and white arms, waving like supple tendrils, floated gracefully with the currents. Jake's mind was doing a rapid-fire analysis. He didn't recognize her, but then, he thought, that doesn't mean anything, the condition this body is in. Still, there was something vaguely familiar about her. Maybe it was the red hair.

He was aware that Hunter had scooted closer to him, and he could feel the small boy's body trembling. Quickly, Jake stowed the fishing pole, turned the key, and started the engine.

"Are—are we just gonna leave her, Granddaddy?"

"We can't do her any good here, Partner, and we've got to go get help. I left my cell phone in the car. Didn't count on needing it out here, and I didn't want to risk dropping it in the water."

As they sped off toward the shore where they'd put the boat in, Hunter turned backward and stared. "That poor lady," he murmured.

"That poor lady, is right," added Jake.

***

After the rescue squad and police had retrieved the body, the crime scene photographer took shots from every angle. As soon as this was finished, Lt. Curtis Ferguson questioned Jake and Hunter about their finding while the coroner did a preliminary examination at the scene. The small man examining the lifeless form, now stretched out on the ground, called to Ferguson over his shoulder. "Did you ID the body?"

Ferguson shook his head. "No, nothing yet, Doc. Checkin' on the boat license now." He turned back to Jake and the boy. "Now, Mr. Tillman, would you please describe just exactly how you found the body."

"We were fishing, see, and Hunter here caught his line on something. We both tugged hard, trying to free the line, and all of a sudden—well, uh, up she came."

xiii

Ferguson nodded as he wrote. "Uh-huh. The body was snagged on a submerged tree branch. Our divers found some of her shirt still on a limb about ten feet down. Your tugging just dislodged her."

Jake nodded and put his arm around Hunter. He could feel the boy's shoulders shaking. "Say, uh, Lieutenant, do you think I could put Hunter here in the car? He's had quite a shock, and he can't really add anything to what I tell you."

Ferguson looked at the child's chalky face, trembling lips, and large, frightened eyes. He looked like one of those caricatured moppets with the oversized eyes he had seen pictured on birthday cards. "Sure. Sure. Go ahead. You can leave, too, in just a few minutes. Soon as I get all this information down. I'll ask you to come to the station later and sign a written statement once I get the report all typed up."

Jake put Hunter in the car, handed him a Pepsi from the cooler chest in the trunk, and returned to where Ferguson was standing. As he was answering all of Ferguson's questions, the coroner, Dr. Fred Watson, approached the men. Watson was a small man with sharp features, penetrating brown eyes, and a bobbing Adam's apple saddled by a bright blue polka dot bow tie.

Ferguson gave Watson a quick nod. "Mr. Tillman, this here's the coroner, Doc Watson. Doc, this is the man that pulled up the body—Jake Tillman. What'd you find, Doc?" Ferguson asked him.

Watson briefly acknowledged Jake with a slight tip of the head and then answered, "Well, right off, Curt, I'd say it's drowning. 'Course I won't know for sure until we do a complete autopsy. By the beginning—and only the very beginning, mind you—of formation of adipocere, I'd say she's been in the water for about five days to a week. Maybe more. Maybe less."

Jake swallowed. "Adipocere?"

"Yeah. That's a yellow-white waxy substance—really an indissoluble soap, if you want to get right down to it—that forms as the decaying process takes place under water. It eventually replaces all the muscles and viscera as well as tissues of the face. Grotesque, really. Makes the body all bloated looking and hardly recognizable as a human being. Takes a long time—about a year to a year and a half—in adults to complete the process. It's just in its very earliest stages in this body, but when you know what to look for, you can spot its beginning signs. It tells me the body has been in the water more than just a couple of hours."

Ferguson's eyes flicked from the pad on which he was making notes to Jake's ashen face. It was a case of TMI, all right. The man, weaving ever so slightly, like an aspen trembling in the wind, was clearly learning more than he cared to know about the decomposition of a body in water. Heck, it didn't bother Ferguson any. He'd seen enough and heard enough to let it roll off his back, and Watson—well, Watson could do an autopsy with a scalpel in one hand and a peanut butter and jelly sandwich in the other. He'd seen him do it. As long as Ferguson had known the sharp-edged little coroner, he was still amazed at Doc's detachment. Maybe that was necessary, though. People tended to do what they had to in order to survive. Ferguson cleared his throat. "Uh, Doc, I think I've got enough here. You can go ahead and take the body. We'll talk later."

Jake suddenly leaned forward and caught hold of the tree near where he was standing. "Sorry. I—uh, I just felt my knees go weak on me all of a sudden." His head began reeling, and he thought he was going to be sick. "I—I—If you're through, Lt. Ferguson—"

Ferguson knew a faint coming on when he saw it, and as tall as this fellow was—he must be six three, six four—that would be quite a fall. "Sure. Sure. You'd better sit down. Better still, if you're up to driving, go ahead and leave. Better rest a few minutes first, though. Be sure your head is clear. I have everything I need. Besides, I've got your contact information. I'll be in touch. Thanks for your help."

As Ferguson watched Jake wobble to his car and then walked back to his squad car, he passed the body, now fully enclosed in a black plastic bag, being loaded into the ambulance. An unsettling feeling—the nagging suspicion that vibrant, healthy, middle-aged women don't just fall off their boats and drown—descended on him that before this matter was settled, he was going to need help, all right. Lots of it.

Book One: The News

Part I: Tootsie

Chapter One

Tootsie Freeman sailed down Interstate 85 toward Durham in her bright red BMW convertible the way she always did: the top down and Kenny Chesney blaring full-blast from her radio. Behind her, the Charlotte skyline, anchored by the imposing Bank of America Building, faded from sight. This was the height of freedom, she thought, tossing her head to get the hair out of her eyes: no confining schedule, no top on the car to coop up her willowy, five-foot-eleven frame. She ran one hand across her head, raking the hair, jet-black but delicately outlined with gray at the temples, between her fingers. In spite of her efforts, the wind blew the wavy chin-length tresses, which she normally kept brushed back behind her ears, onto her forehead and into her eyes. It billowed her long, flowing fuchsia skirt and tinkled the dangling silver geometric designs at her ears. Her skin, as pale and creamy as a magnolia blossom, seemed to belong to a woman half her age as did her extremely svelte figure.

"How do you keep that marvelous figure?" people often asked her, and her answer was always the same: "Three no-fail ways: exercise, exercise, exercise." And it was true. She had always kept fit, swimming at the Duke indoor pool almost every day—that is, every day when she was not gadding about all over the world, which she did at the drop of a hat—playing golf and tennis, or taking classes at the community college. She glanced in the rear view mirror and smiled. With all due respect to modesty, she had to admit that for sixty-something—and she was not about to disclose how many years on the other side of sixty she was; sixty-ish was close enough—she was in fine shape. Yes indeed.

"I'll swanee, Momma," Emma Beth had said many times, "you're in better shape than I am. It's downright disgusting, that's what it is." She had always laughed when she said that because she was proud of her mother and loved that acquaintances often mistook them for sisters. She didn't, however, love it half as much as Tootsie.

This excellent shape was not limited to her physical condition. After her children, Emma Beth and Walt, were grown, Tootsie had taken the advice of her dearest friend, Maggie Palmer, who lived in Mississippi, and had become a real estate agent.

"Look," Maggie had urged, "I sell real estate and deal with other realtors all the time. I know what it takes, and you've got it, kiddo. You're a natural. You have an outgoing personality, plus you have the artistic sense to see the possibilities in property that the clients might not see on their own."

Maggie had been right, Tootsie thought. It did come naturally to her. Once she had her broker's license, she took the real estate market by storm. She regularly topped all sales in Durham and was twice voted Realtor of the Year for the entire Triangle, the area including Durham, Raleigh, and Chapel Hill. Because of the extravagant incomes generated by the high-tech companies in the Research Triangle, homes in the area brought hefty prices, making Tootsie's commissions enormous. She became a very well-to-do lady in her own right.

Then, without warning, her beloved husband, Walter B. Freeman, who had amassed a fortune in a very quiet and unobtrusive way, and who shared it generously with many local charities, died of a massive heart attack. She smiled as she remembered the obits in the paper referring to him as "an insurance and real estate tycoon." Tycoon, indeed! What a hoot! Dear meek, sweet Walter. How he would have scoffed at that! Tycoons were people like Warren Buffet and Jeff Bezos. Walter was just—well, Walter. His idea of an exciting evening was to sit in his favorite chair smoking his pipe with the *NY Times* crossword puzzle on his knees.

Once Walter was gone, she determined not to sit around and feel sorry for herself, but she also determined not to work until the day she dropped either. Life's too short, she decided, not to enjoy it to the max. If Walter's premature death had taught her anything, it had taught her that. Having made that decision, she retired at age fifty-five and devoted herself to enjoying life and helping others do the same. For her many friends, she was the virtual Pied Piper of happiness. She leaned over slightly, keeping her eyes completely fixed on the road, and with one hand fished in her purse and then patiently and expertly lifted a partially unscrewed lid from a jar of peanut butter. This drove her kids crazy. Walt had thrown up his hands in despair, but Emma Beth was determined to change Tootsie's driving habits.

"Momma, you're the classic distracted driver," she had often said. "I don't want to read in the paper that you died while eating peanut butter at seventy miles an hour."

"I am not distracted. I never take my eyes off the road even for a second. I know exactly what I'm doing," Tootsie countered. "That's why I leave the top of the jar—well, ajar." That struck them both funny, and the discussion about her driving ended in gales of laughter.

Retrieving the jar with one hand took considerable coordination, however, but she had practiced often. Jabbing a spoon, which was lying on the divider between the two front seats, into the jar, she pulled it out and popped it into her mouth. "Ah, yes!" she said aloud as soon as she could talk around the glob in her mouth. "That's what I needed: my hourly infusion of peanut butter."

Tootsie's affinity for peanut butter was well known to her family and friends. She spread it on crackers, toast, celery, apples, whatever was handy, but her favorite way by far was a spoonful right out of the jar. P. B. straight up, she called it.

"Momma," Emma Beth had once said, "if that stuff ever starts to make you gain weight, you're going to have a crisis of major proportions on your hands. I declare, you're addicted," she had warned, hands on her hips "That's what you are. Pure T addicted. What would you have done if Walt or I had been born with a peanut allergy?"

"I'd have missed you terribly, darling," Tootsie said.

Speeding down the highway, Tootsie laughed again at Emma Beth's concern. It was always something with that girl. Something to worry about. Something to fret over. Bless her heart. Emma Beth was precious, but she was a worrier, that's for sure. How in the world, Tootsie wondered, did I produce someone so mature, so organized, so structured, so efficient, and so—well, so inflexible? She was reliable to a fault, but she tended to be just a tad—well, let's tell it like it is—predictable. Tootsie mulled this over a minute and then thought: That's a code word for boring. Talk about polar opposites! Had to be Walter's gene pool, she decided with a giggle.

Emma Beth Sinclair, her husband Mark, and their two young children, Livvy and Brent, lived in a neat little house, immaculately cleaned—on a daily basis, Tootsie felt sure—and maintained by Emma Beth herself, in Raleigh, only thirty minutes away from Tootsie's Durham home. It was a perfect distance: close enough for the two women, who enjoyed an unusually warm relationship despite—or perhaps because of—their differences, to have lunch and chat or go

4

shopping, but not close enough for Emma Beth to know—or worry about—all of her mother's escapades. Some of them, but not all.

Just as well, Tootsie thought, that Emma Beth didn't know she had taken off on the spur of the moment for Charlotte to see the "China and The History of the Orient" exhibit at Discovery Place. Tootsie considered what Emma Beth's reaction would have been. She'd have gotten that someone-needs-to-look-after-you glint in her eye and said I shouldn't be going to Charlotte by myself. Too dangerous. Humph! Dangerous, my eye. I could get mugged right in my front yard in Durham. Some people—and she guessed Emma Beth was one of them—seemed to thrive on the what-ifs and kept fear and dread as constant companions. Nine-one-one people, Tootsie called them. Yes, she definitely had to admit that Emma Beth, bless her heart, had a teensy tendency in that direction.

Well, in all fairness, it probably would have been safer to travel with a companion, she conceded, but, heck, it wasn't like she *planned* to go alone. She continued to justify her rashness by recalling that when she had gotten the bright idea of the trip and called her friend Phyllis, she had said she would go, too. Tootsie smiled. Could I help it that Phyll called back and said she'd remembered she had an important meeting of the church worship committee about—gasp!—somebody wanting to put artificial greenery in the sanctuary next Christmas? Could I? Of course not, and I just couldn't *not* go. Especially since the display, "Shoes Through the Ages," was on at the Mint Museum at the same time. It was a twofer, a bargain, and she had never been able to pass those up. Tootsie suddenly realized what she was doing: She was working out her excuse for when she saw Emma Beth—her *child,* for heaven's sake—and told her where she had been. What's wrong with this picture? she wondered.

5

It all sounded logical, she thought. Of course, she could just not mention to Emma Beth where she had gone, but since she'd had lunch yesterday with her son, Walter III, who was a vice president of Bank of America in Charlotte, she knew Emma Beth would know. Walt would have called her. For. Sure. Tootsie was aware that her children regularly kept track of her frenetic pace. It was a source of bemused interest to her that they worried about her so and joined leagues to share their concern about what their mother was up to next. She supposed it was the unasked-for but inevitable reversal of roles that amused her most.

"Well, turn about is fair play, I guess," she said aloud. She had done her share of mothering. Now it was their turn. Let 'em worry a little bit. It won't hurt them. As for herself, she was largely beyond that. At this point in life, she worried about Emma Beth only for her totally uncompromising—and what Tootsie considered almost pathological—bent toward scrupulousness and about Walt for one reason and one reason only: At almost thirty-four, he was not married. He was not even close. Over lunch at the Mimosa Grill in the heart of Charlotte's bustling Center City, she had told him just yesterday that he needed to prioritize and not let his work monopolize his life.

"You're a bit shy and reserved like your father, Walt. That's not a bad thing, but you've got to have some fun, son," she'd said. "Lighten up. Live a little."

"I love what I'm doing, Mom." He looked at his mother, sitting there before him in a bright turquoise skirt and white blouse with beaded trim, enveloped in her usual cloud of Joy perfume. Her earrings, long strips of silver emblazoned with bits of turquoise, cast playful patterns of light and shadow on her cheeks. The manicured nails on her long, thin fingers, which could draw forth the sublime music of Bach and Beethoven from her Mason and Hamlin grand piano, clicked energetically on the table top. Her music was a symbol of one of the many things he loved about her: her breadth. In music, as in everything else, her tastes were inclusive, expansive, eclectic. She loved classical compositions and played them well, but she loved all kinds of music. She could play Beethoven's "Pathetique Sonata" one minute and belt out "I'm Crying in My Beer over You, Lucille" the next. She melted to the mellow sound of James Taylor. Ah, but her favorite music was country, especially Garth Brooks and Kenny Chesney. In the purse at her feet, Walt knew, would be the ubiquitous jar of peanut butter. She was never without it.

Smiling, he thought of her as she often dressed at home: in jeans with a huge turquoise saucer-sized belt buckle and cowboy boots, complete with spurs—her "Western Look," she called it. Or there was what he and Emma Beth referred to as her Native American Princess outfit: suede skirt and shirt with fringe and strands of beads draped around her neck. Or the ever-popular—at least with Tootsie—bohemian look of voluminous swirling skirts and peasant blouse adorned with tassels. She had an outfit for every occasion. He would never forget her accompanying him to a junior high school football game outfitted in what could only be described as midlife cheerleader attire: pleated above-the-knee skirt, letter sweater, and pompons. He didn't know anyone else who could pull off the outlandish outfits she regularly and enthusiastically wore. *Panache. Savoir-faire. Elan.* He guessed that was what they called it. Whatever it was, his mother had it—in spades.

Studying her tall form and her earnest face with its large brown eyes, the color of raisins, dancing behind luxuriant and lavishly enhanced lashes, he sighed. Well, he was forced to admit, her clothing may run to the avant-garde, and her judgment is at times certainly questionable, but if anyone knows how to have fun, to enjoy life, she does. Her many friends would attest to that. He would like to calm her down, make her more—well, settled, mature. So would Emma

Beth, but they both knew that was a hopeless goal. What can you do, after all, with a free spirit like her but love her? That's just who she is, he thought: smart, witty, outrageously confident, sometimes brash, but always kind. To try to tame her insouciance would be a needless and utterly futile frustration for all involved. It just wouldn't work. Walt permitted himself another smile as he wondered what she must have been like as a young girl, full of the unbridled passion for life that characterizes youth. Staggers the imagination, he decided. Almost imperceptibly, he shook his head.

"What?" Tootsie said.

"Excuse me?"

"You're shaking your head, and you have that look on your face like you get when you are thinking about having me committed." Her brilliant smile told him she was kidding.

Walt laughed. "Mom, you're too much. I wasn't thinking that at all. Besides, we both know that there's no place that would take you."

"Well, thank God for that. To paraphrase what Groucho Marx said about clubs, there's no place that would accept me to which I would want to go. Back to what we were talking about—your job and your working too hard—all I can say is that I read a good comment last week. It said that the trouble with the rat race is that even if you win, you're still a rat." She took a bite of her pasta salad and winked at him.

"Mom!" He looked at his mother's impish grin and broke out into the deep, muffled laughter so reminiscent of his father's.

"I just want you to find a good woman, Walt. Settle down and raise a family. That's not too much to ask, is it? By the way, do you know my friend, Lorie Welch?"

He puckered one side of his mouth and raised his eyebrows in a look of resignation. "No, but something tells me I'm about to. Something also just tells me that she has a nice, available niece or daughter or something of the kind, right? I can see it in your eyes: You've got another lead."

Now it was Tootsie's turn to laugh. She threw her hands up in mock surrender. "All right. You've got me. It's her sister's daughter, Walt, and she's precious. Really."

Walt took a gulp of sweet iced tea. "Uh-huh and have you met Miss Precious?"

"Not exactly."

"And just what does that mean? How can you not *exactly* meet someone?"

"I've seen her picture, and I know Lorie's sister. She's very nice. Lorie's sister, that is. Well, I'm sure her daughter is, too. You might say I know her by association."

Walt laughed. "I give up!"

Tootsie smiled as she remembered that look of Walt's. Smiled and stepped on the gas.

Chapter Two

Coming into the darkened house, Tootsie felt something rub against her leg. "Why, Ladybug," she sang out, flipping on the lights, "how nice of you to welcome me home! Did you miss me?" She stooped and patted the tabby cat as it wound in and out between her ankles. "Come on, let's get some more food in your bowl. You've about finished what I left out for you, I see."

After pouring fresh dry food in a bowl marked "The Queen" and filling the large water bowl with fresh water, Tootsie kicked off her shoes, went to the fridge and surveyed the situation. Darn! Talk about Mother Hubbard. "The cupboard is pretty bare," she said to her cat, who blinked at her and went back to eating. She opened the freezer and pulled out a pizza. "Well, look here, Ladybug. Just what the doctor ordered," she said.

She could never stand waiting for an oven to pre-heat. Seemed like such a waste of time, so she seldom fooled with it. She just added an extra ten minutes to the cook time. She popped the pizza in the oven, turned the setting to 400 degrees, set the timer, and poured some salad mix into a bowl. A sudden rumbling in her stomach reminded her that she would have to wait a while. She drummed her fingers on the kitchen counter. *Hmm. Maybe a little something to tide me over while I'm waiting would help. That's the ticket. A little snack, something to stave off starvation.* She took some crackers from a plastic keeper and spread them with peanut butter, poured herself some Diet Coke, and went into her study.

Plopping down in her latest indulgence, a midnight blue Ivan Allen desk chair with so many adjustment levers and knobs that Tootsie had asked the sales assistant how many miles to the gallon it got, she pushed the button to turn on her computer. Lights came to life, and soon the screen welcomed her and invited her to make a choice. *So many things to do*, she thought, *and I don't know how to do most of them. Not yet, that is. But just give me time, and I will.* Without hesitating, she clicked on Google to check her email. It was always wonderful to hear from her distant friends, and email, she felt, was particularly effective at communicating with them. It seemed to combine the immediacy of a phone call with the depth of a letter. Yep. There's mail, all right. Tootsie smiled. Oh joy! It was from Maggie Palmer, her best friend from Mississippi, with whom she corresponded almost daily. She clicked on the letter and began reading.

> *Dear Tootsie,*
> *Well, hi, you gadabout you! Where*
> *in the world are you this time? I haven't*
> *heard from you in ages! Well, okay, so it*
> *was just day before yesterday. Still, I*
> *missed our daily chat.*

Tootsie smiled as she thought of her friend's voice, whispery and elfin, totally out of character for her five-foot-ten athletic frame. Maggie was a world-class talker, though, and she sometimes went on for several breath-defying minutes without stopping for air. Grinning at how much Maggie's written word, rich with hyperbole, sounded like her spoken word, Tootsie scrolled back up and noticed that the email was three days old. *Hmm. She must have sent this right after I walked out the door for Charlotte. I should have written her before I left and told her I was going.* She scrolled back down and continued reading.

> *Hope all is going well with you and you're not missing making the big bucks in real estate any more. ☺ I'm staying really busy and having a good year.*
>
> *I am having a bit of trouble with one client, however. I try not to worry about him and just concentrate on why I'm in this business in the first place: to help people find suitable homes. We've talked about this before, remember? About how real estate is really—or should be— a service profession? Well, anyway, I've got to remember that and quit worrying about this one problem. There's one in every crowd, you know, or a fly in every ointment, as my mother used to say.*
>
> *Okey dokey. So much for the chit chat. I've been building up the drama, in case you hadn't noticed. Insert your own drum roll here. I guess the reason I'm impatient to be in touch is that I have some big news to share with you.*

REALLY BIG NEWS!! Are you sitting down,
Toot-Toot-Tootsie? Silly me! Of course you
are if you're reading this on the computer.
Well, anyway, here goes.

I'M IN LOVE! Yes, me, Maggie Muldoon Palmer!
And I'm going to get MARRIED!!! Okay.
Here you can start humming, "Going to the
Chapel, and I'm Gonna Get Married."
Yes, you read that right. Me, married! After all
these years as a widow—well, I know five years
isn't all that long; it just seems it. Lord! It seems
like an eternity—I am going to be a wife again.
Really, Tootsie, can you believe it!!! I can't.
I honestly can't.

Tootsie stopped reading, aware that her mouth was wide open.
"Well, what do you know!" she said to Ladybug, who had finished
her meal and sat washing her face at Tootsie's feet. Looking back at
the computer, she sighed. *You're right, Maggie; I can't believe it!* She
leaned her cheek on her open palm for a few minutes to let the news
sink in and then continued reading.

I never believed that I'd love anyone
again after my Cam died. How I loved
that dear man! Love him still. I didn't
want to, really, but there you have it:
I'm in love. Love was just dropped
into my lap, so what could I do?

Well, I know you're dying of curiosity,
so here are all the details. Gordon—oh, that's
his name, by the way, Gordon Dawkins—is just
wonderful. He shares my love of children and
animals, and I think he will get involved in the
little program I've had since college to help
disadvantaged children. You know all about
that.

He's also very handsome—drop-dead handsome,
you might say. Yeah, that's exactly what you would
say. I think girls today would call him gorgeous.
He's tall, about six three, very muscular, has
wavy brown hair to die for with a touch of gray
around the temples, which is SO attractive, and
the honest-to-gosh bluest eyes I've ever seen.
Aqua blue. They look like two pools of water
drawn from the Aegean Sea. See? He even
moves me to poetry (something else he likes).
It gives me chills just thinking of him.

I know I sound like a star-struck teenager, but
that's just how I feel. You know, the young think
that they have a monopoly on love and romance.
I've read enough current novels to know that.
They think once you reach a certain age, the
things they take for granted, the things that
are glorified in every novel, magazine,
and movie you see—kissing, hugging, and
just being absolutely thrilled by

14

someone—are thrown out like yesterday's
coffee grounds. They think that the only
interest our age has in sex is that the "x"
counts 8 points in Scrabble. Well, bless
their little hearts! What do they know,
right? Speaking of age, Gordon is almost
ten years younger than I am, but am I
complaining?

Now, I know you're wondering why
I haven't said anything about him before.
There's a very good reason. From the
beginning, Gordon said we must keep
our relationship a secret. He is divorced,
you see, and his grown children wouldn't
approve. He thinks they still harbor the
false hope that he and Jillian—that's his
ex-wife—will get back together (not going
to happen!)

Anyway, it was quite a nasty break-up,
and apparently, the kids aren't over it yet.
My inclination is to be honest and tell them
everything, but not ever having had children,
I don't know what is best in a case like this,
so I'm going with what Gordon thinks.

Tootsie sat back in her chair and took a few deep breaths. *Maggie,
Maggie! What have you gotten yourself into this time?* She reached
down and stroked Ladybug's uplifted chin. "Ladybug, sometimes I

think you have more sense than people." She sat upright again and resumed reading.

> *This is all hush-hush because Gordon*
> *wants us to get married before we tell his*
> *children. He knows they won't approve*
> *because they have made it very clear they*
> *would not welcome anyone else in their*
> *mother's place. He thinks that if it's a*
> *fait accompli, though—that if we just*
> *tell them we're married—they'll adjust.*
> *I guess they'll have to, right? I have to*
> *trust him on this one. He knows them*
> *better than I do.*

Tootsie hit the arm of her chair. *Oh, good grief, Maggie, have you lost your wits? What kind of magic spell has this charlatan cast over you that has caused you to abandon your common sense?* A deep sigh escaped her lips as she concluded the letter.

> *Oh, Tootsie, I am so very happy.*
> *I do love him, and you'll love him, too,*
> *when you meet him. Just you wait and*
> *see! I wish in a way that we were having*
> *a real ceremony so you could be with me.*
> *I wish you could be my matron of honor.*
> *We've been through a lot together, you and*
> *I, since our college days when we were*
> *innocent little Duke coeds, haven't we?*
> *Remember all those confessionals on Giles*

*third floor, north, when we sat on our beds
and told each other everything? I'm pretending
we're there again, and I'm sharing my joy
with you just like old times.*

*Well, what do you think about all
this? Tell me honestly. Well, maybe not
too honestly. ☺ Can't wait to hear
from you.*

*Love,
Maggie*

*p.p.s. Did I mention that he's drop-
dead handsome? I did? Well, it bears
repeating. He is.*

Tootsie sat for a minute in dazed disbelief. Absently, she picked up Ladybug and held her in her lap, stroking the cat's orange and white striped head. "Ladybug, Ladybug, what has she done?" she whispered in imitation of the child's nursery rhyme. "Her heart is on fire, and her sense is all gone." Just then she heard the beeping of the oven, signaling that it had reached the 400 degree temperature to which she had set it. *Good. It won't be long now*, she thought. The next sound would be the timer telling her the pizza was done.

Tapping her fiery red fingernails on the keyboard for a few minutes, she stared at the screen as her mind replayed the letter. *Confessionals on third flour, north, huh? Honest opinion you want, right? Okay, old girl, you asked for it. I always told you back then exactly what I thought, and I'm going to tell you now.* Clicking on Reply, she began

17

writing, her fingers flying over the keys as she poured her heart into her words.

> *Dear Maggie,*
> *I've just returned from a spur-of-*
> *the-moment trip to Charlotte. I know I*
> *was just in Atlanta a week ago, but this*
> *was something I couldn't pass up, and it*
> *was great! I didn't tell you I was going*
> *because I honestly didn't know it myself*
> *until the last minute. I knew Emma Beth*
> *would put up a fuss, so I didn't say anything*
> *to her either. I just went. Saw a simply*
> *marvelous China exhibit at Discovery Place.*
> *(I don't know why people think that place is*
> *just for kids, by the way.)*
>
> *They had about thirty crafts people*
> *from China spinning silk, painting intricate*
> *designs inside tiny glass vases, doing double-*
> *sided embroidery, making paper, writing*
> *peoples' family names in Chinese, and much,*
> *much more. Wish you could have been here*
> *to go with me. Wish you were here for lots*
> *of reasons.*
>
> *Afterwards, I spent the night and went*
> *the next day to the Mint Museum to see their*
> *permanent collection of pre-Columbian art*

and the traveling exhibit that's there right now:
Shoes Through the Ages. Quite fascinating!
We're not the first women who couldn't pass
up a shoe sale, by the way. Imelda Marcos,
eat your heart out!.

Had a nice visit with Walt over lunch.
He's fine—still not serious about anyone—too
committed to his job. How did I manage to
produce such a serious, conscientious child?
Make that two serious, conscientious children.

Okay, I've put off long enough the main
purpose of this letter. Maggie! I am absolutely
FLOORED by your news. You asked what I
thought, remember? And you know me:
I'm going to tell you. Why doesn't that
surprise you, right? You know I've never
been one to shrink from expressing my
opinion and speaking my mind: an act-now-
think-later kind of gal. Why change now?
I know we are both prone to impulsive actions
at times—okay, most of the time—but there
are other times when reason is needed. This,
my dearest friend, is one of those times. Anyway,
pardon me if I step on your sweet little toes.

Of course, I'm glad you're happy. You know
that, but are you sure about this, Mags? I

mean really, really sure? Lots of questions
have popped into my mind, and I'm
going to share them with you. Here goes.

How long have you known this Gordon
Dawkins? Isn't this kind of fast? There's nothing
other than a cake in the oven that a little extra
time won't help. Let's be honest. You and I both
know your romantic nature. While it's one of your
many endearing qualities, it tends to make you
vulnerable, you know? Even to the point of being
naive. In spite of your good business head, you
can be easily swept off your feet in matters of the
heart. Come on, Maggie, admit it. Quit shaking
your head. Remember that SAE at Duke? Huh?

Also, I'm a little wary of a man who wants
to be deceitful about his relationship with you.
Do you really think you will have a harmonious
relationship with his children if you begin with
a deception? Have you even met his children
yet? What do you think of THEM? You're
not the only one who has to pass inspection,
kiddo. It's a two-way street. What do your
brothers think? Have they met him?

Let me be frank about money. Let's
see now, how can I say this tactfully? Oh, heck,
since when have I worried about that, right?
Okay, Does Gordon know about your financial

situation? This is more important: Did he know
you are a wealthy woman before he put the rush
on you? Really, Maggie, that's something to
consider. You mention your "little program"
of giving aid to disadvantaged children. You
are too modest. I happen to know it's much
more than "little." Is Gordon aware of how
much money you give away? Is he comfortable
with that? Will you each maintain your separate
bank accounts? Have you gotten legal advice
about your will?

Now then, those are my concerns and
questions. Please answer them and put my mind
at ease. Meanwhile, don't worry. I'll keep your
secret. My lips are sealed. I'm brimming with
more questions, so answer these, and I'll let you
have the next batch. Remember, Maggie dear—I'm
concerned with one thing and one thing only:
your happiness.

As always, your affectionate friend, (and now
absentee matron of honor),
Tootsie

As she clicked off the computer, she heard the persistent *beep beep beep* of the oven's timer and went quickly into the kitchen, where she removed the cheese-laden veggie pizza, fragrant with the scent of oregano and sun dried tomatoes, from the rack and set it on a mat to slice. As she carried her tray into the den to eat while she watched

TV, she thought of Maggie eating alone, too, and she had a pang of guilt that she had rained on her friend's parade. This eating alone was for the birds. She couldn't blame Maggie, in a way, for grasping at the chance for happiness. Couldn't blame her at all. In fact, there was a little reversal of roles going on here, she had to admit, in even calling Maggie's judgment into question. It was against Tootsie's whole nature to be the voice of reason. It flew in the face of her flamboyant, devil-may-care outlook on life. But this was Maggie, a friend who had been as close as a sister for over forty years. She couldn't let anything bad happen to Maggie. *Maggie, oh Maggie! I just hope you know what you're doing.* As she sank into her burgundy leather recliner, she laid her head back and let her mind drift back to the day she and Maggie had first met. Oh, what a day that was!

Chapter Three

"'S cuse me," the stunning redhead asked a girl on Duke's West Campus, "but can you tell me where the biology building is?" Her voice was tiny, a little girl's voice in a woman's body. Her forehead was lined with concern.

The other girl laughed. "You surely did pick the wrong person to ask if you want information, because I'm a freshman, too. On the other hand, if you want company to the biology building, you asked exactly the right person, because that's where I'm headed."

The questioner's worried brow relaxed a bit. "Really? Oh, good. We'll find it together."

"Yeah, or get lost together, but somehow, this campus doesn't seem as large when there's someone with you. By the way, I'm Tolbert Lincoln Forsyth—my mother's into family names—but my friends call me Tootsie."

"Tootsie? As in 'Toot-Toot-Tootsie, Good-bye'?"

"Yeah, I know, but it's better than Tolbert or Lincoln, for heaven's sake."

Brushing the wild red hair out of her eyes, the girl chuckled and said, "Well, I'm Margaret Katherine Muldoon. My friends call me Maggie." She grinned and made a crooked pucker with her mouth. "Uh, actually, I'll be honest. No one has ever called me Maggie, but I wish you would."

Now it was Tootsie's turn to laugh. "A little away-from-home rebellion, eh? All right, Maggie it is. Glad to know you."

The two stopped right in the middle of the sidewalk, shifted their books to one side, shook hands, and continued on their way, happier than either had been since leaving home for orientation week at college almost a week before. Stopping in front of a building that reeked of formaldehyde through the open windows, Maggie said, "Well, with an aroma like that this has got to be the biology building."

"Either that or the dining hall," Tootsie said. Maggie laughed, and Tootsie went on. "You taking Biology 101?"

Maggie nodded. "Yes."

"Who's teaching it? What room are you in?"

Withdrawing her folded and re-folded class schedule from her purse, Maggie consulted it and said, "Let's see. 214. Professor Brown."

Tootsie smiled before rattling on. "Hey, great. Same here. I have Brown. Do you know anything about biology? I'm not very good at science, not interested in it, really. Thank heavens my verbal scores were good enough to get me in this place. I was really sweating it because Duke is so picky. They took, what this year? Less than ten percent of all applicants? I remember what my father said when I got my letter of acceptance: 'Getting *in* is the easy part.'" She threw her head back and laughed at the memory. "I'm going to major in English, I think. Are you a biology major? Pre-med or anything?"

"Heavens no. I'm a humanities person myself, hopefully an English major, too. I'm just taking this to fulfill my science requirement because I thought it would be more interesting than botany. I couldn't see myself tramping through Duke Forest looking for fern fronds and mushrooms." Maggie stopped suddenly and turned a brilliant smile on Tootsie. "Actually, you want to know the truth? I figured there would be more boys in this class. It's one of the few classes freshman girls can take on West Campus, where the men live, as I'm sure you know."

Tootsie nodded. "Me, too. I figured chemistry was out. I blew up the lab in high school one time. Well, not really blew it up, just created enough smoke that they had to evacuate the whole second floor. Even called the fire department." She laughed. "I thought they were overreacting myself."

Maggie laughed, too. "Bless Dr. Brown's heart. I wonder if the poor man is up to this—both of us, I mean."

***

Taking a bite of pizza, Tootsie smiled as she remembered that first day with Maggie Muldoon so many years ago—her startlingly small voice, her bottle-green eyes, her flamboyant red hair. She remembered how the two of them went to the Dope Shop, as the snack center was called then, for a Coke after class. They had learned in freshman orientation that it derived its name from the fact that Coke, when it was introduced, was felt by many people to contain cocaine and thus be a dope. They had had a good laugh about that. She remembered their feet echoing on the time-worn limestone steps of the gothic building, how they talked all the way during their ride back to the Woman's College campus, how they sensed even at the time that their lives would always been intertwined. And they had been right. They roomed together every year after that, Maggie Muldoon, an athletic, red-haired Roman Catholic from Jackson, Mississippi, and Tootsie Forsyth, a raven-haired, flamboyant Methodist from Bluefield, West Virginia.

They were a striking pair on campus, both tall and willowy, though at five eleven, Tootsie was about an inch taller than Maggie.

The similarities were great: They were both stunningly beautiful, both on the women's swim team, both English majors, and both determined that their considerable IQs, which they downplayed at every opportunity, would not stand in their way of their first goal in life: finding a prince charming. It was not all that unusual a goal among their peers in the fifties and early sixties. *Ah, how times have changed,* Tootsie thought as she munched the pizza. In addition to excelling in academics and athletics, Maggie, with no fanfare or encouragement and utterly defying all traditions of the day, went once a week to the Ebenezer A.M.E. Zion Church to tutor children in the African American community of Durham.

Born into an upper class family in Jackson, Mississippi, Maggie had fallen in love with Campbell Palmer in high school. Cam was the only son of Joanna and Campbell Palmer, Sr., the president of Palmcraft, a highly successful knitting mill that manufactured sweaters, knit shirts, and jackets. By hard work and several good breaks, Palmer, Sr., had amassed a fortune. Just before going away to college, Maggie and Cam broke up, convinced that a long-distance relationship wouldn't work. He went to Millsaps, she to Duke.

In the intervening years, Maggie had one boyfriend after another, but never one for any length of time. To a few, her height was intimidating because when she wore extremely high heels, which she often did, she towered over many of the shorter boys in her class. To others, her Catholicism, not common in the South at that time, was a stumbling block. Even to Cam, a Southern Baptist, it had been a problem. To many, her stubborn morality was another. Still, she never sat in the dorm on Saturday night wondering what the other girls were doing. She changed boyfriends as often as some girls did their bed sheets. Though she still heard occasionally from Cam, she continued to date widely, falling in and out of love many times.

Not far into their junior year, Maggie broke up with her latest boyfriend, Mike Trevor, a boy she had gone with for over two months–something of a record for her–by letter because she didn't think she could face him. She immediately regretted it. "What am I going to do?" she wailed to Tootsie back in their third-floor dorm room. "Once he reads that letter, it's curtains!"

"But, Maggie, you told him you wanted to see other people. What's wrong with that?" Tootsie asked.

"That's just it. I've changed my mind. I don't want to now. More important, I don't want him to either. As soon as I mailed that letter, I knew it was a mistake, but it was too late. Oh, I am so stupid! Stupid. Stupid. Stupid."

"When did you mail it?"

"Just now, after my third period class, why?"

Tootsie looked at her watch. "Where did you mail it?"

"In the West Campus post office, right by the Dope Shop, why?"

"Come on," Tootsie said, grabbing her purse. "We're headed for a little R & R."

"What? I'm not in the mood for rest and—"

"—Reach and retrieval."

"Tell me you're not seri—"

"Hurry! We've got to beat the crowd after fourth period gets out and heads to the Dope Shop."

Maggie grabbed her bag and ran after Tootsie, asking questions all the way. "What are you going to do? Surely you're not thinking what I think you're thinking, are you? What if we get caught? What if Mike see us? Oh, I'd die, just die!"

"Would you rather risk running into Mike or having him read the letter?"

"Tootsie, I—"

"Just hush and come on."

"Tootsie, talk to me."

Tootsie ignored Maggie's pleas and kept walking at a fast clip to the East Campus circle, where students regularly waited to be picked up by other students driving between the two campuses. A ride came quickly. Once they were on West Campus, they hurried down the stone steps to the basement level of the Union Building, which housed the Dope Shop, home of cherry Cokes and hot dogs all the way; a barber shop; a branch bank, and the men's post office. Without delay, Tootsie took off her jacket, stuck her left arm in the mail slot, and began fishing for the letter. Maggie looked nervously up and down the deserted halls. "Are you feeling anything back there?" she asked.

"Yep, the mail is piled up high enough that I can barely touch it—everybody writes home at first, you know—but I can't quite reach far enough down to get hold of the letter. 'Course, it might not be your letter anyway, but then again, it might. Just need to stick my arm in a little bit farther. If I can just reach the pile, I'll keep pulling out letters until we get the right one." After several more minutes of diligent stretching, she heaved a deep sigh and said, "I give up. Sorry, Maggie. I tried. We'll have to take our chances and ask the postmaster if—" It was then it happened. She started to straighten up, but her arm remained caught fast in the mail slot. "Oh no! I don't believe this!"

"What? What?" Maggie's pulse quickened, and her eyes grew large.

"My arm's stuck!"

"You're joking, right?" But Maggie knew it was serious because Tootsie didn't return her nervous smile.

"No, I'm not joking. I'm really stuck."

Maggie began wringing her hands. "Oh, dear heavens! Tootsie! What are we going to do?" She glanced at her watch. "Look at the time!"

Tootsie rolled her eyes.

"Oh, you can't. I forgot. Sorry about that. Well, anyway, it's almost time for fourth period to be out. This place is going to be swamped any minute."

No sooner were the words out of her mouth than a noisy stampede of boys, liberated from class for the weekend and hungry for lunch and mail, came storming down the stairs and thundered toward the post office. In minutes, the two girls were surrounded by at least fifty guys, at first staring, then laughing and hooting. Maggie nervously sought Mike's face in the crowd. It wasn't there. Oh, thank goodness!

Tootsie looked at her friend. "Don't just stand there, Maggie. Go knock on the door and get the postmaster to help us."

Soon, the postmaster had helped free her arm and stood glowering at the two girls. "You *do* know it's a federal offense to tamper with the United States mail, don't you?"

There were catcalls from the assembled group of knights-without-white-horses brigade, as he continued. "Young ladies, I ought to turn you in to the dean of the Woman's College for this." He made an exasperated clicking sound with his tongue. "What's the matter with young people nowadays? No respect for authority. That's what it is." He raised one eyebrow and flexed the muscles in his jaw. Louder catcalls. He turned his head and looked at the boys, then back at the two girls, relaxing his shoulders a bit. "Well, I suppose no real harm was done. But this better never happen again! All right, I guess you can go."

"Thank you, sir, but I'm afraid we can't," Tootsie said.

Maggie cringed. How much longer would her luck hold out before Mike appeared on the scene? What was Tootsie thinking?

The postmaster looked startled. "Can't? Wh—What do you mean?"

"I mean that we can't go without the letter we came for."

29

"Well, I'm sorry, but I can't—"

Tootsie fastened an imploring look on the man. "Sir, please. Just think: a broken relationship, a marriage that will never be, children who will never see the light of day, a spinster alone in the world all because you refused to return a letter written in haste. Sir, have you ever read Herman Melville's story, 'Bartleby the Scrivener'?"

Mutely, the hapless postmaster shook his head, not wanting to be drawn into this little melodrama, but as powerless as a bit of flotsam being swept into a whirlpool to stop it. "I—uh...." He seemed to regain his power of speech just as Tootsie continued.

"Well, it's just so, so sad. At the end of the story, one of the best endings in American Literature, by the way, Melville says that the letters in the dead letter office contain 'pardon for those who died despairing; hope for those who died unhoping; good tidings for those who died stifled by unrelieved calamities.... Ah, Bartleby! Ah, humanity!' " Tootsie blinked several times, as if threatening tears.

Maggie, her flaming face matching her hair, had, for her part, gone past worry and embarrassment to disbelief and amazement at her friend's dramatization. This was chutzpah at its best. Even for Tootsie. Never mind that in Melville's story, the letters were lamented because they were undelivered, and in this situation, the two of them were themselves trying to un-deliver one. It didn't matter to Tootsie. She took the cake! She really did.

The postmaster, sensing the sympathies of the crowd, knew he was beaten. He made a clucking sound with his tongue. "Oh, all right. Come here to the door and identify your letter."

Minutes later, as Tootsie and Maggie emerged from selecting the letter, a roll of spontaneous applause swept through the happy gathering. Maggie, her face burning, tried to hurry by, but Tootsie stopped, faced the crowd, and bowed deeply.

***

Tootsie finished her pizza and sat sipping her Coke, her feet on an ottoman, her head relaxed against the chair. For a week after that post office caper, she had had to listen to Maggie's "I-just-can't-believe-you" sighs. Letting her mind wander, she smiled, remembering the scene and many others that formed a multi-dimensional image in her mind, an image of gothic spires, late-night chats, and wild basketball games in Cameron Indoor Stadium, of rain-puddled slate walkways, of standing-room-only chapel services, of cabin parties. She and Maggie were in all of them. Soon, Cam was in them, too, for during their senior year, Maggie and Tootsie had to make room in their cozy relationship for Cam.

Maggie and Cam began corresponding regularly, and over Christmas of that year, when they were both at home and went out for pizza and a movie, they realized that their love was real, that the ashes of their relationship had been banked but never put out, that their religious differences were not insurmountable, and that compromise was possible. They would join the Methodist Church after they married, they decided. Maggie joked that the Methodist Church had liturgy high church enough to pass for Catholic from which all the fat had been trimmed and church suppers that were Baptist enough to put the fat back on. That might not completely satisfy both families, but it was one they could live with.

It would be a good solution. Love would make everything work. From then on, Cam came to Duke every chance he got. They postponed marriage for a year so that Cam could finish the MBA he would start upon graduation and prepare for the first year of law school at Old Miss. His father wanted him to take over the business, but both of them felt that a law degree, on top of the MBA, would be beneficial.

31

Ah, that senior year! Tootsie smiled. Another image entered the kaleidoscope. It was Walter Baxter Freeman, tall, sandy-haired, quiet. Dimples ringed his mouth like parentheses, and his pale honey-colored eyes seemed to smile all on their own. A Duke alumnus living in Durham, Walter was ten years older than Tootsie and had already established himself in the business community when he met Tootsie. It was during Homecoming at an alumni/senior event sponsored by the Loyalty Fund when their paths crossed. She was smitten immediately—was intrigued, really, by the depth and the reserve of him—but she seemed to make no progress in arousing his attention, try though she did.

Weeks went by, and she finagled another meeting of a sub-committee she volunteered for when she saw his name listed as a member. Shy and unassuming, he finally asked her out, and the relationship swiftly blossomed, so swiftly that Tootsie asked Maggie to be her maid of honor two weeks after graduating in June of 1962. One year later, Tootsie returned the favor as the honor attendant when Maggie and Cam married in Jackson, Mississippi.

The two girls vowed at that tearful parting, as Cam and Maggie prepared to leave for an extended honeymoon trip to Europe, that they would never let their friendship die. To ensure that they would stay in touch, they pledged to send each other a post card every week. "Listen, kiddo," Tootsie had said, "You don't have to write a message. All you have to do is sign your name. I just want to know you're alive." They had both promised and hugged goodbye.

So long ago, Tootsie thought. She laughed at the memory. Post cards did it, too, she thought, until they went online. Though the two friends had seen each other only once since Cam died five years before, their daily email chats and frequent telephone calls kept each other abreast of everything going on in their respective lives. When Cam had died, killed in a car wreck by a drunk driver, Tootsie had flown at once to be with Maggie, returning the favor, as Maggie had driven to Durham two years earlier to support Tootsie when Walter had died of a massive heart attack. Because Maggie and Cam had no children, Maggie was bereft, but she soon threw herself into volunteer work to fill any time left over from selling real estate. She also drew even closer to Tootsie.

What will it be like now? Tootsie thought. Would Maggie have any time left for her if—apparently when—she married this Gordon Dawkins character? Would he resent their friendship? Well, time would tell. She stood and stretched, picked up her tray, and carried it to the kitchen. Pausing to open a jar of peanut butter, she put a spoonful into her mouth, and luxuriated in its crunchy texture. Starting to flip off the lights, she said, "Come on, Ladybug. Let's go to bed. The dishes will wait for another day." The cat stopped and sat down, fixing her with an unblinking eye. "Oh, give me a break. Don't tell me Emma Beth has gotten to you, too. I know she'd never leave dirty dishes in her sink, but just because you stayed with her last week while I was in Atlanta, doesn't mean you can become my housekeeping conscience. Come on." She went up the stairs, soon followed by Ladybug, whose padded footsteps fell in noiselessly behind her own.

She showered, pulled on fresh satin pajamas, and propped herself up in bed to read, a habit she'd started years before. She was trying to finish a mystery she'd been reading for several nights before she went to Charlotte, but tonight her mind kept wandering. Maggie had left her with too many unanswered questions. When would the wedding be announced? When would it, in fact, take place? When and how were they going to tell Gordon's children? What was Maggie going to think about her questions? What if they made her mad? She does have a temper. Finally, she gave up and laid her book down. *All right, Maggie, I'll keep your little secret, but you'd better come through with some answers. And soon.* She pushed Ladybug farther down on the bed and stretched out to sleep. As she drifted off, she realized that a deep worry, like a chill, had settled in her bones.

Chapter Four

Four days later, following a brisk swim at the Duke University pool, after which she drove to Raleigh for lunch and a lengthy talk with Emma Beth, Tootsie returned home and, after spreading peanut butter on several crackers and placing them on a plate, went straight to her study. She had expected every day to hear from Maggie, but as of yet there had been no word. In fact, she had been concerned and had started several times to call her, but she decided that she should let Maggie answer the questions on her own timetable. Maybe there were things she didn't want to talk about just yet. Mustn't rush her, Tootsie kept telling herself.

She turned on the computer and sat munching her crackers as it booted up. Soon, she was online and was relieved when the little light on the mail icon blinked on, indicating that she had mail. About time, Maggie old girl. The only time she had gone this long without getting in touch was when she was in the middle of closing on a huge purchase of land for a retirement home and was being wined and dined by the prospective buyers. Even then, she had warned Tootsie in advance that she would be away from the computer for a few days. Quickly, Tootsie clicked on the mail logo, eager to see what Maggie had to say.

She couldn't believe her eyes. It wasn't from Maggie at all. It was just a ho-hum, newsy letter from Walt, telling about all the business the bank was involved in and how exciting his job was to him. She read the letter carefully to see if by chance he mentioned anything of a social life, but she came up dry. Nothing. Business, business, business. *Honestly*, she thought, *he sounds like a middle-aged man.* How many times had she quoted Oliver Wendell Holmes, Jr. to him— "Life is painting a picture, not doing a sum"? How did she end up with such a dedicated, hard-working, and—go on, she told herself, say it—stuffy son! Charlotte was an exciting city, all right, if you liked finance. Second biggest banking center in the country. Second only to New York City. Skyscrapers, cranes, and businesses everywhere, but a social wasteland. No, that wasn't fair. There were plenty of places for young people to meet. She'd seen them. Sidewalk cafes, bars, sports complexes, churches. But it's hard to meet people at any of those if you're sitting in an office poring over how to increase the bottom line. She laughed and shook her head. *I think I'll send his name into one of these dating services. Hah! That would get his attention and give him something to think about besides money, numbers, and mergers.*

Ordinarily, she would have devoured Walt's letter, however mundane, with great interest. Just not today. Not when she was expecting to hear from Maggie. What in the world? Had she offended her? Surely not. They'd been like sisters too many years for her to take umbrage at Tootsie's curiosity. Maggie knew too well that with her Tootsie said whatever was on her mind. So what gives? She chewed her lip while she thought. And worried. *Well, I guess I'd better do it,* she decided. *I can't stand the suspense. I'd better force her hand and call her.*

Just as she started to pick up the phone, it rang, its cold, shrill ring making her jump.

"Hello."

"May I speak with Mrs. Walter B. Freeman, please?"

"This is she." *Oh great,* she thought, *a telemarketer. What will it be this time—light bulbs that will last longer than I will, aluminum siding guaranteed not to need replacing until I'm one hundred and twenty years old, or a cemetery plot? Big Brother is definitely watching, and he knows when my birthday is.*

"Mrs. Freeman, my name is Chilton Surles. I am the attorney of your friend, Mrs. Margaret Katherine Muldoon Palmer, in Jackson, Mississippi."

Oh, thank goodness, Tootsie thought. *Maggie has gotten some legal advice in this harebrained matrimonial scheme, and she's told him to call and reassure me. She's probably too busy herself right now.* "Yes?"

"I'm afraid—I—uh, that I—well, I have some very bad news."

"Oh, my Lord! Don't tell me Maggie has already gotten married."

"Excuse me?"

"She's eloped, hasn't she?"

"Eloped? No, ma'am, Mrs. Freeman. Nothing like that." There was a long pause. "I'm afraid I—well, I'm very sorry, but—"

Tootsie suddenly felt her blood run cold. There was something in the man's voice that gave her a chill. "What? You're sorry about what?"

"Well, that's what I've called about, Mrs. Freeman. Uh, there's been quite a—a tragedy here. You see, Mrs. Freeman, your friend, Mrs. Palmer...she's...dead."

Chapter Five

Tootsie's arm turned to lead. The telephone suddenly seemed so heavy she couldn't hold it, and she felt that she would surely drop it if she didn't quickly rest her elbow on the desk. At the same time, her head felt as light as a cotton ball, and she dropped her forehead over onto her open palm. Her breath was coming in shallow little puffs now. *No. Not Maggie. Not Maggie. It was impossible. Maggie was too full of life, too excited about the adventure of living, too full of kindness, too helpful to other people, too young. Why, she was going to get married, for goodness sake. No, her mind screamed, it just wasn't possible.*

"Mrs. Freeman, are you there?"

Tootsie tried, but she couldn't make her voice work. It was like being shut inside a glass box where she could see what was going on outside, but she couldn't make contact with it. Leaning her head back against the chair, she took several deep gulps of air and cleared her throat. "Yes," she whispered, "yes, I—I'm—here." This was absurd. There had to be some mistake. She said as much to Chilton Surles. "You can't mean Maggie Palmer. Margaret Katherine Muldoon Palmer? There must be some mistake."

"I'm afraid it's true. I'm very sorry to break such bad news over the phone, but your name was on a list of Mrs. Palmer's friends she had given me some time ago to notify in the event anything ever happened to her."

Tootsie swallowed and took a deep breath. "What—what happened? I mean, how did she die?"

"She—uh, drowned. At least, that's the—"

"Drowned?" Tootsie's mind was reeling. "Maggie drowned?"

"Well, yes, ma'am, that's what the coroner's preliminary report says. The final report from the medical examiner's office isn't in yet. It should be in tomorrow or the day after. I waited to call you until I was able to tell you the funeral arrangements and so forth. Mrs. Palmer's brothers are already in Jackson and have just finished making plans for the funeral at her church, First United Methodist, at 10:00 A. M. Friday. They asked me to express their hope that you can come."

"Of—of course I'll come," she said, swallowing. She was already thinking ahead to flight arrangements, hotel reservations, and clothes. "I'll try to get a flight out tomorrow. Is there a hotel nearby?"

"Yes, ma'am, the Hilton is not far from First Methodist. Shall I call and book you a room?"

"How thoughtful! Yes, that would be a help. Tell them to hold the room for me until 10:00 tomorrow night. Hopefully, I can get a flight out by then. If I'm not there by then, tell them to let the room go and hold one for me the next day."

"Very good. All right. I'll see you then, and, Mrs. Freeman?"

"Yes?"

"Please accept my deepest sympathy. I know you were very good friends."

"Thank you, Mr. Surles." She swallowed and continued, "We were more than friends, really. Maggie was the one person on this planet who understood me, really understood me, and I understood her. That's rare, you know. We've been like sisters for over forty years."

"I know this has been a shock. I'm very sorry."

"Yes...quite a shock. Thank you for your kindness. I'll see you in Jackson."

They hung up, and Tootsie sat dazed, unable to think straight, unable even to cry. She felt like a wooden doll, whose limbs could be moved by a puppeteer but who was incapable of any movement herself. All she kept thinking was *it isn't possible. Just not possible. Not Maggie.* Finally, she shook her head as if to clear it and slowly picked up the phone. She let it ring three times and was just on the point of hanging up, for she couldn't bear to leave a message like this on her daughter's answering machine, when Emma Beth picked up. As clearly as she could, she told Emma Beth what she had been told by Chilton Surles.

"Momma! No!"

"Oh, Emma Beth," Tootsie sobbed, the tears coming freely now, "my Maggie is gone. Whatever will I do?"

"I just can't believe it!"

Tootsie cried, "No, darling. I—I can't either."

"I'll be there in thirty minutes."

Tootsie choked back tears and swallowed hard to keep them from coming again. "No, sugar, really. You've got the children to get ready for school tomorrow, and—"

"Mark can do that."

"Besides, it wouldn't do any good."

"Well, it will do me some good. Don't say another word. I'm on my way, and I'm spending the night."

In thirty minutes exactly, just as she had promised, Emma Beth was in her mother's arms, sobbing, and being comforted by the very one she came to console. Finally, exhausted, the two women sat down

40

on the sofa and held hands as they talked over the news that had devastated them.

"I'm so sorry, Mom. I meant to help you, and it seems to be the other way around." As Tootsie wiped her red eyes with a ragged Kleenex she fished from her pocket, she watched as Emma Beth withdrew an immaculate lace hanky—pressed—from her purse. "I know how close you and Maggie were."

Tootsie, her eyes red-rimmed and heavy, nodded slowly. "Oh, my! We were close, all right."

"And she was so kind, so generous to Walt and me as we grew up and even to my children," she reminisced. "Said we were all her children, too."

"Oh, she loved you as much as if you were. With no children of her own, she felt that spoiling you all went beyond pleasure; it was her duty."

Emma Beth smiled. "I haven't seen Maggie since she came to Dad's funeral. I remember her pulling into the driveway in that big old Cadillac of hers and seeing you run to greet her."

Tootsie smiled sadly. "Oh, yes, I remember. That Maggie! She never got over her fear of flying. Drove everywhere."

"The first thing she did after she got through hugging you was to pick up Ladybug, just a kitten then, and pet her."

Tootsie nodded. "Well, you know how she is...was...about animals. They were her passion. She was on the board of the ASPCA at different times over the years. I think since she and Cam had no children, she decided to become a mother to every stray animal she encountered. Oh, my goodness!"

"What?"

"I was just wondering what will become of her pets. They're all right for the moment because they have a doggy door and, if I know

Maggie, enough food and water in dispensers to last them until the Rapture, but what will become of the pets eventually?"

"Pets? Plural?"

"Oh yes, of course. At last count, she had four cats—two tabbies, one Himalayan, and one Siamese, I believe they were—and two mixed-breed dogs, all refugees from the pound."

"Maybe her brothers will take them."

"Maybe," Tootsie said, unconvinced. She looked down at her lap and bit her lip in an effort to keep the tears at bay.

"I don't understand this, Mom. It's just too unbelievable."

"Yes, that's what I kept saying, but Mr. Surles assured me there is no mistake."

"But you said she drowned."

"That's right, dear. That's what the coroner's initial report said, but Mr. Surles said that was just until the medical examiner completes the autopsy. The final report should be back soon."

"But drowned? How is that possible?"

"What do you mean?"

"I thought Maggie was an expert swimmer. Didn't you tell me that you all were on the swim team in college?"

"Oh yes, Maggie was the best freestyle swimmer on the team—by far. She had a beautiful breast stroke, too. I always envied her stroke—so graceful, yet so powerful. Mine looked choppy and weak beside hers. In fact, she was an all-around athlete. She was good at tennis, too. More than good, really. She always felt she was too heavy, even though she wasn't, and she struggled with that idea all her life. She was so tall, though, and she carried her weight well...had a figure to envy, all right, but she was always trying to lose weight. She felt exercise was the only way to stay ahead of the pounds. Oh, Maggie!" A sob caught in her throat. Sighing deeply, she went on.

42

"She continued to play tennis and swim." Tootsie shook her head slowly, remembering. "Oh yes, she was quite a swimmer."

"Then how could this happen?"

Tootsie closed her eyes and swallowed. "Many good swimmers drown, honey. You know that. It happens all the time. It could have been a cramp, I suppose, or maybe even a heart attack that caused her to drown. I don't know. I guess I'll find out all the answers when I get there."

"It just seems so weird, doesn't it?"

"Yes, it does, sweetheart. Really weird."

Before going up to bed, Tootsie made a reservation for a Delta flight at 10:45 the next morning. Emma Beth smiled for the first time that evening. "That's perfect, Mom. I can take you to the plane on my way home. I'll come over and check on Ladybug once or twice while you're gone, or every day if you think she needs it."

Tootsie shook her head wearily. "No, I'll only be gone two or three days. Just come once and be sure her litter is scooped and she has plenty of dry food and water. She'll be fine."

Once she was in bed, with Emma Beth breathing heavily in the twin bed beside her, Tootsie tried reading for a while, but she couldn't concentrate. Her imagination was going wild. She kept seeing Maggie's face, laughing and gay and full of life one minute and then floating, pale and distended, as she imagined it, in the water the next. The vision made her shudder. When at last she turned out the light and slid down under the covers, she became aware of a tiny feeling of unrest. As she buried her sobs in the pillow, she realized that feeling was more than just sadness at Maggie's death. It was a nagging sense of disquiet, an utter disbelief, and finally, a vague but chafing suspicion.

Part II: Bippy

Chapter Six

There was little cleaning to be done in the ample, white frame house in the Homewood section of Birmingham, Alabama, but Beatrice Priscilla Maas, known as Bippy to her friends, straightened it every day anyway. It gave her a sense of order, much as organizing the books in the rare book room had done when she was head librarian—or as they insisted on calling it these days, Chairperson of the Audio-Visual Department—at Samford University, a few blocks away. Oh, those were the days, she thought. Thirty-five glorious years. Where had they gone? Stooping to pick up a bedroom slipper and aligning it neatly beside its mate on the rack in her closet, she thought of how good life had been. There had never been a husband and children, of course, but the students and faculty at the university had been family enough.

She couldn't believe she had been retired almost five years. It seemed impossible, she thought, putting all the magazines on her bedside table in a well-ordered row. How time flies! Well, she supposed the years had flown because she had been so busy. Busy with things like Roads Scholar. Oh, how she loved Roads Scholar! She'd loved it when it was Elderhostel and loved it even more with the less age-restrictive title. The trips and the classes had been stimulating beyond her wildest dreams. She'd met such nice people, too. Oh yes, very nice people. Nice people are all around us, she often said, if we just take time to meet them. She'd often wondered whether in the midst of hostilities, some mediator could step in and say to the combatants, "Hold it just a minute. You over there. I happen to know you like to draw. Did you know the person you are fighting is an artist, too? And you, you play the trombone. Did you know this person over here plays the clarinet?" Bippy thought that if we could all see that we're in the same huge family, but with different interests and abilities, we might get along a little better.

When she wasn't off on a Roads Scholar trip, she was painting—watercolors usually—and reading, two of her favorite hobbies. Especially reading, and especially mysteries, the more violent the better. Her older sister, Melinda Rose, used to tease her about her reading tastes. Oh, she could hear her right now. "Goodness me, Richard," Melinda Rose would say to their brother, in her mock serious tone. "I wish you would look at that. Beatrice Priscilla is reading another one of those purple prose books that they wouldn't even allow in the library where she works." They would all laugh then. She didn't care. She laughed with them.

She routinely covered the lurid pictures on her paperbacks with makeshift book covers made from brown grocery bags. On the grocery bag book covers, she had carefully printed in large block letters, "Basic English Grammar," knowing full well that if she dropped it, no one would ever pick it up and leaf through its pages. It wasn't that she was ashamed of the books. Not at all. She adored the books and kept one in her purse at all times to read whenever she had a moment to spare. No, it was more a social conscience thing with her. Devout Baptist that she was, she just didn't feel right exposing other people, children especially, to the graphic, bodice-ripping pictures that invariably adorned this type of book. "Why, there's not anything close to that picture in the entire book," she once complained in one of her many letters to the publisher. "It's false advertising, if nothing else!"

And then there were the piano lessons. "Dear Gussie!" she suddenly exclaimed aloud. "I've got to practice. It's almost time for my next lesson, and I haven't learned last week's scales yet." Taking piano lessons was something she had always wanted to do but never had time for. It was her retirement gift to herself. For what, she didn't know. For just having lived long enough to retire, she guessed. Well, why not? People ought to get some reward for that. She laughed whenever she thought of it like that, as if living were some giant obstacle course, and those who made it to the finish line ought to get a ribbon or something. She laughed, too, when she went to her lesson in the music department at the university and sat there in the waiting room with all the prissy little pre-teen girls tying and re-tying their hair bows. Their older sisters were there, too, their garishly painted fingernails flying wildly over texts on their cell phones. When they weren't texting, they were fooling endlessly with their hair, twisting it with giant clips, braiding it, and tying it into pony tails.

And then there were the boys. They were all the same, whatever their age: fidgety, tennis-shoed, and constantly picking at their faces. They, too, were absorbed with their cell phones. They were brought to campus for exposure to what their parents undoubtedly called "the finer things of life." Bippy wondered why, with all these people around them to talk to, these young people were talking to someone else far away. It never made sense to her. She had observed people—couples, even—out to dinner who never exchanged a word but sat texting the entire time. It seemed the height of rudeness to her. It communicated that the person across from him or her was not as important as the person at the other end of the phone.

After every one of these lessons, Bippy went straight home and practiced her heart out, going over the scales up and down, up and down. She was glad the house had no close neighbors. As hard as she practiced the day of her lesson, and as much as she determined that the next week she would practice every day instead of waiting until the last minute, as the week wore on, she got busier and busier. What with cleaning, bicycling, reading, painting, and making trips to O'Carr's Delicatessen, why, before she knew it, it was time for another lesson.

There was also the computer. To no one's surprise, after a few years of retirement, she had become bored with piano practicing, painting, reading, and traveling. She decided she needed a new challenge, so she took some of the very generous love offering collected by an adoring student body on the occasion of her retirement and bought herself a spanking new computer with all the bells and whistles she could find. It was no surprise because everyone knew that although Bippy Maas had not had to use a computer much at school—her assistants did all of that—she was going to keep up with the times. That's just the way she was. Well, you've just got to keep abreast of things, she had said often enough, or get left behind. "Never look back," her mother had said to her once. "It's dangerous. That's not the direction you're going." Privately, she told herself that she had two choices now that she was retired: She could sit at home and knit, something she found exceedingly boring, or she could "get with the program," as that adorable little Sam Kessler, with his big blue eyes and white-blond hair, was fond of saying with a quick wink.

She smiled and sighed as she thought of Sam, a mere boy with his towheaded innocence. How she looked forward to her after-hours sessions with him over in the computer lab on campus! He had been kind enough to help her pick out a computer and had insisted on giving her free tutorials once a week, "just to help you get the hang of it," he had said. This had been going on for some time. Knowing that he felt he owed her something because she had paired him up with Molly Jenkins in the French Department, she tried to let him off the hook.

She had told him over and over that it was her pleasure to introduce them and see them so happy, but ever since Molly had accepted his marriage proposal, Sam just couldn't do enough for Bippy. Heavens, she remembered, he'd even come to her house and set up the computer and volunteered to feed her cat any time she was out of town. Such a nice boy!

She chuckled with contentment when she thought of the young couple. Pairing up people was almost a pastime with her. It just seemed to come naturally. That's why, even now when she went to O'Carr's Delicatessen, a spot well-known and frequented by Samford students, she was constantly being greeted by a familiar voice, for while she was the media specialist at Samford, she did more than help students find books. She often helped them find themselves and occasionally even helped them find their eventual life's partner. It was said that she did more to encourage campus romances than all the sweet-smelling magnolias and warm breezes in Alabama. In fact, the faculty lovingly referred to her, though not to her face, as Marryin' Maas.

O'Carr's! she thought suddenly, straightening up and dropping a magazine on the table by her bed. *I haven't been to O'Carr's yet this week. It's high time, too. A week without cheesecake from O'Carr's is—well, too long,* she laughed to herself. The piano practice would have to wait. She put on a green jacket that always seemed to light up her peach-colored complexion and tied a blue and green scarf loosely around the soft white curls ringing her face. She looked in the hall mirror, dimly illuminated by the old milk-glass sconces on either side, and studied her reflection for a moment. The eyes were okay. Everyone had always complimented her on her sparkling eyes; her hair, though white, was a lustrous cap around her face; and she certainly hadn't put on the weight so typical of many of her friends, but something wasn't right. It was the scarf. "Dear Gussie!" she said aloud, as she did on any occasion of surprise, either positive or negative, "I look like my own granny," and she whipped off the scarf.

Bippy's features were small and rather undistinguished with the exception of her eyes. They were expressive, dark brown—almost black—and warm like two melted chocolates. They offset the tiny nose with the dip in the middle, "like a swag in a mountain," Bippy had often laughingly said of it. The "swag" was where the half glasses usually rested. There was a small mole on her chin that looked like a blot of ink on a piece of creamy vellum stationery, and above it, a small, straight mouth framed two rows of tiny white teeth, all her own. Barely five feet tall and weighing only ninety-five pounds, she looked as if a good stiff breeze would carry her away, but, the very opposite of asthenic, she exercised like a fanatic, as if she were running hard, with osteoporosis and heart disease nipping at her heels. New friends, who wondered how someone so small could eat with as much indulgence as she did, had only to see her exercising to know. One remarked that Bippy was like a hummingbird, constantly feeding, constantly moving. Her small figure, bent against the wind or striding nimbly in the sunshine, was a familiar sight in Homewood. On any given day she could be seen either riding her bicycle or walking briskly on campus, and, unless it rained, even walking to church twice a week, once for worship and once for choir practice.

As faithful as she was to her church, she was equally faithful in her weekly visit to O'Carr's Delicatessen. It was, in fact, about the only place she drove Brother's 1978 Buick, but she considered the drive well worth the effort. She was such a loyal customer that she was afforded an accommodation no one else enjoyed. All she had to do was call O'Carr's and tell them she was coming at such and such a time, and they set out traffic cones, reserving two side-by-side parking spaces to make it easy for her to get her big car parked and backed out.

O'Carr's was, in her words, "a little hole in the wall" on 18th Street, South. Nondescript and hardly noticeable in the shopping strip where it was located, O'Carr's was always filled to its rather small capacity, with lines of people waiting to get in during the lunch hour rush. What made O'Carr's Deli Bippy's weekly destination was what made it the stopping place for many inhabitants of that section of Birmingham: homemade ice cream and cheesecake. O'Carr's had been turning out sumptuous cheesecake and homemade ice cream as long as anyone could remember, ice cream so rich and luscious that milkshakes made with it had to be eaten with a spoon.

As she drove, Bippy thought about those milkshakes and debated which of her three favorite flavors she would have today: chocolate chunk, peanut butter and chocolate, or razzle-dazzle raspberry. *Decisions, decisions, decisions*, she thought, smiling in anticipation. No matter what flavor milkshake she had, she always took a piece of their famous cheesecake home with her. There was no decision to make there. She could never get enough of their hot chocolate cheesecake, creamy cheese so silky smooth it tasted like the thickened custard her mother used to make on Sundays but with a rich, hot-fudge sauce. As a courtesy, O'Carr's always boxed up her cheesecake and fudge sauce separately so she could reheat the sauce at home before pouring it over the cheesecake. Just thinking of it made her sit up a little higher on the cushion that lifted her head barely above the steering wheel and push the gas pedal a little harder.

Chapter Seven

"Yoo-hoo, Socrates, I'm home," Bippy called as she unlocked the door and pushed it open. Just before going in, she rang the doorbell several times, just as Richard used to do when he was a little boy. He had called it "scaring up the spooks." Oh, how they'd all laughed at that. Stepping inside, she quickly turned on the hall light even though it was just late afternoon. Richard was right. An empty house always seemed a little spooky, she thought, as if the very furniture had come to life in her absence and settled back into insentience as soon as she made her presence known. She'd said the same thing many times aloud to her sister. But Melinda Rose would just tease, "You've been reading too many of those murder mysteries, Bippy dear."

It had been so nice when Melinda Rose and Richard were still living. The three of them, none of whom had ever married, had lived together for many years in the proud old, white-frame house on Main Street, the house where their dear Momma and Papa had brought them when they moved from Mississippi. An imposing structure of white columns and wide, welcoming steps, the Maas mansion, as it was referred to in respectful whispers, became more and more demanding as it aged, as if it were determined, like a defiant lady, not to give in to the ravages of time. Painters and plasterers, like efficient plastic surgeons, prodded and patched here and there, staying one day ahead of a total face lift. Bippy knew she couldn't stay here forever, couldn't go on indefinitely plugging the holes in the dike, so to speak, but for now, she was content.

In other days, she and Melinda Rose would always put the kettle on as soon as they came in, and before long, the kettle was rattling away on the gas stove, singing its merry song throughout the house. Melinda Rose, a school teacher, small like Bippy but with more regular features and a decidedly more practical nature, was the oldest of the three siblings and their unofficial leader. Fond of saying "under the circumstances" on just about any occasion, Melinda Rose often shook her head at her younger sister's unabashed gregariousness. "I declare, Bippy," she would say when Bippy stopped perfect strangers on the street and engaged them in conversation, "under the circumstances, I think perhaps a little reserve would be more seemly." What circumstances? Bippy wondered. Age? Gender? Spinsterhood? Oh well. "Perhaps you're right," she would answer and go right on inquiring about the health of everyone from the trash collectors to the policemen along their route.

Melinda Rose, whose school was in the neighborhood, and Bippy, whose job as a librarian at the college was just a short distance away, always got home before Richard did, and by the time Richard left his law office and walked the few blocks to their home, his sisters had tea all ready. He rarely drove his Buick. It seemed a waste of gasoline when his office was so close by, and besides, he pointed out, he needed the exercise. The three of them would sip their Earl Gray—by the fire in the study during the cold months, in the sun room in the summer months—eat their crisp cucumber sandwiches, and talk over their day.

Bippy sighed deeply as she remembered those afternoon teas. There was a time, after Richard died, that she and Melinda Rose carried on the tradition, sitting not by the fire or in the sun room as they had done before—that reminded them too much of Richard—but in the little bay window nook in the sitting room, so intimate and cozy, yet so jolly and cheery in the afternoon sun that it seemed to put its arms around the girls and warm them. But then Melinda Rose fell ill with cancer, and as Bippy watched helplessly, her dear sister faded like a rose plucked from the bush in all its vibrant color, only to curl and wither when left without water in a warm house. After that, Bippy didn't have the heart for tea parties anymore, but she determined not to sit alone and brood, preferring instead to surround herself with the young people at O'Carr's. There were always people to talk to there, people she loved and who loved her. Besides, there was the cheese cake.

"All right, my friend Socrates, here's your supper," she said, leaning down and filling his bowl. "Did you think I wasn't coming home?" The cat, winding itself in and out between her legs, immediately abandoned this pursuit and bent his head over his dish. "Well, I stayed longer than I meant to, really, but there were just so many nice people there to talk to, and well, to be honest, I just lost track of the time." It was not an uncommon occurrence. She regularly went to O'Carr's after the lunch crowd had dissipated and, as often as not, stayed until nearly suppertime. While there, she sat in a front booth, holding court with all ages who came by to speak to her. Children loved her, young people confided in her, and old people trusted her. "Oh yes, Socrates, I had a lovely afternoon even if the time did slip by."

She puttered about the kitchen, opening a can, taking a pan from the cupboard, and continuing to talk softly to Socrates. "And while you eat, I'm going to warm a bit of potato soup and spread some crackers with cheese for my supper, and then for dessert, I'll have this luscious cheesecake I brought home. Mind now, if you're a good boy,

I'll even give you some. Not the chocolate part, though. Mustn't have the chocolate. How's that, hmm?" She bent and stroked his long gray fur and smiled as he purred contentedly and arched his back to meet her hand. "Such a good boy. Okay, now," she said a few minutes later, carrying her tray out of the kitchen, "I'm going into the study to eat my soup while I check my email. You come on in when you're finished," she added, and the cat, stopping to look at her as she left, blinked twice and turned once again to his supper.

Going around and closing all the shutters in the room that had been first Papa's and then Richard's study, Bippy seated herself at the computer and, while waiting for it to boot up, slowly sipped her soup and munched her crackers. This was a grand room, she thought, gazing up at the tall windows, now shuttered securely against the thickening dusk, and the high ceilings outlined with crown molding. It was a room she had played in quietly as a child, while her father, a history professor at the college, went over his lecture notes. She always stayed close by, holding out hope that when he finished, there would be time for a story, and there usually was. Those were the times she loved best of all, when Papa would say in his endearing Dutch accent, "All right, Bippy—for that's the nickname he had given her—let's read together for a short while, shall we?" She settled deeply into his lap, feeling the pleasantly rough texture of his tweed lapels against her cheek, breathing in the aromatic mixture of pipe tobacco, the brown soap with which he scrubbed his face, and the slight hint of lavender that Momma always kept in the drawer with his shirts. On those occasions, she felt like a fairy princess sitting on her throne, and she sat very still, afraid that even the slightest move would break the spell.

The computer's lights signaled that, like a modern genie, it was ready to receive her command, and she felt like a fairy princess once more. *What shall I have you do?* she wondered. *Ah yes, fetch me my mail.* With a giggle, Bippy clicked on the mail icon and was soon scanning her messages. Let's see, she mused, there's one from Sam, one from that friend of Maggie's that she had gotten to know through email, Penelope Caldwell, and, oh yes, good—one from Maggie herself.

Taking a bite of Ritz cracker with cheese, she first answered Sam's note, assuring him that she would see him for her tutorial at the computer lab the next afternoon, then chuckled at the joke sent by Penelope, and at last pulled up the letter from Maggie and began to read:

> *Dear Bippy,*
> *Boy, do I have news for you! Hold*
> *onto your hat, dear friend. I'm getting*
> *married! Can you believe it? It's true,*
> *but I am still pinching myself to be sure.*

Bippy stopped chewing, took off her glasses, wiped them, and settled them comfortably once again into the dip on her nose. Leaning forward, she re-read the words and then sat back in her chair. *Married! Dear Gussie!* she sighed. *How wonderful! How absolutely wonderful!* Bippy appreciated a love match as few people do, and she smiled contentedly as she kept reading.

> *No time for details right now. I'll*
> *write more later. I just wanted to share*
> *my good news. We're not telling people*
> *here yet. In fact, he made me promise not*

*to tell **anyone**, but I just had to tell my
dearest friends, and I am privileged to
count you among them. (Little did we
know that a simple real estate venture
would result in such a beautiful friendship,
huh?) I detected right from the start that
you have my romantic's heart, so I knew
you would understand. Besides, you live
so far away, what could it possibly hurt?*

*Oh, by the way, the groom-to-be is named
Gordon Dawkins. You'll like him, Bippy. He's
tall and drop-dead handsome. Really! And, most
important, he loves me. You'll like this, too: He
sends me yellow roses. Can you believe it? Isn't
that the most romantic thing! He knows how much
I love yellow roses. After we're married, we plan
to take a little trip, and I hope we can come
through Birmingham and stop for a brief visit.
Wouldn't that be fun? I haven't been to see you
since dear Melinda Rose died, and that's been
much too long.*

*Well, I must run. There's much to do. I have
a wedding to plan! Even when I say that, I
can't believe it.*

Talk to you later.
(in) Love,
Maggie

Bippy wiped her glasses again and this time dabbed at the corners of her eyes. *In love. Oh my! Imagine that!* She clicked on "Reply" and began typing:

> *My dearest Maggie,*
> *Your always welcome letter brought*
> *simply marvelous news. I am so very happy*
> *for you I could shout. I know that I will love*
> *Gordon just because you do. He must be*
> *awfully special to have won your heart so*
> *completely and so fast.*
>
> *I am flattered beyond words that you*
> *would want to bring your new husband by to*
> *meet me. What a great time we'll have! Just*
> *let me know when to expect you. I'll serve*
> *some of that fabulous cheesecake I've told*
> *you about and tea. Yes, we'll have a grand*
> *tea party indeed. Your Gordon would like*
> *that, I'm sure.*
>
> *I can hardly wait to hear all the details.*
> *When will the wedding take place? Where?*
> *Has Gordon been married before? If so,*
> *does he have any children? Where will you*
> *live? Will you continue working? Oh, so*
> *many questions. I know you're busy right*
> *now, working plus preparing for a wedding,*
> *but please let me know the answers when*
> *you have time.*

I'll go to bed tonight with a song in
my heart because of your new-found love.
Your happiness is truly mine.
Love,
Bippy

After sharing with Socrates her last bite of cheesecake, from which she had carefully removed all traces of chocolate, and turning off the computer, Bippy returned her tray to the kitchen and tidied up a bit. She picked up her current read, *Death Stalks the Pure of Heart,* and climbed the stairs to her room. She knew that Socrates, asleep on the sofa in the study, where he was happily digesting his supper, would wake up and come later. As she crawled into bed and began reading, she started thinking about Maggie's forthcoming marriage, and the joy she felt interfered with her ability to concentrate. "Oh, for heaven's sake," she said aloud, putting down the book, "I give up! I'm just too excited. There's no use trying to read."

She turned off the light and drifted off to sleep, her mind full of happy thoughts, of wedding plans, of beautiful brides, of handsome grooms. *Wonder why*, she thought, just before sliding blissfully into the peaceful dark of sleep, *they don't want to tell anyone. A bit odd, I'd say. I'd be shouting it to the rooftops, under the circumstances. Good heavens*! She smiled in the darkness. *I'm starting to sound like Melinda Rose, God rest her soul. Maggie said it was Gordon's idea. Well, he doesn't know how lucky he is. He should take out an ad in the paper to proclaim his good fortune to the world instead of trying to keep it quiet. Yes*, she yawned, *a...bit...odd, indeed.*

Chapter Eight

The next day, while riding her bicycle to campus for her computer lesson, Bippy looked up to see Dr. Mac MacLeod, professor of mathematics at Samford, briefcase in hand, walking ahead of her near the school. "Well, hi, Mac," she called happily as she brought the bike to a halt beside him. "How's my favorite sourpuss?" she asked. Dr. McKenzie MacLeod, or M Square, as the students affectionately called him, had been lost in thought, but he now stopped and turned to greet Bippy.

"Hi, yourself," he said, stopping abruptly, his tight lips beginning to part in a smile. He was a tall, strawberry-blond Scotsman with animated, bushy eyebrows, enough freckles for ten people, and a prominent nose. An often solitary figure on campus, he was considered a bit dour by those members of the faculty and student body who didn't really know him. Bippy was not one of them, for though she kidded him about his reserved personality, she knew him well and knew that his rather formidable exterior hid a soul of uncommon kindness.

She also knew that when he was preoccupied, staring at his feet as he walked, he was not being intentionally unfriendly, as those who didn't know him felt, but was more than likely thinking of some way he could help a mathematically-challenged student to pass his course. The students who took his courses soon found it out, too, and they adored him, coming to class a little early in hopes of engaging the reserved M Square in conversation. Though never jocular and always looking like one whose shirt collar was a tad too tight, he occasionally shed his reticence like an old raincoat and talked to the students quietly about his life in Edinburgh and the differences in the two societies, enchanting them, not only with his rolling R's, but with his keen observations.

"What have you been up to lately, Mac? I haven't seen you in a while."

"Not much," he said. He pulled a pipe from his worn jacket pocket, tapped tobacco from a pouch into it, gently tamped in place, and lit it. He leaned forward as he took quick little puffs, and soon he was encircled in a fragrant cloud of cherry-scented smoke.

"Have you been sick?" Bippy persisted.

"No."

"I bet you've been away at a mathematics conference."

"No."

"Oh, busy with the accreditation committee report?"

"No. It's finished." He puffed contentedly on his pipe.

Bippy sighed. "Well, I guess our paths just haven't crossed lately. I'm sorry about that because I always love to chat with you." She said this with a bit of a smile, knowing that "chatting" was hardly the word one could apply to an encounter with Mac MacLeod. It was more like a monologue.

Conversation with Mac was always a challenge, and one had to work hard at it, Bippy knew, to get a dialogue going, so she was willing to try anything, no matter how outrageous, to shock him into responding with more than two or three syllables. "Oh, I know. You've probably been busy squiring around some ravishing redhead or a drop-dead blonde," she said impishly. "Or maybe a beautiful brunette."

Mac blushed, looked down, and shook his head. Then suddenly, he smiled shyly and looked Bippy straight in the eye. "Would I be unfaithful to my best girl?" he quipped.

This was what Bippy loved. It was one of those rare moments when Mac came out of his shell and actually seemed to enjoy repartee with her. "Oh, it's good to know I'm loved," she trilled. "Seriously, Mac, you've been working too hard. I haven't seen you out walking about the campus in almost two weeks."

"Well, you know how it is with us high-paid ivory-tower types."

Oh, this was wonderful. It was one of Mac's coy moods. "Yes, yes, I know. So dedicated. What have you been doing up in that tower of yours anyway? Thinking of pouring molten steel down on the crowds below?"

Mac nodded. "That and throwing student papers up the stairs for grades."

"Oh, same old thing, huh?"

"Mmm-hmm," he muttered through his pipe. "It works better with English papers though, I'm told. Math papers, as a rule, aren't thick enough to land on the 'A' step. Most of them don't go farther than the 'C' one."

Bippy laughed. "I suppose you use that in statistics as an exercise in probability," she teased.

"Not bad, Bippy. You might consider taking my class. Beginner level. Wouldn't hurt you to have some figures up there in that head with all those books."

"You're a rascal, Mac MacLeod. Good thing for you that I like rascals."

"Look who is calling whom a rascal."

"You're just cranky because it's mid-term, isn't it?"

"Yep, and you're right. The reporting period always gets me down."

"Oh?"

"I mean, I don't mind averaging the grades. It's not that. I do have a bit of a way with numbers, after all." He smiled and continued, "I just have a difficult time putting a grade on someone who is trying hard but just not quite getting it, you know?"

Bippy smiled at the rich, sonorous roll he gave the *r* in *grade* and *hard*. "Oh, yes, Mac, I do know. I wonder if your students know how much you worry about them. Maybe you could invent a category for wakeful attention and give all *A*'s."

He removed his pipe from his mouth, threw his head back and laughed then and laid his hand affectionately on Bippy's handlebars. "In spite of your impudence, you're quite the spirit-lifter, Miss Bippy, I'll say that. You really ought to consider taking my class. It would be nice to have a real adult to converse with in class from time to time."

"Uh-huh. I heard what you said about 'beginner level.' You're not fooling me with this sudden Mr.-Nice-Guy routine," she answered. "Well, I'd best be going. Don't want to be late for my lesson with Sam."

"Young Kessler still tutoring you, is he?"

"Yes, and he is probably writing down all the silly questions I ask, like how the computer knows what day or time it is if I haven't typed it in, so he can write a book someday. He's probably also asking himself at least ten times a day why he ever volunteered for this. I think I'm his greatest challenge so far."

Mac laughed. "Well, challenge or not, I'm sure Bill Gates is getting nervous. He's probably making a spot for you as we speak."

"Don't hold your breath, as the young folks say. Well, ta-ta. That's 'cheerio' to you. See you soon." And she was off, pedaling as fast as her small legs could to make up for lost time. As she rode, she thought, *Oh, I'm a challenge, all right*, and she added, *almost as great a challenge as finding you a wife, Mac MacLeod! Hmmm. I wonder how that new professor in the English department would do for Mac—Madeline Wentworth. About his age, I'd say, and quite attractive. Never been married, I'm told. Probably too busy getting her Ph.D. Well, I'll have to look into that, and who knows, maybe we'll have wedding bells one day before too long on the Samford campus with Professors Wentworth and MacLeod saying, "I do."* Even on his worst days, Mac could manage two syllables.

At the thought of marriage, a thought which was never far from her mind, she remembered Maggie, and a smile broke across her face like the rising sun. Maggie was her soul sister is so many ways. They had both always been hopelessly, incurably in love with love. *Oh, Maggie, you dear girl, I remember the first time I ever met you. I knew right then that you were a special addition to my life.*

It had been more than ten years now. She, Richard, and Melinda Rose had decided to acquire a home in Mississippi to retire in when the time came. Not just any place in Mississippi, but in beautiful Jackson, their mother's birthplace. They would have loved to have had the original house their mother grew up in, but it had long since passed out of the family, so they decided that a little place, not too large for the three of them to keep up, preferably all on one floor, would suit their needs admirably. They had thought of staying in Birmingham, but they talked it over and decided that the house was just too large to keep up as they got older, and they couldn't imagine living anywhere else in town and driving by to see other people living in it. Then, too, they loved Mississippi with its warm climate, beautiful landscapes, and gracious people.

They also thought that if all three started fresh together, there would be no entanglements from previous jobs, no calls for help from the library or the law office or the school, no friends pulling them in different directions. Besides, they had thought, a challenge late in life is stimulating, and they had always loved visiting their mother's birthplace. Papa's birthplace, Alkmaar, the Netherlands, was out. A little too much challenge there. Even though Bippy had lived in Jackson only during her first five years of life, she and her brother and sister had listened carefully as their mother talked often and lovingly of the city. So, they had flown out one year, just as Spring, that graceful fairy dancer, was doing her delicate ballet through the gardens and streets of Jackson, leaving rippled ribbons of sweet-scented flowers in her wake.

It was on that trip that Maggie Palmer had first entered their lives. She was the realtor they had picked out of a brochure because Melinda Rose said, "She has honest eyes. Under the circumstances, I think honesty is what we're looking for. I can always tell about a person by the eyes. If they're too wide open, the person is trying to look honest but really isn't. If they're too veiled, the person is hiding something. Hers are just right." She and Brother never argued with Melinda Rose's rather convoluted logic. When they arrived at Maggie's office, located behind her house, they were met by an extravagantly beautiful lady, her red hair and—Bippy had to admit it—honest, green eyes quite overwhelming. But it was her personality and her sweetness that won their trust and affection. She seemed to understand just how much they had loved Momma and Papa, seemed to want to find just the right place for them, a place not too big but with lots of character, a place they could buy now and rent to some nice person until they retired to Jackson.

She had indeed found a place that promised to be perfect, a dear little cottage, white as a sun-kissed beach, with red shutters that had those adorable little heart designs cut out and a sun room, perfect for her to paint in. Bippy sighed as she remembered it, tucked away at the end of a cul-de-sac not two miles from where their mother was born. And the window boxes! At every window there was a box overflowing with vinca vine, geraniums, nasturtiums, petunias, and asparagus ferns, as if the house had put on her finest jewelry for the entire world to see. It was truly perfect.

What wasn't perfect was the way it turned out. Just before Richard was to fly back out to Jackson to close the deal and do all the necessary signing, he complained one night of a pain in his arm. Melinda Rose fixed him a cup of tea and gave him aspirin, but the next day, the pain was back, this time taking his breath away. They took him straight to the hospital, where he was admitted and hurriedly taken away from them on a rolling bed. They never saw him alive again. It was massive, they were told later in a sterile little office with diplomas hanging all over the walls. A myocardial infarction. He had probably suffered cardiac ischemia for some time. Words! Were they supposed to be comforting? Bippy's eyes welled up even now when she remembered hugging Melinda Rose under the bright light of the hospital hallway, where they stood after leaving the doctor's office. "It's just the two of us now, Sister," Melinda Rose had said. "Just the two of us. Under the circumstances, Brother would want us to be strong. We must take good care of each other."

They did, too. They came in from their jobs at the library and school each day and over tea in the sunny little window nook off the drawing room, talked over what they had done that day, what people they had talked with, what interesting things they had learned. It was at one of their little tea times that Melinda Rose brought up the subject of the house in Mississippi. "We have to make a decision, Beatrice Priscilla," she said in her most business-like tone. She always used Bippy's formal name when she was in her business-like mode. "That Maggie Palmer was so dear and so sympathetic when I called her about

Richard—what an understanding person she is!—and said to take our time, but I don't want to take too long to come to a decision. We need to let her know something. I think that under the circumstances we need to forget about moving and stay here."

Bippy sighed. "I suppose you're right," she said. "But, oh, Richard did so love that little house. He couldn't wait to start puttering around in the yard."

"Now, Bippy dear, don't sentimentalize a house we haven't even lived in yet. Besides, this house we're in is ours. We don't need to pay a penny for it, thanks to dear Momma and Papa. We can close off some of the rooms we're not using. Birmingham is our home. Our friends are here. Our doctors. It makes a great deal more sense to stay put now that Richard is gone."

"I suppose so," Bippy said, surprisingly relieved that the decision had been made for her.

"I'll call Maggie right now if you're sure."

"Yes, yes, okay. Let me speak to her, too, though. I love talking to her."

And so it was done. Maggie had graciously gotten them out of the deal and agreed that it made more sense for the two sisters to remain in Birmingham. "But, golly," Maggie had said on the phone, "I'm going to miss getting to know you all better. I just fell in love with all three of y'all." The feeling was clearly mutual. Melinda Rose and Bippy bought two beautiful European pillow shams of Irish linen trimmed with exquisite lace, tucked them about with pristine tissue, and sent them to Maggie to thank her for her extraordinary interest in them. Maggie wrote and even called every now and then after that to express concern for the two ladies and to inquire about their health. It was during one of those calls, several years after Richard died, that Bippy told Maggie that Melinda Rose was in the hospital.

"What in the world! What's wrong with Melinda Rose?"

Bippy hesitated, sighing deeply, and then blurted out, "The doctor says it's...cancer. They operated, but they don't think they got it all." She swallowed. "It's so hard seeing her fade away, you know? She just lies there, and I can see life receding like the outgoing tide a little bit more each day."

Late the next evening, Maggie Palmer, who had no familial or financial connection to these two long-distance friends and had gotten to know them well basically through correspondence, appeared on the Maas doorstep. Bippy heard a car in the drive and was astounded when she opened the door and found her there and wept softly as Maggie bent down and embraced her.

"I can't believe you're here," Bippy sobbed. "We're not your responsibility. You didn't need to—"

"Oh, tush!" Maggie replied. "I needed some time off anyway, and it is a slow time for real estate right now. It was a perfect opportunity for me to jump in the car and come for a visit."

"You drove? All that way?" To Bippy, whose driving range consisted of roughly a ten-block area, the distance from Jackson, Mississippi, to Birmingham, Alabama, seemed enormous.

"Oh goodness yes. It's only about 238 miles. I made it in just over four hours, counting a stop for supper. Besides, I drive everywhere. Flying is—if you'll pardon the pun—for the birds."

"Dear Gussie!"

The next day, Maggie sat with Bippy by Melinda Rose's bed while she slept, her chest rising and falling as her shallow breath escaped in an uneven rasp. "Look who's come to see you, Sister," Bippy whispered softly in her sister's ear when she saw her eyes flutter open. "It's Maggie Palmer, come all this way just to see you, dear. She drove all the way from Jackson in one day. Isn't that remarkable?"

Melinda Rose had murmured then and turned her face, now chalked by the cruel fingers of disease, to Maggie. "You're...the most...unusual friend we've...ever had," she said. "Really, under the circumstances... quite...extraordinary." She closed her eyes then and slept again.

Maggie stayed a week, and in that week she helped Bippy bury her only sister, helped her sort through clothes, taking most of Melinda Rose's things to the Salvation Army, fixed her countless pots of tea, and helped her to begin healing. When she returned to Mississippi, she left behind a devoted friend, one who felt she had known this generous soul all her life, not just a few years. They had continued to write to each other, and then, when Bippy got her computer, she and Maggie had begun emailing. It was an almost daily correspondence, even if just a line or two. Hearts on the same frequency don't need constant reassurance, Bippy knew, but it was comforting, just the same.

Chapter Nine

After her session with Sam Kessler in the computer lab, Bippy stopped by the English department long enough to leave a note in Professor Wentworth's box suggesting that they have coffee in the cafeteria one day as soon as her schedule permitted. Then she was off on her bike, cruising along in the crisp fall air, crunching the golden leaves under her wheels. *If Professor Wentworth agrees, I'll give Mac a call and suggest he join me for coffee at the same time. It will be a good way to welcome a new member of the faculty. That'll work,* she nodded to herself, smiling as she pedaled along. *That'll work just fine. Dear Gussie! If I stand around waiting for Mac to think of it himself, we'll all be tucked away in some moss-covered cemetery for all eternity.*

Why is it, she wondered, *that people are so slow to make new friends? It would be different if we all knew the world was going to end in a few days,* she decided. *We'd see a lot of instant friendships then, all right.* Now Maggie—ah, Maggie was different. She had been so open and warm when they first met that they had become friends almost immediately. Not a bit standoffish. Genuine, too. And now, she has apparently fallen in love just that quickly. Well, that didn't surprise Bippy. That was how Maggie was—warm, demonstrative, and a tad impulsive. That was just one of the things they had in common.

Bippy hoped that her friend Mac would take to the English professor she had picked out for him with just such alacrity, but what if Mac and Madeline didn't make a love match? Oh well, she shrugged. So what? They could at least be friends, couldn't they? No one has enough friends. She hummed a happy tune as she rode. The words, "What the world needs now is love, sweet love," finally bubbled up in her throat and escaped into the air. It was a song she had picked up from her students many years ago. So much time—beautiful time—is wasted on formalities, she determined. Too much. She didn't blame Maggie for grabbing at happiness while she could. No indeed.

She pulled the bike up onto her porch, chained it to the rack she kept there and, ringing the doorbell as was her custom, unlocked the door. She felt a chill as she entered the house and shuddered involuntarily as she stepped into the bedroom slippers which she always left by the front door when she went out. Once she had put up her computer books, she went immediately to the kitchen to put on the kettle for tea. "Well, now, Socrates, O wise one," she said as the cat padded softly into the kitchen after her, "that's done. Let's go see what word we have from Maggie, shall we?" Flipping on the computer, she sat patiently waiting for it to come to life. When she clicked onto her email screen and saw no word from Maggie, she felt an uncontrollable sense of unease creep along her spine. "That's odd," she said, looking at the cat, who now sat on her desk, his tail curled around him like a question mark. "It's not like Maggie not to write back immediately and answer my questions."

Well, she thought, *she is probably busy with wedding plans.* Sitting back, she allowed herself a little smile as she pictured her friend throwing together a wedding trousseau. *Ah, the dear, dear girl. So much happiness, and no one deserves it more.* She drifted away for a moment or two, her mind far away in Mississippi. Suddenly, she was back, and the pale, thin skin around her eyes wrinkled like fine linen as she frowned. Still, she was surprised Maggie didn't write just a line to say she was tied up and would be in touch later. Not like her. Not like her at all.

Bippy turned off the kettle, made her pot of tea, and, after practicing the piano for a half hour, pausing every few minutes to sip her tea from her mother's thin china cup, which she balanced on top of the piano, reclaimed her seat in the study, where she quickly wrote another letter to Maggie:

> *Dearest Maggie,*
> *I was hoping to hear from you tonight,*
> *but I know you're busy, dear, so don't worry.*
> *I can wait. I'm just eager to know all your*
> *plans.*

Maggie's mention of bringing her new husband to Birmingham suddenly popped into Bippy's mind.

> *Oh, and dear, be sure to let me know*
> *when to expect you and Gordon for a visit.*
> *It will be such fun to entertain you both.*
> *Shall we take him out to see the old Sloss*
> *Furnaces? He would probably enjoy that*
> *bit of history, and what about Red Mountain?*
> *The view of the city from the statue of Vulcan*
> *is glorious. After all, it is the largest cast iron*
> *statue in the world. You know you have a room*
> *here with me anytime you want it, but I imagine*
> *since it's your honeymoon, you will want to*

stay in one of Birmingham's fine hotels. I will
understand perfectly. My guest rooms are
adequate, but they are far from the bridal suite.

Bippy smiled and began thinking of all they would do while Maggie and Gordon were visiting her. *Oh, Birmingham is such a lovely city,* she thought, *that showing it to visitors is a pure delight.* Yes, one thing they would surely want to do is go see the statue of Vulcan, the Roman god of metal-working, on Red Mountain. She was glad she had mentioned that to Maggie. Why, at fifty-five feet, it's the largest cast-iron statue in the world. Had she mentioned that fact? Yes, she thought she had. They just couldn't miss that! Another thing they would have to do for sure would be to go to O'Carr's Deli. Oh, yes, indeed. She could serve the cheesecake at home, but then they would miss the ambience of the place.

She rested her head on her hand, thinking of the sunlight streaming through the windows and warming the booths in the front of O'Carr's, of the lovely friends who came and went there, always stopping to speak to her. Suddenly, her head fell forward slightly, snapping her out of her daydream. *Dear Gussie, I must be tired,* she thought. *It's early to bed for me tonight.* She returned to her computer.

Well, I've had quite a full day, my dear,
so I guess I had better put this old body to
bed. Take good care of yourself and don't
overdo. I know you are busy as a bee with
wedding plans, but let me hear from you when
you have time. You are very, very special to me
as you were to dear Sister and Brother.
All my love,
Bippy

After cooking a package of Chicken Voila! and half a package of chopped spinach, she fed Socrates and settled down on the sofa with her supper on a tray, carefully listening as the evening news anchor explained the problems, but never the solutions of the day, followed by the snappy pace of *Jeopardy* and *Wheel of Fortune*. That Vanna White seemed like such a darling girl. *I'd like to fatten her up a bit though*, Bippy thought. A little cheesecake and fudge sauce from O'Carrs would be just the ticket. And Pat Sajak was a love, no two ways about it. He seemed at ease with everybody. In spite of the televised stimulation, she could hardly eat for yawning, and as soon as she had put her dishes in the dishwasher—the kitchen's one accommodation to the twenty-first century—punched the start button, and heard its comforting hum, she scuffed up the stairs, her bedroom slippers slapping her feet in a rhythmic tattoo.

"Come on, Socrates," she called. "I'm going to get a bath and fall into bed. I won't read long tonight."

Once cozily tucked into her bed, the downy comforter puffed all around her, she reached over and stroked the cat, which had lain down on top of the bouffant covers and proceeded to bathe himself. *Tomorrow*, she thought, *tomorrow I'll hear from Maggie, and then I'll start making my plans. Oh, what fun we're going to have! My dear little Maggie, a bride! I couldn't be happier if I were getting married myself. Well, maybe just a bit...*she admitted with a laugh. Just before she turned out the light, though, she shook her head slightly as a question, then a vague sense of disquiet, descended on her.

As the morning sun pried apart the blinds in her room, Bippy slipped on her robe and went straight down the curving staircase to the study. She turned on the computer and waited patiently for it to come to life. With eagerness and expectation, she clicked on her email. Nothing. This certainly wasn't like Maggie. Going into the kitchen

73

to make tea, she decided that she would call Maggie and just be sure everything was all right. *Better wait a bit*, she decided; *it's early yet.* After she had eaten and dressed and sat sipping her tea in the sunny alcove off the study, the phone suddenly jangled. *Oh, my goodness*, she thought. *I'll bet that nice Madeline Wentworth is calling before class to set a time for our coffee. I'll have to get in touch with Mac right away. Strike while the iron is hot, and all that.* Quickly, she picked up the phone. "Hello."

"Hello. I'm calling for Miss Beatrice P. Maas."

"This is she."

"Miss Maas, my name is Chilton Surles. I am Mrs. Margaret Katherine Muldoon Palmer's attorney."

"Yes?"

"I believe you are a friend of Mrs. Palmer's."

"Oh yes, yes indeed. We're very good friends."

"Miss Maas, I..uh, am afraid that I…I have some very...bad news."

"Bad…bad news?"

"Yes ma'am. It's about your friend, Mrs. Palmer. I'm afraid there's been a terrible tragedy."

Bippy's legs felt weak and trembling. Good thing she was sitting down. Why did he keep using the words, "I'm afraid"? What was he afraid of? All Bippy could do was repeat his words. "A…a tragedy?"

"Yes, ma'am." There was a long, deadly silence. "Miss Mass, I am very sorry to inform you that Mrs. Palmer is...dead."

Chapter Ten

Bippy couldn't breathe. She felt her heart racing, and her head made silent designs, swimming with circling planets and rings.

"I'm so sorry to break this news to you on the phone. I know what a shock it is. I'm calling because your name was on a list of friends that Mrs. Palmer had given me some time ago to notify in case of her death. It was part of her will."

Bippy caught her breath. This couldn't be happening.

"Miss Maas? Are you still there? Are you all right?"

Leaning her head back against the chair, Bippy took a deep, shuddery breath. "Yes, I'm...I'm here, but I'm far from all right."

"Could I call someone for you?"

"No, that isn't necessary, but thank you. Now, please, slowly tell me again what you said."

"Mrs. Palmer apparently drowned about a week ago. Her body was found in Serene Lake here in Jackson a couple of days ago. I waited to call you until the funeral arrangements had been made."

"Drowned? Maggie drowned?"

"Yes, ma'am. It looks that way. The final report from the medical examiner's office should be in today. Then we'll know for sure."

"But...but this just isn't possible. Maggie was so full of life and promise she just couldn't be dead. She was quite a swimmer, too, I happen to know. She just couldn't drown. This is unbelievable!"

"I know how you feel, Miss Maas, believe me. I can't comprehend it myself."

Bippy listened quietly while he told her all about the funeral plans and asked if he could make hotel accommodations for her at the Hilton.

"Yes…yes, thank you. The Hilton would be fine. I'll…I'll try to be there sometime tomorrow, just as soon as I can get a flight out."

When she had hung up, she immediately called Sam Kessler at the computer lab.

"Sam, this is Bippy." She had demanded that she and Sam be on equal terms, despite their age difference, and had insisted that he call her by her nickname as he did his other computer students.

"Why, hi, Bippy! How's it going? Computer problems so early in the day?"

"No, no, nothing like that. Sam, a dear friend of mine in Mississippi has died, and—"

"Oh, I'm so sorry."

"Thank you, dear. It has been quite a shock. Well, anyway, I need to leave town tomorrow to attend the funeral. You offered at one time to feed Socrates for me. Does that offer still hold?"

"You bet it does. I'll stop by today after I leave here and pick up the key and get instructions, all right?"

"Oh, Sam, thank you. You are very kind. I hate to impose on you, but I knew I could count on you."

"Bippy, you give me too much credit. There's not a person on this campus who wouldn't walk on hot coals for you. Are you all right now? Do you want me to come over? I can get my teaching assistant to take over."

"No, dear. That isn't necessary. I'll be all right. I'll just putter around here today, making flight arrangements and getting packed and so forth."

"What about taking you to the airport tomorrow?"

"Oh, the idea! Aren't you the sweetest thing! No, I have no idea when I can leave, and it might be right in the middle of one of your classes. The easiest thing is to get a cab. Really."

"Well, if you're sure."

"I am, and I thank you from the bottom of my heart. See you this afternoon."

She hung up and sat for a moment, dumbfounded. Then, a low, almost musical sobbing, like the fluttering of birds' wings, began deep in her chest and finally wracked her small body. *Oh, Maggie, Maggie,* she wept, covering her face with her tiny hands. *Whatever has happened to you, dear?* Suddenly, she longed to be sitting on her father's lap once more, smelling his brown soap and fragrant pipe tobacco and listening to him read comforting stories that had nothing to do with death and drowning. Nothing at all.

Part III: Penelope

Chapter Eleven

"B r-r-r," Penelope Caldwell said, shaking the rain off her umbrella at the door. "Fall is in the air, all right." She slipped off her jacket and removed the scarf tied around her head to protect it from the wind. "And I love it!" In the kitchen, she put the kettle on the burner for tea. October was her favorite time of year, and she gloried in it, walking three miles every day, rain or shine. It was one way she had organized her days since John died nearly eleven years before. She felt that the early morning exercise helped give purpose and direction to her life, not to mention the health benefits, about which she was very, very informed. She read *Prevention* magazine religiously and frequented the health food store, bringing home herb after herb to try, this one for stiff joints, that one for energy, still another for cardiovascular health. She knew that if he were still living, John would laugh at her vitamin regimen, but maybe, she thought, just maybe, she would someday hit on something, some magic combination, that would unlock the mystery of her hearing loss and restore her hearing. What did she have to lose?

She had gradually lost her hearing over the last five or six years and now, at age seventy-two, she was quite "hard of hearing," as she put it, in spite of sometimes wearing hearing aids, which were on the "fritz" as often as not. "Dropped them again," she would say sheepishly when someone asked her where her hearing aids were. The truth of the matter was that more than likely she couldn't remember where she had put them. Because the magnification of background noise was annoying, she was forever taking at least one of them out of her ear and putting it in a pocket. She was a familiar sight at First United Methodist Church in Culpeper, Virginia, where she worshipped regularly, leaning forward and cupping her hand behind her ear to hear. The minister invariably interpreted that as a sign he should speak louder, and by the time the service was over, he was generally hoarse, and most of the congregation was nettled by being yelled at for the better part of an hour.

She stopped by the mirror and patted her hair. *Good thing I'm going to the hairdresser this afternoon*, she thought. In a way, though, she dreaded it. She knew it would be the same old thing. Every Friday, the beautician, itching to experiment with some jazzy new design she had read about in *Mod Hairstyles for Today*, would try to get her to try a different hair style: "Why dontcha' get rid of that net and try somethin' new and spiffy?" Brandy would say, patting Penelope's gray hair and smacking her gum—a habit that annoyed Pen as much as the cracking of knuckles—while looking at her customer in the mirror. "You know, try a new 'do' for a change. Somethin' modern. It'd lift your spirits. Perk you right up." But Penelope would resist. She didn't need perking up, for heaven's sake. Keeping her soft gray hair in exaggerated curls under an invisible net had been her hairstyle for almost ten years, and she didn't intend to change it now.

All the years she taught English at the high school, she had kept her hair neatly trimmed or pulled back in a demure bun, but since then—she had resigned immediately to care for John when he fell ill—she had kept it in this rather low-maintenance style, and it suited her just fine. "There's nothing the matter with my spirits," she would answer sweetly, "but thank you for thinking of me." She wouldn't go to the beauty parlor every Friday and go through the hassle of dealing with Brandy's insistence on ushering her into the new age of hair styles except for the fact that it was the one place she could find out exactly what was going on in Culpeper. The paper told only what the news was, and everyone already knew that for goodness sake. Only at the House of Hair could one get "the rest of the story," as that wonderful reporter, Paul Harvey, God rest his soul, had been fond of saying. She didn't look at it as indulging in gossip; she looked at it as staying informed. It was her duty as a responsible member of the community. It was civic involvement. Indeed, it almost reached the level of patriotism with her.

She leaned closer to the mirror and eyed her skin. Need to powder my nose, she thought. That's one thing dear Mother was always very clear about: no shiny noses. It was important to Mother, and thus to Penelope, whether anyone was around to notice or not. Penelope's fair skin, wrinkled but as translucent as fine porcelain, was daily dusted with a generous sprinkling of dead-white powder, making her small, close-set green eyes, the color of jade, look like two shiny marbles dropped into a flour bin. She pulled a petit-point compact from her large black leather purse on the bench by the door and patted her nose a few times. There now. Mother would be proud.

After turning off the burner under the whistling kettle and pouring the boiling water over the Red Zinger tea bags, she lifted the skirt of her rather damp dress, and, pulling off the tennis shoes that she had reluctantly agreed to use for walking, she slipped her feet into the stretched brown felt house shoes she wore at home. She wasn't at all fond of the tennis shoes, but Gretchen had insisted. "But they don't do anything for my outfit," she had told her daughter in uncharacteristic concern for fashion when Gretchen seemed determined to treat her mother to proper walking shoes.

"But, Mother," Gretchen had countered kindly, "really, most women don't walk in dresses these days. What about a wind suit?" Gretchen knew better than to call it a sweat suit. Not to her mother. "Would you wear one if I bought it for you?"

"Oh, no, dear. I don't need a wind suit. I have a suit for Sundays, and if it's too windy, I just won't walk. But thank you for thinking of me."

Gretchen had thrown up her hands, given her mother a hug, and dropped the subject.

Penelope's taste in clothes, it was true, ran to the frumpish and included a rather sizable wardrobe of ankle-length dresses, left over from the day when the midi-length reigned supreme. The problem was that on her diminutive five-foot-two, though ample, frame, they were maxi, not midi, and made her look like a child playing dress-up in her grandmother's clothes. The usually dark dresses were invariably set off with ruffled collars and cameo pins. She looked like a fashion throw-back to the last century, and she had even overheard someone—a rare feat for her, though it was more lip reading than actual hearing—use the word "rummage sale" and "Penelope's clothes" in the same sentence, but she was not in the least concerned about that. How she looked to anyone else was not even in the sphere of issues to be considered. She dressed the way her mother had dressed, and she felt secure in that tradition. Her late husband John had, on occasion, bought her new clothes, for which she had lavishly thanked him for thinking of her and had promptly put in the back of the closet.

No, what concerned Penelope was not clothes or hair fashions or even food. Learning—knowledge—that was what fascinated and gripped her, what kept her mind as alert as when she was twenty: the never-ending quest for truth. Her hopelessly outdated fashion sense notwithstanding, she kept herself abreast of current events, could converse on many topics, and had a special penchant for quoting poetry. It was as if every line of it she had ever read had been shelved in a tiny library deep within her brain, to be summoned by an invisible librarian at her discretion. Gretchen had often said that her mother could quote poetry at the drop of a hat, and her brother, J. W., had added with a laugh, "She'll even drop the hat."

After changing into a dry dress, sipping her tea, and reading her current mystery for a while by the gas logs that John had installed shortly before his illness, Penelope picked up her crossword puzzle book and quickly worked several puzzles. They weren't much of a challenge. She made a clicking sound with her tongue. Must get a new book. Maybe the *New York Times Crossword Puzzle Book*. "Well, let's see," she said to the empty room, as she often did, dropping the book back on the coffee table, "what can I do now?" She seemed to be at loose ends for some reason. "Ah, yes. I haven't checked my email today."

She went into the small room that had been John's study and turned on the desk light. She never came in here that she couldn't see, in her mind's eye, her beloved husband, tired from a long day of seeing patients, slumped in the burgundy leather chair by the bookcase, his head bowed over the current issue of the *Journal of Bone and Joint Surgery*. "There are so many new advances in orthopedics that every time I pick up *JBJS*, I feel more and more like Alice in *Through the Looking-Glass*," he had told her on many occasions. "And you know what the Red Queen said to Alice: 'It takes all the running you can do, to keep in the same place.' " She smiled as she thought of him sitting there, patiently reading up on the latest techniques and protocols for diagnosing and treating the fractures and joint problems, which he saw every day in his large orthopedic practice. Adored by his patients, often even going to their homes when there was a serious problem involved, he was a Norman Rockwell doctor in a Pablo Picasso world.

It was little wonder that he had been written up in the paper as Culpeper's outstanding person of the year several times. He gave his patients the best of his talent and, Penelope had to admit, most of his time, but she felt pride rather than resentment in that. Oh yes, she readily acknowledged, there were times when the children were little when it would have been nice to have more active fathering on his part, but at that time, women didn't question a man's preoccupation with his work. Running her fingers softly over the head rest on John's chair, she whispered, "His life was gentle, and the elements/ So mix'd in him that Nature might stand up/ And say to all the world, 'This was a man!' " She spoke the lines from Shakespeare slowly, softly to the empty room and swallowed as she thought of all the happy times they had enjoyed together. It had been lonely without John in the rambling white-frame house on Poplar Street—there was no question of that—but Penelope resisted moving to a retirement home. She would one day, she told her children over and over, just not yet. There was so much of her here, but even more important, there was so much of John.

Chapter Twelve

When the computer booted up, Penelope checked her email and was delighted to find mail from her children, Gretchen and J. W., which she read first. It was because of them that she had this computer in the first place, after all. She could still remember the scene when they had presented it to her. They were so excited, but she had resisted. "A computer?" she had asked, incredulously. "Bless your hearts! What in the world do I want with a computer? Thank you, though, for thinking of me."

"But, Mom, everyone is using computers these days," J. W. had said.

Penelope had pursed her lips and shrugged. "Well, all I can say is that Alexander Pope had it right: 'Be not the first by which the new is tried.'"

"Mother!" Gretchen said in good-natured exasperation. "You and your quotes! Actually, I happen to know that one myself, my lady, and the next line is 'Or yet the last to lay the old aside.' How 'bout them apples? Surprised you, didn't I?" She winked broadly at her mother, and her brother laughed.

In the end, Penelope had accepted it graciously, and eventually she even began to be challenged by it as an intellectual exercise. Before long, she had emailed Gretchen and J. W. and conceded defeat. "I'm hooked," she said, "hopelessly, irretrievably, happily hooked. I can no more imagine life without my computer than I can imagine it without a telephone." Both children were immeasurably pleased, not only that they had brought their mother into the new age of electronic communication, but that they had a mother who, in spite of her very long dresses and obvious allegiance to rigid traditions, could be flexible enough to embrace and understand a complicated new tool.

Gretchen Catherine Caldwell, who worked as a stock consultant for Smith Barney in Stuart, Florida, and John Wilson Caldwell, Jr., known by his initials, J. W., who did heaven knows what, as his mother put it, for the Pentagon in Washington, D. C., had pooled their resources and bought her a computer for Christmas two years ago. It had opened up realms of knowledge to her. Since she detested TV, finding nothing on it of intellectual stimulation except *Jeopardy*—and even that, she felt, had been dumbed-down by questions on rock bands and celebrities—and occasional programs on PBS, which her hearing loss made frustrating to watch, she had always contented herself with reading. Even after the children bought her a TV that had closed captioning, she preferred reading, especially mysteries, which were her passion and which, she thought, stimulated her powers of reason; working crossword puzzles; and brewing up new and exotic teas, which she routinely brought home from her favorite shop, Coffee, Tea, and Thee. That was before the computer opened the Library of Congress and the *New York Times* to her. Right in this very room, she could browse through the tomes of the public library of New York or read the news of virtually any large paper in the country. She could also correspond with her friends, both near and far.

J. W.'s children, Wilson and Catherine, were especially fond of writing to and hearing from their grandmother. She heard from them on a weekly basis, things that a ten-and twelve-year old would tell only their grandmother, for fear of being thought silly—or worse yet, "cute"—by their parents. Catherine had once wanted to know why boys act so stupid around girls if they like them. Penelope hadn't had a good answer for that one, but she had reassured Catherine that it had been ever so. "Why, I remember when your grandfather and I were just children that he used to pull my pigtails every day on the way home from school. I thought he hated me for the longest time." Wilson seemed to be the little philosopher in the family, once wanting to know if people in Heaven, especially his grandfather, knew when he did good things. What about bad things, too? he had asked. Penelope had thought about that a long time and had finally reassured him that God would let our loved ones know only the good things—things that made us happy—and not the bad, or else it wouldn't be Heaven, would it? For that answer, Penelope had been rewarded with a return email that read, "I love you, Grandmama," followed by a heart.

She clicked on Gretchen's letter and read:

Dear Mom,

Work is hectic. It seems that every September and October the market goes into a slump, and that's what's going on now, especially with the high-tech stocks. Our customers get all panicked, and everyone seems to want to sell. I don't know why, but this is one product that, when it costs less, everyone wants to sell, not buy. It should be just the other way around.

Oh well...I hope you're okay. Walking every day? Taking your vitamins and reading

*your mysteries? That's like asking a fish if it
swims, right? I know you and your vitamins
and herbs. You're so healthy you'll probably
outlive me!*

*I'll be home for Thanksgiving for sure,
and I may be able to squeeze in a short visit
between now and then. Since Bill and I broke
up, my weekends have been totally free, so one
of these days, I'll take a Friday and Monday off
and come for a four-day weekend. How's that?
My boss tells me I'm working too hard, but
there's really nothing else to do.*

*By the way, did I mention that Bill got
married? Kinda' fast, huh? He met some girl,
the "right" one, he told some mutual friends,
the week after we split up, and that was that.
I obviously wasn't the right one. That's for
sure. I just wish it hadn't taken him over a
year to figure that out. At 35, I'm not getting
any younger. Oh well. I'm better off. I've
heard you say many times that not being
married isn't the worst thing that could
happen—being married to the wrong person
is. I know that. It's just that....well, you know.*

Oh yes, Penelope knew, all right. Knew all too well the loneliness,
the emptiness, the almost frantic need to keep busy. She caught her

mind drifting to the happy days she and John had had together, and, sighing, forced her attention to the rest of Gretchen's letter.

> *I heard from Catherine and Wilson today. They*
> *are so adorable, aren't they? Will they all come*
> *to Culpeper for Thanksgiving, too? Oh, I do*
> *hope so! I know you enjoy them as much as I do.*
> *It's a good thing I have an older brother, or you*
> *might not have grandchildren at all, and wouldn't*
> *life be dull without them?*
> *Love you,*
> *Gretchen*

After worrying about Gretchen's obvious loneliness for a few minutes, Penelope wrote an answer to her daughter's letter, encouraging her to join groups, become active in a church, and volunteer for community programs. Maybe that way she would meet someone worthy of her. Bill certainly wasn't, she thought. She had known that all along, but that wasn't the sort of thing she could tell Gretchen. She had always tried to respect her children's choices and live with them. After she sent off that email, she next read and answered a newsy letter from J. W. and then read with amusement a joke sent her by Bippy Maas, that friend of Maggie's who occasionally sent her jokes by email.

When she first heard from Bippy two months ago and then in quick succession began hearing from two of Maggie's other friends, Tootsie Freeman and Rosemary Harrison, Penelope strongly suspected Maggie of putting them up to it. It would be just like Maggie to write them all and encourage them to write to this "elderly widow up in Virginia who is all alone." A trace of annoyance at the invasion of her privacy, as she thought of it, was immediately replaced by smiles as Penelope thought of Maggie's concern for others. Why, Maggie had even gently suggested to her, on more than one occasion, that she consider a retirement home before she had to, while "you're in such good health and can liven the place up a bit," she had said.

But that was Maggie. She seemed to take on everyone as her responsibility. That was the way she had always been, and Penelope had known Maggie for forty-five years, since John was in medical school and then in residency in Jackson, Mississippi, where their house backed up to the Muldoon's. She had watched Maggie grow and mature and go off to college, and, no matter where they lived, they had stayed in touch over the years.

The last letter was from Maggie herself. Penelope's face, still creased with concern about Gretchen, broke into a smile. Oh, happy day! She and Maggie had been corresponding daily by email for the two years Penelope had had her computer. Why, if she didn't hear from Maggie, it was like a day without sunshine, as the orange juice commercial said.

> *Dear Penelope,*
> *I hope you're doing well and having a*
> *good day. I'm sure fall has come in Virginia,*
> *but it's still very warm here, except at night. The*
> *evenings are beginning to get cooler even if the*
> *days are hot. Thank goodness, it's not as hot*
> *and humid as it was just a month ago, though.*
> *In fact, I have been enjoying my boat more now*
> *that the temperatures are in the low eighties.*
> *Between real estate, volunteer work (did I*
> *mention I've been working on a Habitat*

House?), my board work on the A.S.P.C.A.,
and church, I haven't had too much time lately.

Oh, yes, and there's one more thing that has
been taking a lot of my time. Are you sitting down,
Pen? I have some truly wonderful news to share with
you. I am telling no one but my very best friends, my
four email sisters. I am in love!!!!!!!!!!!!!!!!!!!!!!!

Penelope caught her breath, placing one hand over the cameo pin on her chest, and read on. She couldn't help noticing the string of exclamation points that, like little toy soldiers, marched boldly across the screen.

Now, I know what you're thinking: It's much too
sudden. I'm letting my heart rule my head. Am I right?
Well, hear me out, Pen. Sometimes you know instantly
that someone is special to you. I knew the day I first
came to your door when you and John had just moved
in, that, despite the difference in our ages, we would
always be friends. This is like that.

Anyway, his name is Gordon Dawkins, and he's just
wonderful!!! He's someone I met while showing a piece
of property. He loves children and animals, and you
know how very important both are to me. He even
supports the A.S.P.C.A., just as I do. And guess what?
He brought me yellow roses the first time he came to
call on me. Is that serendipity or what? I know you

90

*are wondering what he looks like, and I'm dying to
tell you. He is tall, has chestnut brown hair that is
just starting to gray at the temples, and robin's
egg blue eyes. In a word, Pen, he's drop-dead
handsome. Wait! That's more than a word, isn't it?*

*Now, here's the part you're really going to like:
he loves poetry. Yes, a man's man who actually
likes poetry!! In fact, he reads it to me all the
time. Isn't that marvelous? You should hear
him read Shakespeare's 18th sonnet. When he
first read, "Shall I compare thee to a summer's
day," I confess I almost swooned. But then, Pen—
and you, English teacher that you are, will love
this—when he told me he loved me and asked me
to marry him, he quoted the 29th sonnet, and you
know the couplet that ends that one: "For thy
sweet love remembered such wealth brings/
That then I scorn to change my state with
kings." Who could resist a marriage proposal
like that? Certainly not I!*

*You must keep my secret because no one
here knows. Gordon doesn't want me to tell
anyone because he is afraid of what his children's
reaction is going to be. In fact, he wants us to
marry secretly and then tell them. The secrecy of
it makes me feel like a star-struck youngster. Oh,
Pen, I do love him so!!!!!!!!!!!!!!*

91

I'll let you know the details later. I just
couldn't wait to share my happiness with a friend
who has been a constant in my life for so long now.
You're my very oldest friend, do you know that?
And I don't mean your age, either. ☺

I haven't mentioned any of this to Clarkson
and Raymond. You know my brothers! They're
much too sensible—to say nothing of protective of
their little sister—and would tell me not to do it.
After it's a fait accompli, however, I know they'll
be happy for me. They always are.

Well, I'll talk to you later. There is much
to tell about Gordon and all of it marvelous.
I love you,
Maggie

Penelope sat for a minute, staring at the screen, not knowing what reaction to give in to. They were all there: surprise, joy, anticipation, skepticism, and even a bothersome one that she couldn't quite name. She pursued that one a while, and suddenly, with an intake of breath, she realized, for a reason she could not pinpoint, that it was fear.

Chapter Thirteen

The next day, after a brisk morning walk, Penelope fixed a pot of her latest tea experiment, chocolate mint, and sat down to send Maggie an email.

> *Dearest Maggie,*
> *As you know, I do not react swiftly to major*
> *issues, especially surprises. Remember calling me*
> *Prudent Pen once upon a time? That was a pretty*
> *accurate description on your part, for I do prefer*
> *to take my time and consider all the facts before*
> *giving an opinion. That way, it is a considered*
> *judgment and not just an off-the-cuff reaction.*
> *That's why I slept on the matter before replying*
> *to the news of your impending marriage.*
>
> *I am very happy for you, my dear, and I*
> *hope this Gordon Dawkins knows how remarkably*
> *fortunate he is to have found you. I share in your*
> *joy and appreciate your letting me know your*
> *good news. I am eager for more details. I do*
> *want to sound a note of caution. My one concern,*
> *and, Maggie dear, you know I voice this only out*

of love for you, is that, if you follow Gordon's
wishes, you would be starting the marriage off
at a disadvantage with his children, it seems to
me. Regardless of your intentions, would they
not see your secret marriage as deceit on your
part, a betrayal of sorts on the part of their father?
Since blood is thicker than water, I'm afraid
they would blame you, not him, for this duplicity.

Besides, if it's a surreptitious marriage,
none of your old friends can be there, now can
we? You know that I don't share your fear of
flying, so I'll be there if you let me know when.
I look forward to meeting Gordon and
hopefully even some of your other friends who
have sent me emails. They seem so very nice
that I truly feel as if I know them, and, of
course, if they are friends of yours, I consider
them friends of mine already.

I hope you will understand and accept my
questions in the spirit in which they are asked.
I want only that which is best for you. I think
after all these years, you know that.
Love as always,
Your "oldest" friend, Penelope

Penelope stared at the screen for a few minutes, hit "send," and
then clicked off the computer, brushing away a feeling of disquiet like
a bothersome crumb.

94

The next morning dawned cold and clear. A brisk northerly breeze rapped on the windowpanes like a forlorn wanderer outside wanting in, and all along the street, houses vented steam like huddled people blowing on their hands to keep warm. Almost whimsically, gold and crimson leaves blew in little swirls under the maple trees in the yard. Penelope dressed warmly in a long, gray wool flannel dress, brewed a pot of tea, and went to the computer to see if Maggie had replied to her questions. She hadn't slept well, worried that her questioning of Maggie might have upset her. As she clicked on her ISP, she was mildly disappointed to see only a forward from Rosemary Harrison, that other "email sister" of Maggie's, as she called them. After reading it and sending a brief response, she thought a minute and then typed Maggie a quick note. Best not to mention the questions again. Wouldn't want to run that into the ground. It will just be a short, friendly note, she decided.

> *Dearest Maggie,*
> *Hurry up with the details. I'm just dying*
> *to know all.*
> *Love,*
> *Pen*

There now, she said to herself, clicking off her computer. Maybe that would soften the edge on the questions she put to her last night. She wouldn't upset Maggie for the world. Lord knows, they'd been friends long enough that Maggie should know she was only concerned for her welfare. Still, she hated to be the only black cloud threatening her picnic.

Grabbing her jacket and scarf, she set out for the high school track, just four blocks away, where she daily walked, but she couldn't get Maggie off her mind. If only Clarkson and Raymond knew! They could figure out what's going on and, if it didn't seem right to them, they could put a stop to it. Well, maybe not exactly stop it, she acknowledged, with a smile, remembering Maggie's fiery determination. Nobody can stop Margaret Muldoon Palmer when she has set her mind on something, but her brothers could come closer to talking sense into her than anyone else. No, she thought, nobody can make Maggie Muldoon do anything she doesn't want to do. Well, I'll just have to wait and see, I suppose. As she walked, Penelope remembered, as if it were yesterday, the ringing of her back doorbell so many years ago.

***

There at the door stood a young girl with flamboyantly red hair gathered into a ponytail and eyes as green as raw emeralds. The child, even standing still, radiated energy. "Welcome to the neighborhood," came the buoyant, but slightly whispery voice. "Doll—I mean Mom; her name is really Laura Gray, but I've always called her Doll—sent you this cake. It's chocolate. Hope you like chocolate. It's my favorite. Doll bakes the best cakes in the world. She really does! She will be over to call on you later. You'll really, really like her. Everyone loves my mom. Well, and Dad, too. We're the Muldoons, by the way. I'm Margaret Katherine, but nobody calls me that—the whole thing, I mean. All my friends just call me plain old Margaret. Our house backs up to yours, see?" she said, pointing at the extraordinarily large house behind her. "The brick two-story with black shutters?"

Penelope nodded, noting that whatever she was called, there was absolutely nothing "plain" about Margaret, and when the child paused to take a breath, she broke in. "Why, thank you, Margaret. How very kind. I'm Penelope Caldwell, and, as luck would have it, chocolate is our very favorite."

"Oh, good," Margaret said, and without pausing went right on. "We're Catholic. Are y'all?"

Penelope shook her head. "No, Methodist."

"Oh," Margaret smiled. "That's okay. Where did y'all move from?"

"Virginia. John—that's my husband—and I both grew up there and met at UVA when I was a third-year student, and he was fourth year. UVA doesn't use class names. Just years instead. Anyway, we'll probably go back to Virginia to settle eventually."

"No kidding! What a coincidence! My two older brothers—I'm the youngest child in my family, by the way—went to prep school at Woodberry Forest in Orange, Virginia."

"Oh yes, I know it well. It's not more than thirty miles from Charlottesville. It's a remarkably fine school."

Maggie went right on. "In fact, Raymond, who's a freshman at Harvard, almost went to UVA himself. He was offered the Jefferson scholarship, but he had his heart set on Harvard."

"He must be quite a good student."

Maggie nodded and smiled proudly, her impossibly red ponytail bobbing up and down for emphasis. "Yes, ma'am. My other brother, Clarkson, is, too. He's a sophomore at Davidson."

"Oh, that's a wonderful school, too. One of the best in the country."

"Yes, ma'am. He won a National Merit Scholarship and a bunch of other scholarships, too. Turned down Princeton for Davidson."

Penelope winced at being addressed as "ma'am" by one not that much younger than she. She suddenly felt very, very old. "What does your father do, Margaret?"

"He's an orthopedic surgeon and teaches a few classes at UMMC in addition to his clinical practice."

"Now it's my turn for a coincidence. My husband John is in medical school here at the University of Mississippi, studying to be an orthopedic surgeon himself."

"No kidding!"

"Yes. It's a long road—two more years of medical school and then four of residency and one additional fellowship year to specialize. Anyway, that's why we're still unpacking wedding gifts. At least, I'm still unpacking. John is gone most of the time."

"You must be lonesome."

Penelope, struck by such intuitive openness in one so young, nodded slowly and responded, "A little."

"Well, anytime you get lonesome, just yell. I'll come right over. Try to yell when Doll wants me to do the dishes, will you?" She grinned broadly. "Do y'all have any children?"

Penelope shook her head. "Why, no. John and I have been married only a very short time. He wanted to get the first two years of medical school under his belt before we got married."

"I thought you looked awfully young. You're really pretty!"

This young girl's forthrightness caught Penelope off guard, and she blushed at the frankness of the compliment. "Well, thank you, but I'm not as young as I look. I'm twenty-three, almost twenty-four."

"Gosh! That old? Well, you don't look much older than I am."

Penelope saw that the child wasn't kidding; she was being completely ingenuous. Remembering when she herself was about this child's age, Penelope could understand how old "twenty-four" must sound to her. "And how old is that?"

"Thirteen. Almost fourteen. Do you like Mississippi?"

"Oh yes, very much. For the past two years, John has been living in bachelor quarters nearer the medical school. I came down several times to visit him, and I fell in love with Jackson. I like it even more now that I've met Margaret Katherine Muldoon."

Margaret seemed pleased and showed her pleasure in a big smile. "Thanks. I like you, too. Well, I'll see you. Call if you need help unpacking or anything. Bye!"

And she was gone. Penelope stood looking after her, laughing at the breath of fresh air named Margaret Katherine Muldoon that had just blown her way.

***

Penelope laughed again, after all these years, as she remembered that first meeting with the friend she now knew as Maggie. She had learned the entire Muldoon family history in ten minutes. Smiling nostalgically, she also remembered all the milestones in Maggie's life that she had been privileged to watch from her backyard: her first boyfriend; her many pets, usually salvaged from the pound or back alleys; her driver's license; her steady sweetheart, Cam, who became a fixture at both the Muldoon and the Caldwell houses; her senior prom; her acceptance by Duke; her leaving home for college, her metamorphosis from Margaret into Maggie. As Maggie moved through all those rites of passage, she shared them with Penelope, and, to a lesser extent—simply because he wasn't around as much—John. It was just before Maggie's sophomore year in college that Penelope and John had bade the Muldoons and the entire neighborhood to which they had grown so attached a tearful good-bye and packed up and moved to Culpeper, Virginia. Culpeper, with one "p," as Penelope liked to say then, was a small community in the beautiful and lush rolling Virginia countryside, a community of friendly people and slow, deep living—a community that had the most important characteristic of all—no orthopedist.

Since that day, Maggie and Penelope had stayed in close touch, both being very faithful to write and call occasionally. Penelope willingly became an older sister to Maggie, and Maggie became the adored younger sister that Penelope had lost to leukemia in childhood. It was quite natural to Penelope that Maggie poured out her heart to her when she was first beginning to realize, early in her senior year in college, that, after many boyfriends, it was Cam she really loved, that she could not be happy without him, and that she was afraid he had forgotten her. Oh, no, Penelope assured her by return mail, he hasn't forgotten you. She had said that with complete assurance because she knew *no one* could ever forget Maggie Muldoon. She was, quite simply, the most extraordinary person of any age that Penelope had ever encountered. Selfless, forward—almost aggressive in her openness and warmth—generous, forgiving, and compassionate to people and animals alike, and so exuberant that life seemed painted in oils rather than pastels when she was around. She was unforgettable. Cam might have found a new love—that Penelope had no way of knowing—but he had not forgotten Maggie. Of that she was quite sure.

After much urging by Penelope, Maggie had written Cam what was in her heart, and not long after that, Penelope's phone rang. "Oh, Pen, you are such an angel," Maggie began. "You were right. Cam still loves me, too! We've realized that we just can't imagine life without each other. We had a long, long talk—by phone and letters and then went out for pizza when we were both home for break. The religion thing is going to work out, too. After we're married, we'll join the Methodist Church. It seems like a good compromise between Baptist and Catholic, and both sets of parents are supportive—well, tolerant—of that decision. Oh, Pen, I have never been so happy in my entire life! And I owe it all to you." Penelope laughed then because she could never remember Maggie not happy.

Penelope and John were in Jackson for Maggie and Cam's wedding, celebrating life to the ultimate with these two young people they had come to love as their own. "What would I do without my big sis?" Maggie had said that day right before the wedding, as she impulsively threw back her encumbering net, veil, and headpiece, letting the red hair tumble wildly into her face, and embraced Penelope. "Whatever would I do?"

It was a question she asked again six years later when Penelope and John flew hurriedly to Jackson to gather her into their arms. She had called, choking out the news between bouts of sobbing. "Doll and Doc...on a trip in Europe...plane crash...oh, Pen, they're gone. Doll and Doc are dead!" Penelope knew the depths of Maggie's despair because she knew how Maggie treasured her parents. Maggie loved and hero-worshiped her father, C. R., a quiet, tall man with luxuriant auburn hair and an Irish twinkle in his eye, and she adored her mother. Close as she and Maggie were, Penelope never kidded herself that she was taking Laura Gray's place. Pen filled the "big sister" role. Laura Gray was definitely the nurturing, encouraging mother, and no daughter ever loved her mother more than Maggie loved Doll.

Once, early in their friendship, Penelope had asked Maggie why it was she called her mother Doll, and Maggie had laughed impishly and said, "Oh, that's because I was such a problem child. Once when I was about three and wouldn't stay in bed at night, crying for Momma to come lie beside me, she gave me a very special doll. 'It's a Mommy Doll,' she said. 'When you want me, just hug this Mommy Doll very tightly, and it will remind you how much I love you.' " After that, according to Maggie, the transition was simple. "As I got a little older, I just started calling Mom 'Mommy Doll.' Soon it was just 'Doll,' and it's been that way ever since. Then, too, I noticed that my father would always come in from the hospital, pick Momma up, and hug her. He always said the same thing: 'How's my doll?' For a long time, I just assumed that was her name." And Penelope had to agree: Laura Gray was a doll by anybody's standards—petite, sandy-haired, unfailingly kind, soft-spoken, eyes always crinkled in a smile—so the grief Pen shared with Maggie was genuine.

That mutual shouldering of grief's almost insupportable burden was shared again when they each lost their husbands. Pen would never forget that Maggie and Cam drove from Jackson to Culpeper when John died. Oh, she remembered it well. Having been called by Penelope when John became so gravely ill that his life was measured, not in months or weeks, as had been the case for a very long time, but in hours, they came immediately. They sat with the family as John's life slipped away, supporting Gretchen and J. W. as well as Penelope, often saying nothing, just lending them the most precious gift of all: their presence. *Oh yes*, Penelope thought, *theirs had been a true friendship, all right, and the bright ribbons of joy, as well as the dark ones of sorrow, were woven all through it. But then*, she thought, *that's what gives it texture and depth.*

Chapter Fourteen

It was two days later when Penelope began to panic. No word from Maggie. *Has she been offended by my questions?* she wondered. *Surely not!* She emailed Maggie again, and the next day when she still had no answer, she decided to call her on her amplified phone. Even with the maximum amplification and now captioning, carrying on a phone conversation was a struggle. If her hearing hadn't been so bad, she would have called Maggie long before now. Quickly, she dialed the number. The phone rang four times before the answering machine picked up, and after the rather long beep, she said, "Maggie? This is Pen. I'm worried because I haven't heard from you. Give me a call when you come in, or better, yet, email me. Love you. Bye." When two hours had passed with no return call, Pen dialed the number again. This time, she could tell by the even longer beep, that Maggie had not listened to her messages since she called.

A day later, when Maggie had not responded, Penelope, by now imagining all sorts of terrible scenarios, decided to email the woman who sent her that cute joke about the gender of computers a month or so ago. "Let's see if I can find her address," she muttered to the empty room. Scanning the list of old mail, she saw it—"Computers: He or She?"—but when she attempted to read it, she was told that it was no longer accessible. Shoot! What now? Wait a minute. She had written her back and thanked her for the joke, Penelope remembered. Maybe her letter to Bippy was still accessible. Scrolling down through sent mail, she suddenly saw it. Yes, there it was: 555bwood@gmail.com. Quickly, she typed in a short message:

> *Dear Bippy,*
> *Although we've never met, I feel as if I*
> *know you through Maggie. Actually, Maggie*
> *is the reason for this note. Have you heard*
> *anything from her recently? I'm a little concerned*
> *because I haven't had an answer to my repeated*
> *emails. I've tried calling, but I get no answer.*
> *Do you know if she's out of town?*
> *Sincerely,*
> *Penelope Caldwell*

As soon as she clicked offline, the telephone rang. *Oh, good,* she thought, *it's Maggie.* "Hello?" she said expectantly. She was so glad the children had recently given her a caption telephone. She didn't want to miss a word of what Maggie had to say.

"Ms. Penelope Caldwell?"

"Yes."

"This is Chilton Surles in Jackson, Mississippi."

Chapter Fifteen

Penelope hung up the phone slowly, failing on the first try to get it back on the hook. Her hand shaking, she pushed and shoved the handset until it was properly seated on the receiver. Her heart was beating so hard she thought it would burst through her chest, and her breath was rapid and shallow. She felt her lips trembling, and soon she was wracked by violent tremors. Wildly agitated, she tried to stand up, but her head was spinning so crazily that she promptly sat back down. "Oh dear God!" she said aloud, resting her woozy head against the antimacassar on the sofa. Thoughts tumbled over themselves in a rush to her head with one horrible thought inserting itself over and over. *Maggie's dead! I've got to get out of here immediately. Maggie's dead! Must call Gretchen and J. W. Have to tell them at once. Maggie's dead! Need to stop the paper and call the post office to hold the mail. Maggie's dead! Have to get a flight reservation right away. Maggie's dead! Dead!*

After resting on the sofa for a few minutes, trying to get her breathing regulated, she picked up the phone and called her daughter at work. She was able to tell the switchboard operator whom she wanted, but when Gretchen came on the line, she suddenly burst into tears. "Gretchen…"

"Mom, what's wrong?" Gretchen asked, her voice high and trembling with anxiety.

For a few seconds, Penelope could do nothing but cry. Even though she heard the rising panic in Gretchen's voice, she just couldn't choke out an answer. Finally, when, above her tears, she heard Gretchen say, "Mom, take a deep, deep breath and let it out slowly," she was able to get her voice under control. "I'm sorry, dear. I'm just so upset. Oh, Gretchen, it's Maggie."

"Maggie Palmer?"

"Yes. I've just received a call that she's...she's...dead."

Now it was Gretchen's turn to gasp. "What! Oh, Mom! What happened? She hasn't been sick, has she?"

"No, not at all. The picture of health. You know how active Maggie is...was."

"Well, what in the—"

"The man who called me, her attorney, said she drowned. A man and his grandson fishing in a cove on Serene Lake there in Jackson found her...her body." She swallowed hard and took a deep breath. "She had been...dead a while. Oh, Gretch, it's just too awful!"

"I can't believe this," Gretchen said. "Listen, Mom, I'll come right home. I'll take the first available flight out."

"Oh, no, no, don't do that. I'm going to leave immediately for Mississippi."

"Fine. I'll go with you."

"No, Gretchen. That isn't necessary, really. I would rather have you come here later—when I'm back. You said you might come for a short visit before you come for Thanksgiving, didn't you?"

"Yes, ma'am, but I—"

"Well, that will help me more than anything. Give me something to look forward to after all this horrid business is over. I will definitely need you then." Penelope meant it, too. She would desperately dread coming back to this house, to this study, especially this computer, knowing that it would never again be enlivened by Maggie's ebullient personality. It was the feeling of being abandoned, the same feeling she had had once as a child when her parents, not realizing she was in her room getting ready to go with them to her grandparents' house, drove off and left her. Though within minutes they discovered their mistake and came back for her, she never forgot that scary feeling of abandonment.

After she hung up, Penelope called the airline at the number listed for hearing impaired customers and secured a flight out of Charlottesville for the next day at 1:24. That would do nicely, she thought. It would give her time to take her early morning walk, which she felt she needed now more than ever, come back for breakfast, have a nice bath, and get dressed. Next, she called her minister, the Reverend L. H. Burns, and asked if he, by any chance, were going into Charlottesville to do hospital visiting the next day and, if so, would he mind a passenger? She relaxed a bit as he said that he was indeed going into Charlottesville to see how Mrs. Reba Land was doing after her back surgery and would be delighted to give her a ride. "I would love the company," he had graciously added. "And I won't just take you to Charlottesville. I'll take you to the airport and see that you get on the plane myself." She let out a deep sigh. That dear man!

All that settled, Penelope got unsteadily to her feet, went to the kitchen and put an egg on to boil. Since childhood, she had always liked a nice, soft-boiled egg with dry toast and tea when she was feeling upset. Her mother had often brought that to her on a tray when she was plagued with bronchitis as a little girl. It was comfort food in the best sense of the word, she thought, running water into the kettle, and the dear Lord knew she needed comfort.

Part IV: Rosemary

Chapter Sixteen

"Have a good swim," Rosemary yelled to two friends, just entering the pool area from the dressing room, as she climbed the ladder at the opposite end. She shook her head, and a circle of water droplets sprayed like a garden sprinkler. Both of the women to whom she called dived in and swam quickly toward the shallow end, where they pulled themselves up to pool edge to join her.

"Why, Rosemary, I haven't seen you in ages," Stacy Parks called back, climbing up the ladder from the pool. "Where in the world have you been keeping yourself, girl? You used to come to the Y after work all the time." She bent her head toward first one shoulder and then the other, hopping on one foot to loosen the water in her ears.

"Oh, mostly just staying busy at the paper, you know. Same old. Same old." She picked up the towel she had left on the bench when she entered the pool and began drying her shoulders. "Haven't had time lately for much exercise. I have been running in for a quick work-out on my lunch hour, but I haven't had time for the after-work swimming routine. Today, I decided to make time. I've missed seeing you guys, too."

"If you're not careful, you're going to lose that model-like figure of yours," Stacy joked. "And then you'll look like the rest of us. Nobody should look as good as you do—not at thirty-nine anyway."

"Hah! What a flatterer! You underestimate the mark by a good six or seven years, but who's counting? And thanks."

"Even more to your credit," Patsy Lewis said, joining them at poolside. Say, by the way, congratulations on your promotion. Assistant Editor of the *Charleston Gazette,* huh? Whoa! I'm impressed."

"Thanks, but don't be."

"Are you kidding me?" Stacy asked, raising her eyebrows.

"No, and don't forget that as of July 2015, it has officially been the *Charleston Gazette-Mail,* but I imagine it will forever be referred to as the *Gazette*—certainly by me."

"Don't change the subject. We are proud of you. Way to go, girl!"

Rosemary laughed. "It's really not that big a deal, but I guess it's not bad for an underprivileged African-American kid from economically depressed Gauley Bridge, West Virginia, huh?" She put air quotes around "underprivileged" and "economically depressed."

"Not bad for anybody, I'd say," Patsy answered, "but seriously, do you miss investigative reporting?"

"You know what? You might not believe this, but I do. It's really my first love. I'm not saying I miss all the leg work I used to have to do and the traveling, but I miss the thrill of the chase, so to speak. In fact, when I find a particularly engrossing story, I still follow it myself even though my real job now is writing editorials. I can't say I'm getting any more sleep, though, because now I stay up nights researching for my op ed pieces."

Rosemary was a high energy person, motivated and fast-paced, sleeping less than six hours a night. Because she was an imminently fair person, she expected as much or more from herself than she did from the reporters who answered to her. She felt her work required the extra digging she did in the evenings after she left the newspaper office. It had paid off, however, because not only was she respected by her peers at the paper, but also her writing had won numerous awards, both as an investigative reporter and now as an editorialist.

The fact that she approached her work—or anything she was engaged in—like one possessed had been an issue between Delorio and her. "You're too pushy and uptight," he had said in the heated argument before she threw him out once and for all five years earlier. That was after he had reappeared following a three-day disappearance with a sweet young thing he had met at the bowling alley where he hung out. "You're always in a hurry, woman," he had complained. It had taken her eighteen years to realize that she *was* in a hurry, a hurry to make something of life, and that Delorio, lazy and complacent, could never understand that, much less match it. Their personalities just didn't mesh, and that, she finally realized, was that.

"How're the twins these days?" Stacy asked. She squeezed the water from her end of her pony tail into which her dark brown hair was gathered.

"Fine, thanks. They're both well."

"Well, come on. You have to give more information than that. What are they up to?"

Rosemary grinned and ran one hand across her brow, wiping excess water from it. Her smooth complexion, the color of latte, shone under the overhead lights, and her dark brown eyes, almost obsidian, were snappy and alive. She smoothed her short, shiny-black hair again with the towel. "Okay. Okay. But remember, you asked." She didn't like to brag about her children, but she was exceedingly proud of them. "Anthony is in law school at Yale, and Dorothy is in veterinary school at North Carolina State. They both tell me they're working way too hard. Of course, when twenty-three-year-olds say they're working hard, I take it with a grain of salt. I tell them they don't know what hard work is yet." Smiling, she hugged herself and chaffed her arms. At five feet, seven inches tall and 120 pounds, she was trim and lithe and had been told often that she bore a striking resemblance to Halle Berry. Her response was always a cheerful, but self-effacing, "Yeah, right."

"What about your life? Met anybody interesting?" Stacy asked. "Come on. Give, girl."

Rosemary hedged. She had been seeing a widowed man in his mid-to-late fifties, a man she really felt was too old for her, but she didn't want to broadcast it in case something should develop later. Or in case it didn't. But since they asked. "Uh, well, I've met a man—Clyde Wexler is his name—with whom I've been going out. You know, to the movies and out to dinner, but I can assure you that we're just friends. Seriously. I'm at the stage of life when companionship counts for a lot," she added, laughing.

"Come on, Rosemary. You make it sound as if you're someone's granny and he's a Labrador retriever."

Rosemary laughed. "Well, I'm not getting any younger, and a dog might not be such a bad idea for company on cold winter nights." The three stood talking for a minute, the water glazing their bodies and pooling at their feet, before Rosemary said, "Well, listen, it's great to see you all, but I gotta run. Let's get together for lunch soon. See you later."

After showering, she dried herself briskly with the thick velour towel that she had brought with her instead of the paper-thin towels provided at the Y. As soon as she got dressed, she pulled her lemon-yellow, vintage Karmann Ghia, an uncharacteristic impulse buy that never ceased to make her feel good, out of the parking lot and headed straight to Kroger. Quickly, she rattled her buggy past the frozen food, tossed in a package of chopped spinach and a box of frozen twice-baked potatoes, then to the produce section, where she got a package of pre-mixed salad. After that, she went straight to the front of the store where the deli was located. Selecting an herb-crusted rotisserie chicken and a package of sourdough rolls, she threw them in the shopping cart and rolled into a checkout lane behind a mother explaining to a particularly insistent two-year-old in diapers why he couldn't have the Chapstick he was reaching for. Once checked out, she was soon on the way to her neat little condo overlooking the majestic Kanawha River.

While the rolls and baked potatoes were warming and the spinach was simmering on the stove, Rosemary went to the den and clicked on her computer, drumming her fingers impatiently while waiting for it to come to life. Once a week, without fail, she heard from the twins. That was a rule. She had told them that it didn't matter to her whether they wrote, called, texted, or emailed, but she expected to hear from them at least once a week, no exceptions. "You can even send a carrier pigeon," she had told them, "but your mother wants—and expects—to know what's going on in your lives. Period. I also expect you to write or call your grandmother and great-grandmother as frequently as possible." There were short messages from both children: Anthony's agonizing lament at an assignment in torts, Dorothy's cryptic reference to a fellow vet student whom she found "interesting."

Rosemary smiled at her daughter's vagueness when it came to revealing any romantic liaisons because it reminded her so much of herself. Ah good, she thought, a letter from Maggie. She clicked and began to read.

Dear Rosemary,
You will never believe it. Never in a million

years! I am in love again!!! Yes!!! And what's more, I'm going to get married!!! Surprised? Well, so am I. As a journalist, you are probably waiting for the five Ws, right? Well, I can tell you the who, what, when, and where, just not the why, unless you count good luck—mine.

Okay, here's the deal: His name is Gordon Dawkins, and he's just the most handsome, most polite, most intelligent, most everything man you can imagine. I mean, really. I have heard the expression "drop-dead handsome" before, but I've never seen anyone who more accurately fits the description. Honestly, Rosemary, he's divine!! And get this: He even sends me yellow roses! Yes!!! We're not telling anyone here yet because he is afraid that his children by his first wife will object. (Did I mention that he's divorced?) He wants to tell them after we're already married. Isn't that exciting? I don't know--it sounds so, so Humphrey Bogart or something. I'll write you details later. I'm not being purposely vague. I honestly don't know them yet myself. I only know he's perfect for me. Oh, Rose, I'm so happy!

Well, that's the scoop from your ace reporter here in Jackson. What do you think? Can't wait to hear from you.
Love,
Maggie

Rosemary clicked on Reply and began typing:

Dear Maggie,

Wow! That's all I can say. Just wow! I knew it must
be big news when I saw all the exclamation points.
When you fall, you fall hard and fast, don't you?
I didn't even know you were dating anyone seriously,
you sly thing, you. You've been holding out on
me. You asked if I am surprised. In a word, yes!

I can't wait to hear all the details. Who, exactly,
is Gordon Dawkins? What does he do for a living?
What does he look like? I know he's handsome
—okay, "drop-dead handsome"—but I want
details. What happened in his first marriage?
When did it end? Speaking of that, where is the
former Mrs. Dawkins? You mentioned his children.
How many does he have? Why not tell them?
Do you think they will approve of his getting
married "behind their backs," so to speak?
Give, girl. I'm dying to hear.

Rosemary read the paragraph she had just written and smiled. Who, what, when, where, and why? I sound like a dad-blamed news reporter.

Wish I had some exciting romantic news to
share, but I'm afraid that part of my life is rather
dull. I am dating a man, Clyde Wexler, but just
as a friend. He is much older than I am by about ten
or fifteen years—probably late fifties to mid-sixties. Oops!

I just realized that's about your age. Sorry. ☺
That doesn't apply to you, Maggie, because you,
my friend, are ageless. I am not saying that just
to say it. It's true. I have always felt that
we were the same age, but then, that's the
effect you have on everyone.

Well, anyway, Clyde is a widower and
very different from Delorio, thank goodness—
hardworking and motivated. He's a senior
partner in Walls, Thompson, Gossett, and
Wexler law firm here in Charleston. We have
dinner or see a movie every now and then, but
it's a matter of companionship for me, and I
hope it is for him as well. It's nothing serious,
that's for sure. That's why I haven't mentioned
him to you before now. Well, actually, I mentioned
him, but not by name. I remember just telling you
I'd gone out with "a friend." Clyde was the friend.
We met about six months ago when our paper
consulted his law firm on a legal problem, but we
didn't start going out until about four months ago.
As I said, it's nothing serious, and that suits me just
fine. Been there. Done that.

I will check my email frequently to see if
you've sent me the juicy details. Don't keep me
waiting. Meanwhile, as kids today say, you go, girl!
Love,
Rosemary

Just before she turned off the computer, Rosemary tapped her long, polished fingernails against the screen. *Speak to me, Maggie,* she thought. *What's going on in your head? Dear Lord,* she prayed silently, as she rose to go to the kitchen, *please help this Gordon Dawkins be worthy of the most wonderful person in the world.* Oddly, she felt the prayer light and aimless, hanging in the air like a helium-filled balloon, but somehow tethered, going nowhere. Suddenly Claudius' words in *Hamlet* came to her mind: "My words fly up, my thoughts remain below: Words without thoughts never to heaven go." That was exactly how she felt. Why, she didn't know. She only knew that, for reasons she couldn't quite understand, it was with a lump in her throat that she sat down to her solitary supper.

Chapter Seventeen

The next day dawned bright and clear. Crimson and golden maples were shouting their colors to the impossibly blue sky. October was, Rosemary felt, the most invigorating time of year. She had always loved the poet Helen Hunt Jackson's phrase, "October's bright blue weather." That seemed to describe it perfectly. There was something in the very crispness of the air and the mellow angle of light suffusing everything it touched with warmth that stirred her, energized her. Always had.

As she wound her way down from South Hills, trees cast their shadows like delicate embroidery in her path. She continued across the bridge, and along the Kanawha River and squinted as the bright sun bounced off the gold dome of the state capitol building. It splintered into golden shards onto the river, which ran like a brilliant ribbon in the valley. She knew she was probably biased, but she thought it was the most beautiful of all state capitols, and in her years as a reporter, she'd seen quite a few. After all, at 293 feet, its dome was higher than the one on the nation's capitol, larger than any other state's capitol dome, and was covered in gold leaf. She had done an article on it when she first started working for the *Gazette,* feeling that local people took it for granted like New Yorkers who said they'd never been to the Statue of Liberty. People tended to ignore what was right in front of them, she thought, so she had suggested an article on the capitol, which was designed by the famous architect, Cass Gilbert. It had been very favorably received, and after running in the *Gazette,* it was published in the state magazine, *Wonderful West Virginia.* That won her special mention by the state historical society and an introduction to the governor.

What a day to be alive, she thought, sipping her coffee from a thermal mug as she zipped along the boulevard. Her grandmother had once told her to begin every day with a prayer of thanksgiving. "If you can't think of anything else, just be thankful you woke up that day." A silent prayer formed within her mind: *Dear God, thank you that I'm alive to see this day*. But the exhilaration that swept over her at that minute was accompanied immediately—almost simultaneously—with an inexplicable melancholy. Maybe it was because her birthday was not far away, and it would mark another year alone, but that had never bothered her before. She had a feeling of dread that she couldn't explain. She shuddered slightly and involuntarily as the feeling passed over her like the trailing shroud of a wraith. Waiting in traffic for the light to change, she puzzled over the swing in moods. It wasn't like her, she thought. Not at all. But still, she couldn't shrug off or forget the eerie feeling of doom that seemed to spring up out of nowhere.

She couldn't forget it then, she couldn't forget it at work, and she couldn't forget it on the way home late that evening. One good thing about working later than everyone else was that she missed the rush hour traffic. Her retro-fitted, hands-free car phone rang as she zipped across the bridge over the Kanawha and began winding her way up the road to South Hills. She wouldn't have answered it if she hadn't been completely alone on this road. She had very strong opinions about people driving distracted from talking on car phones and cell phones—heaven forbid the unfathomably stupid act of texting—and endangering everyone else's lives. It was the ultimate selfishness.

She had even written an editorial about it not so very long ago. She punched a button on the steering wheel. "Hello?"

"Rosemary? This is Clyde. How are you?"

"Oh, hi, Clyde. Tired, but I'm doing just fine. How 'bout you?"

"Great, but I'd be doing greater if you'd have dinner with me tonight. I know it's late, but I have been tied up in court all day and just left my client."

She glanced at the car clock. 8:15. "Tonight? Oh, Clyde, I'd love to, but I'm so tired that I don't think I'd be very good company, you know?"

"We'll go to Manzina's or someplace quick, and I'll get you right home after we eat. Promise. As for your company, let me be the judge of that. What do you say?"

Rosemary hesitated. She enjoyed Clyde. There was no doubt about that, but she wasn't ready to commit to a real relationship just yet, and she was beginning to fear he was. She didn't want to encourage him, give him false hope. The burned child fears the fire, she'd always said, and it was true. Delorio was fire enough to warn her away from men for a lifetime. Still, it was pleasant to have someone to eat dinner with, and Clyde was always a good conversationalist. He discussed legal issues with her and asked about the newspaper work she was involved in, often responding to one of her editorials. In short, he treated her like an equal. None of that "baby" and "yo' my woman" stuff with which Delorio patronized her. "Okay, Clyde. It's a deal, but I really will have to call it a night right after dinner. I'm bushed, and I have to brainstorm with Charles first thing in the morning."

"Sounds important if the editor and assistant editor are meeting."

"It's to discuss our editorial policy regarding elections—what letters to the editor should be published, what ones are too inflammatory, and who decides. We can't possibly publish them all. We need to clarify a position, a fair one, which we can make public and stand behind about how we decide between the insightful and the incendiary. Routine stuff but, yes, important."

"It's that fine line between freedom of speech and yelling 'Fire!' in a crowded theater, isn't it?" Clyde said.

That man could always put his finger right on the legal aspect and articulate it. That's one reason she enjoyed his company so much. "You're exactly right, Clyde. Our first obligation in delivering the news is to protect the First Amendment."

They decided that to save time, Rosemary would just turn around and meet Clyde at Manzina's. "That'll save you driving all the way up to South Hills," she said. He tried to persuade her to let him come pick her up, but she was adamant. She knew that this way, she could leave on her own schedule, not his.

At dinner, over a plate of succulent eggplant parmesan and a bottle of pinot noir, they talked about their jobs. Suddenly, just as Rosemary took a bite of hot, cheesy eggplant, Clyde cleared his throat and blurted out. "Thank you for having dinner with me tonight. I know it wasn't convenient for you, but…ah…well, the reason I was so insistent was that I have something I want to say to you, and once I decided to do it, I was afraid if I didn't do it right away, I'd lose my nerve."

Rosemary stopped chewing and looked at him, afraid to move, afraid to blink her eyes even. What was coming? Oh dear heavens, what was coming? His handsome face, as brown as a berry, as her mother used to say, and wreathed by gray hair at his temples, was uncharacteristically solemn.

"You and I have been seeing each other for what? About four months or so?"

Rosemary nodded slowly, and he continued. "In that short time I have grown very fond of you. Very fond, indeed."

Now Rosemary swallowed. It was all she could do. Speech was out of the question.

"I told you when we first met that I had lost my wife very tragically in a car wreck sixteen years ago. What I didn't tell you is that when Corabelle died, I buried myself, too—in my work. I loved my wife, and I couldn't bear to live without her. So I just quit—living, that is. I practiced law with intensity and went about my duties with tremendous focus, but I quit living. Nothing gave me any pleasure anymore."

"Clyde, I—"

He patted her hand. "Let me finish. Please. Then you came along, and life began to be pleasant once more. I actually looked forward to having dinner instead of dreading the cold solitude of eating alone. Do you know that before I met you, I stood at my kitchen sink and ate a sandwich many times for a meal, simply because I couldn't stand sitting by myself at a table for two?" He smiled tenderly and continued to pat her hand, which had frozen in mid-air, fork still poised to commence eating again. "I hope that I am not deceiving myself that you are enjoying our friendship, too."

Shaking her head, Rosemary said, "No. Not at all. It's been… wonderful."

"Well, I just wanted to say that. I don't want to put you in a corner, make you uncomfortable, you know. I just wanted to express my gratitude to you for allowing me to be a part of your life. I know you're not ready to make a commitment; I didn't think I was either until I decided to be honest with myself about what you mean to me, but I am now. Anyway, I hope you will continue our friendship and allow it to flourish if it will."

Rosemary sat still, not sure that he was through speaking. Slowly, she lowered her fork. She looked at him expectantly and blotted her mouth with the linen napkin. She felt her heart beating faster and felt the pulse throbbing in her neck.

He reached over and stroked her cheek softly. "Well, that's it. That's all I wanted to say. Just that I think very highly of you." He paused. "No, that's not quite true. Let me be completely honest here. I—uh, well, I love you, Rosemary, and I hope someday that you will love me, too. For now, just having you as my friend is enough."

Rosemary struggled to speak. She had to say something. Marriage, if that's what he was getting at, was definitely not in her plans. If he did nothing else, Delorio had convinced her of that. She couldn't let Clyde go on thinking that there was a real future to their relationship, but just as she opened her mouth to speak, he stopped her. "Wait. Don't say anything. Please. I don't want a response from you right now. Just think about what I've said. That's all I ask." Pouring a little more wine into her glass, he said, "Now then, let's finish eating so I can let you get home early as I promised. If I'm on trial here, I want to keep my promises." He smiled then, a beautiful, genuine smile, and Rosemary, smiling back, found herself relaxing, but only because she knew she was off the hook—for the moment.

Later, after Clyde insisted on driving behind her to be sure she got home safely—he was the consummate gentleman—she waved to him as she unlocked the door and went quickly into the house. She leaned against the closed door and caught her breath. Love! That was a word she had purposely avoided for years. Why did he have to mess up a perfectly good friendship with talk of love? In the shower, she let the hot water massage and relax her back, and then she changed into her lightweight flannel pajamas and slippers. After fixing a cup of hot cocoa, she went into the den and turned on the computer. Scrolling hurriedly through her email, she was delighted to see a note from Dorothy, even though it was just the usual complaint about exacting professors and unbearable workloads:

> *Dear Mom,*
>
> *Maybe I had idealized vet school, but this isn't the way I thought it was going to be at all. I guess in my naiveté, I thought I'd be playing with cuddly little animals all day. So far, it's way too heavy on the academics and not heavy enough on the clinical. Maybe the clinical will come later. This place is tough! I have never worked this hard in my life. Plus, I'm frustrated because I want to adopt every dog I see. I can't wait to come home for Thanksgiving.*
>
> *Love,*
>
> *Dorothy*

Why nothing from Maggie? she wondered, as she shot back an answer to Dorothy.

> *Dear Dorothy,*
>
> *Keep looking. The Land of Oz is out there somewhere. Meanwhile, I can't wait until you click your ruby slippers and come home for Thanksgiving.*
>
> *Love,*
>
> *Mom*
>
> *p.s. Don't bring Toto.*

Still puzzled about Maggie, she decided to write her again, this time telling her about the surprise she had received from Clyde tonight.

Dear Maggie,

When I told you yesterday that Clyde and I were strictly friends, I spoke too soon, at least from his standpoint. Tonight over a plate of eggplant parmesan Clyde "declared his intentions," I guess you'd say. Took me completely by surprise. I mean, really blew me away.

I know what you're thinking: What did I say, right? Well, the truth is—nothing. It was all I could do to keep from choking. He told me just to think about our relationship for now. He said he knew I wasn't really ready to make a commitment just yet. I guess he's speaking of marriage here, and if so, he's right. I mean, what else could it be? I know what I'm going to say, though. I'm simply going to tell him that I enjoy his company as a friend, nothing more. I have tried the marriage thing once, and I learned a lot from it. I learned that I don't have to depend on a man for my happiness. The Lord knows, I wasn't all that happy while I was married.

Clyde is a wonderful man, deeply religious, personable, kind, intelligent, handsome, witty, a true gentleman—all the good things you can think of. I just don't want to find out the hard way that there may be a side to him I don't know. I mean,

*look at Delorio. I thought he was heaven-sent, too,
at first. Hah!*

*You are very fortunate, Maggie, if you have
truly found someone you love. I'm happy for you.
Maybe that will happen someday for me, too. Who
knows? I'm not holding my breath, but I'm not
absolutely ruling it out, either. Now is just not the
time. Write as soon as you have time and let me
know all the details. I want to share your joy.*
Love,
Rosemary

As she turned off the computer, Rosemary leaned back in her new, red-leather tufted chair, a luxury she had afforded herself with her last paycheck, and thought about the first time she encountered Maggie Palmer. Well, it wasn't so much an encounter as it was an epiphany. Until she met Maggie Palmer, she had always viewed life in shades of gray and brown. After Maggie burst upon the scene in 1976, Rosemary saw life in shades of brilliant red and gold. Ah, yes, she could remember it as if it were yesterday.

Chapter Eighteen

"Will Rosemary Jones please come to the office," the intercom blared into Rosemary's fourth period calculus class. Rosemary froze and then began chewing on her pencil. She looked up at Mrs. Young's desk, and the teacher nodded her permission. Rosemary was hoping that Mrs. Young would look menacingly at the intercom as she usually did and say impatiently, "Wait until after class," but she didn't. Instead, she smiled and mouthed, "You may go." With shaking legs and the uneasy awareness of eyes burning holes in her back, Rosemary walked up the aisle of desks, down the long hallway, and into the outer office that served the principal, vice-principal, and guidance counselor.

The secretary looked up. "Oh, Rosemary, good. You got here fast. You're wanted in the guidance counselor's office. Go on in. Mrs. Perkins is expecting you."

At least it wasn't the principal! Breathing again for the first time, she was sure, since she heard the announcement, Rosemary walked hesitantly into Mrs. Perkins' office. "Ma'am, you wanted to see me?" she asked, her voice cracking.

"Why, yes, Rosemary. Sit down. I wanted to talk to you about your college plans."

"Excuse me? What college plans?"

"Well, where are you interested in going? You have the grades to go just about anywhere, you know."

Rosemary swallowed. "Actually, I have no plans. College is not an option for me. It's just way beyond what my momma can afford, and I'm not aware of any colleges recruiting an African-American girl from the middle of nowhere in West Virginia, no matter how good her grades are." She spoke, not with rancor, but with shoulder-shrugging honesty. "After high school, I hope to get a job as a veterinarian's assistant and maybe take some classes at the technical college at night."

"Yes, I read that in the newspaper article when you saved the kitten in the flood."

Rosemary nodded. She had been somewhat embarrassed by the furor that little unthinking incident had caused. She hadn't meant to be a heroine; she had just acted on impulse. It had all started when she saw a kitten, clinging frantically to a shutter and mewing piteously, its small pink mouth opening and closing rapidly, its eyes wide and frightened, being swept downstream by the flooding tributary near her Gauley Bridge home. Instinctively, she knew she must try to save it. She had dived in, grabbed the shutter, and, swimming as hard as she could against the exhaustingly strong current, pulled the makeshift boat and its tiny occupant ashore. As luck would have it, a reporter from the *Charleston Gazette* had gone to Gauley Bridge to cover the flooding of the rampaging river and its tributaries and had witnessed the dramatic rescue. The next thing Rosemary knew, the story had been picked up by AP and re-told across the country. Suddenly, she was something of a local celebrity, albeit a reluctant one.

"Would you be interested in, say, West Virginia University?" Mrs. Perkins smiled coyly.

What was she thinking? Rosemary wondered. Surely, Mrs. Perkins knew that there was no way the Jones family, which consisted of Rosemary, her mother Eunice, and her grandmother Clara, could afford the state university in Morgantown. There was not just the tuition to consider but room and board and travel. "Oh, it's a great school, but it's way too expensive."

"Mm-hmm. Well, here's something I think you might be interested in reading," Mrs. Perkins went on.

Glancing down, Rosemary saw that it was a letter addressed to Mrs. Thomas Perkins, Guidance Counselor, Gauley Bridge High School. Quickly, she scanned its opening paragraph:

> *Dear Mrs. Perkins:*
> *This is to inform you that, contingent upon*
> *the satisfactory completion of her senior year,*
> *one of your students, Rosemary Jones, has*
> *been given a full four-year scholarship to*
> *West Virginia University.*

Rosemary quit reading and looked up at Mrs. Perkins in disbelief. "What? But I never even applied to—"

"Keep reading, dear," Mrs. Perkins said.

> *The donor, who is from Jackson, Mississippi,*
> *has specified that Miss Jones should not incur*
> *any expenses during her stay at the university,*
> *nor will she be expected to pay anything back*
> *upon graduation. The donor is making this an*
> *outright gift, free and clear, with no strings*
> *attached. She is providing, in addition to*
> *tuition, room, and board, a generous stipend*
> *for living expenses, travel, clothing, utilities,*
> *and even entertainment. It is by far the most*

generous--and unusual--scholarship we have
ever been privileged to offer a student.

Will you please inform Miss Jones of her
scholarship and instruct her to make
application to the university at the earliest
possible moment? If the donor's impression,
one that she got from an Associated Press
newspaper article, is correct, Miss Jones's
grades are of such a nature that her application
is merely a formality. Once she has officially
been admitted, our office will inform the donor.

The donor did not stipulate anonymity and,
in fact, I feel certain, would love to have an update
from the recipient at her convenience. She by no
means, however, wants her name to be widely
known or publicized. Her one aim, and I quote
her here, is to "reward the uncompromising
bravery and compassionate heart" of the
young woman she read about in the article.

Thank you for your part in bringing about
this happy event. I look forward to hearing from
you in the near future.
Yours truly,
Michael P. Morrison
Michael Paisley Morrison
Dean of Admissions
West Virginia University

Looking again at Mrs. Perkins, now beaming unabashedly from the other side of her desk, Rosemary was aware that the sheet of paper she held in her hand was shaking uncontrollably. Her mouth was open, and her throat was dry and constricted, but she tried to verbalize what she was feeling. Was this a dream? "But why? Why me? I don't even know anybody from Jackson, Mississippi. Mississippi, period. I...I... can't believe it! This is just...oh, Mrs. Perkins!" With that, she burst into tears, and the guidance counselor, pulling a couple of tissues from the box on her desk, came around, offered them to Rosemary, and then leaned down and put her arms around her.

"Well, it's true, my dear, so you'd better start believing it, and I must say, it's well deserved. This lady read about your courage and wants to reward it. It's as simple and wonderful as that. Now, you dry your eyes, go on back to class, and after school, you come in, and we'll get started on that application. Okay?"

Rosemary couldn't speak right then, but she nodded her head vigorously.

"Oh, and by the way," Mrs. Perkins said as Rosemary started shakily for the door, "I've been meaning to tell you ever since that article came out in the *Gazette* that if you ever do anything as dumb as jumping into a raging river to save a cat again, I'm going to turn you over my knee, scholarship or no scholarship." Winking, she fluttered her hand in a good-bye and turned back to her desk.

Rosemary laughed then, the pent-up emotion rolling up from her chest and causing her to throw her head back in merriment, and she had to restrain herself from dancing up the hallway. College! She was going to college, and not just any college but the state university in Morgantown! She still couldn't believe it and pinched herself just to be sure she was not daydreaming in calculus again. *Wait'll Momma and Memaw hear about this*, she thought. *They'll never believe it.* Oh, the day would be long until she could go home and tell her mother and grandmother what amazing good fortune had befallen them. She would even give Molly Brown, for that is what she had named the kitten she had saved, a can of tuna all of her own for her part in this remarkable story.

Once Mrs. Perkins had mailed in Rosemary's application, she revealed to Rosemary some of the details about the donor that Dean Morrison had subsequently divulged in their correspondence. The scholarship was actually in two donors' names: Mr. and Mrs. Cam Palmer, but it was with Mrs. Palmer that Dean Morrison had spoken, and it was because of Mrs. Palmer's extraordinary love of animals that she and her husband decided to become Rosemary Jones's benefactors.

As luck would have it, Dean Morrison's sister-in-law had originally been from Jackson, Mississippi, and he asked her if she had any knowledge of these people. "Oh yes," she had said. "Jackson is a pretty good-sized city, but I think everyone there knows the Palmers—or at least, knows of them and their families before them. They are a young couple, around forty, I think, but regularly written up in the paper for their active involvement in charitable causes. Maggie Muldoon Palmer is a well-known real estate broker, and Cam Palmer is a very wealthy businessman—owns his family's textile plant—but their largest source of income is from Maggie Palmer's family, the Muldoons, who, in turn, inherited it from Laura Gray Muldoon's family, the McIntoshes. Oh yes, everyone in Jackson knows about the McIntoshes, Muldoons, and Palmers. The interesting thing is that, as fabulously wealthy as they are, they are as venerated for their simple, no-frills life-style as for their charitable involvement. Maggie Palmer would never have to work a day in her life, yet she works—works hard—in the real estate business and equally hard at her charitable causes. Her parents and grandparents before them indoctrinated her with a double dose of work ethic as well as a sense of civic responsibility. Oh yes indeedy, those families are quite an institution in Jackson."

Rosemary wrote to the Palmers, and her letter was so full of high ideals, of wonder, and of gratitude that Maggie Palmer answered it immediately. That began a mutual correspondence, which included pictures, grades, and encouragement and culminated in Maggie and Cam's attending Rosemary's graduation from West Virginia University four years later. The first thing Rosemary did when she saw the striking couple get out of their car in Morgantown was to run and throw her arms around both their necks. Before she knew it, she was sobbing.

"Whoa, here, sugah," Cam said, his resonant, deep voice made as rich and heavy as clotted cream by a Mississippi accent. "I didn't come all this way to get cried on. You're gonna shrink my suit. This is supposed to be a happy occasion."

"Oh, it is. It is," Rosemary cried. "I've never been so happy in all my life, and if it weren't for you all, none of this would have happened."

She dried her eyes and introduced them to her mother and grandmother and showed them all around the campus, pointing out the monorail that ferried students among the many campuses. "WVU had a monorail even before Disney World," she said with a laugh. After the ceremony, the five of them went out to eat at Oliverio's, a popular Italian restaurant. During dinner, Rosemary's mother, in expressing gratitude for the Palmers' financial assistance and also for their continued interest in Rosemary, said, "You were so sweet to come all this way for Rosemary's graduation. I know you must be tired. When did your flight get in?"

"Flight?" Cam asked. "What flight? Mrs. Jones, you are looking at one of the last remaining heroes in our country. I accompany my dear wife by car everywhere she goes because she doesn't fly."

"Please call me Eunice. You *drove* from Mississippi?" she asked.

"Mm-hmm. All the way."

"Well, Mr. Palmer—"

"Cam."

"—Cam, some of our mountainous roads aren't the best, so I think you do deserve a place in a highway hall of fame somewhere."

They had all enjoyed a good laugh then. It was a laugh that Rosemary took with her as she departed Morgantown and went to Charleston in search of a job. No matter how many times she was turned down, she remembered the buoying laughter of those four people who believed in her, and her confidence was restored. Finally, after a series of short-term jobs, she secured a starting position in a bank on Quarrier Street and within six months had met and married Delorio Harrison, who had come in to cash a check.

Her quick mind and eager spirit did not go unnoticed, and she advanced rapidly, applying herself with diligence and taking great satisfaction in her work. Within eighteen months, she learned that not one, but two, babies were on the way, and it was with mixed feelings that she quit her job to prepare for and then to care for the twins. Delorio worked at odd jobs, but he could not seem to hold onto anything permanent, or at least, that's what he told Rosemary. Someone, she soon realized, was going to have to earn more money than they had coming in right then. As soon as the twins were old enough for day-care, she got another job, this one even more to her liking. She became first a cub reporter and then an investigative reporter for the *Charleston Gazette*. She did not miss the irony that she would now be working for the very paper that propelled her onto the national stage and into the sphere of Maggie Palmer.

Chapter Nineteen

"Mr. Wexler, please. This is Rosemary Harrison calling," Rosemary said when the secretary answered the phone.

In seconds, Clyde's voice came over the line. "Rosemary! What a pleasant surprise! You are just the tonic I needed today."

Quickly, Rosemary asked him if he could meet her for lunch, and he eagerly agreed. "Let's say one o'clock at the Thai House. My treat this time," she said, signing off.

Over a plate of sumptuous Pad Thai, Rosemary broke the news. "Clyde, I've been thinking about what you said last night, and I have come to the painful conclusion that not to say anything, to let this go on, while certainly easier on my part, would be, nevertheless, cowardly."

Clyde stopped chewing and looked at her solemnly. His shoulders sagged. "I don't think I like the sound of this, but go on," he said.

"You are a wonderful man, the nicest man I've ever dated—by far—but I...uh, well, I just never intend to marry again. I feel it only honest to tell you that right up front. I have found life quite comfortable on my own, and I am not in a hurry to give up my independence. Please understand that it has nothing to do with you personally."

Clyde nodded but said nothing. Rosemary played with her knife a few minutes and then blurted out, "I just don't think I could ever really trust a man again." She looked down at her lap in silence for a few seconds and then looked him straight in the eye. "That's it, I'm afraid. I had one experience of betrayed trust that could last a lifetime. Sounds stupid, but it's how I feel. It wouldn't be a good basis for a lasting relationship."

Later that evening when she drove home from work, she felt both relieved at being freed from an awkward situation and, surprisingly, sad for the same reason. She couldn't understand the tears that kept pooling in her eyes. *This is nonsense*, she said, dabbing at her cheeks with a tissue. *I made the right decision.* Still, she couldn't forget the wounded look in his eyes or the way he smiled sadly and kissed her cheek before she slipped out of the booth in which they sat. *Listen, girl. Get hold of yourself. You're free*, she said to herself over and over. *Free. Free. Free.* It was the best thing that could have happened to her, she decided. Besides, it was the ethical thing to do for Clyde's sake. He was too nice a guy to lead on just for the nice meals and the warm, fuzzy companionship he provided. Her momma had taught her better than to use people.

Feeling much better about herself after the pep talk, she went into the kitchen, slid a low-fat frozen dinner into the microwave, and tossed a salad. Going into her bedroom, she kicked off her shoes and put on her sweats. *Ah, that's more like it.* She went back into the kitchen, assembled her dinner on a tray and carried it to the den, where she turned on the computer to see whether or not she'd heard from Maggie. *Nope. What in the world? Maggie had never taken this long to respond to a message before. Oh well, she's probably involved in some big real estate deal.*

As she sat eating, her eye happened to glance at the answering machine, which she had totally forgotten until this minute. It was blinking. She pushed the button and listened to the message:

> *Ms. Rosemary Harrison? This is Debra Smith.*
> *I'm a secretary for the law firm of Landers, Watson,*
> *Coughlin, and Weller in Jackson, Mississippi. I'll call*
> *back later. Thank you. Beep.*

Rosemary smiled. Probably a mistaken call for Anthony. Maybe it's a prestigious law firm interested in recruiting Anthony when he graduates. Yep, they're calling to get a jump on the other law firms by tempting him with their lucrative starting salary. She smiled as she thought about it. Jackson, hmm? I wouldn't put it past Maggie Palmer to have engineered this whole thing. Sounds like something she would do.

She was still sitting there thinking when the phone rang. She grabbed up the receiver. "Hello."

"Is this Ms. Harrison? Ms. Rosemary Harrison?"

"Yes, it is."

"This is Debra Smith. Hold a moment, please, for Mr. Surles."

After a brief pause, another voice came on the line. "Ms. Harrison?"

"Yes."

"This is Chilton Surles. Sorry to be calling you right at dinner time, but the time difference and your working make it hard to catch you at a convenient time. I'm the attorney for Margaret Muldoon Palmer. I understand you are a friend of hers."

Book Two: The Meeting

Chapter Twenty

Soft lights cast a sickly yellow glow on the tight little groups of people in the Whitesides and Whittington Funeral Home parlor. The lights were suddenly clicked a notch lower by Eddie Lee Johnson, Jr., who stepped out from behind a door marked "Private," swept one hand across his plastered blond hair, and oozed a studied, circumspectly sad smile at all who had gathered. He loved making entrances from that door, especially when there was a large crowd like tonight. It made him feel important, not at all like a lowly assistant manager, which he felt was nothing more than a glorified maintenance man, but like Mr. Whitesides and Mr. Whittington themselves.

"Evenin', Miz Merritt," he said, dipping his head respectfully at the first lady in line to sign the guest register, who happened to have been his first grade teacher some thirty years before. Like most other people in this little section of Jackson, Eddie Lee had stayed in the community instead of going off to seek his fortune. He knew almost everyone around.

"Evenin', Eddie Lee," she replied somberly, transferring her bulging black imitation leather purse to the other arm and picking up the pen to sign. "I just can't believe this, can you?" Beulah Merritt was a big-boned, bosomy woman with tightly-curled iron-gray hair. Enormous daisy earrings, the clip-on kind, only partially obscured large, protuberant ears. Wide-set brown eyes peeped from behind the trifocals that kept slipping down her nose. Her black polyester dress buttoned up the front, a task it strained almost impossibly to do.

"No, ma'am, I sure can't. Nobody can believe Miz Palmer's gone, and that's the truth. It just ain't real."

Pausing a moment, she decided to let the grammar go—it was far too late for Eddie Lee—and nodded. "She was a wonderful woman. All the years I taught at John R. Ridgeway Elementary, which, as you know, is not far from where she lived, she called me regularly to see which children needed what—supplies, clothes, whatever. Always helped out the children that didn't have much, don't you know? Always did, even as a young woman right out of college. She was brought up that way—to look out for others, don't you know." She reached down and tugged up the strap of one of her black, sling-back platform shoes.

Eddie Lee nodded. "Is that right? I never knew that. Well, well," he said, drifting off. Straightening his tie and patting the lapels of his shiny black suit, he dipped his head in the direction of the growing line of people and smiled again.

After he had faded away, his expressionless white moon face blending into the soft pastels of the walls, draperies, and paintings, a man in line behind Beulah Merritt said, "I couldn't help overhearing what you said. I don't know about her benevolence to the school, but I do know that she was the largest supporter we had at the animal adoption shelter."

"Is that right?" Beulah turned and handed him the pen and then watched him sign his name, Billy Ray Boatright. With an arched eyebrow, she took in his large ring, his perfectly coiffed hair, and the heavy perfume which seemed to swirl about him in a diaphanous cloud. Just like Maggie to have gay friends. At the same time, she frowned at the people, who, not stopping to sign the register, went ahead of her into the next room. They were obviously not real friends of Maggie's or they wouldn't be in such a hurry, she thought. They would at least sign in. Let everybody know they'd been and all. Why, she wouldn't think of not getting credit for being there. Such a comfort to the family and all.

"Mm-hmm. It was because of her that we got started in the first place. She couldn't stand to think of all those defenseless little animals being put to sleep just because they didn't have homes, so she got the idea to start an adoption agency that would provide food, shelter, and veterinary care to homeless animals until they could be adopted—or for life if no one adopted them. She gave the money to erect our first building and get us up and running and then endowed the organization to ensure its survival. We wanted to name it for her, but she wouldn't let us. 'Call it the St. Francis Animal Adoption Center,' she said, so we did. No indeed, we'll never forget what Maggie Palmer did for us."

"I'm sure lots of people feel the same way, young man," Beulah said.

As the line moved on, another lady, a tall, striking, raven-haired woman dressed in a turquoise silk pantsuit with a black silk overlay and sporting shoulder-length turquoise and silver earrings, picked up the pen. Beulah Merritt, peering over the back of the register, had relinquished her place in the line moving into the room where the casket lay just to see who this person was. She wasn't from around here. That was for sure. Not with a getup like that.

"You a friend of Maggie's or a relation?" Beulah asked, noting the name: Tootsie Freeman. Didn't ring a bell. She wrinkled up her nose and sniffed slightly. Hmm...It was peculiar, Beulah thought, but she could almost swear she smelled peanut butter.

"Oh, a friend. An old, *old* friend," Tootsie said. *Who is this person*? she wondered. *Probably the self-appointed social director of the Whitesides and Whittington Funeral Home.* "We went to college together," she added, though it occurred to her that she really didn't need to add any more information other than being an old friend. Maggie was dead. Nothing else mattered. She smiled a smile of closure to the woman in front of her and looked past her to the parlor where Maggie's closed coffin rested on a catafalque shrouded not in black, but white crepe. She certainly didn't intend to engage in a lengthy conversation with the neighborhood busybody at a time like this. She wanted time to herself, time to absorb what was happening, time to reminisce, time to think, time to grieve.

As the line moved forward, Beulah stepped out again and let Tootsie pass her. Farther back in the line she had spotted some other people she didn't know—there were many different types of people there of all colors, sizes, and apparent income levels—and she was determined to be at the register when they signed. Someone has to welcome the strangers, she thought. Nodding in greeting to all those who passed her, she watched intently as the tiny little lady with the big brown eyes and funny-shaped nose—Mercy! It looked like a ski-jump—picked up the pen and registered: Bippy Maas.

Beulah leaned in toward the woman. "I don't believe I know you. Are you from around here?" she asked, knowing the answer.

"No, I'm from Alabama. Birmingham, to be exact," Bippy answered.

Beulah thought the stranger would go on to tell how she was connected to Maggie, but she didn't, so not being one to stand on ceremony, Beulah asked, "Were you related to Maggie?"

"No, just a friend," Bippy replied, "a dear friend."

"Oh," Beulah said, with a dismissive flutter of her hand. "Well..."

"I met her when my brother and sister and I came here to look at real estate some years ago," Bippy added.

Beulah breathed a sigh of relief. Finally, some information. "I see. Well, she was quite a success with real estate. One of the biggest realtors in this part of Mississippi, I understand."

Bippy nodded. "Yes, but she was even more of a success at making friends. In no time, she became the closest friend my sister and I had. That was after Richard, my brother, God rest him, passed away."

The line was moving, and Beulah was afraid she would miss some pertinent information. "Did you buy a house here, then?"

"No. That's what I mean about Maggie. After Richard's death, Maggie came to feel that it was not the smart thing for Melinda Rose and me to do, now that it was just the two of us, to buy here. She advised us to stay put in Birmingham. That's what I mean about her putting friendship above business."

Beulah nodded. "Oh, I see. Well, she was wonderful, all right. Just wonderful."

As Bippy made her way into the parlor, the line moved on, and Beulah stood her ground, nodding a greeting and speaking in soft, lugubrious tones to everyone who filed past her. There was Louise Smathers, who had been fixing Maggie's hair for the last forty years. After speaking to Beulah, she twisted her purse handles over and over as she stood waiting to sign. Then came Nora and Charlie Counts, who lived on Maggie's street and fed Maggie's pets when she had to be away. Nora had been crying, and was still dabbing at her eyes with a crumpled Kleenex. Charlie, with one arm around her shoulders, was saying, "Poor Nora. Poor Nora" as if Nora herself had died. After a few more minutes, Beulah, who by now had draped one arm around the back of the guest register stand like a particularly sturdy vine of kudzu, peeped over and read upside down the name of the next entry: Penelope Caldwell. Hmm. Another stranger. This one must have been hiding in a closet for the last twenty years. That hairdo! And that dress! It was down to her ankles, for goodness sakes. Beulah noted with a hint of envy, however, the beautiful cameo pin affixed to the ruffled collar.

"Hello. You must be from out of town," Beulah began.

The small white face turned towards her. "Hmm?" she said, cupping a hand behind her right ear.

"I said you must be from out of town," Beulah repeated slowly as she studied the woman before her. She couldn't have been much over five feet tall, she thought, and at least twenty-five pounds overweight. Her heavily powdered skin looked like alabaster, making her dark green eyes all the more striking. White-gray curls lay under a hairnet like a covey of captured albino butterflies.

"Out of? Oh, yes, town. Sorry. I'm a bit hard of hearing."

Beulah waited for Penelope to finish, to add where, exactly, she was from, but Penelope remained silent. She was shy about conversing with people she didn't know, people who didn't understand her hearing loss, always afraid that she would say the wrong thing or give the wrong answer to a question. When in doubt, she said nothing.

Beulah was not easily dissuaded. "Are you from Mississippi?"

Penelope paused, trying to piece together the sounds she had heard with the lip movements she had observed. Speech-reading, she had read it was called, and, while it was good in most situations, better than simple lip reading, it was not totally accurate. Finally, taking a chance that the question was about where she was from, she said, "I'm from Culpeper, Virginia. That's with one 'p' you know."

"What? Oh, you mean the spelling." Beulah tasted this bit of information as if it were an exotic food and then, after a few moments, asked a little louder, "How did you know Maggie?"

"I...uh. Well, I used to be a neighbor of the Muldoons right here in Jackson. It was when my husband was a medical school student and then a resident."

"Well, I'll be! Well, then, it's welcome home to you." Beulah beamed. She felt that she now knew more about Maggie's friends than anyone here. That was particularly satisfying. She could hardly wait to dazzle the other ladies in her circle with all of this information. "How nice of you to come so far to Maggie's funeral after so many years."

Penelope just nodded, not sure what to say. Finally, she said, "Maggie and I have been close friends since she was thirteen years old. We never lost touch after John and I moved away. I loved her like a younger sister." As she moved on, she patted Beulah's arm, as if acknowledging that Beulah was some sort of fixture at the funeral home like the register to which she clung, some official mourner-in-residence.

The next-to-last person in the line was a striking young African-American woman. After signing the book—Beulah noted that the name was Rosemary Harrison—Rosemary smiled confidently at the lady standing guard over the guest book.

Rosemary stood out, not because of her race, for Maggie had many African-American friends, but because she was so young and attractive. Couldn't be much over forty, Beulah thought. There was nothing common about this person. Her smooth skin reminded Beulah of the cup of espresso—to which she had added a copious amount of cream—she'd had that very morning when she was trying to be so "with it" at Barnes and Noble Books, where she had gone to sit and read without buying anything. The woman's large brown eyes were intelligent and alive.

Beulah decided to try the direct approach. "Where are you from?"

"Charleston."

"Oh, Charleston. I love Charleston."

"Yes. Charleston, West Virginia."

Beulah, who had started smiling at the word "Charleston," suddenly stopped when she heard "West Virginia." Oh. That one. She had taught geography briefly one time when she had been given fourth grade by the new principal, but she had forgotten there even was another Charleston. A little sigh of exasperation escaped her lips. She had been all prepared to ask this lady if she had ever eaten the she-crab soup at 82 Queen Street. That had been one of Beulah's favorite places when her nephew and niece took her to Charleston, South Carolina, a few years ago. Or maybe Poogan's Porch. That was another great place for seafood, especially that wonderfully spicy shrimp jambalaya. And Poogan's Porch even boasted a ghost. But her favorite, hands down, was Hyman's. The shrimp and grits there were pure heaven, and all of the people were so nice. Their emphasis was on attitude, and she liked that. And then there was that gorgeous bed and breakfast over near The Battery—Two Meeting Street. Oh yes, she knew lots about Charleston, South Carolina, and would have loved to tell somebody. Anybody. That would make a good impression and let people know she had gone places and done things and hadn't been stuck in Mississippi as an elementary school teacher all her life. Yes indeed. But she knew absolutely nothing about Charleston, West Virginia, except that it was the state capital—and what was the big deal about that?—so her conversation could go no further in that direction. Instead, she asked, "Did you know Maggie through real estate?"

Rosemary looked surprised at the question and then said, "No, I knew her—well, personally."

"You must have known her really well to come so far. She must have been a very special friend." Beulah looked at her expectantly.

Rosemary bit her upper lip and lowered her head. Finally, she said softly, "She—she changed my life is all."

***

The next day, after a moving tribute to Margaret Katherine Muldoon Palmer at First United Methodist Church—a tribute that called attention to the largess of Maggie's benevolence, the diversity of her friends, the depth of her faith, and the vivacity of her personality—the large crowd of friends, both Catholic and Methodist, looked on silently as she was laid to rest at Elmwood Cemetery beside her beloved Cam. From time to time a hushed sob or sniffling could be heard above the call of the birds. After the ministers had finished the prayers of committal and benediction and had gone to the front row of folding chairs under the tent to speak in muted tones to the family members, Tootsie Freeman stepped forward and laid a single yellow rose on the pall-draped casket. Closing her eyes to try to stop the flow of tears, she felt another presence beside her. Opening her eyes, she saw three other ladies doing precisely the same thing. Each had a single yellow rose, which she was laying on the casket. Looking at one another, the ladies exchanged knowing, solemn glances and, as if responding to some unspoken command, fell back into the shadows behind the tent, waiting until the crowd had left the gravesite.

Chapter Twenty-One

"Listen," Tootsie said quietly, motioning the other three women to come closer, "I'm Tootsie Freeman, and, well, call me crazy, but I have the feeling I know you all indirectly."

Penelope's lips moved as she followed what Tootsie was saying and broke into a spontaneous smile. "Tootsie! So you're Tootsie! I've heard so much about you from Maggie. How she loved you, dear! I'm Penelope Caldwell. Maggie called me Pen. I'd love for you to call me Pen, too." She grasped Tootsie's hand in both of hers, a gesture which Tootsie immediately folded into a hug.

"Oh, my goodness!" exclaimed one of the other women, turning to her. "You're Penelope? I'm Bippy. You've sent me emails, haven't you?"

Penelope cupped her hand behind her ear. "Sorry. I'm very hard of hearing. Let me turn up my hearing aids."

"Oh, sorry." Bippy spoke more slowly, being careful to articulate each word. She knew from experience on campus with hard-of-hearing faculty members that speaking louder usually didn't help—like turning up the volume on a radio that wasn't quite on the station. Speaking slowly and clearly did. "I said you have sent me emails, haven't you?"

"Emails. Oh, yes, just as recently as the day before yesterday," Penelope answered. "I was worried about Maggie."

"Well, ladies," Rosemary chimed in, "that completes the circle. I'm Rosemary Harrison, though Maggie often called me Rose, and I have heard about each of you from Maggie and have even talked with you by email at times, too. I believe the four of us make up Maggie's 'sister list.' "

"Oh, yes, dear," Bippy said, extending her hand, "you have sent me the cutest jokes, which I share with my friends on the faculty at the college. I just loved the one about the Bible in fifty words. I'm so glad to meet you in person."

Penelope turned to Tootsie. "I'm curious. Whatever made you think you knew us?"

Tootsie shook her head. "Oh, I don't know. I think it was the way we all simultaneously put yellow roses, Maggie's favorite flower, on the casket that struck a chord with me. It was like we were her flower girls, but not for her wedding, as we all would have wished." Tootsie paused and swallowed. "There was something so likeminded about that gesture that it gave me the spooky feeling I was among people I already knew. You know that feeling you get sometimes when you think you've done or said or are experiencing the same thing before—atavism, I think it's called? Well, it was like that."

For a minute, the four stood smiling, relieved to be buoyed by any lightness on an almost unbearably heavy day. They patted arms, hugged shoulders, and in general tried to comfort one another and in turn be comforted. Then, one by one, they remembered why they were there in a cemetery, why they were meeting these new friends for the first time, and the realization descended like a smothering blanket thrown over them all. Hushed then by the reminder of their grief and no longer under the burden of having to bear up alone, they cried softly, each in her own way: Tootsie looking straight up toward the heavens, her dangling earrings catching the light; Penelope sniffling into a lace-trimmed snowy linen handkerchief; Bippy covering her face with a small hand, her middle three fingers resting on the little dip in her nose; Rosemary biting on her knuckles and swallowing hard as tears slid down her cheeks. In the distance, the other mourners drifted away to their cars, and silence laid a soft coverlet over the sleeping graves.

"Are...are you all going to the luncheon at the church?" Tootsie asked finally, clearing her throat. When no one said anything, she added, "It's a tradition in the South, you know."

Bippy sighed and shook her head. "Isn't that just for family members?"

"Usually, but not in this case. I spoke with Dr. High, the senior minister, last night at the funeral home, and he said that since the two older brothers are the only family Maggie has—I mean, had—everyone who knew and loved Maggie is coming and bringing a covered dish. He said that applied only to local people—the covered dish part, I mean. We are invited to go as guests of the church. One of the circles is helping, I understand. As Dr. High put it with a wink, 'The Mary and Martha Circle loves to serve bereavement meals. Death is their reason for living.'"

"Well, then, let's go," said Penelope, who had been trying to read Tootsie's lips to follow what she was saying. "We have to eat, no matter what, and I, for one, don't know my way around this city. How did you all get out here to the cemetery, by the way?"

Rosemary said, "I rented a car at the airport. You can all ride with me."

"Oh, good," Tootsie said. "I started to rent a car but took a taxi instead. I told him not to wait because I didn't know how long I would be."

"I took a taxi to the church, but I rode out to the cemetery from the church with some people on my pew, who were kind enough to

148

invite me," Penelope said. "I told them I'd find another ride back to the church because they are going out of town straight from here."

"That's exactly what I did," said Bippy. "A nice lady I saw at the funeral home last night stopped me after the service and invited me to ride with her. She said if I could find another ride back that would be better because she had to rush right back to the church before the benediction was pronounced to help prepare the meal."

"Okay, well, everybody pile in," Rosemary said, motioning to the white Honda Accord now keeping a solitary vigil at the curb. "It's not a limousine, but it's plenty big enough for the four of us."

"This surely is nice of the church to do—serve us lunch, I mean," Pen said, as Rosemary consulted the GPS and pulled into traffic.

"Mmm," Bippy added, "although I don't feel much like eating."

Tootsie smiled. "No, neither do I, but Maggie would want us to go. She would want us to talk to her brothers, enjoy the company of one another, and in general be a part of her world here in Mississippi."

"You're right," Rosemary agreed. "Besides, she told me once: 'No matter what happens, I never miss a meal.' "

As they all laughed, Bippy said, "She did love to eat, didn't she? I remember how much she especially loved collards."

"And cornbread," added Tootsie. "She said that her idea of the perfect meal was collards, black-eyed peas with chopped onions, and cornbread. 'Food for the gods, Southern ones, at least,' she often said."

"Her diet was quintessentially Southern, all right," Rosemary said. "She once told me that if the first Native Americans had given grits a try, hominy would have been the basic use of maize. We might never have had corn on the cob."

"The interesting thing was that she never seemed to gain an ounce," Pen said. "She had a hearty appetite from the time she was a teenager, but she was always slender. I remember the first time I met her was when she brought one of her mother's delicious desserts to our door, and she raved about Doll's cooking. It was justified, too. Her mother was quite a cook."

"Well, she worried about gaining weight and exercised a lot, I know," Tootsie said. "Then, too, she was a type A personality, always burning energy. Even back in college, she walked everywhere—often from one campus to the other and even to downtown Durham. She said the bus was too slow, and the rides were too unpredictable."

Driving towards First United Methodist, they laughed heartily as they continued remembering words Maggie had spoken to each of them. The remembrances made the short trip seem even shorter, assuaging their wounded spirits and keeping Maggie alive in their hearts. Periodically, they would fall silent as each remembered a special encounter she had had with Maggie, an incident, a conversation, perhaps, or just a certain look from the friend she loved.

As soon as they reached the church, they saw the same woman who had greeted them at the funeral home the night before, rushing out to gather them in and welcome them to the lunch her circle had prepared. "Beulah Merritt," she said holding out her hand while she was still a good thirty feet away. "Welcome to First Church."

"I swear, that woman is ubiquitous," Tootsie whispered to Rosemary as they saw her coming.

"And maybe even a little officious," Rosemary whispered back.

"Ya' think?" Tootsie said quietly.

"She's an official?" Pen asked.

Tootsie rolled her eyes. "Thinks she is, anyway"

Rosemary turned so that Pen could read her lips. "No, we said she's officious," she mouthed, "and ubiquitous."

"Oh. Oh yes, she gets around, all right," said Pen, nodding.

By now, Beulah had bounded into them like a battleship with all guns blazing. She gripped each one's arm in turn. "Maggie's brothers are right over there if you want to speak to them," Beulah said. She nodded her head toward two men standing with the minister. "Come on. Do you want me to introduce you?"

The Flower Girls, backing up, all murmured variations of "no" and smiled tight, self-conscious smiles. They chatted with her a few moments and realized as they inched away from her and finally broke free that she had asked them at least ten questions and had told them very little about herself or her relationship to Maggie. Nothing, really, other than her name.

"That's how she finds out all the news," Bippy observed, when Tootsie mentioned Beulah's inquisitiveness. "She's just a harmless busybody."

"I suppose so," said Tootsie. "The busybody part I'm sure of."

"Which brother is that?" Rosemary whispered later as she sat with the other three ladies at a table in the corner eating potato salad and ham. She picked at the shredded carrot congealed salad beginning to melt and pool on her plate. "I never met her brothers. Just heard about them, and we didn't get to speak to them at the gravesite after the committal."

"Yeah," Tootsie said with a quick smile. "We were huddling in the back getting acquainted. Don't you think Maggie would have just loved it?" They all nodded their agreement.

"Let's see, that's Clarkson, the older one, I believe," Penelope answered, rolling her eyes toward a tall man with carefully coifed jet black hair. With chiseled features and large, expressive eyes as blue as cornflowers, he was the kind of man at whom people couldn't help staring. Handsome didn't quite cover it. It was more than that. There was a pure masculinity, a celebrity quality about him, evident in his bearing that seemed to shout: *Look! Pay attention to me.* "I haven't seen the boys in a long, long time, but he was the taller one as I remember."

"That's right," Tootsie said. "He was. I'm like you, Pen. It's been a while. "The only times I've seen them since Maggie and Cam's wedding were the times I flew out for her parents' and Cam's funerals and then not for long."

"They were already away in school when I lived near them," Pen said. "They were a few years older than Maggie, and I saw them only when they came home on holidays and school breaks."

"Well, if that's Clarkson, then Raymond must be the sandy-haired one. Am I imagining it, or is does he have a slight limp?" Rosemary said.

"Yes, Raymond was in a bicycle accident in Europe one summer while he was on a year abroad in college," Penelope said. "He broke his leg badly, and it was improperly set. Some complications set in. I do remember that. It was all the more difficult on his family since his father, R. C. Muldoon, was a well-known orthopedic surgeon. Dr. Muldoon saw to it that Raymond had many operations to correct the damage when he was back in the States, but he always had a slight limp."

"He's quite nice looking," Tootsie said. She studied the tanned face with its square jaw and strong nose and eyes as green as jade. His hair, unlike his brother's, was tousled looking and fell naturally about his face. "He has a certain insouciance, you know? Even under these circumstances, that quality gives him a little boy look. His blond hair has a decided reddish cast that reminds me of Maggie."

"My, but they're both handsome boys, aren't they?" Bippy said, regarding the two men over the edge of her plastic cup. "I wonder whether they are married or engaged." She smiled benignly as she sipped her sweetened tea.

The others looked at her for a minute as if surprised by her question before Tootsie blurted out, "Why, Bippy? You interested?"

Bippy blushed and smiled demurely. "Heavens no! I was just thinking of girls back home who might make them nice wives."

"Ladies," Tootsie replied, "be on your guard. I think we have a matchmaker in our midst."

"Besides," Bippy giggled, "they're too young for me."

"They have sung to you?" Penelope asked.

"No, you misunderstood. I said that they're too *young* for me," Bippy said.

Penelope smiled and shook her head. "Oh. Not really," she said. "Not in today's world. They were older than Maggie, remember. They must be in their mid-to-late sixties. They just look young. Extremely young!"

"Well, they've obviously taken care of themselves," Rosemary said.

Tootise nodded. "Yes, they could both pass for forty-five to fifty, especially Raymond. He seems just a boy."

They turned and looked at Raymond at the very moment he collapsed into a chair and put his head in his hands. From where they sat, they could see his shoulders heaving. They also noticed that no one, particularly no woman, came to comfort him. Tootsie leaned in a little closer to Bippy. "Actually, you all probably know this as well as I do, but Clarkson is a widower with one grown son, who's stationed overseas in the Air Force, and Raymond never married that I know of. Maggie said he was engaged once, and his fiancée was tragically killed in a car wreck three weeks before the wedding. He was absolutely devastated. Whether he's ever had a serious girlfriend since then or not, I don't know. Maggie never mentioned it if he did." The other three nodded.

"Hmm," Bippy said.

"Won't you all have some more potato salad? Bettie Sue makes this special," a large lady in a black crepe dress said, leaning over the table. She ran her hands up and down a red-checked apron. "Puts dill pickles in it. A little onion, too. Or how about some fried chicken? Beulah makes the best fried chicken you ever ate. At least, that's what she says." She laughed. "Calls herself the fried chicken queen." She winked merrily as if, having met Beulah once, they would understand. They did. "We have loads of food. Please go back and help yourselves. And don't forget the dessert table over by the piano." With an arm as large as a small ham, she waved towards a long folding table covered with chocolate pies, German chocolate cakes, peach cobblers, apple turnovers, and carrot cakes with cream cheese icing. "Our circle specializes in desserts." She gave a deep chuckle. "I guess I'm ample proof of that," she laughed.

"Don't worry," Tootsie replied. "The food is too good not to go back for seconds."

"Thanks," Rosemary replied to the lady. "I guess I could have a little more. That is without a doubt the best broccoli casserole I have ever tasted."

She rang the bell with that statement. The lady brightened visibly. "Why, thank you, dear. I made that myself. The secret is lots and lots of cheese, don't you know. Cheddar. Sharp. And just a touch of onion. Not too much." She winked at Rosemary. Smiling, she wiped her right hand on her apron and extended it. "I'm Myrtle Long."

When the ladies seated at the table had each introduced themselves, Myrtle said, "You all must be friends of Maggie's from a long time ago."

"Yes," Tootsie replied. "Some of us longer than others. In my case, from college days, and in Penelope's case, since Maggie was thirteen."

"Oh my. Well, then, you must be as puzzled about all this as I am." She lowered her voice to a whisper and said, "It's all very strange, you know, very strange indeed. Something just doesn't stack up. Beulah and I were talking, and we think—"

"Myrtle," a man in a dark suit called from across the table, "show me which is your famous broccoli casserole." Straightening, she turned quickly and said, "Coming, Mr. Lowden. Be right there." Turning back to the girls, she said, "Well, anyway, we're glad to have you in Jackson and at First United Methodist Church. Any friend of Maggie's is a friend of all of ours. Go on now and help yourself to more food. Don't be shy." She bustled away, stopping to pat Raymond on the shoulder and urge him to eat.

"What do you make of that?" Rosemary said.

Tootsie remained silent and looked pensively off in the distance, chewing her lower lip in an attitude of deep thought.

"Oh, we had a Myrtle in my family," Penelope said, "only her name was Louise. She was always encouraging everyone else to eat. She—"

Rosemary shook her head. "No, no, I mean her response to Maggie's death. Why did she say it was puzzling? Horrible, yes. Unbelievable, of course, but puzzling? I'm not sure exactly what she meant."

"And I wondered what it was she was about to say that she and that Beulah lady had talked about," Bippy added.

Not quite understanding what Bippy and Rose were saying, Penelope shrugged her shoulders and said, "Well, all I know is that I ought to go speak to Maggie's brothers, especially since I knew them once upon a time. And, Tootsie, I know you feel the same." She pushed her chair back and stood up, the others quickly joining her. They walked slowly over to where Raymond sat, his head still lowered. Penelope patted him softly on his back. "Raymond," she said softly, "I'm Penelope Caldwell. I know you probably don't remember me, but I used to live near your family years ago here in Jackson, and these are your sister's dear friends, also." She motioned the others to draw closer.

"And I'm Tootsie, Maggie's college roommate. I last saw you at Cam's funeral."

He looked up, his clear green eyes red-rimmed and moist, and then scrambled to his feet. Reaching out his arms, he hugged first Penelope, then Tootsie. "Oh, yes, Penelope, I remember you. And you, Tootsie, of course," he said. Then turning, he hugged the other two, listening carefully as they said their names. "So you're Rosemary, and you're Bippy. She's spoken of you all many times. You four were her email sisters, as she called you. Thank you for coming. Thank you for…for loving Maggie so much all these years. How she loved all of you!" With that, he broke down completely, and after a period of silence and much arm patting, the ladies moved on and sought out Clarkson, who had wandered away to speak to another group of people.

When Penelope told Clarkson who she was, and Tootsie started to re-introduce herself, Clarkson interrupted her. "Of course, Penelope. And, Tootsie. Who could forget you? You and Maggie were inseparable." As the remaining two in turn told him who they were and what their connection with Maggie had been, he shook each of their hands warmly and said, "I can't tell you how grateful I am that you have come. Your support means so much to Raymond and me. It's just the two of us now—well, except for my son, but he is stationed in Germany. He was home on leave a little over a month ago and came to spend a week with his adored and adoring Aunt Maggie. I told him not to worry about missing the service today. It was more important that he had spent that time with Maggie when she was alive. It absolutely thrilled her that he would spend a whole week of his leave with her. She even put him to work down at her animal shelter for a couple of days. He wants to go to veterinary school when he gets out of the Air Force. She wrote me that she had decided to give him a little advanced clinical experience. Anyway, thank you again for coming. You're every bit the friends Maggie always said you were. How we're going to miss her!"

Tears welled up in Bippy's eyes, overflowing onto her pale cheeks. "Oh, indeed we are," she said softly.

"Everyone is going to miss Maggie!" Penelope said quietly. "Everyone. She always exemplified to me a line from *The Aeneid* as one of 'those who discovered truth and made life nobler.' "

"That's a beautiful tribute, and—I know I'm probably biased—but I think it's well deserved," Clarkson said, his eyes brimming.

Tootsie nodded and breathed deeply. "I...I can't imagine life without her," she said simply. "She's just always been there. Like my arm."

Sighing, Rosemary looked up at the ceiling and clamped her lips together tightly. Her eyes glistened, and her throat pulsed with repressed emotion. Finally, she cleared her throat and said, "This just can't be happening. I keep hoping I'll wake up and find that it was all a nightmare. Maggie just can't be—" She bit off her words as the tears began flowing. Several minutes later, after drying her eyes and blowing her nose and being comfortingly patted, she stood mutely with the others.

They stood in silence for a moment, and just as Raymond, now composed, joined their circle, Clarkson suddenly asked, "Are you ladies staying overnight?"

They all nodded. "Yes," Rosemary said. "I think we all are."

"Do you have accommodations?"

"Oh yes, thanks," Bippy said. "I don't know about the others, but I'm at the Hilton, and it's lovely. I'll be fine. By the way, Raymond, do you ever get to Birmingham?"

He smiled. "No, actually, I've never been. I have been to Mobile several times, though. Why do you ask?"

"Oh, no reason. Just know that you have a friend in Birmingham now if you're ever there in the future. I have loads of friends I'd like you to meet."

He smiled an electric smile that radiated warmth and self-assurance. "I certainly will. Thank you." He squeezed her hand.

"That goes for you, too, Clarkson," Bippy added, smiling sweetly.

"Why thank you. I don't get over that way often, but I'll surely remember that."

Goodbyes said, the ladies walked slowly to the parking lot, discovering along the way that they were all staying at the Hilton.

"Listen, girls," Tootsie said, "I've been thinking. As long as we're all staying overnight in Jackson, do you want to have dinner together?"

"What a great idea!" Rosemary said.

"Yes, maybe it will take our minds off...well, all this," Bippy said.

"What? Oh, dinner? I'd like that," Penelope said. "I feel just so...so—"

"I know exactly how you feel," Bippy said.

"I also know that we need to talk," Penelope said, "to get better acquainted. It's what Maggie would want."

Tootsie lowered her voice and said conspiratorially, "That's true, but it's about Maggie that we need to talk."

Chapter Twenty-Two

Tootsie was already seated at a table for four in the far back corner of the room when Penelope, Bippy, and Rosemary came into the Twilight Room at the Hilton. Motioning to them, she moved her purse off the chair next to her. "I thought I'd come on ahead and save us a table in an out of the way place," she said. "You know, so we can talk."

As she sat down, Penelope said, "I wouldn't have thought I could eat anything after all we've been through today, but as much as my heart is in my throat, I am still hungry." She sniffed the air. "I smell peanut butter."

Tootsie smiled and waved her hand dismissively. "Oh that. I just had a few peanut butter crackers before I left the room. You know, to take the edge off my appetite."

"Well, I wish something would take the edge off mine," Penelope said, and they all laughed softly. They were trying to keep their collective spirit up, and they found a certain comfort in being together, knowing that each of them missed Maggie in a unique way.

The waiter, a muscular man of medium height and penetrating dark brown eyes, hooded by dark, bushy eyebrows, presented the ladies with oversized menus. When he returned with his pad and pen a few minutes later, Penelope ordered grilled chicken with green beans and scalloped potatoes; Rosemary ordered a vegetable plate; Tootsie and Bippy opted for grilled brook trout with parsleyed whole new potatoes, asparagus with lemon-butter sauce, and tossed salads.

"Did you notice the shoulders on that man?" Tootsie asked, after the waiter had taken the orders, retrieved the menus, and left. "Ned, I believe his name tag said. He must lift weights in his spare time. Either that or the trays here are very, very heavy."

Rosemary nodded. "Yeah. I noticed the tattoo, also."

"A tattoo? Really? Where?" Bippy asked, her voice slightly scandalized, a faint smile hinting that she enjoyed being slightly scandalized.

"On his wrist just above his shirt cuff. It was only visible when his sleeve pulled back as he was handing me my menu."

Bippy nodded. "Well, shoot. I missed it. What was it?"

"A skull."

"Oh, my goodness. Rather unusual tattoo for a waiter to have, wouldn't you say?"

"It depends on the food," Tootsie quipped.

Rosemary nodded. "I hope that's not an omen of some kind, you know?"

Before long, Ned was back, and he was indeed carrying a very heavy tray, but he carried it as it were made of papier-mâché. This time, they all noticed the tattoo. Bippy peeked over the rims of her half-glasses and bit her upper lip.

"Will there be anything else, ladies?" Ned asked, scratching his mustache playfully with his pinky after serving the meal. "No? Well, then, bon appétit!" he said, bowing with a flourish and disappearing behind a nearby screen.

"Mmm. Looks good," Tootsie said, eyeing the food that had been put before them. She poured blue cheese dressing on her mixed green salad and tossed it with her fork. "To be honest, as good as the food was today at the church, I wouldn't have been able to tell you thirty minutes later what I had eaten."

"That's the way I feel every time I go to a church supper back home," Bippy said. "I know I have eaten because I'm full, but with so much confusion around me, I can't really concentrate on the food I'm eating."

Penelope thought for a minute, trying to figure out the words she had just heard and then nodded. "Yes, I think tranquility and quiet spell the difference between dining and just eating."

As they sat together savoring their meal, they continued talking in more depth about how each knew Maggie, about how Maggie had entered, and then changed, their lives. When Rosemary told them that Maggie and Cam had paid for her entire college education, they all nodded. Penelope said, "I'm not surprised. It sounds just like them. Even as a child, Maggie had a great heart, always tried to do for others." They grew very quiet.

Suddenly, Tootsie leaned forward and said, "She was murdered, you know!" Forks dropped, and there was a sudden intake of breath. All eyes were riveted on Tootsie.

"Murdered!" Bippy gasped.

"I'm sorry. What did you say?" Penelope asked.

"Maggie. She was murdered," Tootsie answered simply. "I know it's awful to contemplate, but there it is. We have to deal with it."

"How do you know that?" Rosemary asked.

"Yes, what makes you sure?" Bippy added.

"Common sense. What was your first reaction when you learned of Maggie's death?"

"What fraction?" Penelope answered, straining to hear. "I'm sorry, but I'm very hard of hearing." Then she relaxed as the words became clear to her from the context clues. "Oh, my reaction? Shock, of course. I couldn't believe she had died."

"Okay, but after that," Tootsie said, trying to speak more clearly and more slowly. "What was your reaction when you were told *how* she died?"

"Oh, you mean drowning?" Rosemary asked. "I was struck by the irony of it."

"The irony?" Tootsie said.

"Yes, you see, there's more to the story of how Maggie and I met than I told you before. When I was in high school, I jumped into a flooding river to save a kitten, and the incident was written up in the local newspaper. The Associated Press picked it up and carried the story nationwide. When Maggie saw it and got in touch with me—that's how she came into my life, by the way—she remarked at the time that everyone should know how to swim. 'Everyone should know how to save herself in the water,' she said at the time. That came back to me when I heard she had drowned. It just seemed too tragically ironic."

"She was always so fit," Bippy said. "That's why I was shocked. I couldn't believe that anyone as athletic as Maggie Palmer could drown."

Penelope nodded. "She was always a tomboy when she was younger. She could out run, out climb, and out swim any boy in the neighborhood. And she stayed that way over the years. I just couldn't believe that someone like that couldn't survive in the water. I can't conceive of the possibility that she drowned."

"She didn't. That's just what I'm talking about," Tootsie said. "We all had the same reaction. It just couldn't happen. When we were in college, Maggie was the best swimmer on the swim team. I used to envy her strong stroke. She could swim for miles without tiring. I know for a fact that she kept it up in recent years, too. She told me often how much she enjoyed swimming for exercise. No, something about this just doesn't feel right. Didn't from the beginning."

"It's just too tragic. She was getting married. But I guess all of you knew that," Rosemary said sadly. They all nodded.

"Yes, I assumed that she had shared her secret with all of us, her special friends," Tootsie said sadly. "It was so like her to want to share the greatest happiness in her life with those she held dear, even if—"

Suddenly, the waiter appeared at their table. "How about some dessert, ladies?" he said, proffering smaller dessert menus.

After scanning the list of pastries and confections and trying to talk themselves out of dessert on the one hand and justify the need for it on the other, Tootsie spoke up. "Think of it as comfort food. And tonight, my friends, we need comfort food," she said. Finally, the group ordered. The waiter disappeared again behind the screen, and in no time he was back. "Let's see. Here's the orange sherbet for you," he said, placing the dish in front of Rosemary. "And the pecan pie for you," he said as he put a plate bearing a thick slice of pie bursting with pecans and sporting a double scoop of ice cream before Penelope. He leaned over and placed a large slice of chocolate cake in front of Bippy. "And for you, ma'am, the specialty of the house: peanut butter pie," he said, setting before Tootsie a large slice of peanut butter cream pie with chocolate shavings and whipped cream. "Enjoy." Unobtrusively, he poured them all decaf coffee and left the table.

As they ate dessert and sipped their coffee, they gradually opened up, each offering compelling arguments as to why it was impossible for Maggie to have drowned.

"Let me ask you this," Tootsie said. "Did you notice anyone's absence today? Or last night at the funeral home?"

"Wait a minute," Penelope said. "Let me put this thing in." She took a hearing aid from her purse and inserted it. "My children say

163

I should wear both of them all the time, but they worry me to death, make me nervous, especially in a restaurant with all the background noise. I always take at least one out in a noisy place like a restaurant so I can hear the people at my own table. Sometimes, both of them. Still, maybe it will help me a little bit with the conversation. I don't want to miss a word of what you're saying. Okay. Would you repeat what you just said?" she asked Tootsie.

Tootsie smiled. "I asked if you all noticed anyone's absence at the funeral today or at the funeral home visitation last night?"

When no one spoke, Tootsie said, "Well, let me put it this way: Did any of you all happen to meet Gordon Dawkins?"

"No," Rosemary said, shaking her head. "As a matter of fact, I didn't. I kept checking the guest register, but I never saw his name."

"No," said Bippy.

"Neither did I," said Penelope. "I tried to get a good look at the register last night at the funeral home, but that woman was standing guard over it like Horatius at the bridge."

Tootsie laughed. "Oh yes, you must mean the woman we ran into again at the church luncheon today: Beulah—oh, what was her last name? Murray or Merrill or Merritt. Oh yes, Beulah Merritt. That's it. She gave me the once over, too. She was really curious about where I was from and how long I planned to stay."

Bippy and Rosemary nodded. "I thought I was going to have to play 'Twenty Questions' just to get into the room with the casket," Rosemary said. "She was especially interested in when I was going home."

"Me, too," Penelope said.

"So no one met the elusive Mr. Dawkins, huh?" Tootsie said thoughtfully. "That strikes me as very odd. Very odd indeed. I didn't ask Maggie's brothers—or anyone else, for that matter—about him

164

because nobody but the four of us knew about him. Remember, Maggie made quite a point of telling us that Gordon didn't want anyone to know. As far as he knows, nobody even knows he exists. I just tried looking for him on my own."

They sat for a long time after they had finished dessert, lingering over their coffee, chatting quietly. The waiter cleared the table of all but their coffee cups. He lingered in the background for a minute, but Tootsie dismissed him with a polite "Thank you. We'll take our checks now." Before he came back, she leaned in toward the center of the table, and the other three leaned in as well, Penelope cupping her hand to her ear to be sure not to miss whatever it was that Tootsie was about to say. "Well," Tootsie finally said, glancing over her shoulder, "we all know she was murdered. Now the question is: What are we going to do about it?"

Chapter Twenty-Three

"Well," Rosemary began, as the group retreated from the dining room to a little sitting area off the lobby and dropped onto a small sofa and chairs, "I have been an investigative reporter for some time—although it is usually insurance or welfare fraud, bureaucratic inefficiency, and political graft that I investigate, not murder—but my suggestion would be that we start by going to the police."

"Just what I thought, too," Tootsie said. "See what they have, where they're headed with this thing. If anywhere."

"They'll no doubt think we're crazy or interfering busybodies," Penelope said, "since they have probably already ruled accidental drowning."

"Probably," Tootsie countered, "but that's their problem, right? We have no obligation to them—only to Maggie to find out the truth."

"My flight is not until tomorrow evening at 5:47," Bippy said. "When is everyone else scheduled to leave? Could we go in the morning?"

"All right with me," Tootsie said. "I don't leave until tomorrow evening at 7:03."

"My flight isn't until 4:15," Rosemary said.

"Mine's at 3:20," Penelope said.

Tootsie nodded. "Okay. Let's meet for breakfast right here in the dining room at, say, 7:30. Okay with everyone? After we eat and discuss our plans, we'll go right to the police station. Let's see. We should be through here by 8:30, at the police station by 9:00 and back here by 10:30 or so. Eleven at the latest. How does that sound? That will give everyone time to check out, grab a bite of lunch, and get to the airport."

Everyone nodded agreement, and then silence fell once more as they realized the day was at an end. And what a day it had been! Brokenhearted, they had all mourned the loss of their best friend. "Well..." Penelope said, covering a yawn with one plump hand, "I don't know about you all, but this day has worn me out. I'll see you in the morning." She rose from her chair, and the others followed suit.

"Wait, Penelope...Pen," Tootsie said in a surge of emotion. "Don't go just yet...please. I want to say something. I was...ah, well, just thinking how...well, how glad I am we all ran into one another."

Bippy smiled broadly. "So am I," she said.

"I am, too," said Penelope. "Any friend of Maggie's is a friend of mine."

"I think that's how we all feel," Rosemary said.

"I think you're right, Rose," Tootsie said, smiling. "We all seemed to have a certain connection—camaraderie—right off the bat. I was just thinking about how we first recognized one another at the grave earlier today. You remember how we each came forward at about the same time and put a yellow rose on Maggie's coffin? There was so much mental telepathy or common psyche or whatever going on there that it was almost spooky."

They all nodded in assent. "You know, I think I knew who you were even before you called us all together after the committal," Penelope said. "I really do."

"And I feel as if I've known all of you all my life," Bippy said.

"Me, too," Rosemary added. "And it's all because of Maggie."

"You know, we feel this bond that has brought us together and yet we don't really know anything about one another. I mean, for starters, where is everybody from?" Tootsie asked. "We heard Bippy earlier mention Birmingham, so I assume that's where you're from, right, Bippy?"

Bippy nodded, and Tootsie continued, "I'm from Durham, North Carolina. What about you all?"

Pen said, "Near Charlottesville, Virginia."

Rosemary said, "Charleston, West Virginia."

Tootsie caught her breath. "What? No way. I'm from Bluefield. Graduated from Beaver High School, the famous 'Castle on the Hill.' " She placed her hand over her heart and laughingly sang the first few bars of "Beaver High School, Hail to Thee."

"I thought you said you were from Durham, North Carolina," Rosemary replied.

"Oh, I am. At least, that's where I live now and have since college, but I'm *from* West Virginia. I consider myself something of a mountaineer in exile."

Rosemary laughed. "Once a West Virginian, always a West Virginian."

The laughter died, and they stood together in silence then, a tight little knot of emotion choking each throat. No one could think of the right thing to say to sum it all up, to evaluate all that had happened to them in one day's time—-it seemed overwhelming to try—so no one said anything. In the distance, they could hear the mumbled greetings of the desk clerk as a weary traveler checked in. "Well," Tootsie finally said. "That's all I wanted to say—just that I'm glad to have three new friends. Good night. See you at 7:30 in the morning."

168

"For breakfast," Bippy added enthusiastically. Her face immediately flushed, and she said, "I didn't mean to sound quite so eager for breakfast after everything I've just eaten. See you at 7:30."

They all laughed then, these new friends, and their laughter was a source of solace. They hugged and patted and comforted until the silence descended again, and quietly, one by one, they left for their rooms. The group esprit could sustain them just so long. Eventually, they knew they would each take a private memory of Maggie to bed, and each would have to come to terms with the loss—the enormous loss—of her.

***

"You should have seen the look on the desk clerk's face when I asked him how to get to the police station," Tootsie said early the next morning as they walked to the car for the drive to the center of the city. "He blanched and then said, 'Is everything okay, Ma'am?' I assured him it was, but he was still looking at me funny when we left. I didn't know how we'd find it on the GPS without knowing the address of the closest station. Besides, it livened up his day."

The four piled gamely into the rental car and rode in silence for a while, fairly subdued as Rosemary drove through the morning rush hour traffic while Tootsie called out directions from the notes the desk clerk had given her. About twenty minutes into the ride, Tootsie looked again at her hastily scribbled directions. "Turn here. Right here!" she barked suddenly, and Rosemary swung the car around the corner and stopped directly in front of the police station. "Uh, maybe we'd better park somewhere else," Tootsie said. "I'd hate to get a ticket right in front of the station. It might be kinda brazen, even for me." She pointed to a NO PARKING sign.

After parking in back, the four trooped up the steps of the police station, stopped at the information desk, and went down the hall where they had been directed. Stopping in front of a door marked **Investigations--Lt. Curtis Ferguson**, Tootsie knocked. "Come in," the voice barked. As soon as the girls had all crowded into the tiny room, Ferguson, who had jumped to his feet as soon as he saw them, said, "Well, this is a surprise. I don't usually have company, especially from a group of lovely ladies, so early in the mornin'. Uh—welcome, ladies. I'm afraid we're a little cramped for space. Let me bring in a few more chairs." Inclining his head respectfully towards them, he backed out of the office and was soon back with two folding chairs, which he set up by the two chairs near his desk.

This was an unusual coalition, he thought, as he was unfolding the chairs. Damn! What in the world brings a group of biddies down here at this time of day? He dropped into his chair and leaned on the desk, propping his head on his open palms. Probably another flasher incident over at the park. Maybe here to register a complaint about a noisy neighbor. Looks like they brought the entire neighborhood. Or they could live near those new apartments that've been attracting all the young folks. That's it. Kegs. Another drunken party to deal with. Oh me. He pasted a smile on his face as he turned to them. "Now then, what can I do for you ladies this mornin'?"

"We're here about a murder," Tootsie stated simply, sitting erect and confident on the edge of her chair.

Detective Ferguson sat upright. "Murder? What murder? Whose?"

"Maggie Muldoon Palmer's," Tootsie answered.

Ferguson leaned back in his chair and sighed. "And you are?"

"Friends of the deceased," Tootsie shot back.

"Well, I'm afraid you ladies have been misinformed. I'm familiar with that case. I have the preliminary coroner's report." He flipped through some folders on his desk and pulled out a sheet of paper. "Right here. Suspected cause of death: accidental drowning. Mrs. Palmer wasn't murdered. She—"

"Excuse me. We were not misinformed," Rosemary interrupted. "We were told she drowned, but we all have problems with that."

"Exactly what problems?"

Bippy spoke up. "The problem isn't that she drowned. It's how she drowned that we're worried about. It's the word 'accidental' that concerns us. For one thing, we all know her to have been an excellent swimmer."

"Excellent swimmers do drown occasionally," the detective countered.

Tootsie had said this same thing to Emma Beth, but now, when she heard someone else say it, she found herself rebelling against it. Not Maggie.

"But in such cases, the excellent swimmers are often intoxicated. Isn't that right?" Penelope asked. When Ferguson hesitantly nodded, she continued. "Well, that's not the case with Maggie. She was a tee-totaler—didn't drink at all—said it would dull her senses, and she didn't want to miss any of the exhilaration of life."

Ferguson shook his head and sighed. "Now, ladies, let me assure you that, like a lot of other people around here, I liked everything I knew about Mrs. Palmer. There's scarcely a humanitarian or altruistic cause in this whole county that doesn't have her fingerprints all over it. Because of that, I have taken a special interest in this case, a—"

"May we please see the autopsy report?" Rosemary interrupted. "Just to put our fears to rest?"

Ferguson squirmed just the tiniest bit, Rosemary noticed, or was she imagining that? "Uh, it isn't back yet. All I have is our local coroner's report from the preliminary report he made based on finding the body."

"Not back?" Tootsie said. "But her body was found almost a week ago."

"That's true, but when the coroner's office has an unattended death, a case that seems not to be from natural causes, or a case that might involve litigation, they generally send the body to the state M. E.'s office. That's what happened in this case. It takes a little longer that way. Months sometimes. Unfortunately, there are too many to process quickly. "

"But we've already had the funeral."

"That's not at all unusual. Once they do the autopsy and take tissue samples—and they did that fairly quickly in this case—they release the body to the family even though the lab work may take some time to complete. They hold up releasing the autopsy report until it's complete—tox reports and all. That's what we're waitin' for now—test results."

"And when do you expect the lab report to be back?" Penelope asked.

"Probably a day or two at the most."

"I'll wait," Tootsie announced firmly, fastening her startling brown eyes, the color of molasses, on the lieutenant. "I can stay in Jackson another day or two."

With folded arms and glaring eyes, Bippy, Rosemary, and Pen sat straighter in their seats. The message was clear: So can we.

Ferguson drummed his fingers on his desk and nodded his head in resignation. "Okay. Of course, if you prefer, y'all could return to your homes and call back later to see what the results of the autopsy were, or if you'll leave your addresses, we'll get permission from the victim's next of kin and then be happy to send them to you." He leaned back in his chair to gauge their reaction to his suggestion.

Glancing around at the others, Tootsie smiled politely and said, "Thanks, but I think we'd rather stay. We'll be back in touch, Lt. Ferguson. By the way, have you come across a man by the name of Gordon Dawkins in your investigation of Maggie's—uh, 'accident'?" She gave the word an acerbic twist.

"Gordon Dawkins? No, why? Who's he?"

"The man Maggie was going to marry."

"Marry!" He let his chair down with a bang. How could he have missed that one?

Tootsie nodded. "Mm-hmm. Six-three, muscular build, brown hair with graying at the temples, blue eyes, and, according to Maggie, drop-dead handsome. We've been talking, the four of us, and it seems strange to us that we haven't seen hide nor hair of him since Maggie's death. We think it's odd that her fiancé wasn't even at her funeral. Don't you think so, Lieutenant?"

Ferguson's face was a mask, showing no emotion. The tension of the unanswered question hung in the room like a heavy fog.

"Well, we'll go now and make arrangements to stay," Tootsie said. As they rose to leave, she added, "Meanwhile, if you receive any information before we contact you again, we're all staying at the Hilton. I'd appreciate your calling us there."

"I'll need your names, of course," Ferguson said, "and your cell numbers or room numbers at the hotel." He scribbled down the number Tootsie gave him and then wrote as they called off their names, each adding an annotation, telling briefly how she knew Maggie Palmer.

When they left, Ferguson sat for a moment scratching his head and looking at the pad in front of him. How did they know she was going to be married? And, more importantly, how did he *not* know it? That little bit of information was news to him. Neither of her brothers had mentioned it to him. He had interviewed them at length when they first arrived in Jackson. He had specifically asked them for the names of her close friends and business associates in town.

What in the world had convinced these ladies that Margaret Palmer's death was a homicide? *Is it possible?* he wondered. *Was Mrs. Palmer murdered, or are these women, who claim to know her better than anyone, just a bunch of panicky old busybodies?* He realized that he felt better thinking of them in that light, even though only two of them were what you might call old, but for some reason, he couldn't dispel the notion—the fear—that they were onto something, and that the chilling feeling which had enveloped him at the lake the day the body was found was not just an idle hunch.

Chapter Twenty-Four

"Well, so much for getting information from the police. Now what?" Rosemary said, as they trooped down the steps of the police station.

"I suppose it's too early for lunch," Bippy said a little sadly, looking at her watch.

"You have a hunch?" Penelope asked.

"No, I said 'lunch.' "

"Oh, Bippy! I can still touch my breakfast," Penelope said. "How do you stay so little? If I thought about food as much as you do, I'd weigh...well, a lot more than I do." She smiled.

"No, I mean now what do we do about Maggie's death?" said Rosemary.

Tootsie stopped and looked at the others. "Well, I don't know about you all, but I plan to stay until I am satisfied that everything has been explained, and I am comfortable with the explanation. There's no reason I can't. For a few days, anyway. Longer if necessary. I'm going to call my daughter, Emma Beth, and tell her to feed Ladybug—that's my cat—until I get home, whenever that is. First thing, though, is to change my flight."

Rosemary was quiet. Finally, she said, "Well, I'd like to stay. I really would, but I have a job at the newspaper, you know. I just don't see how I can. With two kids in grad school, I can't afford to jeopardize my job. Even with scholarships, there are more expenses than I could handle."

"I understand. That is a problem, all right," Tootsie said. "The rest of us are gainfully unemployed. I guess you just can't." She thought for a moment and then said, "Wait a minute! I have an idea. What about writing this up for the paper from here?"

"This? You mean write about the investigation of Maggie's death?"

"Sure."

Rosemary bit her upper lip and stared off into space as she mulled over the idea. "It might work." Slowly, she began nodding her head. "It's worth a try. I'll call the editor and see what he thinks about my sending columns in from here as things progress. If our hunch is correct, if something is amiss, the thrust of the columns would be an investigative report. That's right up my alley. If not, they would be from a human interest standpoint—you know, what Maggie did for me, how beloved she was by so many people, and so on. Because of my connection to her, it would be of special interest to the people in the Charleston area."

"Great idea, Rose," said Bippy. "Well, I guess I can stay. The only responsibility I have is my cat, Socrates. I have a friend who's feeding him for me. I have his cell phone number. I'll just call and see if he can continue it a while longer. I'm sure Sam—I call him CT, my Computer Tutor—won't mind."

"My children bought me a Smartphone and insisted I needed it to be able to text and email them at all times," Penelope said. "Since I can't hear well enough to use it as a phone, I call it my I-Phony. Anyway, I'll text my children just so they won't worry if they should call on the land line and not find me home. I have no reason to hurry back. No one will miss me." There was a note of sadness in her voice.

"Oh, texting is a great idea! Would you let me use your phone and show me how? Sam will be so proud of me if I do that," Bippy said. "Shocked is more like it."

"Of course," Pen replied, smiling. "The irony of my introducing anyone to modern technology will not be lost on my children. And don't think I'm not going to tell them."

"All right!" Tootsie said. "Well, let's go back to the hotel and arrange to keep our rooms, make our calls, and get our plane reservations changed. I also think we should put a call in for Chilton Surles, Maggie's lawyer. I managed to see his name on the guest register after the funeral, but I never met him. I think it would be good just to touch base with him, know what he really thinks about her death."

"Great idea, Tootsie," Rosemary said. "Want me to call him?"

"That'd be great. And then, I don't know about anyone else, but I didn't bring extra clothes, and I don't want to go about in this black outfit the entire time I'm here. It's so—well, funereal."

"But that's a lovely scarf you have on, dear. So colorful," Penelope said.

Tootsie flipped the bright purple and red scarf back from the neck of her black dress revealing a multi-colored choker underneath. "Thanks. Too much unrelieved black is bad for the psyche," she said. "Anyway, I'm going shopping. Anybody else want to go?" The only other dress she had brought was her turquoise and white silk. She hadn't even brought her omni-present turquoise-studded boots. This was just to be a one-day trip, and the necessity of packing light for the plane had made her uncharacteristically conservative.

An hour later, the women, reservations changed and families and friends notified, piled once again into the Accord and headed to the nearest shopping mall.

"Did you have any trouble with your editor, Rose?" Penelope asked.

Rosemary grinned. "None at all. I told him that I might be onto an interesting piece of investigation that would be of great interest to our local readers from the human-interest angle, since I would be writing about the death of the woman who made it possible for me, a kid from Gauley Bridge, to go to college. He bought it and told me to stay as long as I need to."

"Wonderful! Did you get Mr. Surles?"

"He was in court. I left a message left with his secretary."

"Well, good."

"Oh, look," cried Tootsie, as they passed a strip of shops. "There's a T. J. Maxx. That's one of my favorite stores. It's such an adventure—like a treasure hunt. You never know what you're going to find. Let's go in there, shall we?"

Once inside the store, the girls split up, each pursuing a different size and each, in time, disappearing down the long curtained corridor of try-on rooms. Tootsie reappeared first, in a shockingly yellow dress. Green and orange swirls were splashed about, and interspersed throughout were white and red flowers encircling what looked like a decidedly hung-over eyeball. It was everything Tootsie loved: colorful, dramatic, outrageous. She was looking at herself in the three-way mirror when the others, one by one, emerged in the same dress.

As soon as they caught sight of themselves, all dressed identically in the same ridiculous dress, they burst into laughter, the first genuine laughter they had felt since learning about Maggie. "Oh, dear Gussie," Bippy said. "I wish you would look at us!"

178

"I can't believe it," Rose said. "I just tried it on for a kick because the price was so unbelievable. That must be why they have it in so many different sizes. Someone somewhere in design made a bad judgment call."

Penelope's mouth opened in shock as she looked at herself in the mirror. "I've never had on anything so...so loud in my life," she said in awe. "I don't know what in the world possessed me to try it on. The price and a perverted sense of adventure, I suppose. It does have a nice collar, though. I have a pin that would look nice on it. And the mark-down price is absolutely wonderful."

She was just turning to go back to the dressing room when Tootsie patted her on the back and said, "Way to go, kid." *Kid!* Penelope thought, and all of a sudden, she felt like a kid. Felt like a girl again, not a staid, proper matron; a mother and grandmother; a teacher; a doctor's wife; a widow. Impulsively, she clapped her hands together and said, "You know what? I'm going to buy this silly dress."

By this time, the four of them were laughing so hard they were beginning to attract attention. "Shh," Penelope tried to say through her giggles. "People are looking."

"As if this quadruple fashion mis-statement itself hasn't already drawn more than a few curious stares," Rose said, tears running down her face. "I don't think it's our laughter they're looking at. It's the dress! We look like tacky taken to the fourth power."

"You know," Tootsie said, "I was thinking that since we're newfound friends committed to the common cause of finding out what happened to Maggie and in view of our amazing synchronicity—and, well, this just proves it," she laughed, as she gestured dramatically towards their clothing—"that maybe we ought to have a name. I've been wondering what we could call ourselves—you know to refer to our little group—and I came up with the Flower Girls for the way we spontaneously all put flowers on Maggie's casket. What do you think about that?"

"Flower Girls! I think Maggie would have loved it," Bippy said. "It sounds more like a wedding than a funeral."

"I know she would," Penelope said, "and I feel her presence right here in the midst of us."

"Yes," Rosemary said, "I like it. 'Flower Girls' has a nice ring to it."

"Okay, Flower Girls it is."

"I have an idea," Bippy said, giggling. "Let's all buy this dress. It will remind us of this day, of this moment of temporary insanity, and of the beginning of our new friendship. It'll be the official Flower Girls dress."

And in that frantic moment of hilarity, they all agreed that it was a memory in the making. "Too good to pass up," as Tootsie put it, wiping her eyes.

They piled their dresses in their respective buggies and split up once more to secure the other things they needed. In addition to the dress, Tootsie bought lingerie, jeans, a denim shirt, new boots—why in heaven's name had she left her boots at home, even for a short trip? That's okay. A girl couldn't have too many turquoise-studded boots—a couple of skirts and blouses in brilliant shades of aqua and green, a belt she couldn't live without, and two brightly colored cardigan sweaters and went happily to the check-out. Penelope soon joined her with a dark paisley skirt and shirt and a little black sweater and a few other items of clothing. "I'd love to dress a little more youthfully," she confided to Tootsie, "but I don't have the nerve. Maybe in time. Lord knows, this dress is a good start."

Tootsie looked her right in the eye and said, "Pen, my friend, dress the way your heart tells you to dress. You're all right just as you are."

In that instant, Pen felt such warmth and love for this woman—a woman whom she barely knew—that she couldn't speak. Here was a person of obvious glamour and sophistication, a person totally unlike her, who wasn't trying to change Pen's hair or her weight or her dress. She was doing the hardest job of all: She was simply accepting her as she was. Shaking her head in disbelief, she grabbed Tootsie's hand and squeezed it. Soon, Bippy and Rose appeared, each with pajamas, two pairs of slacks and several tops, and, after cramming all the packages into the trunk of the car, they were on their way.

"Did everyone remember to buy underwear?" Tootsie asked from the front seat.

"Yes, dear," Pen answered. "I think we all did."

"Me, too," Tootsie said with a laugh, "although I've always considered it a colossal waste of money."

The girls, whose hilarity threshold was by now quite low, erupted again into boisterous laughter. "Oh, Tootsie," Bippy said, "you are too much!"

"I haven't laughed this much in years," Pen said.

"Let's all try on our new dresses as soon as we get back to the hotel," Bippy suggested. "Maybe they'll look less conspicuous with our own accessories."

"Good idea," said Tootsie.

Rosemary drove along with the traffic and soon pulled into the Hilton lot.

Tootsie smiled. "Home sweet home. Want to meet in the lobby in our new outfits in, say, fifteen minutes?"

"And then have lunch?" Bippy asked.

When Rosemary finished putting on her dress and stood looking in the mirror, trying to tone it down with a black belt and shoes, she noticed in the background the blinking light on the phone, indicating a message. Quickly, she picked up the phone and listened to the message:

> *This is Debra Smith. I am calling for Chilton*
> *Surles of Landers, Watson, Coughlin, and Weller*
> *law firm. He's sorry to have missed your call, but*
> *he was in court. Mr. Surles would like to speak*
> *with you at your earliest convenience. Would you*
> *give us a call back at 601-555-1016? Thank you.*

When Rosemary called the number, the secretary answered and in seconds, Chilton Surles came on the phone. "Oh, Ms. Harrison. Thanks for returning my call. I'm sorry I wasn't available when you called earlier, but I guess my secretary explained that I was in court."

"Yes."

"I was surprised that you were still in town."

"Something came up."

"Could you possibly come by my office today?"

"Come to your office? Today?"

"Yes. As you know, I am the attorney for the estate of Margaret Katherine Muldoon Palmer. While Maggie's brothers are in town, we've decided to go ahead with a reading of the will. It will save them from having to return to Jackson immediately, and they can decide what to do with Maggie's property at a later date. They just called and asked me to do this a few minutes ago, and I was afraid you would have already left. If I had missed you, we would all have had to get together later on."

"That's fine. I'm not leaving today, after all, but I don't understand why I should be there for a reading of the will."

"Because, Ms. Harrison, you are in it."

Rosemary couldn't think of anything to say. Finally, she stammered, "Me? But this is preposterous. Why should I be in it? Are you sure?"

"Quite sure. Can you be here by four o'clock?"

"Yes, yes, I'll...I'll be there, but....Well, thank you."

After receiving directions to the law firm and without changing her dress, Rosemary walked slowly to the lobby. This must be a dream, she thought. Maggie had already given her a new life—a college education, a job, self-respect. She had even suspected Maggie's hand behind the wonderful scholarship Dorothy had received for vet school at N. C. State. What more? The hunger pangs that had been nudging her that it was time to eat had suddenly disappeared. She felt too much emotion to think about eating. She would just excuse herself from lunch.

When she reached the small sitting area off the main lobby, there sat three copies of herself in flaming yellow dresses, lined up on a long sofa like goldfinches on a fence. They were not, she noticed, jabbering as usual. Bippy was not perusing a menu. In fact, their faces wore masks of disbelief and shock. "What is it?" she asked. "Is anything wrong?"

Tootsie spoke first. "The lawyer, Mr. Surles. He called and wants to see me. He said that Maggie...uh, well, Maggie left me something in her...will." She swallowed and looked at the floor.

Bippy wiped at her eyes. "He told me the same thing."

"Me, too," sad Pen, biting her lip.

"And me," added Rosemary.

***

At five past eleven, the phone on Curtis Ferguson's desk jangled while he was pecking a report into his computer, muttering at his mistakes. He grabbed up the receiver impatiently. "Yeah? Ferguson here."

"Curt, Doc Watson. I've got the completed autopsy on that body in the lake we found a week ago. The Palmer lady? Just got the fax from the state medical examiner's office. You want to hear it?"

Ferguson looked at the report in his computer. "Uh, listen, just fax it to me, and I'll read it soon's I get through this report on the ring of house break-ins over on the south side. This is due on the chief's desk by 5:00." He picked up a mug of coffee and, leaning back in his chair, began sipping the hot, black brew, burning his tongue as he did so. He cursed silently.

There was a hesitation at the other end of the line. "Well...okay. But, uh...there was a bit of a surprise in the autopsy, though."

"Oh yeah? What?"

"The victim didn't drown as I first thought."

Ferguson slammed his chair to the floor, sloshing the hot coffee onto his hand. "What! Didn't drown? What do you mean?" He transferred his cup to the other hand and shook his scalded hand to rid it of the burning liquid.

Watson said, "Just what I said. She didn't drown. There was no water in the lungs."

"Then how—"

"Broken neck and severe blow to the head, either of which could have been fatal, and both of which occurred before she entered the water."

Ferguson stopped drinking and plunked down his coffee mug, sloshing some out on the papers spread out before him on his desk. "Damn! You're tellin' me it's a homicide?"

"Not necessarily. The M. E. doesn't go there. The lack of any forensic evidence would make that hard to prove, at any rate. My guess is that she fell while attempting to hoist the sails, struck her head pretty hard, and broke her neck. Or maybe after she was unconscious or dead from the blow to the head, her neck got caught in the loose rigging. That could account for the broken neck. Later, she was rolled off into the water by the tossing and turning of the boat. It wasn't anchored, you know. There was no sign of abuse in any way. Other than the broken neck and head injury, I mean. No evidence of sexual molestation. Her clothing was intact, except what had caught on the submerged limb. Nothing under her fingernails. "Of course, being in the water would probably have removed every trace of that, but... No defensive bruises or cuts. It's inconclusive, but it's been ruled accidental death for now, and that will stick unless something startling turns up down the road."

"Yeah, yeah, okay, Doc." He sighed and leaned back in his chair. "This is goin' to be very interesting to a group of biddies—er, ladies that came to see me this mornin'. Really going to set them off. They're convinced it's murder. Well, fax the final report to me A.S.A.P. And thanks."

Ferguson hung up and sat staring at the phone for a minute. Then, leafing through the pile of folders stacked in disarray on his desk, he pulled out one. Ever since he had found out the identification of the body, opening the pages of that report had taken on an almost reverential air. He'd had what he guessed might be described as a secret crush—or maybe it was just raging curiosity—on Maggie Palmer for a couple of years now. Not that he really knew her. He had just seen her picture in the paper and read about her. Who hadn't? He'd just—what was it they called it?—worshipped from afar? Yeah, that was it. He'd worshiped her from afar. He and about a thousand other men. She was beautiful and extremely well-liked. Hell, if everything he read was true, everyone who knew her loved her. That's just the way she was—gorgeous, bright, vivacious, generous, captivating. The closest thing Jackson had to a celebrity.

Flipping through the papers, he came to the pictures at the end. He studied them a minute. He never would have recognized this as the Maggie Palmer he had seen in the newspapers. In one photo, the pale body, eyes now closed by the coroner, seemed to be asleep. In another, a close-up of the face, Ferguson thought for a fleeting moment that it looked as if she were crying. I wonder what you're crying about, Maggie Palmer, he thought. And as he put the folder back to await the medical examiner's report, he felt a curious mixture of sadness and foreboding sweep over him, and for the first time in a long, long while, he, too, felt like crying.

Chapter Twenty-Five

"Come in," Ferguson said as Clarkson and Raymond Muldoon appeared at his door. He rose to greet them and expressed once again his sympathy in the loss of their sister, all the while shaking their hands warmly. He had interviewed them days ago and had seen them at the service the day before, but he had needed to get back to the office afterwards and hadn't lingered to speak to them.

"You said you'd gotten the final report about Maggie's death?" Clarkson asked as he stepped into the room. He and his brother glanced at each other.

It was obvious to Ferguson that these brothers of the deceased were ill at ease in a police station. It was probably their first visit to such a place. Or maybe they were just distressed about their sister. His experienced eye took in everything about the two brothers' apparel. Clarkson, his black hair smoothed impeccably to his head, was dressed in a dark-blue, lightweight wool pin stripe suit with a pale-blue button-down shirt, red tie—Brooks Brothers, probably—and Cole-Hahn wingtips. Expensive. Ferguson noticed the elegant monogrammed gold cufflinks as Clarkson extended his hand. The other brother, Raymond, the shorter, more muscular one, was much more casually dressed. He was wearing khaki trousers and a red and green plaid shirt with a red pullover sweater. Ferguson had seen the type before. Jaunty. Sporty. The perpetual jock. Looked as if he had fallen right out of a Land's End catalogue. His reddish-blond hair was windblown and in mild disarray, and his eyes were full, worried, and outlined in red.

"Yes, I called you as soon as the report came in. Here, have a seat." He scooted two chairs closer to his desk and returned to his chair on the other side.

Raymond cleared his throat. "After you called us, Lieutenant, we got to talking, and—uh, we were just wondering—well, what the report could have to say that we don't already know? I mean, Maggie's dead, and—" He paused and took a deep breath. "Well, what I mean is, um, Maggie drowned and uh—" He looked away, and Ferguson saw him swallowing, attempting to choke back his emotion.

Clarkson broke in. "What my brother means, Lieutenant, is that we probably don't want to know all the graphic details. It's just too much. What matters is that Maggie is gone. Nothing we know can make that any easier."

Ferguson nodded. "I understand. I am not gonna read you the details of the condition of the—uh, the body. I just want you to hear what the M. E. lists as the cause of death."

"Cause of death? I thought that had been established. Maggie drowned," Clarkson said. "She was found in the lake, after all."

"True," Ferguson answered, "but things are not always as they seem. In fact, your sister died from a blow to the head or a broken neck. The M. E. is not sure which one killed her. Either could have."

"But—"

"There was no water in the lungs. Drownin', therefore, has been ruled out as the cause of death."

"What are you saying, Lieutenant?" Raymond asked, rubbing his brow as if trying to iron the worry from his face.

Clarkson's face went chalky. "Wait a minute. Are you saying Maggie was murdered?"

Ferguson looked sharply at Clarkson. Strange he would jump to that conclusion. What could that mean? He shook his head. Hell's bells! Those crazy ladies were getting to him. "No, no, not at all! The evidence points to accidental death, just not drownin'. The M. E. said there is no indication of foul play at all—no cuts or bruises on her arms or torso, no torn clothing, no sexual attack, no residue under her fingernails that would indicate a struggle. The M. E. thinks she might have gotten her neck caught in the riggin'."

Both brothers sighed deeply. Was it Ferguson's imagination, or did they seem relieved? Maybe just glad they don't have to go through the ordeal of a trial down the road, he decided. That was probably it. "It looks as if she got tangled in the riggin' of the boat and either fell and hit her head or was strangled by the ropes and then buffeted about, sustaining the head injury. Later, her body rolled off into the water—perhaps was held under by the boat itself, which was driftin' freely—hit the tree below the surface and was snagged."

"I see," Clarkson replied.

"Let me ask you all something. When we talked earlier, right after your sister's death, I asked you for the names of her business associates and local close friends. You didn't mention any romantic relationships at that time. Were there any?" He didn't want to come right out with what the ladies had told him. He wanted to see how much information he could elicit from the brothers first.

Ray shook his head. "No, none that I know of. How about you, Clark?"

"No. Not that I was aware of. There was no one since she lost Cam."

189

"She and Cam were extremely close. I think that part of her life shut down after he died," Ray added.

"So, no boyfriend or fiancé or anythin'?"

Both brothers shook their heads.

Why would they lie? Ferguson debated asking if they knew a Gordon Dawkins, but something held him back. The women could have gotten that wrong. Wouldn't surprise him a bit. Amateur detectives! He'd do some checking on his own before confronting the brothers with a name. No point in causing them distress or opening a kettle of fish if it turned out to be nothing. He knew how to get in touch with them in case he needed more information. No, best to let sleeping dogs lie right now.

Everyone was quiet then for a few minutes. Finally, Clarkson said, rising, "Well, I guess that's all, then. Thank you, Lieutenant. You've been very helpful." He shook hands with Ferguson and walked quickly out of the office. Raymond tarried a minute, looked at Ferguson with great anguish in his eyes and said, "I...uh, I just can't believe this has happened, you know. That Sis is really gone?"

Ferguson nodded. "Yeah, I do know. It's hard to accept when someone we love dies, especially prematurely and especially under these circumstances." He hesitated, cleared his throat, and then added, "Your sister was a much-beloved person in this city. But I guess you already know that."

Taking his hand and shaking it slowly, Raymond said, "Yes, thank you. She was...much-beloved...by everyone." He gave Ferguson a searching look, opened his mouth to say something, but then turned abruptly, and followed his brother.

After the Muldoon brothers had left, Ferguson sat thinking for a minute. He was at constant war with himself, always trying to tone down his suspicions, to shade the bright, critical eye of the investigator that he'd inherited from his policeman father with the subtle rose-colored lens of compassion that his gentle mother, a mother who had caught ants in the house and put them outside so they wouldn't get stepped on, had instilled in him. It wasn't easy. Why, for instance, didn't they tell him about her boyfriend, if indeed there was one? And why would a brother jump to the conclusion that his sister had been murdered? Why wouldn't he assume she'd had an accident? Yet Clarkson had done that very thing. Why? And why did Raymond look at him so pitifully just now? Genuine grief or an urge to tell him something? Ferguson shrugged and then shook his head. Well, the medical examiner had ruled: It was accidental. It was not for him to second guess the official medical ruling. There was nothing to do now but inform the friends of the deceased. He picked up the phone, dialed the number written down at the top of the page that the ladies had left, and waited.

When he was connected with Tootsie Freeman's room, he said, "Ms. Freeman? This is Curtis Ferguson with the Jackson Police Department. You were in my office this mornin'? I have the report we spoke of in my hand. It came back sooner than I expected."

Tootsie, who, like the other girls, had gone back to her room to compose herself a few minutes before lunch, was holding the phone to her ear with her shoulder while she screwed the lid on a jar of peanut butter, her appeasement of the delayed lunch. Suddenly, she tossed the jar on the bed, grabbed the phone with her hand and said, "Call me Tootsie, and we'll be right there, Lieutenant. And thank you for calling."

Before Ferguson could even tell her on the phone that there was really no reason to come to the station, that the death had been ruled accidental, Tootsie had rung off and was busily buzzing the other Flower Girls' rooms. "Don't even change clothes. We'll do a late lunch

191

afterwards," she said. "The important thing is to get down there as soon as possible." In ten minutes, they were on their way downtown.

As they marched through the police station in their screaming yellow dresses, looking like a singing group from the local retirement home, they gathered open-mouthed stares along the way. Pen insisted on holding her dress up slightly with her right hand as if she were getting ready to make a curtsey, and Bippy was swirling hers about like a four-year-old in a new Sunday frock. The police dispatcher leaned over the desk to look at them as they went by.

"Not used to haute couture in the J.P.D." Tootsie said to the others. "Too much navy blue. Warps the fashion sense."

The girls giggled and followed Tootsie down the hall.

"Well," Tootsie blurted just as soon as the four of them had trooped into Ferguson's office, "what's the news? What does the report say?"

"Please. Sit down." Ferguson gestured toward four chairs. He tried not to let his startled reaction to the dresses be noticeable, but suddenly he realized that his mouth was open. When everyone had been seated, he took a deep breath. "Now, I don't want you to jump to conclusions when I tell you what the report says." Tootsie didn't respond, so Ferguson began leafing through the papers on his desk and finally picked up a stapled report. "Okay, first: your friend, Mrs. Palmer, did not drown. There was no water in the lungs."

"I knew it! I knew it!" the ladies murmured. Rosemary pulled a small pad from her purse and began writing.

"She was murdered, wasn't she, just as we thought?" Tootsie said.

"No, ma'am, on the contrary. There is absolutely no evidence at all to suggest foul play. No bruises or cuts, no sexual molestation, no ripped clothin', nothin' under the fingernails, no defensive wounds to suggest she fought off an attacker."

192

"Well then," Rosemary began, "what does the medical examiner think caused—"

"Her death," Ferguson interrupted, "could have been caused by one of two equally lethal acci-*dents*: a broken neck or a severe blow to the head." He pronounced the word "accidents" with a decided emphasis on the last syllable. "The medical examiner found it impossible to establish which occurred first. As I said, either could have been the cause of death." He looked up from the papers, which he held in his hand. "It appears that she struck her head on the mainsail and then caught her neck in the riggin' or vice versa. After a while, with the tossin' of the boat, she rolled overboard."

"Impossible!" Tootsie said.

"It happens sometimes in sailin'," Ferguson countered. "When we found the boat, the sail was still flappin' freely. We had a lot of wind the week she died. Sailin' would have been rough. Real rough."

"My point exactly!" Tootsie responded. "She wouldn't have done it."

Bippy and Penelope had sat quietly, stunned by the revelation. Now Bippy said in her sweetest voice, "Excuse me, Lieutenant, but was Maggie wearing a life preserver?"

"No," Ferguson said, "she wasn't."

"That's odd," Bippy said. "She was a stickler for taking precaution. She said to me one time that if the airlines would let her fly wearing a parachute, she might consider flying. She said, half jokingly, that it only made sense. I remember that she said, 'I'd never go out on my boat without a life preserver, after all, so why should I fly without a parachute?' No, it just doesn't sound like her."

"Lieutenant, have you told her brothers this?" Tootsie asked.

"Why, yes, I did. They came in earlier, and I went over the report with them."

Tootsie nodded slowly. "What was their reaction?"

"What do you mean?"

"I don't know exactly. Were they surprised or skeptical, maybe?"

"Why do you ask?"

"Just curious."

"Well, in answer to your question, they didn't seem to feel it made much difference. As Clarkson said, 'All that matters is that Maggie is gone.'"

"I see," Tootsie said. She sat chewing her lip for a moment and then said, "All right, Lieutenant Ferguson, you've been very helpful to call us and put our minds at ease about the way Maggie died. Thank you." She rose from her chair.

"Will you ladies be goin' back home now?" Ferguson asked, rising with her and trying to keep the hopeful tone out of his voice.

"Not right away. We have to meet with the lawyer late this afternoon," Penelope said. "He wants to read the will while Maggie's brothers are still here...while we're all still here."

Ferguson nodded, hitched up his pants, and hooked two thumbs into his belt. He wasn't about to bring up this Gordon Dawkins character again now that it seemed the ladies might be slacking off. He'd investigate that on his own without their input. "Well, it's been a real pleasure meetin' you ladies. I know you'll be in a hurry to get away after that, and I probably won't see you again. Y'all hurry back to Jackson, you hear? I hope your next trip to our fair city will be more pleasant."

Outside, on the steps, the girls again stopped to reconnoiter.

"Was it my imagination, or was he hurrying us out of town?" Rosemary asked.

"It may *be* imagination, but I got the same feeling," Penelope said.

"Yeah. It was like 'Here's your hat. Here's your coat. There's the door. What's your hurry?' " Tootsie added. "Wonder why?"

"Could be that he just sees us as a nuisance," Rosemary said. "Wants us out of his hair. We ask too many questions. Take up too much of his time."

"Yes, I think he sees us as gadflies," Penelope said.

Tootsie nodded. "I suppose so. Still, there are many questions that I can't help asking."

"What do you say we go have a bite of lunch and talk this over before we go see the lawyer this afternoon?" Bippy suggested.

"What bunch?" Pen asked.

"Lunch," Bippy repeated.

"Oh, lunch. I was about to suggest the same thing," Pen said.

Once they had piled into the car, Bippy said, "Dear Gussie! Maggie out alone in her sailboat in rough winds with no life preserver. It just doesn't make sense."

"It doesn't to me either," said Tootsie. "It doesn't to me either."

Chapter Twenty-Six

"Well, what's your impression of Lieutenant Ferguson?" Tootsie asked.

"Other than his accent, you mean?" Rosemary said, laughing. "I mean, it goes beyond Southern, doesn't it? Way beyond."

Tootsie nodded. "Been drinking out of too many Dixie cups."

"Oh, I don't know," Penelope began. "He seems nice enough, I guess."

"A little hard-boiled, if you ask me," said Bippy. "I'm famished. Where are we going to eat, by the way?" Suddenly, she spotted a quaint little sidewalk cafe. "Oh look at that precious little restaurant," she said, reading the sign. "Stratford Upon Avon Tea Room and Sidewalk Cafe."

"Sounds like an Englishman does Paris to me," said Rosemary.

Bippy smiled. "What a blending of cultures! How darling! I love it."

Tootsie laughed. "Bippy, I do believe you're the only person I've ever known who could call a restaurant 'precious' and 'darling' and mean it."

Bippy smiled at the good-natured teasing. "But, listen, it does look like a good place to eat, doesn't it? I mean, with the little umbrellas over the tables and everything."

"Is it going to rain?" Pen asked. They all looked at her.

"Who said anything about rain?" Bippy laughed.

"You said something about umbrellas."

"Oh! I was saying that this restaurant with the umbrellas over the tables looks like a good place to eat."

"It does indeed," said Pen. "Want to stop here for a sandwich?"

"Why not?" said Rose, wheeling into the small parking lot beside the white stucco building.

Tootsie got out of the car and surveyed the scene before her. "Well, I wouldn't have described it as precious, but I have to admit it does have a certain *élan*. Oh my gosh, I've succumbed to the French suggestion already. *Panache*, then. No, wait. This is getting no better. Save me, Shakespeare! Let's think tea pots with delicate roses painted on them and cups thin enough to see through."

In the small plot of grass in front of the building, tables with colorful umbrellas bloomed like an array of errant wildflowers. Stepping stones connected one table to the next, and white-aproned waiters were bustling about on the winding paths as if playing a childhood game of hop-scotch. There was a comforting old-world charm about it, a charm that evoked tea in dainty little porcelain teapots and watercress finger sandwiches with the crusts cut off. Tootsie had to agree, as they followed the path to a table, that this was just what the doctor ordered—food for the body and for the soul.

Soon a waiter came to pour water and, noting the outlandish dresses, which he referred to as "happy," asked shyly if they were members of a choir. Tootsie exclaimed, "Lord yes, honey. You may have heard of us. We're called the Flower Girls. We have done gigs at all the assisted living places in the South." They all laughed, and he laughed with them, not sure whether he was being put on or whether they were just enjoying a moment of hilarity. Eventually, after he had taken their orders for the English tea and watercress sandwiches that seemed quaintly predictable for such a place, they fell silent.

"What are you thinking, dear," Bippy finally said, looking at Tootsie.

"Oh, I was just thinking about all the things we don't know about Maggie's death. We don't know anything about the man who found her. He could be a person of interest in her death. We don't really know her brothers. Well, maybe you do, Pen and Tootsie, but the rest of us—"

"—Not really. It's been so many years, I don't feel that I know them either," Penelope interrupted, slowly shaking her head.

Tootsie nodded. "Mmm. Same here. And we don't know the mystery man, Gordon Dawkins; we don't know how much Gordon Dawkins' children knew about his involvement with Maggie or what their true feelings were; we don't know why Maggie listed us in her will. But most of all, we don't know why Maggie would suddenly throw caution to the winds and go out on her sailboat alone on a windy day without a life preserver."

"There are a lot of unknowns, now that you mention it," said Rosemary.

"Too many," said Tootsie, sipping her Earl Gray tea, "entirely too many."

***

Tootsie went first through the revolving door at First Union, the others right behind her, and scanned the elevator listing. The office of Landers, Watson, Coughlin, and Weller was on the twelfth floor. She pushed the up button and after a few minutes, a ding signaled the doors' opening. When the doors parted, the ladies gasped in surprise. Clarkson and Raymond were already on the elevator. "We rode up from the parking garage below," Clarkson said, after re-introductions were made all around.

"I haven't trusted those since the first World Trade Center bombing, the one in the parking garage," Rosemary said, as the doors closed, "so we parked in the lot across the street. I know, I know. If I really thought something like that would likely happen here, I wouldn't be riding up in the elevator, right? But still...." They all mumbled understanding.

"We're on our way to see Maggie's lawyer," Tootsie blurted out. She felt some kind of an explanation was demanded. "He...he called us."

"Really? For a reading of the will? So are we," Clarkson responded.

A silence descended on the mirror-walled elevator as it whooshed its way to the twelfth floor. As it stopped periodically to let someone on or off, Tootsie noticed those who entered the elevator, as well as Clarkson, sneaking discrete peeks in the mirrors. Every time she caught his eye, he looked at his feet. Finally, she could stand it no longer and burst into laughter. "It's the dresses, right?"

"Excuse me?"

"I know you're probably wondering what's with the get-up." When Clarkson demurred, she continued. "Oh, come on now. I know we look like an aging rock group, a kind of female Rolling Stones. Actually, most of us are younger or not much older than Mick Jagger, come to think of it." Clarkson and Raymond both smiled, and she continued. "We call ourselves the Flower Girls, and the dresses just seemed to fit. What can I say? They were an impulse of the moment, a frantic attempt to cheer ourselves up."

Bippy said, "It was...our desperate effort to bring the Maggie who loved such fun and spontaneity back to life. She would have howled.

Oh my." She giggled and then quickly drew a handkerchief from her purse to dab at her eyes.

"It was...a...a...moment of hilarity," Penelope added, beginning to chuckle.

"It was...insanity is what it was," added Rosemary laughing until the tears streaked down her face. Then, biting her lip to regain control, she added softly, "It loses something in the translation. You...you just...had to be there."

When the Flower Girls pushed open the tall mahogany door and trooped into the prestigious law firm of Landers, Watson, Coughlin, and Weller, with Clarkson and Raymond in tow, they made quite a spectacle. "May I help you?" the startled receptionist asked.

Tootsie thought she seemed poised to direct them to some other office, perhaps mental health, preferably in some other building. Preferably in some other town. "We have an appointment with Mr. Surles at 4:00." She checked her watch. Three minutes 'til four. Tootsie smiled. She liked being on time. It didn't happen all that often—it wasn't something she worried about or got uptight about like her son and daughter, bless their hearts—but when it did, she liked it because she knew Walter would have.

The receptionist spoke into an intercom, and in a few minutes, a legal secretary, dressed in a smart, royal-blue suit with gold, twisted knot buttons, emerged from behind a series of doors. With a complexion as smooth and pale as cream and golden hair pulled back neatly into a French twist, she was a picture of efficiency and professionalism, but she smiled warmly enough, and if she noticed the outlandish appearance of the ladies, she gave no hint of it. "Hello. I'm Debra Smith," she said, extending her hand to each of the ladies and then to Clarkson and Raymond. "I believe I have talked with each of you on the telephone. Thank you for coming in. Please come this way." She glanced back quickly at the receptionist as if to send some fleeting mental communication about the unusual attire of their clients, then turned, and led them into a large, book-lined office. Bippy noticed that Debra smiled very directly at the man seated at a large desk as she introduced the visitors and pulled the door shut after her.

Chilton Surles came from behind his desk and greeted them warmly. He was about thirty-five, Bippy guessed, a tall, lanky, pleasant-looking man with sandy hair, hazel eyes, and round wire-rimmed glasses. His arms were long and dangled at his sides as if attached to his shoulders by strings. Bippy noticed immediately that he wore no wedding ring. *I wonder if he and Debra Smith are more than boss and secretary*, she mused. *If not, maybe they just need some nudging.* She smiled at the thought.

Surles extended his hand and took each lady's hand in his, holding it affectionately for a few seconds. Finally, he shook hands with Clarkson and Raymond, saying, "Good to see you both again."

Bippy leaned closer to him. "Mr. Surles," she said, "your secretary, Debra, is quite a nice representative for the firm. Efficient and warm at the same time."

"Well, thank you, Miss Maas. I'll be sure to tell her."

"Pretty, too."

"Ma'am?"

"I said she's pretty, too."

Surles's face reddened noticeably, and he seemed at a loss. He cleared his throat. "Yes…ah, well, won't you all sit down."

Once they were all seated in a semi-circle, Surles, once again seated at his desk, took a deep breath, swallowed, and began. "First, let me once again express my condolences to each of you in the loss of your sister and friend. Mrs. Palmer was truly an exceptional person, always helping others. In fact, she insisted on my drawing up her will, which is larger and more complicated than most, because she wanted to demonstrate confidence in me, help me make partner in the firm, something, which, I'm pleased to tell you, is now in the process of happening, thanks in large part to her." Bippy smiled and nodded. He paused and cleared his throat. "Now, uh, as I said, Mrs. Palmer had a very large estate, and she gave long and careful thought to its distribution, changing the wording several times. This is a recent will. Very recent. Mrs. Palmer and I discussed her wishes for bequests at length. I drew it up, and she read it, approved it, and signed it not more than six weeks ago." When no one said anything, he again cleared his throat. "Okay. Here we go. Once I read it through, feel free to ask me questions."

I, Margaret Katherine Muldoon Palmer, being of sound mind and body, do hereby will and bequeath the following:

(A) One million dollars to Duke University, Durham, North Carolina, and one million dollars to Woodberry Forest School, Woodberry Forest, Virginia, to be used by both institutions to establish a scholarship fund for deserving students who evidence high moral character, exceptional academic ability, and established need.

(B) One million dollars to First United Methodist Church of Jackson, Mississippi, to be used in whatever ways best enable the church to serve the community and the world.

(C) One million dollars to the St. Francis Animal Adoption Center, also of Jackson, Mississippi, and an additional one million dollars to the American Society for the Prevention of Cruelty to Animals.

(D) To my beloved brothers, Clarkson and Raymond,
I leave my home in Jackson and my beach retreat at
Gulfport, and all other real and personal property
with the exception noted below, share and share alike.
In addition, to each brother shall be given the sum
of two million dollars.

(E) To my dearest friends: Penelope Caldwell, Tootsie
Freeman, Rosemary Harrison, and Bippy Maas I leave
the sum of five hundred thousand dollars each. In
addition, I leave them each a personal memento,
to be selected by Clarkson and Raymond.

As Surles droned on, adding the legal requisites at the end, the Flower Girls sat in stunned silence. *Amazing,* thought Tootsie, *and just like Maggie to be so generous.* Penelope swallowed. *This can't be happening,* she thought. Bippy dabbed at her eyes and muttered under her breath, "Oh dear, I'm going to cry." Rosemary covered her eyes with her hand. She had lost count, but she knew the bequests totaled somewhere around eleven million dollars plus real and personal property. She knew Maggie was well-to-do, but she never dreamed she was as wealthy as all that. Despite all the thoughts that swirled in their minds, no one seemed able to speak. For several minutes, nothing could be heard except the ticking of the antique Seth Thomas clock on one of the bookshelves. Finally, Surles broke the silence.

"Are there any questions?"

"Why us?" Rosemary finally asked, numb with disbelief. "We're not family. Penelope and Tootsie go way back with Maggie, but Bippy and I don't. I don't understand." Her voice cracked. "I mean, did you all expect anything like this?" she asked, turning to the other Flower Girls. They shook their heads slowly.

Surles rose and came around his desk and stood near them. "Mrs. Palmer told me at great length what each of you had meant to her and why she wanted her relationship with you to continue after she was gone. Of course, at the time we talked, this was something way off in the future. We had no idea that her life would end so tragically and so soon in such a horrible accident."

"It wasn't an accident," Tootsie said abruptly. There was a slight, but perceptible, intake of breath in the room. "And we plan to stay here until we can prove it."

Just then, Clarkson, who had been clearing his throat since the reading of the will, was seized by a violent coughing spell. Mr. Surles went to pour him some water from the carafe on the table by the window, but Clarkson had already hurried from the room to the water fountain in the hallway. Tootsie shot Rosemary a quick look. Raymond's mouth opened in surprise, though whether because of what Tootsie had said or because of his brother's violent coughing, Tootsie couldn't be sure.

Surles flushed and quickly changed the subject. "Uh, well, I know Maggie's death is hard for any of us to comprehend or accept."

He reached out to take Penelope's hand and guide her to her feet. "I'll be in touch with all of you and will be sending you a check as soon as the estate is probated and settled. It may be a while—maybe almost a year—because of the sheer magnitude and complexity of Mrs. Palmer's bequests, but I will expedite things as rapidly as possible. Meanwhile, if you have any questions, do not hesitate to contact me." He smiled and nodded thoughtfully, obviously ready for them to go. "Well, thank you again for coming in."

And just like that, the Flower Girls found themselves very mystified. And very rich.

Chapter Twenty-Seven

"Ladies, excuse me," Clarkson said, stepping in front of the Flower Girls after they had all left the thickly carpeted quiet of Chilton Surles's law office and clicked down the tiled hall towards the elevator. "I...uh, I wonder whether I...that is, we...might have a word with you."

The ladies stopped walking and looked at him. Bippy, who had tarried behind to speak quietly with Debra, came quickly to join them. "Certainly, Mr. Muldoon," Tootsie said. Just then, the elevator yawned open, and two men in business suits and identical navy and yellow polka-dotted power ties got off, looked aghast at the girls' dresses, gave them a surprised little smirk as if the girls were the welcoming committee or something, and walked quickly down the corridor to the door of Landers, Watson, Coughlin, and Weller.

Tootsie nodded toward the identically dressed men and said under her breath, "We're all alike. It's just our costumes that are different."

Clarkson motioned the ladies toward the elevator. When the door closed with a soft sigh, he punched the button and spoke. "Raymond and I want to thank you again for all you have meant to Sis over the years." He glanced at his brother, who was nodding his head in agreement, and continued. "We didn't know she had mentioned you in her will, but I want you to know that we think it is marvelous that she did, and…uh, well, we thought it might be nice—that is, it's what Maggie would want—if we got better acquainted with you."

The ladies stood motionless, not even breathing, waiting to hear what this was all leading up to. Finally, Tootsie said, "Well, Mr. Muldoon—"

"—Please," he interrupted, "call me Clarkson. That would be a start anyway." He smiled at the tall, flamboyantly attractive woman before him, her glossy black hair waved back behind her small ears. He found himself eyeing her svelte figure, not completely hidden by the garish dress she wore, her exquisitely smooth complexion, and her eyes as brown and soft as velvet. She could pass for forty, he thought, but he knew—because she was Maggie's age—that she was just a few years younger than he. He ran one hand across his smoothly coifed hair and then, with the slim fingers of his right hand, unconsciously straightened the knot in his already perfect tie.

Tootsie looked directly into the deep blue eyes—the color of light denim, she thought—that he turned on her and smiled guardedly. "Okay, Clarkson it is. Now, what did you have in mind?"

"Well, for starters, why don't you check out of your hotel rooms and come stay in Sis's house with us?"

Penelope, who had been carefully reading their lips, turned wide eyes on the two men. "I beg your pardon."

"What my brother means," said Raymond hurriedly, "is that Sis thought the world of you and would want us to extend you every courtesy, to invite you to stay in her home the rest of the time you're here. You said in there"—he tossed his head back, indicating the law office that was now stories above them—"that you weren't leaving right away, so come stay at Maggie's house. Please. We'll be leaving tomorrow. We'd rather have someone in the house than not. It's quite large, and it's…it's the least we can do for her." He swallowed and looked down.

Tootsie, looking at his strong nose and square jaw, was struck by the difference in the two brothers. Physically, they were opposites. Clarkson, aristocratic and elegant, was cut from the tall-dark-and-handsome piece of cloth, the epitome of the well-groomed man, dressed for success. Raymond, on the other hand, with his tousled reddish-blond hair, square jaw, and tan face looked as if he would be more at home on a boat than in a board room. In spite of his limp, or maybe because of it, he projected a surging masculinity, enhanced, not hidden, by the loose clothing he wore like an afterthought. The differences didn't stop there. Their personalities were no more alike than their physiques. Clarkson was so in control, so unemotional, that he seemed almost aloof, distant, but this Raymond, Tootsie thought, seemed ready to cry at the drop of a hat. Still, it could be fake, she decided. She didn't know them well enough to judge. Yet.

"That's extraordinarily kind of you. Sounds like a good idea to me," she said. "What do the rest of you all think?" she said, turning to the other three Flower Girls.

Rosemary nodded. She would relish getting to dig out more information for her story. Getting into Maggie's house and getting to know the brothers better was the perfect way to do it. "Sure. Suits me." She wondered as she said it if her motivation were the same as the brothers' intent. Did they want the girls where they could keep an eye on them? Pump them for information? Were the investigators themselves to be investigated?

"How about you two?" Tootsie asked Bippy and Pen.

This suited Bippy just fine. A little change of venue to cheer them up—get their minds off Maggie's death—was just the ticket. She felt as if she were embarking on an adventure, stepping into one of her paperback murder mysteries. "You know me," Bippy smiled. "I'm game for anything."

"That's very nice of you," Pen said, smiling at Clarkson and Raymond, "very nice indeed. Southern hospitality at its best."

***

Later, after checking out of the hotel and following the instructions given them by Maggie's brothers and by both Tootsie's and Pen's memories, the Flower Girls pulled up in front of a long, gated drive, completely walled in by tall bushes. "This is it," Tootsie said, as Rose pulled the car up to the gate. "Haven't been here since Cam died, but I remember this long driveway."

Rolling down her window, Rose pushed the buzzer, and waited until the intercom crackled on. "It's the Flower Girls," she said confidently into the speaker. That brought giggles from the other occupants of the car.

Immediately, the gate opened, and they drove up the long driveway, pulling into the parking area behind the house. They piled out of the car and had just begun pulling their suitcases from the trunk when Raymond and Clarkson appeared and insisted on taking over that chore. "No, no," Clarkson said. "You all just go right on in. Your bedrooms are the four upstairs. Raymond and I are staying downstairs. Sis added a wing last year with two bedrooms and baths. She wanted to have a downstairs bedroom when she got older and be able to have overnight guests, who also might not want or be able to climb the stairs. We'll bring your suitcases right up. In the fridge you'll find some lemonade that the neighbors brought. Sandwiches and desserts, too. Help yourselves."

The four friends made their way upstairs and, walking down the hallway, peeked in at each room. One, the walls a rich cream, had a Shaker four-poster bed with canopy, an oval braided rug, and a fireplace in the corner. Bippy exclaimed when she saw it. "Oh, would you look at that. It looks like something out of *Southern Living*. And I wish you'd look at those pillow shams." She recognized them instantly as the ones she and Sister had sent Maggie.

"Why don't you take that one, Bippy," Tootsie said. "I like this sunny yellow one right across the hall." Yellow, orange, and red poppies and field flowers decorated the floor-to-ceiling drapes that hung at the large windows.

After Rosemary and Pen chose their rooms at the end of the hall, one a soft blue with chintz curtains, and the other a pale pink with Victorian flowered spread and drapes, they accepted their suitcases from Raymond and Clarkson with smiles and thanks.

"I'm afraid we don't have any help at the moment," Clarkson said. "Maggie liked her privacy and wouldn't hear to live-in help. She did most of the work herself and had a cleaning lady only about once a month to do big cleaning—more if she expected company. Since Mattie isn't due for about three weeks, things are just as Maggie left them."

"After Mattie comes in and cleans thoroughly, I guess we'll put the house on the market," Raymond added.

"What about Maggie's pets?" asked Rosemary.

"The neighbors are taking care of them for the time being while they try to find good homes for them. If they can't, of course, they'll take them to the St. Francis Center, where they'll be taken care of for life. The neighbors have been incredible. They all say they can't do enough for Maggie."

"It's little wonder," said Pen. "She inspired that kind of loyalty."

"She was the most innately good person I've ever known," said Rosemary.

Tootsie nodded. "You hear it said a lot that a person was one in a million, but in this case, it is absolutely true. There was never a person like Maggie Muldoon Palmer."

"Oh my!" Bippy said. "She was the best friend I ever had. She never stopped doing for other people."

"Thank you," Clarkson said. "I have to agree with you there. She may have been my sister, but she was...was really...something else."

A snuffling sound caused them all to turn around and look at Raymond. He was furiously mopping his eyes with a handkerchief, and his reddened face was contorted and drawn. "I'm sorry," he said from behind the white hanky. "I...I just can't...get the picture...of her tagging around after me when we were kids out of my mind. It just makes me so sad that I—"

An awkward silence descended on the little group in the hall, a silence into which no one dared trespass. No one knew quite what to say to comfort him. He was far away in a childhood past, struggling with his own personal grief, and no one could have reached him anyway.

"Well, listen, why don't you all get freshened up," Clarkson suddenly suggested, "and we'll all go out to dinner together. Cheer ourselves up a bit."

***

On the way to the restaurant—they had decided on Chili's because Bippy thought the name was cute—the girls began talking. Clarkson and Raymond were ahead of them in Maggie's car, since neither the rental car nor Maggie's BMW would hold all six of them comfortably.

"Well, what do you think?" asked Tootsie, relieved that they were at last alone and could talk over all that had happened in the lawyer's office and since.

"Hmm? Oh, think? About what, dear?" said Pen.

"About 'the boys,' " she answered with a grin. "What do you make of their reaction when I said we didn't buy Maggie's death as being accidental?"

"That was quite a coughing spell Clarkson had back in Chilton Surles's office, wasn't it?" said Rosemary.

"Yes, it was," said Pen. "He must have a terrible cold."

Tootsie shrugged. "Funny, I didn't notice any other signs of a cold."

"I was too busy watching the lawyer to notice," said Bippy. "Dear Gussie! He turned so red in the face I thought he was going to have a stroke."

"Hmm," Tootsie said. "Do you suppose he knows something he's not telling us?"

"Who? Mr. Surles or one of the brothers?" asked Rose.

"Well, maybe all of them," Tootsie said, looking out the window. "Maybe all of them."

***

Clarkson picked at his chicken-fried steak and finally laid down his fork. "I have to ask you ladies something." They all paused their eating in anticipation. Every eye was on him. "What did you mean, Mrs. Freeman, by saying in the lawyer's office that you don't think Maggie's death was an accident?"

"Just that," said Tootsie, removing a small jar of peanut butter from her purse. "It doesn't make common sense. And please call me Tootsie."

211

"And me Bippy."

"And me Rose."

"And please call me Pen."

He nodded. "That sounds lots better. My friends call me Clark, by the way," he said with a smile. "My brother goes by Ray to his friends, and I do hope we can call you our friends. Right, Ray?"

It was the first time he had used the shortened form of his brother's name, and Tootsie thought it made them both seem warmer, folksier, especially Clarkson. Maybe Mr. Perfect is human, after all, she decided, or at least wants to appear that way. She found herself smiling a cautious smile.

Ray nodded. "I'm speechless at the idea of Sis's death not being an accident, but I second what Clark said about our being friends."

"Absolutely. Anyway," Tootsie continued, "looking at this from a common sense standpoint tells me that it violates everything we know about Maggie to think that she would take her sailboat out alone on a very windy day and not wear a life jacket."

"She was very cautious, as you know," said Pen.

"Very cautious indeed," added Bippy.

"And extremely smart," said Rosemary.

"You're right about that, but, well, supposing what you say is true," Raymond said, "do you have any idea who could be responsible for her death?"

Suddenly, it was as if they had all stepped inside a sound-proof booth to answer some sixty-four thousand dollar question. Not a person breathed, much less spoke. The only sound that could be heard was the faint tinkling of silverware off in the distance somewhere. Rosemary made a mental note to ask the other girls later why they thought Raymond's question was so daunting. Was it threatening? Defensive? Accusative? She honestly didn't know.

Tootsie spread a chunk of peanut butter, deftly spooned from her purse onto the bread on her plate, took a bite, daintily patted each side of her mouth with her napkin, cleared her throat, and, looking down, toyed with the spoon at her place setting. Finally, she lifted her eyes. "Let me answer that by asking you a question, Ray," she said. "What do you think of Gordon Dawkins?"

"Who?"

"Gordon Dawkins. The man Maggie was going to marry."

If the silence had been profound before, now it was dizzying. Finally, Raymond, whose mouth had dropped open at her words, took a huge gulp of water and said, "Wait! What? Marry? Maggie was getting married?" He looked wild-eyed at his brother.

"I take it you didn't know," said Rosemary. "You're surprised."

"That may just be the understatement of the year."

"Of a lifetime," corrected Clarkson.

"She emailed us all about him, but she said he didn't want her to tell anyone. He was afraid his children would object because they wanted him to reconcile with their mother. Wanted to spring it on them after they were already married."

"That doesn't sound like Maggie," Clarkson said. "She was the soul of integrity. She would never be a party to deception."

"Ordinarily, no," said Tootsie, "but in this case, she said she had to trust that Gordon knew how to handle his children better than she did. She was willing to play along in the interest of family harmony."

"Oh, dear God!" sighed Raymond. "What was she thinking?"

"I wish she'd confided in us," said Clarkson. "We could have talked her out of it."

"That's precisely why she didn't tell you, Clark," said Pen. "She didn't want to be talked out of it. And, don't worry. We tried to."

"I surely raised the question about starting off married life with a deception," Tootsie added.

"No, all she wanted was to be happy and make this Gordon Dawkins happy," said Bippy. "It was true love."

"I take it that neither of you met him at the visitation or the funeral," said Rosemary.

"No. I never heard his name until just this minute," said Clarkson. "Never."

Rosemary nodded. "Neither did we—see him at the visitation or the funeral, that is—although we realize we could have missed him, especially if he didn't sign the guest register. Could be too overcome, I guess, but all of this has left us seriously wondering about him—where he is and if he's on the up-and-up."

"I have an idea," Tootsie said suddenly, slapping her hand on the table in such a way as to make Raymond jump just a little. "Why don't we look him up in the phone book and pay a call on him? You know, share our grief."

"Good idea," Clark said. "I'll be right back."

When he returned, he was carrying the Greater Jackson phone book. He plopped it on the table and began ruffling through it. "Daniels. Davenport. Davis. Hmm. The only Dawkins is an Ellen Dawkins on Shady Rest Retirement Home Road. What do you make of that?" he asked, closing the book.

"I think we can safely assume that's not it," said Tootsie.

"Could be he was not from here or had just moved here," said Raymond, "and was staying in a hotel."

"Or might have an unlisted number. Or no land line. What about this?" said Rosemary. "Why don't we run an ad in the paper asking anyone with information about Maggie's last days—any information at all—to come forward? We could offer a reward. That might be a strong motivator to anyone who is reluctant to share anything he or she knows."

"Great idea!" exclaimed Tootsie. "I wish I'd thought of it! What do y'all think?" she said, looking across the table at Ray and Clark. "It's really your call since she was your sister."

Clarkson rubbed his chin thoughtfully. "You know, I have to tell you that when you mentioned at the lawyer's office the possibility of Maggie's death not being an accident, it made me very nervous."

"I noticed that, Clark," Tootsie said forthrightly. "Why?"

Clarkson swallowed. "Well, Mrs.—Tootsie," he said, "You certainly pull no punches"

Tootsie flashed a smile. "I tell it like it is."

"So I noticed." Clarkson studied this woman before him. Tootsie had changed to a turquoise and white silk dress with long billowy sleeves and a belt of silver that cinched in her tiny waist. On her feet she wore chocolate brown boots with flecks of turquoise. A blend of the Old West and New York Boutique, bordering on the outlandish, it was not a typical run-of-the-mill, off-the-rack dress. Certainly, nobody he had ever dated would have worn such a garment, but on Tootsie, it looked right. It seemed to play up that gorgeous complexion and jet-black hair. It also seemed to match her shoot-from-the-hip personality. "Well," he said finally, "I suppose it's because an accident somehow seems more bearable than murder. The very word 'murder' makes my blood run cold. I guess I was just upset by the idea that anyone could purposely harm Maggie."

"Maybe he didn't," Tootsie said.

Clarkson looked surprised. "He?"

"Or she."

"What do you mean?"

"Maybe someone killed her, but not on purpose. I mean, maybe it didn't start out that way. Maybe it was an argument that escalated. Maybe it was an accident that got covered up."

Clarkson sat silently and regarded Tootsie through narrowed eyes. What did she want? What was she after? What was she picking at? What did she know that he didn't?

Finally he spoke. "You may be right. Unfortunately, I can't remain in Jackson any longer right now. We'll be back later to sell the house, but I have an investment banking commitment back in Houston the day after tomorrow that I must honor. Much as I'd like to, I can't stay to field any calls that might come in as a result of the ad. If you all can stay a while, though, I think it's an excellent idea. What do you think, Ray?"

Raymond nodded. "Sure. It's a great idea. We might not get anything, but it can't hurt."

"I figure that maybe there are some people who would rather not talk to the police who might talk to us," Tootsie said. She smiled and added. "And I think Rosemary's right. I think those people would be further encouraged if a reward were offered."

Raymond said, "Mm-hmm. You're probably right. How much?"

"What about a grand?" Clarkson asked. "We could go up to five, depending on the amount of information,"

"Good idea," said Rosemary. "Gives us some bargaining power."

Raymond nodded. "Since Clark and I are co-executors of the estate, either of us can withdraw the money. That's no problem, but who would take care of the calls or tips, if there are any, and see that the money gets to the person with the information? I'm afraid my time here has run out, too. I have a flight out tomorrow morning. I need to

216

get back to Atlanta. The business won't run itself without me forever, although I have four hundred and thirty-six employees who would probably like to think it would," he grinned.

"You're too modest, Ray. I'm sure they'll all be glad to have you back. Meanwhile, we'll take care of answering the ad," Tootsie said. "That's no problem."

"I hope it won't be," he answered. "I also hope it won't be dangerous."

An unusual thing to say, Tootsie thought, but she said nothing.

"We'll go with you to the airport," Rose said. "We'll follow you in our car and bring Maggie's car back and put it in the garage."

"That's very nice of you, but we could call a cab," Clarkson said.

"Oh, no," Tootsie said. "It will give us something to do."

"Okay, if you're sure. I wish Ray and I didn't have to leave, but we really do."

"I understand completely, but I intend to stay until I feel at peace with Maggie's death," Tootsie said. "You both have jobs and responsibilities. We have nothing but time—well, except for Rosemary, that is, and she has that worked out. I am, however, determined to stay until I get to the bottom of this."

"So are we," the other girls chimed in.

"Fine. Stay at Maggie's for as long as you like. Actually, it will help to have someone in the house. You can close up the house when you leave and just leave the keys in the house," Clarkson said. "Mattie's not due to clean for another two or three weeks. She has a key. Do you want me to call and see if she can come in earlier?"

"No, not at all," Tootsie said. "We'll be just fine, and, really, I think we'd prefer to be left alone."

Well, then," Raymond said, "It's all settled. Let's do it. Tell you what. Right after dinner, we'll word the ad and call it in, even though it probably won't appear until the day after tomorrow, okay? What do we have to lose? The worst that can happen is that we'll find the police are right, that her death was an accident."

It is not, Tootsie thought, with a strange sense of foreboding, the worst that can happen.

Chapter Twenty-Eight

At 8:00 the next morning, as they waited at the airport for their flights to be called, one going east, and one going west, Ray and Clark went over a few things with the girls. "Here are both of our numbers, both at home and at the office," Clark said, and, lowering his voice, he added, "and here is a thousand dollars to use for reward money. Ray and I had some cash with us, and we just went ahead and made up the difference by withdrawing it from our personal accounts so there wouldn't be any red tape at this point." He handed Tootsie a small manila envelope, which she immediately slipped into her purse.

"And please don't hesitate to call us at home or at work if and when you need more money for the informant," Ray added. "We'll wire it immediately."

"Let me write you a receipt for this," Tootsie said, withdrawing a pen from her purse.

Clarkson shook his head and placed his hand on her arm. "That won't be necessary. We're friends now, remember? We trust you. We'll each call you from time to time to see how things are going." He took Tootsie's hand. "And, whatever you do, be careful."

Tootsie's cheeks flamed as an uncharacteristic blush spread across her face. She had to swallow before she could reply. "We will."

"Promise?"

"Promise."

"Call us at any time if you need anything," Raymond said, glancing at the flight board and seeing his flight to Atlanta was running on time, "and good luck. Clark, we'd better go."

Goodbyes said, the men hugged each of their sister's friends in turn, picked up their carry-on luggage, hurried to their respective gates, and got in line to go through security.

***

"Here it is," Rosemary said the next day as she brought the paper in the front door and headed to the kitchen, where the roasted-nut aroma of coffee filled the room. Pen was just taking out of the oven some canned crescent rolls she had found in the refrigerator and slathered with butter and cinnamon. "Mmm. Smells good in here." Rose had gotten up early, thrown on a pair of tan slacks and butter-cream sweater, and walked three blocks to a newspaper machine to buy a paper. "Let's see: classifieds are in section C. Here we go. Okay, listen."

INFORMATION SOUGHT
Anyone having knowledge of the last week of Margaret Muldoon Palmer's life or of facts surrounding her death is asked to call 555-7578, email mmp555@yahoo.com or write Estate of Margaret Muldoon Palmer/1523 West Haven Lane/Jackson, MS 39213. A reward will be offered for information which results in clarifying the manner in which Mrs. Palmer died. Anonymity guaranteed.

"I couldn't hear everything you read. May I please see the paper?" Pen said. After reading the write-up, she put the paper down on the kitchen counter and said, "Sounds wonderful, dear. Very concise and to the point."

"Yes, I hope the perp squeals," said Bippy.

Rosemary and the other two, still clad in their pajamas, stopped what they were doing and turned astonished eyes on her.

"Pfft!" Tootsie spewed the coffee she was sipping. "What did you say?" she gasped, laughing.

Rosemary was laughing so hard, she put her coffee mug down hard, sloshing the coffee onto the counter. "The perp?" She smothered a guffaw. "Squeals?" She dissolved in laughter again.

Bippy blushed. "Sorry. I love to read murder mysteries, and in them the suspect is referred to as a perp. That's police jargon. Short for perpetrator, I suppose. I guess I got carried away."

"Why, I love murder mysteries, too, Bippy," Pen said, "but I brought only three with me, *The Gruesome Twosome*, which I've almost finished, *Murder Squared*, which I've read before, and *Something Rotten in Denmark*. I just grabbed a handful on the way out the door. Want to trade books when you finish the one you're reading?"

"What a grand idea!" said Bippy. "Just a splendid idea! It reminds me of when we were children and traded comic books. You're so resourceful, Pen dear. Anyway, I hope the ad brings us some helpful information."

"I hope so, too," said Tootsie, as she continued chuckling to herself while slathering peanut butter on a piece of toast. "I just hope we did the right thing in putting the address in the ad."

"Well," Rosemary said, "I think you had a good point about some people being afraid of traced calls or even the Internet, which the police computer experts can hack. They can write anonymously if they don't want to call or email without fear of being traced."

"True," Tootsie said, spreading more peanut butter on the next piece of toast.

"It's a good thing you don't have a weight problem, girl," Rosemary said, eyeing the toast. "Don't you ever get tired of that stuff?"

"Peanut butter? Heavens, no!" exclaimed Tootsie. "It's my energy food."

"Well, it must be. It's as regular as the morning paper. I never saw anyone—" She suddenly caught her breath. "Wait a minute."

"What?" Bippy asked.

"The morning paper. I went down a few blocks and bought one from a machine. Wonder why it isn't being delivered? In fact, why isn't there a pile of them somewhere from the day Maggie disappeared?"

"Probably Clark or Ray had it stopped," Pen said, "or one of the neighbors called. The boys said they'd been awfully helpful."

"Yeah, maybe," said Rosemary slowly. "Maybe." She made a mental note to ask Ray and Clark when they called, as they promised to.

Later that morning, a conference call came in from the brothers, and the Flower Girls, with much excitement, told them about the ad's appearance in the newspaper. Rose read them the ad and said, "It looks good, the way it's boxed and everything. Let's hope it draws some attention."

"But not the wrong kind," Clark said somberly.

"Say, speaking of papers, let me ask you all something," Rosemary said, as her friends huddled nearby listening to the speaker phone. "Where did you all put the back papers that came after Maggie disappeared? We would love to read the accounts of her disappearance."

"Papers?" Clark said. "You know, that's odd. There weren't any papers there, were there, Ray?"

"Nope."

"You didn't have them stopped?" she asked.

"No," both brothers said at once.

"Actually, never thought of it," Ray continued. "Why?"

"Just wondering."

Clark answered, "Well, as I said, there were no papers there when we arrived, so they hadn't been delivered for some time, apparently. I guess that's why we didn't think to stop delivery."

Tootsie, Bippy, and Pen then took turns moving closer to the speaker phone to talk to Clark and Ray. Pen, struggling to hear the conversation, suddenly exclaimed: "What? You're doing what? Oh, my goodness!" She turned to her friends, who had stepped back and let her be right up close to the phone, and whispered. "Ray either said he's frying some bacon or lying down naked. Dear me."

Laughing, Tootsie moved closer to the phone and said, "Ray, what did you say? Pen couldn't understand you. Oh, okay. I'll tell her." She turned to Pen and said, "Raymond is on a private plane flying to Macon on a business trip and will be back in touch as soon as he returns."

"Oh, flying to Macon," Pen said, and her voice was a mixture of relief and disappointment. Then she brightened and moved in closer to the phone. "Ray," she giggled into the speaker, "my conversation is a lot more interesting than yours."

They said their goodbyes, and the phone call had no sooner ended than the doorbell rang. "My, that was fast," Bippy said. "Who says newspaper advertising doesn't work?"

They all went into the front hall as Tootsie opened the door. Before them, in a lime-green polyester dress and matching hat, looking as surprised to see them as they were to see her, stood Beulah Merritt.

"Well, I'll swanee! What are y'all doing here?" she exclaimed. Before they could answer, she went on. "I'm Beulah Merritt. I met y'all at the funeral home and then at the church lunch after the funeral."

"Of course, Mrs. Merritt," Rosemary said. "We remember you." She permitted herself a little sigh. Who could forget her?

"Beulah, please," she said. "Mrs. Merritt sounds like what my school children called me all those years. Makes me feel old. I bet y'all never thought you'd see me again."

To cover her friends' stammered response to that statement, Tootsie quickly said, "It's a surprise, all right, but that's what makes life interesting, isn't it? Well, Beulah, what brings you out our way this morning? Could I get you some coffee?"

Beulah had already begun edging her way through the door. "No, thanks. I've had my limit of caffeine this morning. I just came by to check on the house. See if everything was all right here, don't you know. Thought maybe Maggie's brothers might need me to help them go through things and all." Her eyes scanned the space behind where they were standing and took in the stairway. "My, isn't that a grand staircase," she said. "I've never actually been in the house before. Well, anyway, I didn't expect to find y'all here. Are y'all busy right now?"

"Uh," Tootsie stammered, "no, of course not. Come right in." It was a redundant invitation, as Beulah had already worked her way into the hall and was fast making her way to the living room, looking from floor to ceiling as she went. Her head nodded up and down like an elevator gone berserk.

"The gate was open down at the end of the drive," she called over her shoulder, "so I just came right on up. I hope that's okay. Are y'all helping the boys go through Maggie's stuff?" She preceded the other women into the spacious living room and dropped into the first seat she came to, a geranium-red, down-filled wing chair. Pen, Rosemary, Tootsie, and Bippy exchanged glances and then settled down in chairs all around her.

Pen smiled. "Oh, Beulah, our dear Maggie didn't use snuff."

Beulah looked at her as if she had just landed from Mars. "What?"

Bippy intervened. "Penelope is very hard of hearing, Pen," she said, "Beulah said 'stuff,' not 'snuff.'"

A smile of relief spread across Pen's face. "Oh, thank you, Bippy. You're always so kind to tell me what's going on. You really are." She patted Bippy's small hand.

"Actually, Beulah," Rosemary said, "Raymond and Clarkson have gone, and we have moved over here from the hotel."

Beulah's eyes widened, as she turned to look at her. "Y'all are staying *here*? In Maggie's house? Do her brothers know?"

Tootsie squelched the impulse to say, "Of course, they know, you dingbat. Do you think we would just move in on our own?" Instead, she said calmly, "Yes. As a matter of fact, they invited us. Insisted, actually, that we stay here for the duration of our visit."

"Oh, I see." She didn't see at all, but the way she pursed her lips told the Flower Girls that she was determined to find out just what was going on. "Now, tell me again how y'all knew Maggie."

As each recited her connection to Maggie, Beulah nodded, taking mental notes. "I see. How interesting. Isn't that wonderful?" she said after each report. "Well, it was mighty nice of y'all to come so far to honor Maggie, but I guess you'll soon be returning home." When there was no answer, she tried again. "So, how long do y'all plan to stay in Jackson?" She nonchalantly patted her purse, which was shaped like a tired saddlebag, and then brushed a bit of lint from her dress, as if the answer meant little to her one way or the other.

"We...uh, we're not sure," Bippy responded.

"Oh?" Beulah arched her eyebrows. "I assumed you'd be going home right after the funeral."

"We planned to," Bippy said, "but things changed."

That was like waving a red flag in front of a bull, Tootsie decided. Better just come out with it, but there was no need to tell her more than she needed to know. "We plan to stay until we know all the details of Maggie's death. We just decided that we would all feel better waiting until the autopsy report was back. You know, put our minds at ease. That's all."

"Oh, well...." Beulah, for once, seemed at a loss for words. "I see." When nobody said anything, she finally patted her knees and said, "Well, I guess I'd better be going." As one, the four sprang to their feet with her. As they walked her to the door, she said, "Now, y'all be sure to call me if you need anything. I'll be glad to come over and help you if you decide to go through Maggie's things. Here's my number." She scribbled on a wrinkled grocery receipt that she fished from her purse and handed it to Penelope. "Really, it's no imposition at all. I wouldn't mind a bit."

As Tootsie, Pen, Rose, and Bippy edged their guest toward the door, Beulah suddenly stopped. The foursome stopped just short of banging into her. "I know! I'll bring you some food since you're going to be staying a bit. You'll like my fried chicken. I don't mean to brag, but everybody does. Like it, that is. I'm more or less famous for my fried chicken, don't you know. They call me the Fried Chicken Queen of Jackson."

"Oh, no, please don't do that!" Tootsie said, a little too quickly. As Beulah turned to look at her, Tootsie went on hurriedly, "I mean, we're all on special diets, so it would not help to have something we couldn't eat. Too much temptation. Really. We'd just have to find someone to give it to. Thank you, though." She gave Beulah an appeasing smile and shrugged her shoulders as if in great disappointment.

"Special diets?" Beulah sounded unconvinced.

"Oh, yes, high cholesterol, high blood pressure, salt-free, gluten-free, food allergies, diabetes. You name it; we've got it. We shouldn't have broken over at the church lunch, but we did, and now we're all paying for it."

"How 'bout deviled eggs?"

Tootsie smiled politely, but she was firm. "No, really. Thank you, though."

"Well...." Beulah hesitated at the door. "You're sure now?"

"Positive. Thanks just the same," Rosemary said.

"Yes indeed, but thank you for thinking of us," Pen added.

"Well, you've got my number. You can call me if you change your mind," Beulah said as she stepped onto the porch.

After the door was closed, Rosemary motioned the Flower Girls into the kitchen, where they burst into laughter. "She wouldn't mind a bit going through Maggie's things," Rose said between guffaws. "Really she wouldn't."

"I'll just bet she wouldn't," said Tootsie as she took the grocery receipt with Beulah's number from Pen and dropped it in the trash. "I know her kind. She's hoping to get her hands on Maggie's clothes and jewelry. The old biddy!"

"Did you see how fast she left after you told her why we are staying?" asked Rose.

Tootsie nodded. "Yeah."

"What do you make of that?" Bippy asked.

Rosemary laughed. "She missed her calling. A busybody like that should have been in the journalism business. She couldn't wait to spread the news."

"What views?" asked Pen.

"The news, Pen," Bippy said. "She's a gossip."

"Oh, yes," Pen said, nodding her head. "That's exactly the impression I had of her, but wasn't that a nice dress and hat?"

Tootsie rolled her eyes. "I guess. If you like wearing lime jello."

"And that fried chicken and deviled eggs surely sounded good," Bippy said quietly.

Tootsie patted Bippy on the back. "I know, Bippy, but that was just her excuse to get back in this house and see what we are doing. The food might be good, but it wouldn't be worth it to have to put up with her again."

As soon as they wiped the tears of laughter from their eyes, the girls fanned out into the neighborhood, talking to neighbors, seeking information, hunches, ideas, anything. When they returned shortly before noon, they compared notes.

"No one I talked to picked up the papers," said Bippy. "Is anybody besides me hungry?"

Rose said, "The neighbors I talked to said there were never any left lying at the gate."

"That's the same thing I heard," said Tootsie.

"Me, too," said Pen.

"Tell you what," said Rosemary. "I'm going to run down to the newspaper office and see what I can find out. There's some reason a newspaper hasn't been delivered here since Maggie disappeared."

"Maybe she didn't have the paper delivered. Maybe she just bought one every day," Pen suggested.

"Well, I can find that out, too," Rose said. "They'll have a list of subscribers. I'd call, but if I go, I can show them my credentials as a journalist, and I think they'll open up their records to me. Be back soon. And, Bippy, I'll bring some lunch. How's that?"

While Rosemary was gone, Tootsie decided to check out Maggie's office. "Want to look through Maggie's office? See what we can find?" she asked Pen and Bippy.

The three walked out back to the neat little cottage that served as Maggie's real estate office, and Tootsie unlocked the door with the keys Clark and Ray had left and turned on the lights. When she saw Maggie's empty desk chair, a lump formed in Tootsie's throat. *Oh, Maggie, Maggie*, she sobbed silently, running her hands over the back of the chair. *How often you sat in this very chair to write to me!* She glanced at Bippy and Pen. Bippy was chewing on her lower lip, and Pen was wiping her eyes. After a few minutes, Tootsie took a deep breath. "This isn't helping Maggie any," she said.

"You're right," Bippy agreed.

Tootsie cleared her throat. "Well, let's see what we can turn up. While you two see what you can find on her desk—and in it—I'm going to try the computer," Tootsie said. Bippy and Pen started rummaging through the desk drawers and rifling through the stacks of papers on top, while Tootsie dropped into Maggie's chair, turned on the computer, and waited for it to boot up. Tootsie stared at the screen, which was adamantly demanding a password. She tried several, but each time, access was denied. "Shoot!" she yelled in frustration.

"What's the matter, dear?" Pen asked.

"I can't get the right password. Not long ago, she emailed me a guide to choosing a secure password. I remember that the article, which she probably followed, said it should be at least six digits, and it should probably have some capitals and some numbers for security. I remember that she said she thought a four-letter word was enough if you added some numbers and capitals to make it harder to crack but not too hard to remember. We've got to think of a four-letter word that had some significance to Maggie and some numbers or capitals also with significance. I've tried 'Duke' for our alma mater plus the year we graduated, 'real' for real estate plus the initials MP and the number in her family. I even tried 'aspca+St. FranAAC' short for A.S.P.C.A. and the Saint Francis Animal Adoption Center plus all the variations of those three I could think of. Nothing works."

"What about 'camP63' for Cam Palmer and the year they married?" Pen suggested.

Tootsie's fingers flew as they clicked in the four letters and date. Nothing.

Suddenly, Bippy almost screamed. "Look! Here's her appointment book," she said, clutching a small black notebook that was hidden between stacks of real estate listings.

Tootsie smiled. "Good! I knew it had to be here somewhere. While you two see what you can learn from it, I'm going to keep trying to crack this password."

Bippy and Pen pulled up two chairs, lined up neatly along the wall to accommodate real estate clients, and started going through the small handwritten entries in the book. Suddenly, Pen caught her breath. "Look at this," she exclaimed. "Here's an entry for October 9. The last day I heard from her was October 8. What about you all?"

"Same here," Tootsie and Bippy agreed. Tootsie turned in her chair to face them. "What's it say?" she asked.

"She has written on that date: 'Picnic, weather permitting. G. D.'"

"G.D. Gordon Dawkins?" asked Bippy.

"Seems like the most reasonable explanation to me," said Tootsie.

"How very interesting," Bippy said, pushing the little glasses back into their natural saddle on her nose, "that she schedules a picnic with her would-be husband on October 9, and no one ever hears from her again."

"I agree," said Pen, "very peculiar."

"It seems likely that she would have emailed us all after she returned," mused Tootsie, fingering the edge of the notebook. "She'd have wanted to share the latest news with us."

"What I want to know," said Bippy, "is why the police are so sure Maggie's death was accidental. Why won't they even pursue a lead or check out this Gordon Dawkins? Seems fishy to me."

"Did you say they'd gone fishing?" asked Pen.

Bippy laughed. "No. I said it sounds fishy."

"Decidedly," added Tootsie.

Chapter Twenty-Nine

"Y'all! Y'all!" Rosemary shouted. "Guess what!" When there was no answer, she set a bag of sandwiches and drinks on the kitchen counter, walked straight through the kitchen, out the back door, and into the little office with small yellow mums in the window boxes. Bippy, Pen, and Tootsie turned to look at her. "I brought lunch, by the way. Veggie subs from Subway. They're in the kitchen. Now, here's the news: Maggie *did* get home delivery of the paper, and someone *did* discontinue it on October 9th. How 'bout them apples?"

"What did you say about apples?" asked Pen, her hand cupped around her ear.

Rosemary spoke more slowly. "I said that Maggie's paper was discontinued on October 9th."

"Oh, I thought you said something about apples."

"But if her brothers didn't cancel it, and her neighbors didn't," puzzled Tootsie, "who did?"

"Exactly!" said Rosemary.

"Maggie herself?" asked Pen. "Maybe she planned to go somewhere."

"She would have told us," Tootsie said.

Bippy almost shuddered with anticipation. "This is getting more interesting all the time."

"It reminds me of *Headlines of Horror*. Did you ever read that one, Bippy?" asked Pen.

"Was that the one where the victim's paper was stopped so no one would find her body?"

"That's the one."

"Yes, I did read that, and you may have something there, Pen."

"Okay, girls," said Rosemary, "here's what I think we should do."

"Eat lunch," suggested Bippy, as they all laughed.

It was decided that the first order of business—after eating—was to check back papers for weather reports at the time of the scheduled picnic, to see whether the weather was suitable for picnicking and especially sailing. "Pen and I will go to the branch library and check," Bippy said.

"Here are the car keys," said Rosemary.

"Nonsense, my dear. It's only about a mile or mile and a half. I saw it as we drove in. It'll be a nice walk. I, for one, have missed my exercise."

"Me, too," said Pen. "I'm used to walking three miles a day, rain or shine. Helps me keep my girlish figure," she said with a grin, patting both of her ample hips.

"Okay, if you're sure. While you all are doing that, Tootsie and I will be calling all the hotels and motels in the area to see whether anybody by the name of Gordon Dawkins was a guest there during this time," said Rosemary. "Tootsie, you want to use this phone out here, and I'll use the one in the kitchen. They're two separate lines, I noticed."

***

"Well?" Rosemary asked as Bippy and Pen returned from the library late in the afternoon, their cheeks pink from the wind. "Any luck?"

"I'll say," Bippy answered, her magnified dark eyes peering out from her glasses like two black mollies in a fishbowl. "We checked all the papers since the day we last heard from Maggie, and guess what? It has rained only one day, October 11th, which was three days after we last heard from her. It's starting to rain now, by the way."

"And the weather on October 9th was perfect for picnicking, with clear skies and temperature in the low 70s."

"So we can assume the date with Gordon took place," said Tootsie.

"Maybe for picnicking, but not for sailing," added Bippy. "It was not a good day for sailing at all. The paper reported high winds on October 8th and 9th, gusting up to 30 miles per hour."

"Maggie would never have gone sailing in such wind," Tootsie observed.

"Speaking of wind, it's getting pretty brisk out there right now," Bippy said. They listened as the wind rattled the windows.

"Yeah, I think we're getting ready for a storm," Tootsie said, looking out the window at the darkening sky.

Rose smiled. "Memaw—that's what I call my grandmother—has always said, 'It's comin' a cloud.' It's a West Virginia-ism, I guess. I've always thought that was such a quaint way to describe a storm."

Pen shook off her jacket. "The reason it took us so long at the library is that we made copies of all the newspaper accounts of Maggie's disappearance...and...of the discovery...uh, of her body. Also, the obituary. Here." She handed half of the pages to Rosemary and the other half to Tootsie, who immediately bent their heads and began reading. "What about you all? Did you have any luck finding Gordon?" she asked.

Rose and Tootsie looked up from their reading and shook their heads. "No," Tootsie said, "I'm afraid not. We called every Holiday Inn, Hilton, Marriott, Radisson, Howard Johnson, Hampton Inn, Red

Roof Inn, Clarion, and Quality Inn listed in the phone book. None of them has or has had in the past month a guest by the name of Gordon Dawkins. Of course, there are still more—second or third-tier local motels, I guess you'd call them—to reach, but we came up empty on all the national chains. And, of course, he could have stayed here—in one of Maggie's guest rooms."

"But not at first. Not when he came to Jackson on business before he even met Maggie. I mean, he had to stay somewhere."

"It took some doing to get that information, though," Rose said. "Lack of information, I should say. The first one I called seemed hesitant to give out information about their guests until I said that I was supposed to have met my college sweetheart, whom I hadn't seen for fifteen years, for a reunion and couldn't remember at which hotel he had said he would be staying. I said that he was supposed to be in town by October 8th, and yet I never heard from him. When he didn't show, I was afraid something had happened to him and wondered if they would mind checking for me to see if he had been there within the last couple of weeks. At least that way I would know if he just didn't want to contact me—and here I sighed heavily—and would move on. After that, it was easy. I used it every time. Everyone was very helpful."

"All the world loves a lover," Bippy said dreamily.

"Now what?" asked Pen.

"Well, he was here at least a week ago," said Rosemary. "I mean, we know that on October 9th Maggie planned to be with him, don't we?"

"Since he was in her appointment book, I think we can safely assume that," Tootsie said.

"Well then, where do we go from here?" Bippy asked. She thoughtfully stroked the mole on her chin like a gypsy rubbing a crystal ball.

"Let's sleep on it and start fresh in the morning, what do you say?" said Tootsie.

"Good idea," said Bippy. "Maybe we'll have a new perspective in the morning. Now, where shall we go for dinner? I noticed a darling little restaurant yesterday as we were driving. It has the cutest name: Guys and Dolls. It advertises great cheesecake, and I just love cheesecake. I've missed my trips to O'Carrs. I jotted down the address so we could be sure to find it."

When, following the directions she entered into her cell phone's GPS, Rosemary pulled the car into the parking lot off South Venture Street, and the headlights of the car illuminated the white brick wall before them, there was an audible gasp. Black silhouette cutouts of unclad recumbent, nubile young women, their backs arched in painful contortions to thrust their generous breasts all the farther northward, adorned the side of the building. On the roof, sure enough, was a sign that read: Guys and Dolls. On the marquee in front, also sure enough, were the words that had so fascinated Bippy: Jackson's Best Cheesecake. No one said anything as the windshield wipers rhythmically whack-whacked, blurring and clearing the amazing scene before them.

Finally, Rosemary broke the silence. "Uh, Bippy dear, I don't think this is the kind of cheesecake you would like."

Bippy, unable to speak for looking at the pointy breasts and slim hips of the figures on the wall, could muster only two words as she slowly shook her head: "Dear Gussie!"

Seeing Bippy's little chin quiver, Tootsie suddenly said, "Well, I don't know about you all, but I've always been curious to see what one of these places is like. I say we give it a try."

"You're not serious," Rosemary said.

"Why not? It's pouring rain, we're hungry, and they do serve food. If we don't eat here, we'll have to look for another place in the rain and the dark."

"But..." Pen started, and then the unusual mood that had seized her at T. J. Maxx, a damn-the-torpedoes-full-steam-ahead mood, settled on her soul again. "Why ever not?" she said, suddenly.

As the four figures, clad in yellow rain slickers purchased at a Target on the way, burst in at the door, the manager, a massive, barrel-chested bullet of a man in a T shirt with the name tag "Buster," intercepted them. "Whoa, ladies! Where y'all think you're goin'?" His heavily tattooed arms were thrust out from his sides, and his shirt and pants didn't quite meet in front, revealing a prodigious belly.

"I beg your pardon," Pen said, lifting her hands to her ears.

Grinning, Buster rubbed the earring in his left ear and said, "This is a...a—"

"Yes?" Tootsie said. She was eager to hear how he defined this particular establishment.

Bippy hung back, muttering to herself about wishing she'd never gotten them into this, while Rosemary consolingly patted her arm.

Finally, after mulling several descriptions over in his mind, Buster had it. His shoulders relaxed a bit. "This is an entertainment place," he said. "You know, *adult* entertainment." He winked broadly.

"Well, guess what, Buster? We're adults," countered Tootsie. She winked back.

"Yeah, but—"

"But what?"

"Y'all can't come in here."

"You do serve food?"

"Well, yeah, but—"

Turning to the other Flower Girls, Tootsie said, "What about that table over there in the corner, girls? Does that suit everybody?"

"Listen, lady—"

Tootsie's eyes flashed, and her voice lost all of its excitement, but none of its edge. She was clearly on a quest now. She spoke very deliberately, as if speaking to the village idiot, and her words were etched in ice. "Am I to understand you are refusing to serve us food? On what grounds? Would you like to call the police to have us put out? If so, do it because we're *not* leaving!"

At the word 'police,' Buster colored and, sputtering, motioned them toward the table. "Okay. Okay. Look, take it easy. Suit yourselves. I'se just tryin' to look out for y'alls' feelin's, you know? Geez!" Making fists as he led them to the table, he flexed the muscles of his arms, causing the naked lady on his right biceps to wiggle and squirm. Bippy and Pen averted their eyes. Tootsie quickened her step and strained to see.

While the girls sat at the table waiting to be served the four hamburgers—Buster Burgers, the menu said—they had ordered, Rosemary motioned with her eyes toward the opposite corner. Through the smoky semi-darkness, they could make out several male patrons at another table. The "entertainment" was draped all over them in the form of a straw-haired blonde with long legs and an exaggerated bust. Her red blouse was midriff, being tied in front as if she had stopped by here briefly on her way to a hayride somewhere. Her trim little behind was barely concealed by a short, black leather skirt, which had hiked up to reveal the curve of her buttocks when she leaned over one of the men to stroke the face of another. As she did so, a third man reached over and ran his hand up and down the back of her thigh, going higher each time.

"Oh, dear Gussie," whispered Bippy, adjusting her glasses. "I wish you'd look."

"Don't worry, we are," said Rose.

"Why do I feel as if I'm saying the blessing in a bus station in a Norman Rockwell painting?" said Pen.

They began giggling then and couldn't stop. Finally, their laughter, which they had tried to squelch, erupted and filled their side of the room.

"Somethin' funny over there?" one of the men asked roughly.

"Actually, yes," Tootsie said. "We're laughing about incongruity."

"Huh?"

"About our being here, you know?"

He mumbled something, which the girls couldn't hear, and turned back to take a gulp from his beer bottle. Slamming the bottle down, he reached for the blonde again, but the spell was clearly broken. After rising from the man's lap on which she had been sitting, she sidled off provocatively, casting a pouty look over her shoulder at the women clustered on the other side of the room.

"Aww, I don't think she likes us," Bippy said.

"Silicon Sal, you mean? Actually, I think this is where we're supposed to discover that she really has a heart of gold and take her home with us. Put her in the church choir or something," Tootsie said through giggles.

When their order came, Pen said, "Shall we have a silent blessing?" Her face, dutifully dusted with white powder before she left home, was even chalkier than usual. She fiddled with the cameo pin at her neck and then raised one hand to arrange her hair, hair that wasn't going anywhere. It was already securely anchored under a net.

Tootsie said, "Why not? We may as well live up to that Norman Rockwell painting."

After finishing their hamburgers and fries, which were, they agreed, surprisingly tasty, the ladies left a generous tip, paid their bill, and left the table. Tootsie sidled up to Buster as they headed for the door and said, "Thanks, Big Guy. It was—fun." She left him chewing on his mustache. Once in the car again, they dissolved into laughter.

"Did…you…see…Buster's… expression"—Rose gasped for breath—"when… Tootsie …said…to…call…the…police?"

"Yes!" said Bippy, "and when we said the blessing, I peeked, and—you're not going to believe this—he had his head bowed."

"Either that, or he was trying to get a better look at his tattoos!" said Tootsie.

Pen wiped her eyes. "Dear Gussie—Oh, Bippy, now you've got me saying it—I haven't had so much fun in years."

"Maggie would have loved it," Tootsie said. "Just loved it."

***

Tootsie tossed and turned, unable to drift into the deep sleep she so much needed. The near-miss they had in the car after leaving Guys and Dolls had excited them all. "Why, that fool almost hit us," Pen had said in a moment of unusual anger. It was true enough. They had been driving slowly through the rain on the long, deserted road that led to the area where Maggie's house was located, when all of a sudden, out of nowhere a car came flying right up behind them and pulled ahead, cutting directly in front of them. "Dear Gussie!" Bippy yelled, as they swerved and ran off the road. Even though she was buckled in, she was thrown against the door and bruised her head, but other than that, no one was hurt. The other car didn't stop. After putting rocks under the rear wheels for traction in the mud, they had gotten back on the road and had driven quite cautiously the rest of the way.

They all talked quite a bit after returning home about their near miss on the road. "It was almost as if he was trying to hit us," Tootsie said.

"Trying to scare us, you think?" asked Rose.

"Who?"

"I don't know. Maybe someone who didn't like the ad we placed and followed us from home and waited outside Guys and Dolls until we left and it was totally dark. Or could the mysterious Gordon Dawkins have finally appeared and decided we needed to leave before we found out something?"

"Should we mention it to Lt. Ferguson?" Bippy asked.

"Uh, no," Tootsie said. "I don't think so, at least not now. We have no proof, and it would just give him more ammunition for shooing us home."

Their talk eventually turned to the adventure at Guys and Dolls, mentioning how much Maggie would have hooted at their escapade, all of them reminiscing about her love of a good time. In talking and remembering so many forgotten capers that she and Maggie had been involved in together, Tootsie had become agitated again over the whole question of Maggie's disappearance and death. After they had all had showers and turned in, Tootsie found herself staring at the ceiling, reliving many of her escapades with Maggie as well as the night's adventures. No matter how hard she tried to relax, she kept seeing that car cutting right in front of them.

Finally, she turned on the light by her bed and rummaged through a book shelf for something to read. A family photo album caught her eye, and she took it back to bed with her, plumping up her pillows as she did so. As she turned the pages of Maggie's childhood, she read with a smile the captions Maggie had carefully put under each photo. Suddenly, she zeroed in on a picture of Maggie's parents. They were much younger in the picture than when Tootsie met them for the first time when they came to Duke to visit Maggie, but she recognized them instantly. Under the picture were the words from Anthony Trollope's

Doctor Thorne: "He argued that the principal duty which a parent owed to a child was to make him happy." Beneath that quote were these words in Maggie's distinctive handwriting: "Doll and Doc—they did just that!"

Doll, Tootsie thought. *I'd forgotten Maggie called her mother that. Doll.* She tossed the album on the bedside table, and turned off the light once more. A rumble in her stomach told her that she was hungry. *Wish I had some peanut butter and crackers*, she thought. The jar in her purse was empty, but there was one downstairs in Maggie's pantry. She'd already checked. Oh well. She tried to get her mind off her hunger by thinking about her need to access Maggie's computer tomorrow. There might be something in Maggie's computer files or in her email, both sent and received, which would give them a clue about her death.

She must find that password. What could it be? Maggie's brothers' names, even in their diminutive form, wouldn't fit the four-letter format that Maggie had mentioned and still allow for numbers. Neither would her parents' names, Laura and C. R. What about.... Wait a minute! Suddenly, she sat straight up in bed. What about "Doll"? Could that be it? It was a four-letter word that Maggie could well assume nobody but her most intimate friends would remember. With the right combination of numbers, it just might be the password! After tossing and turning a few more minutes, she gave up sleep as a lost cause and made a decision.

Nudging her feet into the slippers by the nightstand and grabbing her bright coral silk robe, she slipped quietly down the long staircase, hugging the banister as she went, and, without turning on a light, groped her way into the kitchen. She didn't want to wake up the whole house just because she couldn't sleep. The soft whoosh of the swinging door behind her billowed her robe. She felt her way along the counter until she came to the silverware drawer. Gently guiding it open, she felt for a knife. Next, to find the pantry, she inched her way along until she felt the doorknob. She opened it, went in, closed the door softly behind her, and then turned on the light. After spreading several crackers with peanut butter and putting them on a paper plate, which she found with some other picnic supplies on one of the shelves, she turned off the light, and started for the back door.

Removing the office key from a hook by the back door, she took the night latch off the kitchen door so she could get back in and walked quickly through the cool night air toward the little cottage. Lucky thing the rain had stopped, she thought, trying to avoid the puddles illuminated by the mercury vapor light suspended on a tall pole by the garage. Just as she was fumbling the key into the lock, the door pushed open under her touch. That was funny. She didn't remember leaving it unlocked, much less ajar. Hmm. They must not have pulled it all the way shut. Oh well. Now to try out her hunch. She couldn't wait to see if "Doll" was the password. Her curiosity was killing her. Just then, she caught sight of movement in the shadows of the office, but it was too late to dodge. Suddenly, a dark figure loomed over her, banged her head against the door sill, and threw her roughly to the floor. The last thing she thought, as she hit her head and passed into unconsciousness, was *my curiosity is...really...really...killing ...me.*

Chapter Thirty

Bippy lay awake for a long time, twisting and turning, but failing to slip into the arms of the god Somnus. The thought of that awful place where she had steered the girls for dinner made her face burn in the dark. She couldn't let go of it. How embarrassing! How humiliating! They were good sports about it, all right, especially Tootsie, but Bippy would be a long time getting over her idiocy. She rose up on one elbow and plumped her pillow. *And I thought it would be like O'Carr's. How could I have been so mistaken?* she asked herself over and over. *I guess I'm just a naive, silly old fool.* And then there was that awful driver who nearly hit them on the way back from Guys and Dolls. Had someone followed them from the time they left home and waited until they left the restaurant to run them off the road? That was a scary thought.

Thoughts of O'Carr's summoned up the vision of her huge old home on Main Street and her happy life in Birmingham, and Bippy was suddenly struck with a strange feeling. At first she thought it was homesickness, but suddenly she was filled with what she realized with a start was dread. She sat up to sort this out. As much as she loved her friends on campus and her treks to visit with the patrons at O'Carr's, the thought of going back to that rather solitary existence after the camaraderie she was enjoying with the other Flower Girls made her sad. It hadn't been the same since Brother and Sister had died. No, not the same at all. Oh, yes, she had friends—loads of them—but she still went home alone after each outing, still ate breakfast alone, still sat and read in the quiet old house, alone.

Well, there was no use worrying about that now, she decided, and turned instead to trying to figure things out about Maggie's death. Were she and the other Flower Girls being overly suspicious? Had they all gotten caught up in a type of group hysteria, as that Lt. Ferguson suggested? Had Maggie's death really been an accident, after all? *Oh dear, I wish I knew.* She straightened her gown, which had gotten twisted around her small body, and lay back down to finish sorting things out.

Now, let's see. Where was I? Oh yes, Lt. Ferguson seemed determined that Maggie died accidentally. He seemed particularly adamant about that. Maybe he knew what he was talking about. After all, he has been at this longer than any of us. She lay very still for a few minutes, willing herself to relax. Tomorrow, she would suggest to the other girls that they re-examine what had caused them to be so sure Maggie's death was murder. Right now, she couldn't quite remember. Was it just that she went sailing without a life vest on a windy day? People do tend to be careless at times, she thought. In fact, she had remembered reading one time that it's usually good swimmers who drown. They get overconfident and become reckless. Wait. They had already discussed that with the nice police lieutenant. *Oh, I need to get some sleep*, she admonished herself.

But nagging thoughts wouldn't let her sleep. Why had Gordon Dawkins so completely disappeared? If he was as devoted to Maggie as she said—if, in fact, he was planning to marry her—wouldn't he have been very visible at her funeral? Wouldn't he have made some contact with Maggie's brothers? They didn't even know he existed. Wouldn't he have gone to the police with his concerns? Maybe he didn't have any, Bippy conceded. Maybe he was behind whatever happened to Maggie.

And her brothers. Why had they behaved so strangely at the lawyer's office? Oh dear, this was just impossible. She had to get some rest, but she couldn't clear her mind long enough to fall asleep. Maybe a cup of warm milk would help. There might even be some Ovaltine in Maggie's cupboard. She had always loved Ovaltine at bedtime. Snapping on the bedside lamp, she pulled on her knitted bed socks, wrapped herself in a warm fleece robe, and headed quietly down the stairs.

In the kitchen, Bippy picked a dainty shell pink flowered cup and saucer from the cabinet. Afraid to put such a delicate cup in the microwave, she warmed some milk and Ovaltine to the scalding point in a saucepan, poured it into the pink cup, and took the pan to the kitchen sink to run cold water in it. As she looked out the window, glancing first at the nimbus around the mercury vapor light and then at the puddles in the yard, to see if the rain had stopped, her eye fell on the door to Maggie's little office building. Were her eyes playing tricks on her? Was the door open? She was sure they hadn't left it open. And what was that dark form on the floor half in and half out of the doorway? Just a shadow?

Bippy set her cup and saucer down gently and went to the back door. She turned the door knob and noticed that the night latch had been taken off. That was strange. She knew they had locked all the doors before going to bed. Slowly, she eased the door open and peeped outside. As her eyes grew accustomed to the darkness, she blinked and looked again at the doorway ahead. In the dim glow, she could just make it out. *Oh, dear Gussie*! she breathed. It was a person! Gathering her robe about her, she ran quickly to the door of the office and knelt beside the body. Gently, she turned the woman over. She could hardly believe her eyes. It was Tootsie! Bippy stepped over the form sprawled across the door sill and dashed to the phone in the office. Her shaking fingers dialed 911, and she quickly gave the dispatcher all the information including the address. "I can't stay on the phone," she said to the voice on the other end of the line. "I have to go back and check on her. I don't even know whether she's...alive or not. I just ran straight to call you."

"Ma'am, please stay on the line. Ma'am?"

Dropping the phone on the desk, Bippy heard the voice urging her back to resume conversation about the accident victim, but she ran instead to Tootsie's side. "Tootsie! Tootsie! Oh, please hear me. Please answer me," she sobbed, patting Tootsie's hand.

For the first few seconds that Bippy rubbed Tootsie's hand and cried for her to awake, there was no response. Then, suddenly a groaning and slight stirring caused Bippy's heart to flutter. She was alive! Bippy breathed a silent prayer of thanksgiving and continued to chaff Tootsie's hand. "Tootsie," she called. "Tootsie, can you hear me?"

"Bippy?" The voice was groggy and uncertain. "Is that you?"

"Yes, oh, Tootsie! Thank God you're okay. Don't move. Lie still. Help is on the way." She ran back to the desk and filled in the dispatcher, who was still hanging on, with the latest on Tootsie's condition and was assured that help was indeed on the way.

***

"Well, that was some scare, wasn't it?" Bippy said on the ride home after Tootsie had been transported to the hospital emergency room by E.M.T., examined, observed, and discharged with headache medication in hand. "One I wouldn't like to have every night."

"Be honest, now, Bippy," Tootsie teased. "You loved it. It was like one of your mystery novels in action." Laughing, she reached over and patted Bippy's hand.

"Tootsie! How can you say such a thing?" Bippy said, and then she, too, broke into nervous laughter, following the release of tension.

"The most unnerving part of it all was that ride in the ambulance," Tootsie observed. "Honestly, it's a miracle we didn't have a wreck on the way. I'm glad our ride home with Rose as the driver is much more uneventful. That ambulance driver is a lunatic. Right, Bippy?"

"Oh, dear Gussie! I thought we were goners a couple of times."

"I started to do a little back-seat driving, but I decided I'd better keep quiet. Besides, even though by the time the medics arrived, I was feeling much better, my head really started throbbing when I sat up, and it hurt so much on the way to the hospital, I wasn't inclined to talk much. By the way, thanks, Bippy, for riding with me in the ambulance and helping me answer all the policemen's questions, and thank you, Rose and Pen, for following behind us and bringing us all home. Thank goodness Lt. Ferguson wasn't notified. This would give him just the ammunition he needs to tell us to stop meddling. I can hear him right now: 'Ladies, when are y'all gonna' accep' that Maggie Palmer's death was an acci-*dent*.' "

"Well, I hate to tell you, but he'll know about it by morning. You can take that to the bank," Rosemary said. "In spite of his down home accent, he impresses me as the type who doesn't miss much."

"Me, too," Tootsie said. "That's why I can't figure out why he is so reluctant to believe that Maggie's death was a homicide."

As Rosemary pulled into the driveway, the police were still there, going over everything with a fine-toothed comb. Her headlights fell on them and on one plainclothes detective in particular. "Uh, Tootsie, I think we can forget about the morning. Guess who's here?"

"Ms. Freeman," one officer, Cliff Manning, who had interviewed her briefly at the hospital, said, leaning in the car window, "could you tell me again what you were going to do in this office—an office that isn't yours—in the middle of the night?"

"Well, I—"

"Thanks, Cliff. I'll take over here. I know these ladies," Lt. Ferguson said, approaching the group. "Well, well, well. Hello again, ladies. My, my, don't we have a way of gettin' around now? You ladies do keep things interestin' for sure. How about we get out and go into the office and sit down? We're through takin' prints and pictures in there. The officers can finish writin' up their reports outside." His flushed face indicated an impatience simmering just below the surface like little bubbles around the edge of a sauce pan of fudge just before it comes to a rolling boil.

After they were all seated, he said, "Now, would y'all care to answer Officer Manning's question? What *were* y'all doin' out here in the middle of the night?" As Tootsie patiently explained that they were living in Maggie's house at the suggestion of her brothers and that she was going to attempt to use the computer to see whether she could fill in any of the missing pieces of the puzzle of Maggie's last days, Ferguson held up his hand to stop her. "Y'all just won't let that go, will ya'?"

Tootsie sat up a little straighter and shook her head. "No, quite simply, we won't."

Ferguson sighed, walked to the window, turned around, and paced back to the girls. After taking a deep breath, he said, "Is anythin' missin' from the office?"

"Missing?" they said together. Until that very moment, the thought hadn't occurred to any of them that this had been a bungled theft. They had all been so intent on the attack that they forgot why the attack had been carried out in the first place, assuming it was just an attempt to scare them off. "Well," Tootsie said, "As a matter of fact, I don't know." She had to admit grudgingly that Ferguson was a keener observer than they were. Maybe what they had seen as his hesitance to investigate was just thoroughness. Maybe.

"Would you check, please?" He spoke slowly, obviously controlling himself.

The Flower Girls fanned out in the office and checked the desk top, the drawers, and the filing cabinet. All at once, Tootsie frantically patted the papers on the desk. She and Rosemary looked at each other. "It's not here," she said simply. "Lt. Ferguson, Maggie's appointment book is gone. We were looking at it earlier, so I know that it was here."

After the officers had finished their reports and left, and Ferguson had given another lecture on the subject of civilian interference in police matters, the girls walked slowly back into the house and went upstairs to take off their hastily put on clothes and get into their gowns and robes once more. Tootsie took a shower and changed into a fresh gown she found in one of Maggie's drawers. In no time, Bippy had put on a pot of decaf coffee, and the girls were seated around the kitchen table sipping the hot brew and talking. "This is just like a pajama party," said Pen, her normally death-white cheeks flushed and pink.

Bippy smiled. "It is, isn't it, Pen?"

"See. I told you that you were having a good time," said Tootsie.

"Oh, Tootsie!" Bippy said with cheerful exasperation.

"Well," Tootsie said, "at least now we know that we're onto something. Why did someone want Maggie's appointment book? If her death had been accidental, there'd be no reason to break in and steal that. There was an expensive computer in there, but the only thing taken was her appointment book. Strange. Of course, the thief could have planned to take it, too, but was scared off after the ruckus with me."

"That's right, and I'll tell you what's been bothering me," said Pen at last. "I just have to go with the feeling I had when Maggie first wrote about her involvement with Gordon Dawkins. I don't trust a man who would ask his fiancée to hide the fact that they were getting married."

"Me either," said Rosemary. "That's been gnawing at me, too."

"Hmm?" said Pen.

"I said that had been gnawing on me."

"Yeah, I think it has on all of us," added Tootsie.

"All the more reason we should try to get any information from whatever sources we can about what was going on," said Pen.

"We need to try to figure some things out—like who would have wanted Maggie's appointment calendar?" suggested Rosemary. "Who didn't want us to know something?"

"Excellent question," Tootsie said.

"You think whoever did that murdered Maggie?" asked Bippy with a shudder.

Tootsie sighed. "I don't know. The murderer could have been anybody, I suppose: Gordon Dawkins is a prime candidate, but it could have been someone we don't even know. What about his ex-wife? You want a long shot? It could even have been Lt. Ferguson, for that matter. He could have removed the appointment book before we got back from the hospital."

"Why?" Rose asked. "Why in the world would he do that?"

Tootsie shrugged. "I don't know. To keep us from finding out something? I said it was a long shot. He just seems awfully eager for us to go away."

"Or Clark and Ray," said Pen. "Let's not forget about them. After all, they'd have had the most to gain from Maggie's death."

"But they are in Texas and Georgia now," Bippy said.

"How do we know that?" asked Tootsie. "I mean, for sure?"

***

"I think y'all probably know why I've called you in," Lt. Ferguson said to the Flower Girls the next morning after they were all seated in his office. "Ms. Freeman, Ms. Maas, Ms.—"

"Uh, Lieutenant? It would save time if you'd just refer to us as the Flower Girls," Tootsie interrupted. That's what we're calling ourselves."

Lt. Ferguson cleared his throat and continued. "As I was sayin', I think you probably know why I've called you in." No one replied, so he continued. "It's not to find out any more facts about the break-in. It's this," he said, rising and dramatically throwing the newspaper he was holding on the desk. Their eyes fell on the ad they had placed. It had been circled in red. "Did y'all place this ad?"

They nodded silently.

"Y'all have been busy little bees, haven't ya'? Just what in blue blazes do y'all think you're doin'? I can't believe this, 'specially after the scare y'all had last night." His face was beet red, and his fists opened and closed as he paced in front of them.

"Well, of course, we didn't do it in reaction to that. We placed that ad the day before the attack, Lieutenant," Tootsie said.

Ferguson was not appeased. "You know what I mean. I mean I especially can't believe—oh, you know what I mean. Look. This is not the wild frontier where vigilante justice takes over, ladies. Here in Miss'ippi we do things through the correct channels, and that means the police department investigates all homi—I mean, suspicious deaths."

"Wait! What? You started to call this a homicide."

"I corrected myself."

"By calling it a 'suspicious death.' So you do admit this is a suspicious death?" said Tootsie quickly. It was all she could do to suppress an "Ah-ha!"

"I'm not admittin' anythin' at all. I just want y'all—you Flower Girls, as you call yourselves—to lay off. Let the police do the work they're trained for."

"But, see, that's the problem, Lieutenant. The police do not admit there's anything to investigate," said Rosemary defiantly. "That's why we're frustrated. That's why we've taken it into our own hands."

"I want to tell y'all somethin', ladies: If and when I decide there is somethin' to investigate, I will do it and do it thoroughly, but I won't be badgered into wastin' valuable police time on women's intuition or a hunch."

Pen whispered to Bippy, "Did he say something about lunch? Isn't it a little early?"

Bippy patted Pen's hand. "No, dear. He said 'a hunch.'"

Rosemary said, "Lt. Ferguson, we are not trying to badger you, as you put it. All we're doing is just trying to get enough facts to present you with a reason for investigating."

Ferguson's pacing stopped, and he leaned threateningly toward Rosemary's face. "Listen. I'm warnin' y'all to let this go. Let Maggie Palmer rest in peace." He slammed his fist on the desk with such force that all four of the girls jumped, even Pen, who heard the noise all too well. If he was fudge at pre-boil stage last night, he was at full, rolling boil now. Hard ball stage.

"Maybe when you understand our thinking," said Rose, unintimidated by his theatrics, "you'll see why we ran that ad." As a reporter, especially when she investigated the fracking industry, she had been ignored, cursed, even pushed once or twice. This man didn't scare her. "We figure that there are a lot of people who, for one reason or another, don't feel comfortable coming to the police."

"Imagine that!" Tootsie said with wide-eyed innocence.

"People who might be able to shed some light on Maggie's death," continued Rosemary.

"Back off!" warned Ferguson. "I'm tellin' you, this course y'all are on could be dangerous." He took a deep breath. "Even deadly."

"Why," Bippy asked, "if Maggie's death was accidental, as you claim?"

"Because the people who will answer that ad are unscrupulous, cold-hearted, and vicious. Criminals who want to make a fast buck. They're the ones you'll be dealin' with, not some little shirt-and-tie pansy who wants to sit and sip tea with four little—" he took another deep breath and swallowed—"little ladies."

"I think what you were about to say," said Tootsie icily, "is 'four little *old* ladies.' Well, let me tell you something, Lieutenant. Some of us are not that much older, if any, than you are—Rose, in fact, is quite a bit younger—and, with the exception of Bippy, we are not especially little. Even if we were, that would in no way diminish our intelligence, interest, or commitment. Rest assured that we consider ourselves properly warned, but we are *not*—repeat *not*—leaving here until we are satisfied that everything possible is known about the way our friend died. It will take a heck of a lot more than a bump on the head or an angry diatribe by a local policeman to chase us off." With that, she picked up the beaded and tasseled purse by her side, a purse that looked like a Native American saddlebag, and, with all the deliberate bravery of her distant Choctaw ancestors, flounced from the room, followed silently, but defiantly, by the other three.

Chapter Thirty-One

Tootsie still had a mild headache as she typed in the four letters for the password as fast as she could: D-o-l-l. But what could go with it? Maybe her father's name, too? That would be more than the four digits Maggie had said she was capable of remembering, but she wouldn't have trouble remembering both of her parents' nicknames. What did Maggie call her beloved father? It was "Daddy" sometimes, but not always. She had a pet name for him that she used with Doll. What was it? It seemed to go with Doll. Doll and what? Doll and what? What was it Maggie had called Dr. Muldoon? All of a sudden, she remembered meeting Maggie's parents for the first time when they came to Duke for parents' weekend. "These are my folks, Dr. and Mrs. Muldoon," she had said proudly to Tootsie. "You can call them anything you want, but I love to call them Doll and Doc, so you can do that, too, if you like." Tootsie had never felt comfortable doing that and soon forgot about the nicknames, but she remembered them now. That had to be it! Now if she could only think of a number. What about the number of members of the Muldoon family? Eagerly, she typed in Doll&Doc5. Immediately, like a sleeping genie, the screen blinked and opened up to await the next command.

"Eureka!" she called at the top of her voice. "That's it!" Pausing to scribble down the password so she wouldn't forget it and take a bite of the peanut butter crackers and a sip of fragrant Earl Grey tea, which she had taken out to the office with her, Tootsie began the tedious process of checking all of Maggie's email and files. "Well, here goes nothing," she breathed as she started scrolling down the list of files. Hours later, after turning up only lots of real estate quotations, many email letters, descriptions of properties, and some research on a chemical company by the name of Rexco, she began to despair of finding anything helpful. She kept reading.

"How's it going?" Rosemary asked as all the Flower Girls trooped out to the office and stood around the desk like a group of superannuated cheerleaders.

"Not good," Tootsie replied. "Not good at all. I can't find anything." Rosemary sighed. "Nothing?"

"Oh, her letters to us are all here, all right, under sent mail; apparently, her computer was set to store them indefinitely, but they shed no new light. In her files, she has lots of entries—you know how much she liked keeping a journal—detailing her concern about the environment, toxic waste, the ozone layer, and especially her animal center. She was really protective of that land, but she makes a vague reference to selling a portion of it. It seems she owned acres and acres of the land adjoining the preserve set aside for her animals and had very strong feelings about parting with any of it. I have only plowed through about half of her journal entries, but the words are starting to run together. I'll finish it later. Her entries are beautiful prose concerning things about which she felt deeply. The only file that doesn't quite make sense—that seems a tad out of place—is this one of statistics about Rexco Chemical Company. Does that ring a bell with anyone?"

The girls shook their heads. "Never heard of it," Bippy said. "What does Maggie say about it?"

"Oh, nothing, really. She has just saved to file a report by the president of Rexco that she apparently got from the Internet."

"What's the report say?"

"I haven't finished reading the whole thing. I just started skimming it and got bored. Didn't seem important. You know, it was the traditional pep talk to the shareholders. Earnings this quarter up or down, I can't remember which right now, but the usual rah-rah, everything-is-going-to-be-all-right talk you'd expect from the president of a company to the troops. I'll read it all later. I was just thinking...."

"What?" asked Rose.

"That maybe we should run another ad in the paper."

"Another ad? About what?" asked Bippy.

Tootsie smiled. "Oh, about a certain tract of land for sale adjacent to the animal adoption center."

***

"Why don't we take in a movie?" suggested Bippy the next day after the take-out containers and dinner dishes had been cleared from the table. They had all used the computer to email their friends and relatives to notify them that they were staying on in Mississippi a while longer, and they were now feeling a bit restless. It had been twelve hours since their ad, seeking information about a "tract of land adjacent to the St. Francis Animal Adoption Center, owned by Margaret Muldoon Palmer," had appeared in the paper. So far, there had been no calls, no emails, and, of course, it was too soon for letters. "It will get our minds off things, and maybe we could stop in at the Double Dip afterwards for a bit of something sweet. I noticed it the other day."

"Can you guarantee that this is going to be as much fun as Guys and Dolls, Bippy?" Pen asked.

Bippy blushed and laughed. "Dear Gussie, wasn't that place awful?"

"Actually, it's a good idea," said Tootsie, who was popping a bit of peanut butter into her mouth as a meal chaser. "Right after we clean up the kitchen."

"No, you all go on," Rosemary said. "I need to stay here and do some work on the article I'm supposed to be writing about Maggie for the *Gazette*, remember? I'll even clean up the kitchen. Go on, now. You won't get an offer like that every day. Scat."

***

After the girls left, Rosemary cleaned up the kitchen, thinking as she did so about all that had happened since she left Charleston. Charleston. That seemed so long ago and so far away. She pictured the beautiful view of the winding Kanawha River stretched in front of the state capitol like a long piece of satin ribbon, the gold dome of the capitol building itself gleaming in the morning sun, the dark mountains rising all around like protective arms. She thought about her children, her mother and grandmother, her job, her friends, her cozy life, and, suddenly, out of nowhere, she thought about Clyde Wexler. *Where did he come from?* she wondered. She hadn't thought about him in days. Yet, when she was alone, there he was, his smiling face, his kind touch, his rich voice. Rosemary didn't know how she felt about him. Maybe she just didn't want to deal with how she felt about him. She brushed that thought out of her mind. Now was not the time to make her life any more complicated. Maybe one of these days...

She had come so far from those days in Gauley Bridge that it was dizzying to look back. Momma and Memaw were getting older now, and Rosemary was glad that living in Charleston meant she was only about an hour away from them. She smiled as she thought of them happily ensconced in a new house that Rosemary was paying for. They had protested fiercely when she proposed moving them farther back from the river, but Rosemary had insisted. It's for my peace of mind, she had told them, and, in truth, it had given her the most pleasure of anything in life.

They had been in their previous little house for over forty years, and it was a warm and sheltering home to them, but periodically, when the river went on a rampage, they had to evacuate and watch as Memaw's well-tended and much-loved garden was swept away. Now, in the tight little three-bedroom brick house on the hill, they looked down on the spot where the New and Gauley Rivers formed the Kanawha River from a safer vantage point. Memaw had a vegetable garden out back and a flower garden in the front. She was happy as long as she could dig in the soil, and though her joints ached after all her bending and kneeling among the rows of onions, tomatoes, and snap beans, gardening was what kept her going.

Momma, retired now from cleaning the funeral home and other businesses, was a reader, had always been a reader at heart, though all the years she was working, she never seemed to have the time to bask in a sunny spot with a book. Rosemary knew that her mother read when she could, though, for she always had a book by her bed. Momma sat now for long hours and absorbed everything from the works of Shakespeare and Milton to James Weldon Johnson and Toni Morrison. Her favorite piece of reading, hands down, though, was the editorial page of the *Charleston Gazette*.

Rosemary wiped her hands and pumped some rich, yellow lotion on them from the dispenser on the counter. She imagined Maggie standing here doing the same thing, and the thought suddenly saddened her. She felt sorry for Maggie. Felt sorry for her in spite of her goodness, her wealth, her friends. Felt sorry that Maggie had been widowed in middle age and had no children to enrich her life as she grew older. What a blessing children would have been for her! And for them! The thought of her own children made Rosemary smile. Anthony, bespectacled, impressively intelligent, his ebullient spirit constantly in the "on" position and Dorothy, introspective, shy, her sympathetic nature making her a natural to be a veterinarian, were the joys of her life. Their father had dropped out of sight when he and Rosemary divorced, and they had heard nothing from him since then. *His loss,* Rosemary sighed to herself.

She went into the dining room and settled into a chair at the table, spreading her legal pad out before her. With the other girls gone, the house was finally quiet, as quiet as an old house can be. It creaked and moaned like an arthritic old lady getting up from being seated too long in one position. *I know how you feel,* Rosemary thought, unbending her legs, which she had tucked up under her while she wrote. Although she was only forty-six, Rosemary felt the twinge of stiffness as she unkinked her legs. She had often winced when her mother and grandmother had waddled, stiff-legged across the room after getting up from a chair, but Memaw would always make her laugh by quacking like a duck. Rose, too, had occasional mornings of inflexibility, particularly in her ankle joints. Probably the beginnings of arthritis, the doctor had told her, giving her renewed motivation for her swimming. She stood now and stretched, holding her arms high over her head. Suddenly, she thought she saw something at the window out of the corner of her eye, but when she turned her head, there was nothing there. *Boy, is my imagination fired up! Good for my writing, I suppose.*

She was still standing, still stretching, when the lights went out.

Chapter Thirty-Two

Rosemary glanced out the window at the inky sky. Probably getting ready to storm again, she decided. She had thought she heard a slight rumble of thunder a little bit ago. Maybe the lightning had already struck a transformer somewhere. That happened, on occasion, she knew, sometimes well in advance of the actual rain. She had read that if there was thunder, lightning was likely present, whether it was visible or not. Still, she wasn't absolutely sure the noise she had heard was thunder, so she decided to check all the doors just to be sure. Her hands felt the widow's lock on the front door and then dropped to the deadbolt. All secure. As soon as she felt the deadbolt, her mind immediately leaped to the kitchen. The deadbolt on the back door! She remembered that when the girls had left, she had not followed them and locked the door behind them. The kitchen door was locked only with the night latch, which was not, she knew, all that secure. Tales of thieves easily opening such locks with credit cards flashed in her mind, and she turned, grasping the backs of chairs, and felt her way into the kitchen. *This is silly*, she told herself all the way. *It's really, really sil*—Her words died on her tongue.

Through the window in the back door, she saw a large, dark figure sliding something in-between the door and the sill. As she watched, frozen with fear, she heard the faint click of the doorknob. Whoever it was had opened the door! She felt as if her feet were nailed to the floor, but she knew she couldn't stay there. She had to move—had to—but she had to do it quietly. Whatever she did, she must not attract the intruder's attention. Her legs, though as limp as two strands of cooked spaghetti, carried her quietly back, back toward the dining room door. Her hands groped behind her for the swinging door, for she dared not take her eyes off the shadowy figure. Scarcely breathing, she was thankful she had on her black turtleneck and black and green plaid pants and hoped she blended in with the darkness well enough for camouflage. Just as her fingers found the door, the figure, his eyes now used to the dark, apparently spotted her and lunged.

Rose ducked through the door, swung it hard behind her, and heard the satisfying grunt when the man struck his head against the door. The thud and his cry of pain told her that she had hit him solidly. The fight-or-flight syndrome never reared its head. Fighting was not even a consideration; flight was her only thought, her only chance. Instinct took over as he fell, and she ran. She tore towards the front of the house, bumping into chairs as she went. She lost her balance and teetered for a minute, but she righted herself and kept going. She could not fall. She kept going, racing, stumbling towards the door, but as she did so, she knew she would never be able to unlock all those locks on the front door and get out in time. In a split second, she thought of the irony that while those locks may have kept intruders out, they also kept the victims in. As soon as the man got up, he would be right after her. No time for locks.

There was also no time to stop and consider her options. She had to do something to save herself. And do it immediately. In a split second, she realized the time it would take to get out the door was time she didn't have. Instead, turning towards the steps, she grabbed the banister, took the steps two at a time, and dashed into Tootsie's bedroom, which was the first room on the left. She couldn't outrun him, nor, judging from his size, could she best him in a confrontation. Her only hope was outthinking him. She hoped that he would assume she had run to the end of the hall, as far away from him as she could get. That's what most people would do. The natural inclination would be to put as much distance as possible between her and her attacker. She had to fight that inclination. She left the door open, which he would not be expecting. She hoped that he would assume if the door was open, she hadn't run in there. It was a risk, but it was all she knew to do. Quickly flattening herself behind the open door, pushing herself against the wall, and turning her feet sideways to take up less space, she held her breath, hoping that the man would check this room first, not discover her, and thus buy her some time to get away to the downstairs while he went into all the other rooms. It wasn't much of a chance, but it was all she had.

She heard his rapid footsteps on the stairs and his voice. He was cursing about his head. He wasn't trying to be quiet. Why should he? Since there was no car in the drive, he must know she was in the house alone. Just then, she felt a tickle in her nose and a pooling of tears in her eyes. With horror, she realized a sneeze was coming on. It happened whenever she ran. *Please God! Maybe if I get my mind on something else...* Shutting her eyes and willing the sneeze away, she swallowed hard and waited. She heard him go in Bippy's room first. *Darn!* That was one less room for him to check while she made a run for it. Just as she expected, though, he just gave the room a cursory glance, and soon she heard him coming across the hall. His flashlight swept the room where she hid, playing quickly over the floor, and she ceased breathing. He was inches away from her, just on the other side of the door, and she could hear his breath coming in puffs after his run up the stairs. If only he wouldn't check behind the door. If only. What was he doing? All she could hear was...nothing.

Suddenly, the flashlight swept out of the room, and she began breathing again. Now was her chance. She had to time it exactly right. She had to slip out of the room and down the staircase while he was in one of the two remaining rooms. If she came out of her hiding place while he was in the hallway.... She wouldn't think about that. Couldn't think about it. Slowly, she pushed the door far enough away for her to get out from behind it and peeked into the hall. She could see the flashlight in Pen's room, so this was it. Now or never. If she could do this quietly enough, maybe he would go on to check her room at the back before he started over. Almost paralyzed with fear, she had to will her legs to work. She streaked swiftly and as silently as she could for the stairs and, thankful that she had changed into her elasticized lounging slippers before starting to write, tiptoed quickly down the stairs, being careful to avoid the especially creaky steps she had noticed earlier.

She made her way to the kitchen and, resisting the urge to grab a knife, picked up instead the cell phone she'd left lying on the counter. She could hear the man upstairs, running now back into each bedroom, probably looking under beds and in closets again, sure he'd overlooked her the first time. She could tell by his shouts that he was becoming more and more agitated. Carefully, quietly, she pulled the door shut behind her and made her way outdoors. It was so dark. Where could she go? The trees behind Maggie's office offered her only chance, and she made her way there as stealthily and quickly as the pitch darkness would allow. She couldn't risk running down the long driveway toward the street. Out in the open like that, she was sure to be seen. She ran first behind a slender oak, decided it didn't offer enough protection, and slipped quickly into the shadowy embrace of a magnolia, its limbs covered in broad leaves reaching all the way to the ground. Gasping, she leaned against the tree and tried to get her breathing under control.

Her hands were shaking so badly she could hardly dial, but finally, after getting her breath, she pecked out 9-1-1 and almost gave way to sobbing while waiting for the dispatcher to answer. It seemed to take forever.

The words, when they finally came, sounded like the voice of God. "This is 9-1-1. What is your emergency?"

"Please," she whispered into the phone, "please help me. This is an emergency. Send the police. Hurry! Someone—a man—is in the house, and I think he's trying to kill me. He's chased me all over. I'm outside now, and I think he's still inside. I don't know, though. He could be outside now. He could be anywhere." She was jarred by a snapping sound like someone stepping on a twig. She sobbed again into the phone. "Please help me. Where? Oh, I'm—I'm at—"

"I'm sorry. I didn't get that address. Tell me again where you are. Ma'am? Stay on the phone. I need the address please. Ma'am? Where are you?"

Rosemary didn't finish—couldn't finish—because that very same someone of whom she had just spoken had her by the neck and was slowly choking the life out of her.

***

Pen and Tootsie walked beside Rose, who was seated in a wheelchair pushed by a nurse, as they left the hospital two days later. Bippy had gone to bring the car to the front of the hospital. "You drive, Bippy," Tootsie had said on the way into the hospital. "Pen and I are larger and can support Rose better getting her into and out of the car."

Bippy had thought a moment and then said, "Well, I guess I can. I do take Brother's Buick out every now and then to keep it running—have to go to O'Carr's you know—and it's larger than this car." She pulled the car to the loading zone and got out to watch, while Tootsie and Pen helped the nurse transfer Rose from the wheelchair to the front seat, where they thought she would be more comfortable. When Rose was settled in the front and Pen and Tootsie in back, Bippy climbed into the driver's seat. Seated on a cushion so she could see above the steering wheel, she drove slowly out of the parking lot.

The doctors had told them all that Rose was a very lucky lady. Her windpipe had been severely bruised, but not crushed. While the airway was constricted, enough air was able to get to her brain so that she would not suffer any lasting consequences from the near-strangulation. Lucky for her that the assailant thought he had finished the job. "With rest and some TLC, you'll soon be as good as new, but I surely wouldn't want to come any closer than that, ma'am," the attending E. R. physician had said.

"How're you feeling?" Bippy asked, looking over at Rose, seated in the passenger seat.

Rose rolled her head toward Bippy. "You've heard, no doubt, of a sore throat? Well, let me tell you, my friend, that what you have with a cold isn't a sore throat. It's a tickle, a minor irritation. *This,*" she said, pointing at her neck, "is a sore throat!"

"We're just all so thankful that the 9-1-1 operator could trace your call and that you didn't...that you survived the attack, Rose," said Pen. "If anything worse had happened to you, especially while we were out enjoying ourselves, I would never have gotten over it."

"Well, it could just as easily have been one of you. The two policemen who investigated think the man was watching the house and knew you all had left. They said he probably thought there was no one in the house. The police said it could have been an attempted burglary that went bad. This is some big house, you know, and everyone in

Jackson knows it's empty now. They said there might be no connection between this and Maggie's death. Could be just a coincidence, they say, or could be an opportunist who read about her death in the paper and decided to burgle an empty house."

"Well, Ferguson certainly didn't think it was random, nor a burglary attempt. He was a little steamed, wasn't he?" Tootsie said.

Rose nodded ever so slightly. "Oh, to be sure. He's convinced that the attack was the direct result of our newspaper ad. He really blessed me out in the hospital. Once he found out I was going to be okay, that is. He said our 'meddlin'—that's the word he used—was getting us in more and more trouble. He said again that with the coroner's report of an accidental death, his hands are tied; that he would investigate when he had something solid to go on and not before."

"Doesn't the man understand that's what we're trying to give him?" asked Bippy.

"I just wish I could have seen the attacker's face, but it was as dark in the house as it was outside, and besides, he grabbed me from behind."

Bippy nodded. "Well, I think it's clear that the perp was trying to send a message for us to drop the investigation of Maggie's death."

Tootsie smiled. "I think the phone call pretty much clinches that."

"Phone call? What phone call?" Rose asked.

"An anonymous call that came in while you were in the hospital, warning us to go home and 'let Maggie Palmer rest in peace,' to quote the message exactly."

"What? No way! Did you mention it to Lt. Ferguson?"

Tootsie shook her head. "Do I look like a crazy person to you?"

"Any idea who it was?"

"Not really, but..."

"But what?" Rose asked.

Tootsie shrugged. "Oh, just that the wording interested me. Do you remember what Lt. Ferguson told us?"

"Sure. He told us to drop this investigation and go home."

"Yes, yes, I know, but do you remember his exact wording?"

Wincing at the pain, Rosemary turned and looked at Tootsie in the back seat. She spoke very slowly. "He said we...should...let...Maggie... Palmer...rest...in...peace!" she gasped. After that, they rode home in silence.

Once they were in the house, the girls put on the tea kettle and sat around the kitchen table talking about where they were in all this. Tootsie spoke first. "We've got to covenant right now that (a) we're going to change the locks on this house first thing tomorrow—today, if possible—(b) we're never going to leave one of us here alone again under any circumstances, and (c) we're going to figure out how to use the security gate at the end of the driveway. Agreed?"

They all nodded and placed their hands, one on top of the other, in the middle of the table. "Agreed. There's safety in numbers, so they say," Rosemary said.

"Back to what you said in the car...I wonder if Lt. Ferguson really could be in on this," Pen said.

"Well, if he is, it would be just like *Double Dose of Death*," Bippy said animatedly as she pushed the glasses back into the swag on her nose. "In that book, the policeman who was investigating the murder of a woman's doctor/husband, decided he wanted the widow for himself, and when she rejected him, he killed her."

"Oh, I read that one, Bippy," Pen said. "Didn't he discover that the widow had killed her husband and threatened to turn her in unless she...well, unless she gave in to him?"

"Yes, but she said it was self-defense because her husband had found that she had been unfaithful and started beating her. Then she threatened to turn the policeman in for blackmailing her. She thought she could beat the murder-one rap, using the battered-wife syndrome as her defense, but the cop killed her."

Pen nodded. "That was a good book," she said simply.

"Sounds like a real classic," Tootsie teased.

The conversation died off, and they sipped their tea with great bands of silence stretched between them as they thought. Finally, Tootsie spoke softly. "Okay. I've been knocked down; Rose has been attacked and nearly killed. You all want to quit?"

"Quilt what, dear?" Pen asked.

"Not quilt, quit! Quit investigating Maggie's death and accept that it was an accident. Quit stirring up things. Quit trying to figure everything out. Quit meddling, to use everyone else's word. Nothing we can do will bring her back anyway." Tootsie bent her head and fought for control. Staring at her in surprise, the other girls saw two large tears overflow her eyes and streak the makeup on her soft-as-down cheeks. The group was shocked into silence at seeing Tootsie, their unflappable leader, give way to her emotions.

Finally, Pen said, "Do you remember the passage from the *Aeneid* where all of Aeneas' followers are discouraged and feel beaten? They are ready to quit when Aeneas says to them:

> *O comrades, we have been through worse,*
> *Together before this.... This, too, the god will end.*
> *Call the nerve back; dismiss the fear, the sadness.*
> *Some day, perhaps, remembering even this*
> *Will be a pleasure. We are going on*
> *Through whatsoever chance and change, until*

We come to Latium, where the fates point out
A quiet dwelling-place, and Troy recovered.
Endure, and keep yourself for better days.

"Well, that's what I think we need to say to ourselves now. Better days will come. We just have to endure until then." Then, she blushed and said, "Sorry. My children say I quote things at the drop of a hat. In fact, they say I'll even drop the hat. It's a problem with English teachers, I guess. English teachers never die; they just quote away."

"It's not a problem at all, Pen," Tootsie said, patting her hand. "It's beautiful, and it's just what we need to hear. Support across the centuries! A pep talk from Virgil! I'm just worried that I might be encouraging you all into something that's dangerous. Maybe for safety's sake we should quit."

"Why, Tootsie, honey," Bippy said, "We can't quit now. We're onto something. I think that's obvious. We've stirred something up. We've got to find out exactly what happened. But we can't do it without you. You're the leader of this merry group. I think you need a fix." Everyone turned and looked at Bippy as she calmly rose, walked to the pantry, and returned with a jar of peanut butter. "Here, dear, this will make you feel better."

It started with a snicker, but as humor often does, it took on a life of its own, and soon all four of them were holding their sides and wiping the tears away. This time the tears were of joy. "You're right, Bippy," Tootsie gasped between laughs, "I do need a fix."

Just then the phone rang. Tootsie grabbed it up, hopeful that it was an answer to their ad. The other three listened as she spoke.

"Why, Clark. What a nice surprise!" She paused and listened to him. "No, I'm sorry. Nothing yet. Oh, no, we're not giving up." She looked at her friends, huddled at the table. They smiled and nodded encouragement. "Not a chance. Listen, while I have you on the phone, will you tell me how to use the security gate at the end of the driveway? I mean, how do you talk to someone there and let them in? We've just been leaving it open." After thanking Clarkson and assuring him that they would be in touch the minute they learned anything, Tootsie hung up.

"Was he calling from Texas?" Rose asked.

"He didn't say, and unfortunately, Maggie didn't have caller ID, so I don't know."

"I guess he was," Bippy said uncertainly. "He stayed in this house for a few days, though, so he would know the phone doesn't have caller ID. He could have been calling from anywhere."

Tootsie nodded. "I guess. I decided not to tell him about the two incidents," she said with a wink. "He might join forces with Ferguson and make us leave."

"Is that the real reason or are you hoping to find out by his tipping his hand whether or not he had anything to do with them?"

Tootsie smiled sadly. "A little of both, I guess."

While Rosemary called a locksmith to come change the locks on both front and back doors, as well as the office door out back, Bippy sorted through the mail that had been left in the box at the street and which she had gone out to collect. She picked up a small white envelope and exclaimed, "Look, you all. This could be an answer to our ad. It's addressed to The Estate of Margaret Muldoon Palmer just like we said." She tore it open and read:

I might have information that you want. If you're
interested, meet me in the back booth at Lulu's on

272

Highway 19 on Friday at 10:00 p.m. Come alone.
If any cops come with you, the deal is off. Bring the
money. One grand.

"Ohhh! Gives me the shivers just reading it," Pen said, with a shudder. "It sounds like a scene from *Fantasy of Fear*. Have you read that, Bippy?"

Bippy nodded, her lips clamped together in a solid line of certainty. "Yes, and I was just thinking the very same thing. Friday. That's tonight."

"Wonder why this person wrote instead of calling or emailing? We gave the phone number and email address, too," Pen asked.

"Might have been afraid it was a set-up, and the call or email would be traced," Tootsie said. "Safer to write, and we did give writing as an option."

"What's to keep him from fearing that our meeting him will set him up, too?" Bippy asked.

"Oh, I expect he'll check that out very carefully. Be sure no police are anywhere around before he makes his appearance. He has named the place. It's obviously his territory, so he would know if anyone strange were there."

"Well," Rose said, "what do you suppose we should do?"

"There's only one thing to do," Tootsie said, looking at her watch. "I'll go."

"Alone?" the other three said. "But, we just decided last night that—"

"Alone. You heard the man. Now, praise the Lord and pass the peanut butter."

Chapter Thirty-Three

Picking her way along Highway 19 in the pockets of fog, Tootsie wished for a booster on her headlights like the one on her mixer at home. Whoever described this stuff as pea-soup surely hit the nail on the head. In between periods of dense fog, when she had to put her beams on low to focus them on the road directly ahead of her, she still had trouble seeing. "Darn! I can't see my hand in front of my face," she muttered aloud, as much to keep herself company as to vent her frustration. The road, a black ribbon, could have been a strip of blotter paper, as thirstily as it soaked up her lights. Even on bright, with no moon at all, they did little good. She also realized with a sinking feeling in her stomach that she had gone off and left her cell phone charging on the kitchen counter. Shoot! She hit the wheel in exasperation. *How could I have done something so stupid! Oh well, chances are I won't need it.* She wasn't meeting this person in a secluded place after all. Lulu's would probably have lots of people. What was it Rosemary had just said last night? There's safety in numbers.

She had driven a long stretch, running in and out of dense, scary places where the fog had settled, without meeting another car. Suddenly, she saw up ahead, tucked back from the road, a parking lot full of rusty pick-ups and Jeeps. *This has to be it,* she thought, swinging abruptly off the highway, and then added, *but I wish it weren't.*

Oh, Lord, help! Once she had pulled into the gravel lot, she could see the center of all the activity. The building itself, a squat, dingy cinderblock affair with no windows and a neon sign flashing Lulu's, was less than half the size of the pool of trucks and mud-splattered four wheel drives that surrounded it. Squeezing into a space between a truck that flew the Rebel flag from the antenna and one that had a bumper sticker reading, "When guns are outlawed, only outlaws will have guns," she turned off the car and shrugged her shoulders. It figured. Every Billy Bob and Bubba in the county must be here. What a dive! They had places like this back in North Carolina, places she studiously avoided. She guessed every state had them. Taking a deep breath, she gripped her purse firmly by the handles and opened her door. Spanish moss dripped in swaying tendrils from the enormous oaks that towered over the building. Involuntarily, Tootsie shuddered as she walked in the shadows towards the building. *Not exactly the safest place I've ever been. Oh well.* She pushed open the door of Lulu's with resolution. *Here goes nothing.*

It took a moment for her eyes to adjust to the smoky haze that hovered like low-lying clouds inside, but soon she could see that everyone was looking at her as she stood uncertainly just inside the door. What was the matter? Had they never seen a woman in a skirt before? A quick look around convinced her that the answer was probably no. She had worn a long aqua skirt, one that clung to her slim figure and made her easily look like a woman in her early forties. Maybe even younger, she had decided honestly when she looked at her image in the mirror in her bedroom. She had topped it with a white and aqua blouse and her beloved wide belt studded with real turquoise. She realized quickly that she should have dressed in jeans to avoid standing out like the proverbial sore thumb. Everyone continued to stare, but no one approached her. What! No *maître-de*? She suppressed a smile in spite of herself. Just then, she heard someone calling to her in a loud voice.

"Hey, lady! You want somethin' or you just sight seein'?" It was the bartender, who was slapping bottles of beer on the counter as fast as the customers' outstretched hands popped up. It occurred to her that it was like alcoholic whack-a-mole.

Tootsie squared her shoulders, ready for anything, and walked over to the bar. "Uh...I'm supposed to meet someone here," she answered, giving no hint of the shakiness within. "Let me have a Diet Coke. You got any sandwiches?"

"Yeah, sure. Whatcha' want?"

"Peanut butter and jelly will be fine."

The bartender looked at her in disbelief and then barked through the little window behind him, "Hey, Bertie, one p b and j. Yeah, you heard me." He turned back to Tootsie and said derisively, "Will that be white or wholewheat, madam?" Several men leaning on the counter guffawed.

Tootsie shot them a confident smile and said to the bartender, "White please and with the crusts cut off. Can't stand those nasty little things." She flipped one of her dangling earrings with her finger for emphasis and winked. "I'll be in the back booth." No one laughed this time, but she felt their eyes burning into her back as she turned and walked towards the rear of the establishment, and she distinctly heard the word, "babe." *Not bad for a sixty-something-year-old*, she thought with a smile. There were five booths lined up in a row, but they all seemed to be empty. Once she had slid into the last booth, she looked around and realized why. In one corner was a Foosball table, and around it were gathered roughly ten pairs of faded and ripped jeans. The jeans were all she could see because their owners were bent over, fixed on watching the game being played. In another corner from a TV tuned to a heated NFL game between the Atlanta Falcons and the New Orleans Saints, blared the sportscaster's amazed "Did… you…see…that? What a catch!" and clustered around it, leaning back on rough wooden chairs, were approximately fifteen men, some with scruffy beards, some with pot bellies, some with long hair pulled into pony tails, most with tattoos, but all of them cheering for the Saints.

In a few minutes, Tootsie's sandwich and Coke arrived, brought by an extremely well-endowed twenty-something with badly bleached blonde hair and wearing faded denim shorts. The shorts were fringed, but even the fringe stopped twelve inches above her knees. The term "shorts" had never been more appropriate. *She's got to be cold,* Tootsie thought. "Darlene" was pinned over the left breast of her too-tight blouse. "You ordered a p b and j, hon?" the girl asked, setting the plate on the edge of the table, as if ready to grab it back if Tootsie didn't pass inspection.

"That's right, darlin'," Tootsie said, giving her a broad wink and sliding the plate closer to her. "There might be something else. I'm expecting someone."

She noticed the girl's fixed smile and the self-important swagger as she walked back toward the bar. Tootsie thought such hardness must be necessary in a place like this. *Her only defense is a good offense.* Trouble is that such a stance usually makes a person both defensive as well as offensive. Pity. *Oh well,* she sighed, and began eating. *Mm-mm. One thing you can say about peanut butter. It's no respecter of environments. Ambience doesn't mean a thing. It's as good in a dive as in a diner.*

She hadn't finished her sandwich more than five minutes when he came in. She sat facing the door, nursing her second Diet Coke, brought by Darlene, who this time had asked with a striking lack of real interest, "You're not from around here, are ya'?" When Tootsie shook her head, Darlene asked, "Whatcher' name, hon?"

Tootsie mumbled her name, but she was too engrossed in the man who had just entered to engage in further conversation, so Darlene left. He stood at the door a few seconds, almost like a shadow, looking around cautiously, scanning the crowd, and then made his way straight to the back booth. "Gimme a Bud," he yelled to the bartender as he went by. He slid in across from Tootsie, lit a cigarette, and said nothing until Darlene brought his mug of beer.

Fighting the impulse to fan away the smoke—how could people smoke those nasty things?—Tootsie studied the small, rather wizened man across from her. Not big enough to be the figure Rosemary described. He didn't look imposing, certainly, but that didn't mean anything. Nothing at all, she acknowledged. Forget it, Charles Atlas. Size doesn't matter anymore. Any two-bit punk with a gun can be imposing if he chooses to be. A large scar slashed a pale streak across his left cheek from the outside of his eye to the corner of his mouth. His arms, which were bare, bore several tattoos, one of which caught Tootsie's eye. Its incongruity fascinated her. It was a spinning globe, little squiggly lines indicating motion, with the inscription, "Love Your Mother." *What*? she mused. *I've got a conservationist here*?

He took a big gulp of his Bud, wiping the foam away from his upper lip with the back of his hand. "You the dame placed the ad?" he asked, grinding out one cigarette and lighting another.

"I'm the dame," Tootsie said, smiling. Maybe she could establish some kind of rapport with this man. As she was growing up, her mother had often quoted Ben Franklin on the efficacy of catching flies with a teaspoon of honey versus a gallon of vinegar. "I'm glad you wrote, but I'm a little puzzled. Why didn't you call or email?"

He leaned closer, letting the smoke escape his nostrils like a Chinese dragon. "Calls are too risky. I ain't got a computer. Listen. I don't want no trouble with the cops, see? Me and them don't—well, I just like to keep my distance from them. Understood?" He looked Tootsie straight in the eye.

"Perfectly," she said.

He studied her a minute and then said, "Okay. You got the money we agreed to?"

"Well, I don't know that we actually agreed, but—"

"A thousand or the deal is off."

"I have it," Tootsie said quickly, patting her purse. "Let's see what you have first." When he hesitated, she said, "Okay. Fair is fair. What about this?" Very surreptitiously, she pulled a few large bills from her purse and laid them in her lap. "Half now. Half after I hear what you have to say. Fair enough?"

He nodded, and she motioned for him to reach under the table. With one deft move, he found her hand and pocketed the bills. "Okay. Here's the deal. On the night of October ninth, over at the lake, I seen three men—"

"Three?"

"Yeah, three. Let me finish before you ask your questions. Anyway, these three guys was rowing out in the lake in the dark."

Tootsie ignored his warning to hold off with her questions. "But is that all that unusual? I mean, couldn't they have been going fishing?"

"Yeah, 'cept for one thing. They'se pullin' a sailboat behind 'em. That just struck me odd, you know? People goin' out fishin' don't pull a sailboat along, especially for night fishin'. It'd just be in the way."

"What were you doing in the vicinity, Mr.—"

"Jacko. Just call me Jacko. I'se gettin' ready to do some fishin' myself early the next morning. That's how I happened to see 'em, you know? I'se diggin' worms up on shore when I looked up and seen 'em gettin' the boats in the water and then rowin' out real quiet-like in the moonlight. I wouldn't a' thought nothin' of it if it hadn't a' been for that sailboat. That seemed kinda strange, you know? I started to call out to them, but I didn't. Figured they couldn't see me in the dark since I'se up on shore under the trees and by now they'se out a pretty good ways on the water."

"Can you give me a description of the men?"

"Well, they'se big. I know that. Tall fellows. At least two of 'em was. One was a little short guy. It was dark, you know, so I couldn't really see their faces."

Tootsie sagged with disappointment. "Anything else?"

"Just one. One of the guys was limpin'."

Chapter Thirty-Four

Tootsie peeled the remaining bills as if separating the rings of an onion, feeling each one, trying to keep them under the table as she counted. No sense making things more dangerous than they already were by flashing big money around. She was already dreading the walk back to her car under the shadowy canopy of those moss-draped trees. An involuntary shudder shook her shoulders. When she had finished counting, she gestured with a slight jerk of her head towards her left shoulder that Jacko should reach under the table, and when he did, she put the money into his hand and gripped his fingers before he could pull away. "Listen, Jacko, in case you've thrown the ad away, I've put my phone number on a slip of paper with this money. I want you to think very hard about that night, and if you think of something else—anything at all—I want you to call me. I'll make it worth your while. Don't take time to write me a note. Do you understand? The phone has not been tapped. You'll just have to take my word on that. The police do not have any idea what's going on, and I want to keep it that way."

He nodded, took one last swig of his beer, ground out his cigarette, and left as quietly as he had arrived, blending into the smoky haze and then just melting away. After he had disappeared, Tootsie motioned to Darlene, who sashayed over to the table, and with an arrogant lifting of her brows and a barely perceptible sigh, inquired what the devil she wanted now. Well, Tootsie admitted to herself, she didn't actually say that in so many words, but she communicated it loud and clear. She tugged on one corner of her blouse, which was tied, mid-riff fashion, in the front, displaying an elegantly pierced navel. Tootsie could read her unspoken annoyance like the morning newspaper. This is too much, she seemed to say. I mean, waiting on tables is bad enough, but bringing a peanut butter jelly sandwich to a strange woman decked out like some high falutin' western model! Really.

Darlene obviously wasn't used to being put through her paces by a woman. Given her circumstances, though, Tootsie acknowledged that she didn't know what she would be like if she were in Darlene's situation, and she put enough money in the girl's hand to cover her tab and Jacko's, plus a generous tip. When Darlene nodded a grudging thank you, Tootsie gathered her purse, and braced for the walk to her car. She was dreading leaving the place, but she knew she couldn't stay there all night. Now was probably the best time while all the men were engrossed in the game. She made it to the door unobserved. So far, so good.

She couldn't give in to fear, Tootsie kept telling herself over and over, as she picked her way quickly across the gravel lot. *I can't. I can't. If I do, I'll break out into a run, and who can run in gravel? Must walk slowly. Carefully. What is it the police are always saying? Appear confident, aware of your surroundings.* In this case, the two were mutually exclusive. To consider these surroundings was to lack confidence. The feeling that someone was right behind her, almost breathing down her back, caused cold prickles to creep up and down the back of her neck and finally forced her to turn around. Nothing. A bad case of nerves. That's all it was.

Still, as she walked, more quickly now, she could have sworn she heard something. Something like footsteps in the gravel. Was it more than one person? Was she imagining it? She glanced over her shoulder. Nothing. She started on towards the car and heard it again. She had her remote ready—she remembered that much from the class the Durham police had taught on self-defense—and when she got nearer the car, she clicked the unlock button on the remote quickly, jumped in, and hit the lock button after her. She threw her head back against the head rest and took a deep breath. What a relief to be safe again! Taking several more deep breaths, she finally restored her breathing to an even keel, and, as she backed out, turned, and pulled onto the highway, was disappointed to see that the fog had thickened.

She glanced in her rear view mirror and saw nothing behind her. Apparently, she had just imagined that she had heard someone following her in the parking lot. Her imagination was working overtime. Soon, the car was enveloped in fog, and Tootsie decreased her speed as she lowered her light beams to focus on the road directly in front of her. A suffocating sense of aloneness made her heart pound. A sudden burst of light caused her to glance again in her rear view mirror. A car was directly behind her! Where in the world had it come from?

No one had pulled out after her at Lulu's. At least, not that she had seen. Probably someone who was flying along Highway 19 and then hit this fog. Well, she didn't blame him for sticking close to her, following in her path. *I'd do the same if there were a car in front of me,* she conceded. Fog was one of those many times in life when two were better than one. She tried to convince herself that it was a comfort to have someone right behind her, but then a niggling fear began pricking her brain. *Why didn't I see his lights coming on that long straightaway of 19 before I pulled out of Lulu's?* Was the fog that bad all the way up the road? Had someone pulled out after her with his lights off? Was it her imagination or was the car getting closer and closer? Despite her care, had someone seen her peeling the bills off and giving them to Jacko and assumed there was more where that came from? Had Jacko himself hidden until she left and then decided to see if she had any more money on her? Money for info was a good deal. Money for nothing was an even better deal.

She was just trying to convince herself that the fog was playing tricks on her perception of distance when a hard bump sent her lurching forward. Her neck jerked sharply, and she gripped the wheel a little tighter. There was no longer any doubt. The car behind her had deliberately bumped her! Suddenly, all of Lt. Ferguson's speeches about the danger of their involvement were running through her mind—and making sense. She picked up her speed as much as she dared, but she realized that until she ran out of this fog, she was helpless to lose him by speed alone. It would have to be something else. Still, she had managed to put enough distance between them that only the faint glow of his lights showed right now, though she could tell they were getting brighter with every second. But if she could get off the highway fast enough and remain hidden, maybe she could lose him. There was a chance. Just a chance.

Suddenly, right around a curve, she saw a secondary road off to the right. He wouldn't be able to see her turn off because of the curve. Quickly, she made a sharp turn and bounced down the dirt road, immediately turning off the engine and dousing her lights. She could only hope that she had hit the lights before he noticed her turning. She was down so far that she couldn't see the highway. The darkness was terrifying but not as terrifying as the unknown threat that followed those two headlights. She sat still, scarcely breathing. All around her, the dense fog draped an eerie silence over the darkness, shutting out everything except the sound of her pounding heart.

Her hands were shaking so hard that she gripped the wheel until her knuckles ached. On her forehead, beads of perspiration gathered and slowly trickled into her eyes. She could feel the cold breath of fear blowing down her neck, raising chill bumps and resulting in a violent shudder that shook her shoulders. Leaning her head back against the seat, she held her breath and waited. From habit, she felt for the reassuring presence of her cell phone in her purse, but with a piercing stab she remembered that it was back at Maggie's house. But whom would she call anyway? She certainly wouldn't have wanted to call the other girls—at least not yet. She didn't want to worry them needlessly when maybe this would turn out to be nothing. The police? Just when she had begun getting somewhere on the investigation of Maggie's death? Admit to Lt. Ferguson that he was right and be forced to drop her quest for the truth? Much as she hated to admit it, though, she needed the police, needed them desperately, and longed for her phone.

When, after a few minutes, nothing happened, she made a decision: She would start the car and get back to the main highway. Chances were, he had gone on by unseen in the fog, and anyway, she was beginning to think that it was safer there on the highway than on this Godforsaken road out of sight. Maybe she had read too much into that bump from behind. Maybe it was purely an accident caused by the fog, after all, and whoever bumped her was too cowardly to stop. Yes, that had to be it. She grasped at a fact she wanted desperately to believe. Her trembling fingers reached for the keys. Hesitating, she breathed a prayer into the silence and then started the car. Quickly, she turned the wheel as hard as she could and pulled forward. Throwing it in reverse, she backed up, and then started forward again. When she reached the main road and felt the reassuring hardness of asphalt under her tires, she began breathing more regularly.

She was just beginning to work some of the tension from her shoulders by rolling them forward and backward when, all of a sudden, a glance in the rear view mirror confirmed her worst fears. The lights were behind her again, this time not quite as close as when she had been bumped, but menacing all the same. She had not lost him. "No!" she screamed aloud. She stepped on the gas. Fog or no fog, she would have to try to outrun him. What else could she do? Stop and wait for him to attack and rob her? Or worse? She muttered and fumed as her fear morphed into a blind anger. *Not on your sweet life!* She could only hope, as she sped through the fog, that nothing would suddenly loom ahead of her. Unable to see where she was going more than a few yards ahead, but reassured by the white line that she was in her lane, she sped on. *Please! Please!* she breathed. Behind her, the lights followed like two sinister yellow eyes. She was checking her rear view mirror when it happened. In one simultaneous second, she realized that she couldn't see the white line anymore, that the car was out of control and going down a hill, and that a fence was dead ahead. After the impact, but just before she lost consciousness, she was aware of someone running to her car, pounding on her door, but she couldn't see who it was. Didn't want to know, really. Just wanted to sleep.

As she sank into oblivion, pictures swirled before her eyes, pictures of Emma Beth and Mark, of Livvy and Brent, of Maggie, of Ladybug, of the new friends that she felt she had somehow led into a dangerous cul-de-sac. And then, there was blackness.

Chapter Thirty-Five

"She's coming around," an EMT said.

Tootsie blinked her eyes open, stared around her, and immediately attempted to sit up on the gurney. "What happened?"

Another EMT restrained her. Another voice, a familiar one, chimed in. "Please. Lie down. You ran off the road. Hit that very sturdy fence. Timber, wire, and stone. Really more of a wall. Good thing I saw you. You're one lucky lady."

"Lucky?" Tootsie shook her head slightly and turned to see who was talking. It couldn't be! "Lt. Ferguson!"

"Yeah, it's me all right. Like I say, you're lucky. If you hadn'ta hit the fence, you'da gone in the river down there or maybe plowed into that tree over yonder."

"Lieutenant, someone was following me."

He started shaking his head. "No. No. That was me. Nothin' sinister there. I saw you go off the road and down the embankment. I called 9-1-1."

"You?" She shook her head. She realized then that it was he who had run to her car and pounded on the window just before she blacked out. "No! I mean, thank you—really, thank you—but there was another car. Before you. Miles before I ran off the road. He was right on my tail. He bumped me from behind. Check my rear bumper if you don't believe me. When I got far enough ahead of him and thought he wouldn't see in the fog, I pulled off onto a secondary road that went down a steep hill and cut my lights. He went on by. When I thought it was safe, I pulled back on the road. I saw lights behind me and thought he was after me again, but he must have gone on. I was speeding to try to get away from him. That must have been you."

Ferguson nodded.

"Thank you again. I owe you big time."

"No problem. Glad I was in the right place at the right time."

"But the man who bumped me—I think he followed me from Lulu's."

"Lulu's!" Ferguson said. "Hold it right there. That's somethin' we gotta chat about. What in hell—'scuse me, ma'am—tarnation were you doin' at Lulu's in the first place?"

"It's a long story."

"I got lots of time," he said.

After the EMTs ran some on-site tests and checked Tootsie's eyes, one of them called the hospital. "GCS is fourteen," he said into the two-way radio.

"Fourteen. Not bad," the second EMT said to Tootsie, "for a head injury like you've had, your GCS is great, in fact."

"My what? What's a GCS?"

"Glasgow Coma Scale. Three is the worst. Fifteen is considered normal. You're almost there. Shock has lowered it a tad, but that's to be expected. Okay, let's go."

"Go?"

"To Lake View Hospital."

"Wait! Hospital! Is that necessary? Look, I'm not even cut or anything." She attempted to stand and was struck with a sharp pain in her head. "Ow!" she sighed, sinking back down.

"You'd better lie back down," Ferguson said.

Tootsie winced. "Yeah, maybe. I can't believe this. Two times in one week. It's, as Yogi Berra said, 'Déjà vu all over again.'"

"You keep this up, you're gonna need a revolvin' account at the hospital," Ferguson said, trying to coax a smile.

"Well, I must say you're being awfully jolly about all this."

"I'm not the one with the bump on my head. Besides, I think now y'all will finally listen to me and stop all this sleuthing nonsense." When she started to answer, he continued. "You want me to call anyone? What about your friends?" Ferguson asked.

Torn between not wanting to worry the girls with either the news that she had been in a wreck or with the worse worry of simply not returning, Tootsie finally gave him the number of Maggie's house. "Tell them I'm all right and have been unavoidably detained. Oh, and Lt. Ferguson, tell them I'll be home soon."

"Look, Ms. Freeman—"

"Tootsie, please."

"Okay, Tootsie, then, your friends are gonna know somethin' is up. I'm gonna to have to come up with somethin' better than you've been 'unavoidably detained.'"

"Well," Tootsie paused, "okay, tell them that I've had car trouble, and I called you for help since I had your number." She hoped they wouldn't remember her phone charging at home. "And that's the truth, you know? I have had car trouble. Big trouble."

He sighed and under his breath muttered something, of which Tootsie heard only "...a piece of work."

Hours later, after a thorough exam in the E.R., which included an M. R. I., an X-Ray, and a period of observation, Tootsie was finally told she could go home. "It's about time," she fumed, after pushing open the front door of the hospital and walking out into the cool night air. "In the paper when it says an accident victim was 'treated and released,' it sounds so quick. Almost like drive through. Hah! I've had babies in less time!" She was speaking to no one in particular, but suddenly Ferguson was at her side, matching his stride to hers.

"Where's my car?" Tootsie asked him.

"Out front. I had it towed here. Hope that's okay. All you got is a good-sized dent in the door on the passenger side. It drives fine. I checked it out. You cut the wheel just enough to avoid hitting that fence head on. Bubba Stallings towed it. I told him you'd be good for it."

"Yes, of course. Thank you. I have Triple A."

"He'll come out tomorrow and get you to sign for it. He's a good body man, too, if you want him to fix that door. You can open it all right, but it sure doesn't look too good."

"It's a rental car, so I guess we'll have to call the rental company first. See what they want to do about it." Tootsie suddenly turned to him. "Did you check the back? My bumper?"

Ferguson nodded. "Yeah, you had a bump back there all right, but it's hard to tell whether it was deliberate or not. Coulda' happened some time ago in a parkin' lot, say. Nothing definitive there. I finally told your friends what happened, by the way. They were wantin' to get a cab over here—they'se just hoppin' up and down—but I told them that you were gonna be treated and released and for them to just sit tight. No need havin' a bunch of hysterical ladies descendin' on the hospital at this hour of the night. They didn't buy the 'car trouble' bit, which surprised me not at all, so I had to tell 'em. Now, you want to tell me that long story you mentioned earlier?"

Tootsie chewed on her lip and let the "hysterical ladies" remark go. At least he didn't preface it with "little old," so there was that.

She knew—had known from the beginning—that Ferguson lumped them all under that category, but there was nothing she could do about that. That was his problem. They had stopped at her sedan, and she suggested that they sit inside the car while she told him everything. As she was recounting the part about the car tailing her, she suddenly stopped. "I was just thinking. How did you happen to be behind me on Highway 19 tonight anyway, Lt. Ferguson? That was quite a coincidence when you think about it."

Ferguson shifted his weight uncomfortably. "Uh, well, it was just luck, I reckon."

"Luck?" said Tootsie, unconvinced.

"Well, yeah, kinda'."

"What do you mean 'kinda'? Would you clarify that, please? Why were you on that particular road tonight?"

"Wait! Who's conductin' this interview anyhow?"

"I'm waiting," Tootsie answered, lifting her eyebrows in anticipation.

"Okay. I drove out to the Palmer house to check on you ladies. You know, be sure y'all were all right. Hadn't heard a peep from you since your friend Rosemary was released from the hospital. Y'all are makin' a habit of this, you know." He winked and made a clicking sound as if he were telling a horse to giddyap. "Anyway, just as I was fixin' to turn down that street, you went sailin' by, so I just followed at a discrete distance to see what you were up to. Curiosity may have killed the cat, but it is a detective's major personality trait. I followed you out into the county and couldn't believe it when you turned into Lulu's, but then, nothin' should surprise me now. I donned this Ole' Miss baseball cap to blend in if I had to go inside, which, luckily, I didn't. I parked way off at the end of Lulu's lot under some trees and waited." He cleared his throat. "Uh, unfortunately, I missed seein' you leave. I'd—uh—briefly gone to the men's room that's around back of the place. When I came back, I looked for your car. It was gone. I started drivin' the way I knew you'd go—towards home—hopin' I'd be able to follow at a safe distance, and you'd never know I'd been behind you. I was gonna see that you got safely home. I lost you in the fog. Never saw you or caught up to you. Thick as pea soup. I was pickin' my way along when I suddenly saw car lights go down the hill off the road towards the river."

Tootsie, her tongue clamped tightly between her teeth, nodded thoughtfully. His mood had definitely improved at the thought that the Flower Girls would take this latest scare seriously and go home. Finally, she took a deep breath. "I see," she said. She hesitated for a minute, not fully trusting him and yet needing to confide in someone, and then said, "So you never saw the car that was behind me. The first you saw of me was when I went down the hill. Well, let me finish telling you everything."

When she finished telling about everything that had happened from home to Lulu's and afterwards, including meeting an informant, he said, "I hate to be an I-told-you-so, but that's what I warned you would happen by running those ads, didn't I?" His tone, scolding and parental, annoyed Tootsie. "Y'all are mixing with riff-raff doin' that." He took a cigar from his pocket and chewed on its end for a minute. "Pure T riff-raff. And to go to Lulu's at night by yourself!" He blew a little puff of exasperation. "That's plumb crazy!"

Tootsie chewed on the inside of her cheek and then said, "Well, since you know everything, you probably don't need me to tell you that whatever happened to Maggie—"

He let out a deep sigh. "Are we back to that again? When in the name of goodness are y'all gonna accept that her death was an acci-*dent*?" As always, he emphasized the last syllable and pushed his hat back on his head.

"If her death was an accident, why in heaven's name is someone trying to scare us away? Hmm? Where is that detective's curiosity of yours now?" When there was no immediate answer, she continued. "As I was saying, whatever happened to Maggie could have been caused by Raymond."

He took the damp cigar from his mouth. "Raymond! As in Raymond Muldoon? Her brother?"

"The same."

He gave a slight shake of his head. "What in the—whatever gave you that loony idea?"

"My informant said that one of the men he saw that night was limping." It gave Tootsie a small thrill to see Ferguson dumbfounded as he very obviously was.

"Limpin'?" he repeated.

"That's right."

"Well, what in the world would Raymond have stood to gain by his sister's death?" Ferguson asked.

"You mean aside from his inheritance? Isn't that enough? Maybe he needed the money. Maybe his business is in trouble."

"There's only one thing wrong with that little theory. Raymond—and Clarkson, too, for that matter—inherited the same amount from their parents that his sister did. It's a matter of public record. Go check it. I did."

So he *had* done some investigating. Tootsie was impressed in spite of herself at his detective work, but she shot back. "It wouldn't be the first time one sibling ran through his inheritance."

Ferguson put the unlit cigar back into the corner of his mouth. "No," he drawled, "I s'pose not." He thought for a few minutes and then said, "Of course, you're operatin' under the assumption that somethin' criminal *did* happen to Maggie Palmer. That she didn't just meet with a very unfortunate acci-*dent*."

Tootsie turned and looked at him. "Yes, Lieutenant, that's exactly what I'm assuming, and everything that has happened to us since we started investigating Maggie's death has just confirmed it for us. I think we're making somebody very nervous."

"Yeah, me," he said.

"Oh?" She had not noticed before how unusual his eyes were. Even this late at night, she could see them, their hyacinth irises iridescent under the street light where they sat. The thought crossed her mind that she could easily be mesmerized and comforted by them, but in the same instant, she also realized she could just as easily be like a rabbit gazing into a snake's eyes.

"I can't help it—I worry about you ladies, like y'all are my personal responsibility or somethin'."

"Well, thanks, but we don't want your worry, just your help. And I'll tell you another thing: The more someone tries to scare us off, the more determined we'll be to establish that this was not an accident and to find what or who is at the bottom of it."

"Is that so?" A hint of a smile played at the corners of his mouth.

"That's so."

"Well," he drawled, "I don't s'pose it'll hurt to do a little more checkin'." He reached over and patted her hand. "Now, little lady, we'd better be gettin' you on home or those friends of yours will be formin' a posse, and Lord help me. I can't deal with that." He winked broadly and gave her a little grin as he opened the door and got out, walked around the car and motioned for her to slide over to the passenger seat.

"What? You're driving me home?"

"It's the only way the hospital would let you leave. They didn't feel comfortable with you driving after that bump on your head. While they were workin' on you, I signed a paper that I was a responsible party and would be drivin' you home. I'm off duty." He winked. "Nothing better to do."

"How will you get back to your car?"

"Not a problem. I'll call one of the black and whites in the area to pick me up and drop me back here. Now scoot. Let's get the heck outta Dodge before that posse of yours figures a way to get here."

The mental picture of a posse of Flower Girls—Pen, in her long, dark dress, with a sheriff's badge replacing the cameo pin at the neck; Bippy in jeans and holster, her tiny glasses sliding off her nose, a lurid paperback gripped firmly in one hand; and Rose on horseback, clinging to her ever-present legal pad, sent a charge of laughter like a current of electricity through Tootsie's body. She began chuckling, and, feeling the tension of the long night drain from her body, she rested her very sore head against the headrest, unable to speak—for the fits of laughter that controlled her. She was still laughing when they pulled into backyard and were immediately surrounded by her three very worried friends.

Chapter Thirty-Six

Tootsie, her head throbbing, sat at Maggie's computer. After being welcomed home by her worried but relieved friends and filling them in on the entire evening, she said, "Well, that's that. We know more now than we did, and that was the point of it all, so in spite of what happened, I'm glad I went. From now on, though, I think we should all stick together at home or away. Four of us together are less likely to be a target. Besides, now we know we're on to something. Let's see the police try to rationalize this away the way they did the intruder who choked Rosemary."

Bippy nodded. "Or the person who knocked you up against the door. Something is rotten in the state of Denmark, all right."

"Have you read that one, Bippy?" Pen asked.

"*Hamlet*?"

"No, *Something Rotten in Denmark,*" Pen answered. "I'll let you have it. It's really good. It's about the murder of a famous TV chef in Copenhagen."

Tootsie smiled and ran a hand through her thick black hair. "You all go on to bed and try to get some sleep with what is left of the night. I'm too keyed up to sleep, and besides, I'm eager to see what I can find in Maggie's correspondence. I want to see if there is any clue about her relationships, especially with Gordon Dawkins, and I'm going to read that entire article she saved about the Rexco Company. There has to be a reason she saved it."

"Didn't you just say we should all stick together after this? I couldn't sleep right now either," Rose said. "I'm going to stay out here in the office with you and work on my article."

Bippy leaned over and patted Tootsie's shoulder. She had fluttered around and fixed her friend a snack of skim milk and crackers spread thickly with crunchy peanut butter, which she put on a delicate blue-flowered plate. "I think in our present state of excitement, sleep is a long way off for all of us."

"That's putting it mildly," Pen said.

Bippy smiled at Tootsie. "Do you want us to stay out here with you?"

"No, no. Rose is staying, and we'll lock the door after you. We'll be fine."

"Well, dear, you go ahead and finish. Pen and I are going to be reading in the living room of the big house. We've traded books, and I can't wait to get started on *Murder Squared* or *Something Rotten in Denmark*. Haven't decided which one to read first. They both look great. So many books, so little time. Call us if you find anything."

After Pen and Bippy left, Rosemary settled down to another, smaller desk in the office, took out her yellow legal pad, and began writing.

"You need the computer, Rose?" asked Tootsie. "I can stop for now."

"Good heavens, no! I much prefer this," she said, tapping her paper. "I have a laptop at home, which I use when I write a final draft, but I didn't bring it with me. Didn't figure I'd need a computer just to come to a funeral. Anyway, I'm one of the few remaining journalists,

I suppose, who actually prefers to write a first draft in longhand. I can circle ideas in pencil, draw arrows from one thought to the other, and just scribble while I'm thinking. I can't do that on a computer—at least not on mine. I'm just brainstorming ideas for my article about Maggie. You go ahead." Deep in thought, Rose had closed her eyes and sat leaning back in her straight chair when Tootsie's sudden intake of breath grabbed her attention. "What? What?" she asked, lowering her chair.

"I don't know if this means anything, but there's a paragraph toward the bottom of the Rexco report addressing what the president calls 'hysterical governmental interference in the necessary elimination of surplus by-products.' In other words, toxic waste. From what he says, the company has apparently been the target of some governmental studies. This Ed Winslow, the president, is fearful that if the government cannot be convinced to back off, Rexco is going to lose some money. Big money. His tone gets a bit threatening, I'd say."

"Why do you suppose Maggie copied that address into her files?"

"Beats me," Tootsie sighed. "It really beats the heck out of me. I'm going to go back through her sent email and see if I turn anything up. The first time I went through it, I just looked for letters to Clarkson, Raymond, Gordon Dawkins, or the four of us." Humming softly to herself, she once again began scrolling and reading. Impatiently, she tapped her bright red fingernails on the side of the monitor. "Well now, isn't that interesting?" she muttered. "Hey, Rose, here's a letter to Ed Winslow, the president of Rexco Chemical."

"Why was Maggie so interested in chemicals all of a sudden?"

"I can't imagine." She grew quiet as she began reading the letter.

"Well?" Rose asked.

"Wait just a minute. I want to read his response. Then, I'll tell all."
After she finished reading, she turned her chair toward Rose and said slowly, "I think I'm beginning to get an idea."

"And?"

"Listen to this and see what you think." She scrolled back up and began reading from Ed Winslow.

Dear Ms. Palmer:

I understand you want to diversify your investments and appreciate your interest in Rexco Chemical Co. We would be pleased to have you as a major investor. Although I cannot tell from your email where you live, if you happen to live nearby or if you are ever in our vicinity, I would welcome you to tour our facilities. I think you will find our company both efficient and impressive.

You inquired about toxic waste disposal and expressed concern that our company could be held accountable by Washington to the point that the company would not be profitable. I share your annoyance at the perversion of democracy as seen in governmental interference in private industry. Let me assure you that we have no intention of bowing to bureaucratic pressure and will continue to dispose of our waste in ways that seem most profitable to maintaining the health of this company.

We are, by way of information, in the process of acquiring a site in Mississippi—near Jackson, to be precise—at the present time, a site which will enable us to dispose of much of our backlogged surplus.

"Near Jackson!" Rose interrupted. "Are you thinking what I'm thinking?"

Tootsie nodded her head. "Um-hmm. Go get Pen and Bippy, will you? I'm going to print this out as well as Maggie's original email to him and the file on Rexco she had downloaded. There's also one more thing I want to check."

Minutes later, with all the Flower Girls standing around, Tootsie spread out the printed letter from Ed Winslow of Rexco Chemical as well as the report he had made to the stockholders and Maggie's letter of inquiry, claiming to be interested in making a major investment in the company. After they'd all finished reading, Tootsie said, "You'll notice that in the speech to the stockholders, while giving the usual rah-rah speech about the company, Winslow is urging them to use pressure—by writing to their representatives and senators—to get the government to back off, saying their dividends would fall if they didn't. He indicates that the company has lost money—lots of it—in trying to clean up former toxic waste sites, and he doesn't intend to spend another penny on such foolishness. Foolishness! He threatens, and I quote, 'to use whatever means are necessary to preserve and maintain the health of this company.' How do you like that! Forget the health of the United States!"

"Do you think that Rexco was trying to buy land near Maggie under false pretenses, and Maggie somehow caught on?" Pen asked.

"Spacious as her property is, there's not enough land around her house for something like that," Rose said.

"What about out near her beloved animal rescue station?" Bippy said.

Rose nodded. "Possibly. There's certainly enough space on that property, but even if she didn't think the company was coming here, she would have fought this tooth and nail, wherever it was located. I think she pretended interest in becoming a share holder to find out what was really going on. She was just getting ammunition for the battle."

"You're right there," Tootsie said. "She never backed off from a good fight if she thought the cause was just. Look," she said, picking up another piece of paper, still in the printer tray. "This is the last email I got from Maggie. I pulled it up and printed it. Listen to this."

> *I am having a bit of trouble with one client,*
> *however. I try not to worry about him and just*
> *concentrate on why I'm in this business in the*
> *first place: to help people find building lots*
> *and suitable homes. We've talked about this*
> *before, remember? About how real estate*
> *at its best is really a service profession? Well,*
> *anyway...I've got to remember that and quit*
> *worrying about this one problem. There's*
> *one in every crowd, you know.*

Bippy caught her breath. "How interesting! I wonder if she's referring to the land deal that Rexco was trying to pull off?"

"I wonder," Rose said, "if the client she was having trouble with was not one she couldn't sell to, but one she wouldn't sell to."

Tootsie exhaled slowly. "If so, I also wonder who was behind it, who was giving her trouble, and just how Gordon Dawkins fits into all this. Where is he, by the way? Doesn't it strike you as peculiar that we haven't met him *yet,* this love of Maggie's life?" She turned back to the computer and began scrolling down through Maggie's files again.

"I wonder if there was a conspiracy of some sort—a front man trying to buy the land by posing as a friend, perhaps," Rose said.

"Or as a boyfriend?" Bippy said. "Rexco would have definitely had to pull the wool over her eyes to get a toe-hold in here."

Rose nodded. "Yes, and one way to do that would have been to appeal to Maggie's romantic side. She was a great believer in the capitalist system and private business, but she also had quite a commitment to the common good. Maggie would never knowingly have sold land for such unconscionable purposes."

"But people will do things for love they wouldn't do for any other reason," Bippy said. "And you know what a romantic Maggie was."

"She still wouldn't have sold that land near her beloved animal shelter unless she had been convinced that it would be properly taken care of and would not impact the environment in any way," said Rose. "Besides—"

"Oh, my gosh!" Tootsie suddenly exclaimed. "Will you look at this!" As the girls gathered around, she clicked on print, and in seconds a page fluttered into the tray of the printer.

"I was just re-checking when I decided to look at the sent mail again. The letters whose subjects were real estate, I had skipped before. I didn't see how they could be important. But listen to this. This is a letter, dated the 9th of October."

Dear Gordon,
Though we will meet shortly for what I am sure

will be a sublime afternoon together, to keep
things legal and professional, I am hereby
putting in writing that after careful consideration,
I have decided not to sell the parcel of land adjacent
to the animal shelter or to allow its use for construction
purposes. As you know, I told you of a particularly
insistent client, determined to get me to sell shortly
before I met you. Apparently, I have finally succeeded
in discouraging him, as I have heard no more from him
since my last refusal.

As to your proposal for the land, I understand
the desirability of the lot for the large home you plan
in the area. The fact that you say you eventually want
to share that home with me makes it all the more tempting.
However, there is no reason we can't live in my present
home, or buy another one, for that matter, without
disturbing the tranquility of that secluded spot near
where my animals already make their home.

I do not wish to impact them negatively in
any way. I know you will understand my thinking
here and respect my decision. I am bringing a copy
of this letter to you, my dear, and will be happy to
discuss it with you, though my mind is made up and
at peace on the issue. I am bringing not only the letter
but also my love. See you soon!
Maggie

Tootsie put down the paper and sat looking at the floor. The room was quiet except for the breathing of the four friends. Finally, Rose spoke. "So, now we know. Gordon Dawkins was trying to get land away from Maggie for some reason or the other. Probably *not* to build a house on."

Bippy chimed in, her face flushed and her granny glasses on the slide. "And she decided against whatever it was he was proposing."

"And he killed her," said Tootsie sadly. "Maybe they quarreled over her decision, and he lost his temper, accidentally killing her, or maybe he was just angry at her for standing in his way."

"We still don't know why he really wanted the land," Rose said, "but I'd be willing to bet that Rexco is behind it."

"So would I," said Tootsie. "So would I. That's probably the client that was badgering her before. She mentioned that it was shortly before she met Gordon. Rexco probably withdrew, reorganized, and tried subterfuge to get what it wanted. With something of this scale, there are bound to be some other people involved, either directly or indirectly, too. I'd be willing to bet one of those other people is our very own mysteriously absent Gordon Dawkins."

Pen nervously clasped and unclasped her cameo pin. With all the excitement, she still hadn't dressed for bed and wore her usual dark dress with a wide, white collar. "Directed at what?"

Tootsie smiled patiently. "No, I said others are probably involved, directly or indirectly."

"Oh. How are we going to find out?"

"There's got to be some way of pulling this Gordon Dawkins and the perps out of the woodwork where they're hiding," Bippy said.

After a long silence, Tootsie said, "Are you all thinking what I'm thinking?"

"Another ad?" Rose questioned.

Tootsie nodded. "Another ad."

"Dear Gussie!" Bippy said.

The next morning, actually just a few hours after the middle-of-the night confab in Maggie's study, Tootsie phoned the ad into the paper. Bippy, Pen, and Rose sat huddled around the breakfast table, sipping tea and munching on the doughnuts Bippy had bought at the small store three blocks away. Tootsie had just hung up the phone, when it rang. "That was fast," she said.

"Talk about good advertising," Rose added.

Grabbing up the receiver, Tootsie answered, "Hello," and then corrected herself. "I mean, Palmer residence."

"This is Lt. Ferguson. Which one of you ladies am I talkin' to this time?"

"This is Tootsie Freeman, Lieutenant. Long time no see," she added with a laugh. "What can I do for you?"

"Thought it sounded like your voice, Ms. Freeman, but I'm surprised you're up and about so early after what you went through last night."

"It's Tootsie, remember? And, actually, I never went to bed. It takes more than that to get me down, Lieutenant."

"So I noticed." His tone became very folksy. Tootsie could picture him chewing on his cigar and winking those hyacinth-blue eyes. "Say, I'se wonderin' if you ladies would mind comin' down here to talk to me a bit."

"Whatever for?"

There was a significant pause, and then he said, "We—uh—we found a man's body this morning."

"A body!" Tootsie exclaimed. She looked at the other girls, who had quit eating mid-chew and were glued to her end of the conversation. She saw Bippy mouth, "Dear Gussie!"

"Yeah, and I thought maybe it would help if we went over a few things, strictly to aid our investigation, you understand. I'd—uh, I'd consider it a favor," he added.

"Wait a minute, Lieutenant." Tootsie's mind was still reeling. "This *is* the same Lt. Ferguson who's been trying to get us to go home, isn't it? A body? You found a body? And you want help from us? Why?"

There was a deep sigh and then Ferguson spoke, "About five o'clock this morning, we found a body, like I said—male, about six-three, brown hair—shot in the back of the head and thrown in the lake. When Tootsie didn't say anything, he went on. "I think you ladies might be interested in this."

"I repeat: Why?"

"From what we can piece together, this man just might be your friend's sweetheart—"

"You mean—"

"Yep. Gordon Dawkins."

Chapter Thirty-Seven

"If there was no ID, what makes you think this is Gordon Dawkins, Lieutenant?" Rose asked, when they were all standing around a draped body in the morgue. Ferguson lifted the sheet from the dead man's face, and there was a collective gasp as they all took a step backwards. Rose tried to concentrate on the man's once-handsome face and not the cloying smell of sweet disinfectants that hung in the air like cheap perfume. She had never liked the artificial cover-up of air fresheners. They reminded her too much of the Brooks and Jones Funeral Home, where she used to help her mother clean on Saturdays. They had cans of spray in every room at that place even with all the lilies and mums in the viewing rooms. She could remember running out into the alley behind the funeral home, on the pretense of shaking her dust mop, to gasp for a breath of fresh air. She could remember her mother, too, crinkling up her nose and saying that "true cleanliness doesn't need camouflage." Rose could picture her mother's face, her winking eye, as she said it. "If a place is clean, there's no sense gilding the lily, and in this place there are plenty of lilies to gild."

Ferguson replaced the sheet over the corpse's face and motioned for the ladies to follow him up the stairs, down the hall, and into his office. "I'll answer your question in my office," he said to Rose as they climbed the steps. As they started into his office, a man in his late fifties, who was poised on the edge of a chair by the door, stood and turned towards them. He smiled at each of them in turn, but when he came to Tootsie, who had paused to smile back at him, he bowed slightly and said, "Ma'am."

Tootsie flashed her signature smile, tilted her head toward him, which made the long, dangling silver stars at her ears spread streaks of light across her face, and extended her hand. "Tootsie Freeman," she said.

"I'm Jake Till—

Ferguson stepped forward and said, "This is Jake Tillman, the man who found the, uh, Maggie Palmer's body." He always hesitated to say the word "body" in front of the Flower Girls as if they would dissolve like sugar cubes in hot water at the very mention of it, even though he had to know by now these were not the dissolving type of women. "Mr. Tillman, these are the friends of the deceased that I told you about."

Tootsie winked at Rose. "I'd give my eye teeth to know what else he told him," she whispered under her breath as they found chairs.

When they were all seated, Ferguson said, "I asked Mr. Tillman to come down today, too, to view this latest body, just to make sure he'd never seen this man before—say in the area around the lake on the day he found Mrs. Palmer's body—and to give you his account. Now, as to why we think this is Gordon Dawkins: He picked up a piece of paper from his desk and glanced at it. According to the description you gave me of what your friend, Mrs. Palmer, said Gordon Dawkins looked like—tall, about six three, very muscular, handsome, brown hair with a touch of gray around the temples, blue eyes—we think this might be the guy."

"Think?" asked Tootsie, secretly impressed that Ferguson, for all his protestations of the accidental nature of Maggie's death, had, in fact, jotted down the description of Dawkins after the Flower Girls had left his office that first time. Tootsie studied the lieutenant's face. When he was concentrating, as he was now, and not chewing on that infernal unlit cigar, he was really quite nice looking. Why hadn't she noticed it before?

"Well, it's just a guess right now, but I'd say it's a good one. We don't have any missin' person reports, and he doesn't fit the description of anyone we're lookin' for. We took prints, and we're waitin' to hear back from the FBI. I'd lay you odds, though, that his name isn't—wasn't—really Dawkins."

Tootsie replayed the ebullient email from Maggie in her mind:

> *He's very handsome. Drop-dead handsome,*
> *you might say. He's tall, about six three, very*
> *muscular, has wavy brown hair to die for with a*
> *touch of gray around the temples, which is SO sexy,*
> *and the bluest eyes I've ever seen. They look like*
> *two pools of water drawn from the Aegean Sea.*

She thought about this man who had so captured Maggie's heart and now lay lifeless in the morgue downstairs. Was this a case of drop-dead handsome or drop dead, handsome? "It's all a matter of punctuation," she said.

"Excuse me?"

"Sorry. I was just thinking out loud."

She glanced at Jake Tillman, who sat on the edge of his seat, his hat in his hands, his red hair tousled. Seeming to sense her gaze, he raised his eyes briefly to meet hers and immediately looked back at his feet. Tootsie was struck with the color of his eyes. She'd always been an eye person. It was the first thing she noticed. Next to Maggie's, they were absolutely the greenest she had ever seen—almost the color of pale emeralds, she decided. She'd always liked emeralds.

But Bippy had not let go of Ferguson's hunch that Gordon Dawkins was not who he said he was. "What makes you say that?" she asked. "What makes you suspect he was using an alias?"

"The fact that he had no ID on him. Most unusual. Usually people have a driver's license, credit card, or even a receipt of some kind on them. He was as clean as that ole whistle people are always talkin' about. It appears that he—or someone else—wanted to make sure he wouldn't be identified by his real name."

Slowly nodding her head, Pen said, "So, he could have come into town posing as Gordon Dawkins, and no one would have been the wiser. Without his real name, he couldn't be traced back to whoever sent him."

"That's right!" said Bippy enthusiastically. "Maggie wrote us that he hadn't lived here long, though we didn't know whether that meant a couple of years or a couple of months, and he didn't want her to tell anyone about their relationship."

"Wait a minute!" Ferguson exploded. "You've left out quite a bit. Why would someone send him and why would someone want to kill Maggie Palmer's boyfriend?"

Tootsie, Bippy, Rose, and Pen spilled out all the tidbits they knew: the letter to Gordon, the letters to them about Gordon's reluctance to let their relationship be known, the land, the Rexco report and letters, and the general suspicion they had based on what they knew—but wouldn't admit to Ferguson—was nothing more than "woman's intuition."

On the way home, Rose said, "Thank goodness the rental company gave us a new car. This one is lots roomier than the other one. They were very nice. I'm glad I took out the kind of insurance that covered whoever drove the car. I think that helped."

"Yes, you're right," Tootsie said. "Hey, what did you all think about the man who found Maggie's body, Jake something-or-other?"

"Take what, dear?" Pen asked.

"Jake. I said how did you like Jake?"

"Oh, he seemed very nice, I thought," Pen said. "He was very polite and seemed genuinely grieved over Maggie's death? What did you think?"

"I thought he had the most gorgeous eyes I've ever seen," Tootsie said.

Bippy giggled. "Still think he might be involved?"

"I could be wrong, but I don't think he could be involved in anything any more serious than digging fishing worms on public property."

"Yes," Bippy said, "he certainly has an engaging air about him, doesn't he? By the way, Tootsie, you didn't tell the lieutenant about the new ad we placed in the paper."

"Oh, darn! Didn't I?" She smiled. "I didn't want to distract him from the leads we put him on to. Besides, I didn't want to listen to another lecture. Maybe he won't even see it."

"And maybe hell will freeze over," Bippy said. For a few seconds everyone just turned and looked, open-mouthed, at Bippy, and then they all burst into laughter.

***

The next day, Rose went out and brought in the newspaper. "Here it is," she said, opening it up to the classifieds.

Will all persons interested in purchasing land belonging to the late Margaret Muldoon Palmer please meet in the outbuilding at the rear of the property adjacent to the animal shelter on Sunday night, October 30, at 6:00 P.M.

"My, that ad looks nice, boxed and all," said Pen, reading over Rose's shoulder. "It's very noticeable."

"I'm not sure whether that's good or bad," Rose said.

"Well, we'll soon find out," Tootsie observed.

The time dragged until after supper when Pen said, "Don't you think we should be going? It's already 5:15. It'll be getting dark soon."

They all put on warm sweaters and slacks, even Pen, who, without calling attention to it, had bought a pair on their shopping trip, and piled into the car, a dark green Honda SUV. As they drove to the outskirts of town, and night began making serious threats of descending imminently, Bippy said, "Why didn't we make this meeting for the middle of the afternoon?"

"I was just thinking the same thing," Pen said.

"Because," Tootsie said, "I thought it would be better to have it after working hours—some people have to work on Sundays—to be sure everyone could come. There may be people right here in Jackson involved in this, too. We want everyone who knows anything to come. This is an equal opportunity trap."

"What map?" Pen asked.

"Trap, Pen, trap," said Bippy. "We're setting a trap."

"Oh. What fun!"

"Besides," Tootsie continued, "some types seem to like the cover of darkness better than the light of day."

"Yeah," Rosemary said, "like cockroaches."

The car bumped along the dirt road leading from the tall bushes at the front of the lot, across a broad expanse of meadow, to a little wooden house on the other side of a thick clump of tall magnolia and pine trees. It was where Maggie stored the hammock and lawn chairs that she used when she entertained friends out here in "the deep, dark woods," as she called it. Tootsie smiled as she looked at the hammock draped over a hook and remembered seeing Maggie sprawled in it, her long legs dangling over the sides, her red hair cascading from her head thrown back in laughter. She could almost hear Maggie's incessant, bubbling chatter, and the memory caused a wave of sadness to wash over her.

After sitting for fifteen minutes, talking and sighing about their memories of Maggie, the girls suddenly heard a noise. "I think someone's coming," whispered Rose.

Bippy peeped out the tiny window. "Yep. It's a car, all right. No, wait. It's a van."

Pen, Rose, and Tootsie peered over her shoulder. To their amazement, they saw not one, but three men, two of them very tall, pile out of the van and make their way up the path to the storage house. The thing that struck all of the Flower Girls at the same time, the thing that made them all draw in their breath, was the way the last of the men, the second tallest of them, was walking.

He was limping.

Chapter Thirty-Eight

Tootsie went to the door as the men approached. "Hello. How ya' doing? I'm Tootsie Freeman, and these are my friends, Bippy, Rose, and Pen. Y'all must be here for the Palmer real estate," she said heartily. "It didn't occur to me that all the people answering the ad would car pool. How environmentally sensitive of you!" Behind her, the girls tittered. The men stood still and looked past her into the small room. Two of the men were large, tall—one about six seven and one about six two—and well built. The other was short, not more than five nine, and had a slight frame. "Well, we're glad you came," she said as they hesitated. "Right now it's just us chickens, but maybe someone else will come."

"Uh—I don't think so," murmured the largest man, who had a neatly trimmed black beard and mustache and piercing eyes the color of onyx.

"Oh? What makes you say that?" asked Rose, stepping forward.

Suddenly, before Tootsie or Rose could react, the men had pushed roughly past them and were inside the room. The last one in, the slightly built one, slammed the door and quickly leaned against it. He wore khakis and a blue-checked button-down shirt. Behind tortoise-shell glasses, his eyes were beady, shifting back and forth from the ladies in front of him to the men beside him. His brown hair was neatly combed and his clothes boasted the familiar logo of a man playing polo, but even though he was well dressed, he had the look of an unmade bed. His shirt and pants were rumpled, and his belt buckle was three inches off center.

"Well, ex-cuse me," said Tootsie. "Come right on in, why don't you?" She turned and whispered to the girls standing behind her, "Whatever happened to manners?"

"Lock that door, Billy," barked the first man, the one apparently in charge.

Tootsie was momentarily distracted. So now Mr. Unmade Bed had a name. "Oh," she began, "I don't think that's necessary. It's safe enough out here. Besides, what if other people do come, then what—"

"Lock it!"

Billy, apparently used to taking orders, turned quickly and did as he was told. "Hmm," he said as he slipped the wooden peg into its slot, "I wonder why the Palmer dame had a peg lock like this on the inside of a storage shed."

The Palmer *dame*? Tootsie felt a cold sensation slowly begin to creep along her backbone, but she was determined not to lose her head. "Billy, is it? I think I can answer that one," she said, trying to remain calm and proceed as rationally as possible. Maybe her hackles were getting raised for no reason. She was alarmed by the imperious nature of these men, and, though every womanly intuition bell she had was ringing frantically, she told herself rationally that she had no reason to push the panic button. Yet. "Maggie loved to 'camp out,'as she called it. She knew it wasn't safe for her to go tent camping by herself, so she brought her dogs with her out here in the spring before it got too hot, and again in the fall, and she slept in her sleeping bag right in this shed. That's what that cot over there is...was...for. She often wrote me about the quiet and the peace she felt here. Now let me repeat my question: Why won't anyone else come?"

"Because," the largest of the three men said with a twisted smile, "We...uh...left a little sign back at the highway." He stroked his beard as if petting a cat.

"Oh really? What sign?" asked Bippy.

The middle man, who up to now had said nothing, took off his Atlanta Braves cap, revealing dirty blond hair, as stringy as it was receding. He scratched his head and returned the cap to its perch. A pair of jeans and a red plaid shirt did nothing to camouflage his huge, well-muscled frame. Lounging against the wall, he smirked. "A sign that said: 'Meeting about land sale from Palmer Estate has been canceled. Watch paper for re-scheduling.'"

"Why...why on earth would you do that?" Bippy asked, feeling the hairs on her slender arms stand up. It was a question to which she really did not want an answer.

The man in the middle nodded. "Tell 'em, Thurston."

They all looked at the large man who had entered the room first. Tootsie was making some mental notes while waiting for the answer to Bippy's question: Short man was Billy, apparently the lackey. The big guy was Thurston and the obvious spokesman for this unholy trinity. In addition to being the tallest, he was also the most striking looking. He had a white collar look about him, educated and intense, with a certain edginess that made him interesting. Put a briefcase in his hand and a suit on his back, Tootsie thought, and you've got yourself a lawyer. He turned his penetrating black eyes first on Tootsie and then on Bippy. "What Tom here is referring to is privacy, you know? We wanted to have a cozy little chat with you. Just you and us."

"No, dear, we wouldn't fuss," Pen said.

Thurston turned a look of irritated incomprehension on her. "Huh?"

Bippy said, "She didn't understand. She's hearing impaired. Pen, listen. He said, 'us,' not 'fuss.'"

316

Tootsie was turning things over in her mind. She now knew all their names: Billy, Tom, and Thurston. What she didn't know—what they were up to—was the most important thing. And that bothered her. A lot.

"Thurston," Billy said, "what are we gonna' do now? I didn't know it was gonna be all four of 'em." He blinked his eyes repeatedly, and his shoulders twitched nervously.

Thurston ignored Billy's question and instead posed one to Tootsie. "What did you ladies have to go pokin' around for? Why couldn't you just accept that Maggie Palmer drowned and let it go at that?"

"I beg your pardon?"

"Why didn't you just leave well enough alone?"

"Well enough?" Tootsie exclaimed, her voice getting higher and higher. "Well enough! Our friend is dead. I don't call that 'well enough.'"

"Wait! Are you interested in acquiring property from the estate of Maggie Palmer or not?" Bippy asked.

The three men exchanged glances. "Yes ma'am," Thurston said, unsuccessfully squelching a grin. "You might say that. We most definitely are interested in acquiring it."

"Are you a real estate agent?" Pen suddenly asked.

"Actually," Thurston replied, "I am. Yes indeedy. A gen-u-wine, bone fide real estate agent. Not, however, too successful of late, I might add, but one who promises to do real well, real soon."

Hoping to quell the rising fear within her, Tootsie said, "What does the way Maggie died have to do with your interest in this land anyway?"

"And what did you mean by asking why we didn't accept Maggie's death as accidental?" Rose added.

"Just what I said," Thurston replied. "Why didn't you?"

"Because it wasn't," Rose said forcefully. "She didn't drown. We know it, and"—she took a deep breath—"apparently you know it."

"I think," added Tootsie boldly, "that not only do you know she didn't drown, but maybe you know more than that. You obviously have some interest in her land or you wouldn't be here." When no one said anything, she added, "Maybe so much interest that you killed her for it or know who did."

There was a long silence. Finally, Thurston said, "She wouldn't listen. I approached her about buying this whole property, but she was so hell-bent on preserving her precious animals in that pest farm of hers—the other two men laughed at his corruption of 'pet farm'—she wouldn't listen. Rexco was willing to pay a fair price. At two million dollars, more'n fair, I'd say."

"Rexco?" Bippy asked.

"Yeah. They wanted to buy the land adjacent to the St. Francis Animal Adoption Center."

"For?" Bippy asked.

"For an industrial by-products management facility," replied Thurston.

"In other words," Rose said, "a toxic waste dump."

"Tsk. Tsk. You use such ugly words," said Tom. Billy guffawed.

"No wonder Maggie wouldn't sell," said Tootsie.

"Oh, she didn't know that at first—about the toxic waste, I mean. You think I'm crazy? Everybody around here knew what a tree-hugger she was. I tried buying it as a rustic retreat for a client who wanted a 'dream home' in the country. See, what happened was I had been approached by Rexco to see if I could acquire some land out in the country. They made me a very generous offer. Let's face it: Real estate's been slow lately. I can use the extra income right now, so I said, sure, I'd find 'em some land. I did, too. Trouble was, the Palmer dame wouldn't budge. She didn't want any building on that piece of land. Not near her precious animals! I couldn't let some bleeding-heart animal lover stand in the way of progress, now could I?"

"Whose progress?" Tootsie said acidly.

"Mine, of course." Thurston grinned and looked at Tom and Billy for approval.

"Hmm? What process?" asked Pen.

"Progress, Pen, progress," said Rose sharply. Then, seeing the wounded look on Pen's face, she patted Pen's hand and said, "Sorry. I'm just a little tense."

"So?" asked Bippy. "Maggie wouldn't sell. Then what?"

"Well, then I got Billy here, who's in insurance, and Tom, who's a builder, to help me. We put our heads together and tried everything. We tried telling her that insurance rates were going to go up, and she'd need lots more insurance for the animal adoption center—she had continued to pay the insurance premiums on that place even after she gave it to the society—as well as the land that adjoined it. There are lots of trees that can fall on that piece of land. Do some damage. You know what I'm saying? She'd be needing the nice income from the sale of that land. She didn't buy it. Then, Tom here tried convincing her that if she'd sell to my client, he'd build a huge brick wall all the way around the 'dream home' I told her my client wanted to build there. Told her it would be in such a secluded way that you wouldn't even know it was there. We even promised to landscape and camouflage it with trees. Still, no dice. That was one stubborn lady."

The Flower Girls stood stock still, gripped by what they were hearing. "And?" Tootsie said.

"Well, it was time to outsmart her," Thurston said. "That's when we brought Les Cartwright in."

Rose said, "Let me guess: a.k.a. Gordon Dawkins?"

Tom smiled. "You catch on quick. Les—or Gordon, as the Palmer woman knew him—was an army buddy of mine. We served together in Afghanistan. That's where I got my leg nearly blown off. Anyway, I knew he had a way with the ladies. Always did. He was supposed to court her up a storm and even promise to marry her if he had to. That way, he could talk her into selling him the land to build them a love nest on. Then, the four of us would split the money, and he'd split the scene."

Thurston, clearly warming to his subject, jumped in. "He was good, too. Damn good."

"He was that, all right," interjected Tom. He looked at the floor and slowly nodded his head.

Thurston nodded. "He quoted poetry to her, sent her flowers, charmed her, and—you know—swept her off her feet. For a good businesswoman, she sure was easy to fool. Told her he knew it was fast, but he'd fallen head over heels in love with her. Couldn't help himself. They saw each other every day and every night. At first, he approached her as an ordinary client wanting to buy a parcel of land to build a country retreat on. But soon, he told her he was madly in love with her, wanted to marry her, and wanted her to share the huge estate he was planning to build with a lake, woodland, and rustic mansion. I think she saw it as a way of protecting those animals. Knew she'd be nearby to look out for their interests. Course, she fell for him, hook, line, and sinker, and she told him that if they built their home out there, she could keep an eye out to be sure nothing encroached on the acreage set aside for the animal center. He told her he shared her vision for the center. Told her it would be their animal kingdom, and she would be the queen of the kingdom. Oh, yeah, he was good, all right."

They had come too far to turn back now. The Flower Girls knew it. The men knew it.

"Then...then why is Maggie dead?" Bippy asked.

Billy shuffled his feet and looked at his toes as if checking to make sure they were still attached to his body. He wouldn't meet Bippy's gaze. Instead, he shifted his eyes quickly from Tom to Thurston and ran his hand through his hair, messing up the one neat thing about his appearance. After fiddling with his glasses, he swallowed, and his Adam's apple bobbed nervously.

"Well?" repeated Bippy, looking straight at him.

"I'll answer that," Thurston said. "Billy is a bit shy. Doesn't get out of the office much, do you, Billy?" He winked in Billy's direction and then looked straight at the girls. "You want to know why your friend is dead, do you? Well, the day before her 'accident,' she discovered a note from Billy in Les's car, a note that alluded to our little partnership and our connection to Rexco."

"So you killed her because she found out Gordon Dawkins was a phony?" Tootsie cried.

"Not quite. She met Les—Gordon—for a picnic that day, and she confronted him with what she'd discovered. It seems she did a little checking on Rexco on the Internet. Tsk. Tsk. You know what they say about curiosity. Well, anyway, she wasn't absolutely convinced that Les had been lying to her, that he was part of it. Probably didn't want to believe it. She just wanted an explanation of what the note meant. Les lost his cool. Admitted his complicity. Became enraged. They argued. She started stomping off, vowing to make his treachery known and to expose to the city what the group had planned. He said he panicked. He couldn't let her leave like that. Not just go off and blow the whole thing for us. So, he hit her over the head from behind with a large fallen tree limb that had been knocked down by the wind that day. Hard. It broke her neck."

"Oh dear Lord!" Bippy gasped, sinking down on a chair nearby.

Thurston leaned against the wall and put both hands in his pockets. "She never had a chance to struggle. That night, Tom and Billy here helped him take her body out in a johnboat and dump it. They left her sailboat, which they'd towed behind them, and rowed back to shore."

Tootsie, her heart sinking within her, got some perverse satisfaction from seeing Billy fidget. Thurston and Tom seemed to have nerves of steel, or, more likely, no conscience at all. Maybe both, she thought. But Billy, his close-set eyes wildly flitting from one of his accomplices to the other, seemed about to come unglued. Tootsie decided to pick at the sore. "So, Billy, you did that, huh? You murdered a perfectly innocent person. A woman, too. She must have been about the age of your mother. You must be very proud."

"I did not! I didn't murder anyone," he shot back.

"Oh, ex-*cuse* me," she replied. "Point taken. You just dumped her poor, lifeless body into the lake like so many pounds of potatoes. You'll probably get the humanitarian of the year award. Not to put too fine a point on it, Billy, but you're still an accessory to murder."

"Shut up!" Tom said.

"I want to know one thing," said Rose. "If he did such a bang-up job, why did you kill Les Cartwright? You did kill him, right?"

"Les was a loose cannon," Thurston said. "He rattled around a lot after Maggie's death. I don't know what came over him. He changed."

"Murder will do that," Rose said.

"I think maybe he really fell in love with her...a little bit," Billy said meekly.

Tom joined in. "Maybe. Whatever, he still panicked and killed her, putting us all at risk. That wasn't in the plans. He had to go. Just had to. I hated it. I mean, he was an old army buddy, but still.... We couldn't afford a possible tie-in with us. You never know what the police will unearth once they get to sniffing."

"So handsome had to drop dead," Tootsie said.

"What?" Tom said.

"I was just remembering something Maggie said in describing him."

"Is that the only reason?" Rose prodded.

A dark smile creased Thurston's face like a knife slash. "That and the fact that with one less, there'd be a bigger piece of the pie for each of us. It was going to work out okay. With Palmer dead, we figured we could buy the property from her estate—no problems now. Of course, that would take some of the money we'd been promised by Rexco. That would now have to come out of what they'd agreed to give us for our part in securing the land—whatever way we got it. But with Cartwright out of the way, we'd split it only three ways."

"I see," said Tootsie. "So, this all comes down to greed, doesn't it?"

"Doesn't everything?" Thurston said. "I mean, really now, doesn't everything?"

"No," said Tootsie firmly, "I think not."

"Well, I hate to draw this little chat to a close," Thurston said. "I can't tell you how much I'd love to stay and continue this philosophical discussion, but you know what they say about all good things." From his right pants pocket, he withdrew his hand.

Tootsie, Pen, Bippy, and Rose all stared silently at his hand. In it was a shiny silver .357 Magnum.

Chapter Thirty-Nine

Like a cat on padded feet, Ferguson, still hidden by the trees, crept closer and closer to the back of the small building tucked within the arms of the forest. He had hiked in from the far corner of the property instead of coming from the front where the dirt road cut through. There he would surely have been observed. Instead, he came in farther down, nearer the animal center property, where he had to crawl through thickets and vines, which tore at his hands and face. Drat those women and their damn newspaper ads, anyhow! He could have been at the Longhorn Steakhouse right about now enjoying a nice juicy porterhouse coated with fresh-cracked pepper if he hadn't had to come trailing after them. Visions of the steak and its accompanying baked potato—crispy outside and fluffy inside, a crown of butter melting on its fat, pooched-up middle, just the way he liked it—flitted behind his eyes.

And it was more than likely all for nothing. Hadn't the coroner ruled Palmer's death accidental? Still, Ferguson had not had a good feeling about this case from the very beginning—something he attributed privately to his mother's intuition, which he seemed to have inherited. His investigation, which he had not bothered to share with the women, had failed to turn up anything definitive, however. What more could he do? Were there any real facts upon which to base a homicide investigation? Facts which he could use to justify a full-fledged investigation to the commissioner and subsequently the D. A.? He permitted himself an exasperated shake of the head. He wasn't often one to indulge in "what ifs," but this was one of those times. If those dizzy dames had just gone on home after the funeral.... A quiet sigh escaped his lips. Oh well, they hadn't, and that was that.

He had tried to discourage them, even bully them into letting go of their suspicions for their own safety, but instead, here he was, in the middle of the woods with dark coming on fast, getting a little chilly even in his lightweight jacket—the coolest night yet this fall—waiting to see what, if anything, would happen next. Of course, there was always the possibility, he admitted to himself, that the women just might be onto something. After all, he didn't for a minute buy the fact that the burglar who conked Tootsie over the head at the door of the office or the intruder who attacked Rosemary were after valuables at the Palmer residence. What were they after? And what about Tootsie's being run off the road, as she claimed? Coulda' been her fault. She coulda' just gotten disoriented in the fog, but she was insistent that someone had been following her and bumped her. He saw her go off the road, but whether she just lost control or whether she was speeding from fear that she was being followed once again by the one who bumped her, as she claimed, was another question entirely. Could someone have gotten between her and him following her from Lulu's? Could be. Could be. There were a couple of other pick-ups leaving Lulu's after she did. He held back until they were gone so he wouldn't be spotted, and he couldn't be sure which way they had gone in that fog. It was the worst fog he'd ever seen. There *was* a dent in her bumper, just as she'd told him there would be. He'd just have to wait and see.

He didn't have to wait long. From his position, crouched low in the bushes, he could see a van snaking its way up the long, dirt road. He stayed perfectly still as the vehicle parked and three men got out. Even in the semi-darkness, he thought he recognized one of them. Thurston Mansfield. Who could miss him? What in blazes was he doing here? Nothing good, of that Ferguson was certain. How could the perennially bankrupt Mansfield possibly hope to buy the Palmer property? Mansfield, a slightly shady realtor, who had been suspected of lots of things, but convicted of nothing, was hard to miss. At six seven, he towered over just about everyone else. Local gossip had it that he had played basketball in college somewhere in the Midwest but was kicked off the team and out of the college in a point-shaving scandal. He seemed to be one of those people, who, like a dark suit, attracted only the things you didn't really want. He always seemed to be one step behind what Mansfield had been quoted in the paper as calling "a really big deal." He was one of those people who was always *going* to make it, but never did. Ferguson had been to see him on a couple of occasions. As chief detective, he had questioned Mansfield about a racketeering ring. Mansfield came out of that as innocent as a choir boy and then had given Ferguson quite a tongue-lashing, threatening to sue for false arrest. Never mind that he was never arrested, only questioned, something Ferguson pointed out when Mansfield drew a breath, but he had made quite a scene anyhow. Had gone on TV to excoriate the bullying tactics of the local police! Even though it had been several years, Ferguson remembered him. Oh yeah, he remembered him, all right. Quite the sleaze.

Once the men were inside the building, Ferguson, his suspicions raised by the presence of Mansfield, left the cover of the woods and, his gun drawn, stole quietly right up to the shed. There was no window at the back, so he knew he couldn't be seen by those inside. Hunched over, he crept along the side of the small outbuilding until he was right beneath the side window. Kneeling, scarcely breathing, he listened. Because it was now fully dark, he was able to stand slowly and peek in at the window every now and then without being observed. He heard them discuss the whole thing: the plans, the murders, the goals. The cold metal of his revolver was comforting.

"So, now we know," Tootsie was saying sadly.

"Yep," Thurston replied, "now you know. Why didn't you all leave when we tried scaring you off? Four times we tried. You're slow learners, you know it? I thought forcing you off the road night make you go on back home."

"On the way home from the restaurant. So that was you," Rose said.

"Then, I thought when Tom retrieved the appointment calendar and in the process knocked one of you dames down, you'd take the hint. But no-o-o. That would have been too easy. We had to send Tom back over to the house to put a scare into you at night. Then, when that didn't work, we tried scaring one of you on the road by bumping your rear bumper. Nothing seems to get through to you broads. Like I say, slow learners."

"I suppose you're going to kill us with that," Rose said.

Thurston looked at the gun in his hand and smiled. "This? No, actually, I'm not."

"Whew, that's a relief," Bippy breathed. "I was afraid there for a minute that—"

"Not unless I have to. You're going to have a tragic accident, all the more tragic because it's the same way your dear friend died. I can see the headlines now: 'Friends Die Re-enacting Palmer's Death.' "

The Flower Girls all seemed to gasp at once. "Dear Gussie!" Bippy exclaimed with more than her usual emotion.

Rose gasped. "The same way Maggie—"

"—You heard him," Tom cut in. "You're going to be out on the lake trying to find out what happened to Maggie Palmer and have an unfortunate boating accident. You panic and drown. It happens."

"Billy, you're getting to be quite good at this, aren't you?" Tootsie said, looking at the small man cowering in the corner. Instinctively, she knew he was the weakest link in the men's murderous chain.

"You've got quite a mouth, dontcha', lady? Ignore her," Tom said, slapping Billy on the shoulder. "Let's go."

Ferguson quickly thought of his options. He could surprise them, try to get the drop on them, and just hope he was successful. If not, and if there were any gunfire, the Flower Girls would be at risk. He was outnumbered, after all, and, of course, he was no match for the three men size-wise. The other choice was repugnant in that it meant he had to abandon the girls, temporarily anyway. If he could just get to his car, he could call for help. He surely couldn't call now. He couldn't make a single sound. Not even breathe.

There didn't seem to be any immediate danger to the women since the plan was to make their death appear accidental. That plan wouldn't call for them to be killed here, so he made a quick but calculated decision. He had to get help. To do that, he would creep back to the woods as quickly and as quietly as he could. Once there, he could stand and run without danger of being seen. The undergrowth would slow him down, but he would just have to do the best he could. He had to make it to his car, hidden behind some bushes, before the van pulled out onto the highway. He knew they were headed for the lake, knew they were going to try to stage a second accident in the same spot, so if he couldn't tail them without being seen, he'd go there on his own. He knew a shortcut.

Twenty more feet, and he'd be out of sight of the shed. He picked his way along at first, not daring to switch on his flashlight. Once in the safety of the forest, knowing the light would be swallowed up by the woods, though, he quickly clicked it on and began running as hard as he could. Vines tore at his jacket, slit the backs of his hands. A low branch gouged his cheek, narrowly missing his eye. His lungs burned, his legs cramped, and his throat ached as he gasped for breath. He knew there was all manner of wildlife in this area and tried not to think of what eyes were watching his progress. He particularly didn't want to think about snakes. He had never been one for snakes. The very thought of them made his blood curdle. All at once, he tripped over a root, stumbled, and crashed to the ground, hitting his forehead hard against a log, but after feeling to make sure he wasn't cut, he stood, shook his head, and ran on. Just when he thought he couldn't run any farther and would have to stop and rest, he saw his car up ahead. Sliding into the driver's seat, he jerked up the phone and, panting, dropped his head back against the headrest. His breath came in deep gasps as he waited for the police dispatcher to answer. Up ahead, the lights of a van poked holes in the blanket of black that had draped itself over the countryside. Poked, turned, and were immediately replaced by the soft red glow of tail lights.

Chapter Forty

Ferguson sped along the dark road, his headlights sweeping bravely ahead like fearless scouts. "Come on, baby," he said aloud. "Let's get there." He often talked to his car, urging it, coaxing it, as one would a horse. It didn't do anything for the car's performance, he knew, but it made him feel less alone. He couldn't remember another time when he felt so stressed, so afraid that things were going to go wrong. The presentiment of danger, of doom, and of guilt was due to the decision he had made back there at the shed. Was it the right one? Second-guessing himself was part of his personality, and he engaged in it with vigor. He could have intervened right then, but it was just too risky. Too much danger that one of the women could get hurt. As likely as not, one of the perps would have grabbed at least one of the women to use as a shield. Then where would he be? Where would they all be? He would have had to stand there and let them go.

On the other hand, he might have gotten the drop on them and spared the women this risky ordeal. He was gambling, he knew, and the stakes in this little game were four innocent lives. Shaking his head, he thought how many times a policeman is called on to make a split-second decision with no do-overs. In an instant-replay world, we're expected to make snap decisions without error that will stand up to public scrutiny. In the real world, the world of police work, it just doesn't happen that way. Hell, he thought, it doesn't even happen that way in basketball games.

He could no longer see the van in the distance, but that was okay. That meant they couldn't see him either. He knew where they were going, the only place they could go to recreate Palmer's murder, and he would be ready for them. Quickly, he whipped off the highway onto a back road that would cut minutes off his time to the lake. That would put him there ahead of the van—slightly. If only the backup arrived before...before the murders were carried out. If not, he would just have to go it alone. If worse came to worst, he'd throw a light on them and order them to surrender their guns. He would shoot if he had to. Maybe they would assume he had reinforcements in place. That would be a last resort, though, because of the danger of hitting the women. No, by far the best thing would be to outnumber them, surround them, and get the drop on them while they were occupied getting the women out of the van and into a boat. If there was just time!

Ferguson glanced at the luminous glow of his watch in the darkness as he pulled off the road about two hundred yards from the entrance to the boat ramp at the lake. He eased into a little picnic area with an outdoor grill, a picnic table, and a space wide enough to park three or four cars. Because of two large bushes blocking the view, he knew he couldn't be seen from the lakeshore. He had asked for at least two black-and-whites to meet him here and had been assured they were on the way. Should be there at the boat launch in about ten minutes, the dispatcher had said. That was five minutes ago. *Hurry up*, he breathed to himself. *Hurry the hell up.*

He sat quietly for a while, his headlights off, but his engine idling, and waited, running through in his mind the different scenarios that might be awaiting him. Looking again at his watch, he saw with near panic that time was ticking away. He had been here almost four minutes. Four minutes that could well mean the difference in life and death for those four women. Where was his backup? If they didn't come in another minute, he was moving in on his own. No choice.

***

Pen was pushed roughly into the back of the van. *What have I done? What have I gotten myself into*? she thought, as she pressed the unfamiliar slacks down on her legs. She missed the comfort of her long skirt, which she often wrapped about her legs like a blanket. Oh, to be back in Culpeper taking her daily walks, putting the kettle on for tea, going to church, going to the House of Hair where Brandy would gently insist on trying a new hairstyle! That was such a good life. Lonely maybe, but good. She saw that now. She had often wished that she could break away from the silent memories that held her a reluctant, if willing, prisoner there, could meet people and discuss ideas, could see more of the world while she was still able to get around well. Though she had the financial security to travel, she lacked the one thing that would make it possible: confidence. She couldn't possibly travel alone. Couldn't begin to understand announcements over the public address systems of the world's busy terminals. Couldn't dare to see loneliness as it appeared in the face of every stranger. Couldn't bear to feel it dragging like a weight behind her as it followed her from Culpeper to the ends of the Earth.

Pen's life, which had revolved for so many years around the children and especially John and had blurred into insignificance since his death, came sliding into focus as she thought about what lay ahead for her just down the road. The last fifteen years had been hard.

First there was John's illness. Then, his death. The loss of him, of his warmth, his companionship, his personality wounded her in more ways than she could have imagined. She lost confidence in herself, lost her enthusiasm for new things. Finally, there was her loss of hearing. That had been the final blow. She had more or less given in to her deafness, she realized. She was forced to admit that she had capitulated to a disability. Understanding what people were saying was just too much of a struggle, too tiring, so she had mostly withdrawn into her own comfortable house, her own secure world, muted and stagnant though it was.

She never indicated to the children that she was anything but happy in the large home in which she and John had invested their lives, never shared her loneliness with them. She had heard her own mother say too many times that she "never wanted to be a burden to the children," and Pen had unconsciously adopted that as her own philosophy, too. It's always a mother's instinct to protect her children, she supposed, even from herself. Gradually, she had become a martyr to her condition, not wanting her children to feel that she was burdening them, and so had insisted that they not come to see her because she didn't want to intrude on their busy lives, when all the while she would so have loved to have had her grandchildren come and have tea parties with her in the gazebo on the grassy lawn behind her house. Martyrdom is the loneliest of conditions. And greatly overrated. If she only had life to live over...

She looked at Bippy's small form beside her, shivering with cold and fear. How to comfort her? "Bippy," she whispered, "Endure, and keep yourself for better days." Bippy tried to smile. Pen looked at the other two. Tootsie, her head thrown back, had her eyes closed, and Rosemary was talking. Pen couldn't quite make out what she was saying, but she knew it was to the men in front because Rosemary

333

was leaning forward, talking earnestly. How amazing, Pen thought, that she was about to come to the end of her life's journey with these people who, a short time ago, were perfect strangers. Yet, she couldn't have chosen to die with closer friends. What warmth she felt for them! Adversity quickly destroys the barriers between people and makes them friends. Pen shook her head. Why do we waste so much of life's precious time?

With a shudder, she thought about the dark, cold waters of the lake, about how the news of her death would finally make its way to her children and grandchildren, about how they would react, and that made her sad. The overwhelming feeling of sadness that possessed her, however, was not of her impending death, but of missed opportunities, overlooked joys, postponed pleasures. She turned her head toward the side of the van and wept silently. Suddenly, feeling Bippy's hand patting her knee, she looked up and smiled at her new friend. Just as she did, she saw two of the men, the two biggest ones, climbing between the seats and holding on as the van raced down the highway. They were heading for them. In their hands they held something she couldn't quite make out, but something that she knew instinctively was to be instrumental in her death.

***

"Okay. It's gonna' take all three of us to get this done," Thurston said.

The Flower Girls, rendered unconscious by the administration of a drug as they streaked through the darkness in the van, now lay like sleeping children in the back. They had struggled, fought, kicked, cried, and clawed, but they were no match for Thurston and Tom. Billy had driven down the long road on the Palmer property and along the highway to the lake while the other two did the dirty work. But now they were at the lake's edge, and the time had come.

"I--I don't know," Billy said. "I don't think I can do this. You know, 'off' little old ladies."

"Nobody asked you to think," Tom replied. "You didn't back out before."

"That was different. That woman was already dead."

"Well, these are gonna be, too, pretty soon. Simply a matter of timing. Just do what you're told and before you know it, you'll be lying on a beach somewhere in the South Seas sipping a cool drink with some smooth-skinned native girl glazing you with coconut oil while you are trying to think of ways to spend all your money. Now come on. Give us a hand. These broads have gotta drown. That's the only way the story will make sense. We've got to get them out in the lake and hold them under water before the drug wears off."

"And that's another thing. What about the drug you knocked them out with? An autopsy will show it," Billy protested, "and then suspicion will be aroused about the Palmer woman and then Cartwright, and we'll be implicated in all the murders. Sooner or later it'll get back to us."

"Not this one, my man. This little drug—courtesy of Rexco Chemicals—just renders the person unconscious and then goes away. Poof. No tell-tale residue. It's perfect."

"Sure, perfect," Billy muttered. "What if somebody hears us going out into the lake? Won't that cause curiosity? Somebody's sure to notice."

"Electric motor, Billy Boy," Tom replied. "Quiet as a breath. Now relax. Thurston has thought of everything."

As the men lifted each of the women's bodies out of the van and piled them into the bottom of a medium-sized boat, Billy said, "I don't like it. Long time ago my daddy told me to drown a sack full of kittens somebody'd left at our place. I disobeyed him and let 'em go up the road a bit. This is kinda' like that. I feel like we're about to drown a sack full of kittens, only worse. Way worse."

"Gawdamighty, Billy! You're starting to sound like that loony Palmer dame herself."

Chapter Forty-One

Sunlight flooded the room and lay in a pool of gold on the floor. "Where am I?" Pen asked. She turned her head groggily and looked at the form under the sheets in the other bed.

Bippy leaned on one elbow. "Pen? Are you awake? It's about time. I've been lying here waiting for you to come to, Sleepyhead."

"Oh no! Who's dead?"

"Oh, dear Gussie. Bless your heart. I didn't say 'dead.' I said 'sleepyhead.' "

"Oh. Bippy? Where are we?"

"Lake View Hospital. We were held overnight for observation. I've already talked to the nurse. She says once the doctor comes around, they're going to release us."

Suddenly, Pen tried to sit up. "Where are Tootsie and Rose?"

Bippy smiled. "Relax. They're in the next room. They peeped in at the door a little bit ago, but you were still sleeping, so they didn't come in."

"Oh, my head!" Pen said, falling back onto her pillows.

"Mine, too," Bippy said. "I'm going to ring the nurse now and tell her you're awake. See if she can give us both something for a headache. I'll ring Tootsie and Rose, too."

When Rose and Tootsie, still clad in flapping hospital gowns and thin-as-paper robes, came into the room, they went to Pen's and

Bippy's beds, hugging each one silently for a long time. It was not until now that they could all release the weeks of wondering, the days of grief, and the hours of pent-up fear. And release it they did. When Lt. Ferguson walked into the room, it was to be greeted by four women hugging one another and bawling like newborn babies. "What in the world is the matter, ladies?" he said, his voice considerably more upbeat than it had been in his previous encounters with them.

"Nothing's the matter," Bippy said between sobs. "Nothing at all. That's just it."

"We're just so thankful to be alive," Rose said.

"What happened, Lieutenant?" Tootsie asked. "The last thing I remember is riding in that van headed to the lake and two of the men coming back towards us. What happened next? How did you get involved in this?"

"This might come as a surprise to you all, but I read the paper, too," he said, smiling, and then frowned at them. "That reminds me. What did I tell you about—"

Tootsie held up one hand. "Please! Spare us the lectures right now," she said. "My head hurts too badly. What I want to know is how we got from the van to the hospital."

The Flower Girls listened, rapt, as Ferguson recounted how he had read the ad, arrived at the shed, listened to the conversations, and, once back in his car, summoned help. "Well, I arrived on the scene at the lake shore–I knew a shortcut–just before y'all arrived in the van. It seems you had each been given a drug to render you unconscious. If my backup hadn't arrived when it did, I was prepared to make the arrest myself, but I've gotta tell you, I sure was glad to see those squad cars pull in."

"Did you arrest the perps?" Pen asked.

Ferguson raised his eyebrows and then relaxed his face into a smile and nodded. "Yes, ma'am, we did. The perps are all in custody."

"Did you have to use torture to get the truth out of them?" asked Bippy.

Ferguson grinned. "No, ma'am. No bright lights, cattle prods, or rubber hoses, but one of them, Billy Adams, has offered through his lawyer to testify against the other two—and even against Rexco—in return for a lighter sentence. That's the one I'd really like to get, that Rexco outfit. I've already talked to the D. A., Monica Adams, this mornin', and though it's early yet, and she can't promise anythin' until she has read all the reports, I think we have a deal. Adams—can you believe this guy?—says he didn't think it was 'right' to kill women. I believe his exact words were—pardon me, ladies—'off little old ladies.' "

"How very courtly of him!" Rose mocked.

"And I thought chivalry was dead," Tootsie said. "Silly me."

"It appears we owe you—owe you big time," Rose said. "If you hadn't followed up on that ad, we would be...dead right now."

Bippy shuddered. "Ohhh, don't talk like that!"

"I don't even like to think about it," Pen said, touching a trembling finger to her lips.

"Well, it's true," Tootsie said, beaming at Ferguson. She raised her hand to her head in a shaky salute. "Congratulations, Lieutenant. A nice piece of police work, I must say."

Ferguson colored and turned his head, stretching his chin as if to free it from a too-tight collar. "All in a day's work, ladies. Glad I was there to help. Now, I have somethin' to say. As it turns out, I owe y'all, too."

"Oh?" Tootsie said.

"Because of y'all, I wrapped up two murder investigations that might otherwise have gone unsolved, at least for a long time. Even though I had checked things out at the beginnin' and thought I was on top of it, I was wrong about Maggie Palmer's death. I wasn't suspicious enough. I allowed my head to overrule my heart."

"What do you mean?" Tootsie asked.

"I had suspicions at the scene, a gut feelin' that a healthy woman just wouldn't fall off her boat and drown. Then, when the coroner said she hadn't drowned but had broken her neck, but that there was no evidence of foul play, I beat back that gut feelin' again and took the autopsy report as gospel. I clearly wasn't suspicious enough."

"Well, maybe we were *too* suspicious," Tootsie said, laughing. "At one point, we even suspected you."

"Me!"

Tootsie shrugged. "Well, we just couldn't understand your reluctance to investigate. We didn't know you were quietly 'checking things out,' as you put it. At that point, we suspected everyone. Clarkson. Raymond. Even Jake what's-his-name."

"Tillman. Jake Tillman. Oh, by the way, he's waitin' to say hello to you all. He's been here quite a while—all night, in fact."

Tootsie's mouth opened in surprise. "You're kidding! How did he know what happened?"

"I called him. He came right over and spent the night out in the lobby pacing the floor."

Tootsie couldn't hide a smile. "Well, I'll be. Girls, it appears we have a new friend. Maybe he can get a Hawaiian shirt to match our dresses."

"Clarkson and Raymond are on their way here, too. They had all asked me to keep them apprised of how the case was developin', so once we wrapped this up last night, I gave them all a call. Clarkson and Raymond are both flyin' in this mornin'. Should be here soon. They told me to tell you all to save dinner tonight. They want to take us all—Jake and me, too—out someplace special to celebrate."

***

That evening, after another trip to T. J. Maxx for just the right thing to wear for the celebration, Tootsie, Rose, Pen, and Bippy sat at a table for eight with their dates for the evening: Jake, Lt. Ferguson, Clarkson, and Raymond. The girls were surprised and delighted when they each found at their plate a yellow rose, a gift from Maggie's brothers.

"How extraordinarily sweet!" Pen said over a lump in her throat.

"How very thoughtful you are!" added Bippy.

"How did you know about the yellow roses?" asked Tootsie.

"We have always known that Sis loved yellow roses, and then we saw you place them on her coffin at the cemetery. It was such a moving gesture at the time that—well, who could forget it?" Clarkson said, clearing his throat.

"Speaking of forgetting," Raymond said, taking a deep breath, "I'll never forget any of you, especially you Flower Girls."

"Me either," said Jake. "We—and I include everyone in Jackson—owe you more than we can say for getting to the bottom of what happened to the one and only Maggie Muldoon Palmer. Everybody in this city loved her."

Suddenly, a vaguely familiar voice rang out from the other corner of the dining room. "Yoo-hoo. Well, would you look who's here. I do declare! Y'all just keep turning up in the most unexpected places." Beulah Merritt was making her way hurriedly across the room, her sensible shoes tapping on the polished hardwood floor. "I'll swanee, if this isn't a coincidence! I *never* dine here, but tonight I came with three other ladies from the Mary and Martha circle to talk about plans for our church-wide bazaar next spring. I want to get the jump on the other groups in the church because I think our circle should be in charge since we do all the work, don't you know, especially with the bereavement committee. Anyway, here you are."

"Yes, here we are," Tootsie said without enthusiasm. She shot a look across the table at Ferguson and, as Beulah turned around to signal to her friends that she would be along in a minute, mouthed, "Arrest her. She's stalking us." Her face relaxed in a grin.

Immediately, as Beulah turned back to the table, all the men stood. "Hello, Mrs. Merritt," Raymond said. Turning to his brother, he said, "Clark, you remember Mrs. Merritt from the church." He went on hurriedly introducing the other men at the table as if trying to relieve himself of the burden by pawning her off on the next in line.

After the introductions were made, Beulah motioned to the men. "Now, now, please sit down. You're such gentlemen, but I won't hear of disturbing your meal."

Tootsie looked at Rosemary and smiled. The same thought was going through both their minds: *That's why she came over here, right? Not to disturb our meal.*

She looked at Jake and said, "I haven't seen you around before. Are you Mrs. Freeman's beau?"

Tootsie coughed and covered her mouth with a napkin. Jake grinned shyly and said, "No, ma'am. I live here, but I stay out pretty much at the lake. Unless you fish, we probably wouldn't have run into each other."

"Oh, I see. Well, never mind. I'm glad you've met Mrs. Freeman, though. Maybe you two can get to know each other better while she's here." She winked broadly at Tootsie as if they were co-conspirators in the eternal woman-seeks-mate scheme.

Bippy let out a little gasp. "Dear Gussie!" she whispered under her breath. Such brazenness! She herself would never have been so tactless. She much preferred using finesse and subterfuge in fixing up couples. *This woman obviously has no sense of subtlety,* she thought.

When Jake murmured something and then fell silent, Beulah said, "Well, I guess I'd better be going. You'll want to be ordering soon. Be sure to try the squash supreme. Needs a little more salt, if you ask me, and a tad more cheese, but it's still the best thing on the menu." Then she lowered her voice and muttered out the side of her mouth as if speaking to an accomplice. "I wouldn't order the chicken if I were you. I think I'll come over and offer to teach them how to fry chicken." She winked again. "Well, toodle-oo. You girls come back to Mississippi soon," she said to Pen, Rose, Bippy, and Tootsie.

As she retreated and left the restaurant with her friends, there was an almost palpable sense of relief at the table. "You know what they say about a bad penny?" Tootsie laughed. "Beulah Merritt is our bad penny."

"She's missed her calling, all right," Raymond said. "Should have worked for the police."

"Oh, Lord no!" Ferguson yelled. "What did we ever do to you? The CIA."

Raymond nodded. "Now, where were we before we were so...so..."

"Rudely?" Rosemary offered.

Raymond smiled. "Interrupted."

"You were saying that you would never forget us," Bippy said.

"That's right. And, Bippy, one of these days, I'm going to take you up on that offer to come to Birmingham."

"Marvelous!" exclaimed Bippy. "We'll have a grand time. I have loads of folks I'd like you to meet. You, too, Clark."

Turning to Jake and Ferguson, Raymond continued. "And I'll come to see you both whenever I'm in Jackson."

"So will I," said Tootsie, "if I'm ever in Jackson again."

"Well, I'll be here. That's for sure," said Ferguson, "and you must come back. All of you."

Jake's red hair, softened at the temples by streaks of gray, and the emerald eyes that had so stunned Tootsie upon first meeting, made him appear years younger than he was and gave him a boyish, insouciant air. Still, the smile he turned on Tootsie seemed basically sad. "I want to stay in touch, too, but I'm, uh, not sure I'm going to stay here. In Jackson, that is."

"Oh?" asked Tootsie, spreading a cracker with peanut butter from a jar, which she had produced from her purse. "Where are you planning on going, if I may ask?"

"Well, I'm not sure yet, you understand, but since my grandson Hunter left, I've been doing some thinking. I've come to realize that now that my wife is gone, there's nothing here for me anymore. It's too lonely. My only son lives in Charlotte, and if I ever want to spend much time with my grandson, I guess I'm going to have to put myself a lot closer."

"Wait! You're moving to Charlotte? North Carolina?" Tootsie exclaimed. Her eyes flashed with excitement. "Why, that's just about two and a half hours from Durham, where I live."

Jake nodded. "Yes, I, uh, I know." He blushed and added quickly, "It's not certain yet, but, yes, that's what I'm thinking. I've talked to my son and daughter-in-law about it, and they think it's a great idea. John, that's my son, suggested I get a place on Lake Norman, where I can keep my boat. I can fish whenever I like. Take Hunter with me."

344

"Your children are right: It is a great idea!" Tootsie said, smiling. "Sounds wonderful."

"What about you, Rose?" Clarkson said. "Where is your life headed now?"

Rose looked down at her lap and thought for a moment. Then she turned a brilliant smile on the group. "I'm going back to my job in West Virginia—back to the grind on the *Charleston Gazette*—and to some unfinished business."

"Oh-ho. Does this unfinished business have a name?" Clarkson prodded.

Rosemary laughed outright. "Now, who should be working for the CIA?" They all laughed. "Clyde Wexler," she added simply.

"Well, all I can say is he's a lucky man."

"Thanks, Clark. I just hope his offer is still on the table."

He patted Rosemary's hand and nodded slowly. "I said he's lucky, not foolish. Of course it will still be on the table. What man with half a brain would let someone like you get away?"

"Thank you, Clark. You're too kind. Let's hope you're also right."

"He usually is," Raymond quipped, smiling broadly at his brother. "At least, that's what he's always told me. And you, Pen?" he asked. "What will your life be like once you're back in Virginia?"

Pen, her hand cupped around her ear to focus her hearing on her companions rather than on the rest of the restaurant, sighed. "Well, to be honest, it's going to be quite a come-down after this. I'm afraid it's rather boring there," she said. She had never admitted that to anyone, had never expressed her interest in seeing other parts of the world. "Oh, I know I sound like a dotty old woman. I'll be all right, really. It's just that—well, I don't like to complain, but I do get lonely. My daughter is in Stuart, Florida, and my son is in Washington, D. C. Since there's no direct flight to Culpeper, and they're so busy, they can't come often. I've never told them this because I don't want them to feel that I'm a burden, but I would dearly love to travel, to see things, to meet people. You know?" Her eyes shone with anticipation. Just as quickly, she sighed and dropped her voice. "My deafness, though, makes it all but impossible for me to travel by myself. I don't mean to sound sorry for myself. I'm not. That's just the way it is."

Suddenly, Bippy pushed her glasses up on her nose and leaned forward, speaking slowly so Penelope could hear her. "Pen, listen, I just had a brainstorm. Don't give me an answer right now, but just think about it, okay?" After nodding her head affirmatively as if to generate the same response in Pen, she swallowed and then blurted out, "What about coming to live with me?"

"What!" Pen clapped one hand to the cameo broach at her neck. "Live with you? Oh, no, Bippy. Bless your heart, but I could never—"

"I told you not to give me an answer right now. Listen now. I rattle around in a big old house. Really big. Some people refer to it as the Maas Mansion, though not to my face. I overheard that one day. They don't know I know. Imagine! Anyway, you could have your own apartment there. We could see as much or as little of each other as we like, and I promise I would only practice the piano when you're out."

"Or when I wasn't wearing my hearing aids?" Pen laughed.

Bippy laughed, too. "Well, sure. It would be nice to have someone else in the house. I'd love the companionship. Think about it. We could travel together. You know, go to Roads Scholar trips together all over the world. Walk together. Read our mysteries together. Go to O'Carr's for that delicious cheesecake I've told you about together. You'd be closer to your daughter in Florida and probably, while farther, just as conveniently located for your son in Washington. He could get a direct flight right to Birmingham. If you don't want to give up your home right now until you see how this works out, what about renting it? You said Culpeper isn't that far from Charlottesville. I bet you could get some nice faculty member from the University of Virginia to rent it. Just think about it. Please?"

"That sounds terrific, Pen," Tootsie offered. "You ought to take Bippy up on it."

Pen sighed and looked down at her lap. Then, she picked up her rose, turned it in her fingers, and ever so slightly began smiling. Soon, her face was wreathed in smiles.

"What?" Bippy pressed.

"Before I met you girls, I would never have even considered such a drastic move, but now? Well, I'll certainly think about it, Bippy. Yes indeed. What a generous offer! You're very kind. And thank you for thinking of me."

"And you, Tootsie," Raymond said. "What about you?"

"Oh, that's easy enough. I plan to head back home. Since one of my children is in Raleigh and one in Charlotte, I keep the road hot between Durham and those two places." She glanced at Jake and was pleased to see him smile shyly. "What about you two, Clark and Ray? What will you do with Maggie's house and estate?"

Clark said, "We've been talking about that quite a bit. Both Ray and I have decided that we'd like to keep the house and meet here periodically for R and R. It's roughly halfway between Houston and Atlanta and an easy flight for both of us. In fact, we want to invite all of you to join us for some get-togethers. I think we should plan at least one a year, a time when we can all stay in the house that Maggie loved and renew our friendships. Sort of a reunion. In between those times, you're welcome anytime."

"And, someday," Ray added, "when we retire, who knows? We're thinking we might even live here again."

"That sounds marvelous. Meanwhile, we can all still keep in touch by email," Bippy suggested, "no matter where we go." She glanced at the men. "We must all be sure we have everyone's address before we leave this place."

"That's a wonderful idea," said Raymond, "especially since it was email that indirectly brought us all together in the first place." He lifted his glass of extra-sweet iced tea. "In fact, I'd say it's a perfectly splendid idea. Here's to email." They all raised glasses of iced tea, clinking them together in good-natured merriment.

The conversation went on for some time, lively and cheerful, full of laughter and repeated toasts. Tootsie, regaled in a crimson wool-knit dress with black trim that perfectly defined her elegant figure, suddenly put down the peanut butter cracker she was nibbling on and raised her glass of iced tea. "While we're at it, I have two more toasts. First, here's to dear Maggie, who blessed us in life with her presence and in death with new friendships."

"Hear, hear," several murmured. "To Maggie!" There was a clicking of glasses all around, and Bippy set her glass down to wipe her eyes. "And now," Tootsie continued, "a toast to the one without whom this happy moment would not have been possible. The one to whom we owe our happiness, our peace of mind, and"—her voice faltered—"our...our very lives. Here's to you, Lieutenant Ferguson."

Ferguson swallowed and cleared his throat. A hint of color crept from just above his collar all the way up to his hairline. "Thank you, but please, it's Curt," he replied. "Tonight I'm just Curt, celebratin' with friends."

Tootsie suddenly felt her eyes fill with tears. Friends. That's what this had all been about. Friends. Her dearest friend was gone, and her heart still ached with the absence—she would always have an empty spot where Maggie had been—but now she was surrounded by seven new friends, people she hadn't even known a couple of weeks ago, people who had changed her life.

How strange life was!

And how wonderful!

#

About the Author

Rebecca was born and reared in West Virginia and, though she has lived many other places, considers herself a Mountaineer in exile. She earned undergraduate and graduate degrees in English from Duke University and taught college literature, composition, grammar, and journalism.

She wrote weekly newspaper columns (humor), some of which were syndicated, and has won awards for drama, short story, and a children's story. (Sadly, there were no awards for raising the children, which was a much harder job.) Her work has appeared in *Saturday Review*, *Explore!*, *High Point Enterprise*, *Savannah Literary Journal*, and *Novello*.

She and her husband Julian love to travel and, determined that their children would, too, dragged them all over the United States and Canada. (Pets went, too, but that's another story.) They have traveled extensively by tent and camper, visiting many of the National Parks. For a year, she and Julian lived in Edinburgh, Scotland, and traveled around Europe. They now live in North Carolina, where they travel to the western part of the state for hiking and mountain climbing in the summer months. In addition to reading, writing, and sewing (definitely not arithmetic), she enjoys all sorts of animals, including a wild bird (an Eastern Phoebe) that she has trained to eat from her hand. Most of all, though, she enjoys precious time spent with her family.

This is the first in a series of Flower Girls mysteries.

Made in the USA
Columbia, SC
20 February 2025

54144123R00219